Josephine Seaton

William Winston Seaton

Josephine Seaton

William Winston Seaton

ISBN/EAN: 9783337372231

Printed in Europe, USA, Canada, Australia, Japan

Cover: Foto ©Raphael Reischuk / pixelio.de

More available books at **www.hansebooks.com**

WILLIAM WINSTON SEATON

OF THE "NATIONAL INTELLIGENCER."

A Biographical Sketch.

WITH PASSING NOTICES OF HIS ASSOCIATES
AND FRIENDS.

BOSTON:
JAMES R. OSGOOD AND COMPANY,
Late Ticknor & Fields, and Fields, Osgood, & Co.
1871.

PREFACE.

THE following pages are simply extracts from a
memoir of Mr. Seaton, written for his family, to
be preserved for his descendants, that they may know
him as he lived, — his domestic and social surroundings, — and understand in a degree the love and honor
that hedged about his living steps. His name is still
a household word by many a hearthstone, and it has
been thought that these recollections of him, his home
and virtues, may be acceptable to those of his countrymen who yet cherish his memory. This sketch does
not venture within the domain of politics; still less,
assume to be a history of Gales and Seaton, ample
materials for which were placed in the hands of the
late Edward William Johnston, the brilliant journalist,
who was for a series of years literary editor of the
National Intelligencer, and whose knowledge of public
men and events, the rise and decline of political parties,
and his personal friendship for Mr. Seaton and Mr.
Gales, pre-eminently fitted him for the task.   His

death frustrated this design, which, however, it is hoped will yet be accomplished by a competent pen, and an essential ·chapter of our political history preserved for posterity.

Washington, July 15, 1870.

WILLIAM WINSTON SEATON.

MR. SEATON was lineally descended from that historic family whose name during many centuries has been inwoven with the annals of Scotland. There were few surnames in Scotland previous to the reign of Malcolm Canmore, who bestowed on the gallant gentlemen of his time especial surnames after that of their land. Among those so distinguished was one Dougall, the founder of the Seaton family, whose patronymic was thus derived from the possession of lands and a town hard upon the sea. The silvery Firth of Forth nearly encircles this beautiful and widespreading domain, where yet stand the stately home, the ancient *toun*, and the venerable collegiate church of Seaton.

Devoted adherents of the exiled Stuarts, for whose throne and restoration they had stanchly fought and unceasingly striven, the Seatons opposed the Prince of Orange, making themselves peculiarly obnoxious to the government by their complicity in the Jacobite schemes for its overthrow. Finally, convinced of the futility of any further resistance to the measures and authority of William III., Henry, the eldest son of John Seaton, of Gair-miltoun in East Lothian or Haddington, with a number of other gallant Scotch loyalists, or *rebels*, as they were dubbed by the Orange party, sought refuge, in 1690, in the colony of Virginia. Henry Seaton settled first in Gloucester County, on the Pyanketank, where for some years he continued to reside, during which period he married Elizabeth Todd, daughter of a gentleman of standing in the same county.

Mr. George Fitzhugh, of Rappahannock, — a gentleman remarkable for his wit and abstruse learning, — in his valuable papers on the "Valleys of Virginia," quotes Bishop Meade's list of the early justices and vestrymen, — at that time offices of mark, — among whom in Petworth parish is named Henry Seaton, and says : "None but men of substance and consideration were made vestrymen, and the reader will find that the descendants of these gentlemen have retained their high social position. Mr. Seaton, of the Intelligencer, is a great-grandson of the Seaton mentioned above, having been born in the adjoining County of King William, at an old ancestral seat. His family is of the Scotch Seatons." Henry Seaton subsequently removed to an estate on the Mattapony, which for several generations continued to be the home of his descendants, and where in 1711 was born his only child, George Seaton.

By a deed a century and a half old, in possession of the family, "An Indenture Tripartite, made in the first year of the reign of our most gracious Sovereign Lord and King, George the Second, between Colonel Tayloe, George Seaton, only son and heir of Henry Seaton, and Elizabeth his wife, now wife of Augustine Moore, gentleman," we learn that Henry Seaton's widow had re-married. Among the children of this second alliance was Annie Moore, afterwards the wife of Charles Carter, who purchased the estate of Shirley, by which designation himself and numerous descendants of his prominent family have been since well known in Virginia, and whose ancestress was thus Mrs. Henry Seaton.

In 1734 George Seaton married Elizabeth, daughter of "Leonard Hill, of King William, gentleman," and seems to have maintained the family dignity, holding large properties in Spottsylvania, besides the paternal estate, which, at his death in 1750, he bequeathed to his son Augustine. By the "inventory of the estate," still in possession of the family, we get an interesting glimpse of the belongings and "habit as he lived," of a gentleman of fortune in colonial times. There, "three dozen gilt coat buttons" of the courtly flowing suit, do not disdain contact with "three pounds of shoe-thread," with which doubtless to repair the "high heeled pumps"; while homely "stone porringers and earthen pipkins" are neighbors to the aristocratic "silver table service and caudle cup." "Two spinning wheels" speak pleasantly of stately dames in pinner and kerchief, notably engaged, seated the while in the "large high-backed leathern chairs"; and the imposing culinary array, and still more significantly the "stone, china, glass, and silver *punch-bowls*," conjure up a vivid picture of the generous hospitality of that old Virginia household. The folio family Bible, Burkett's commentaries on the Testament, and "ye morning exercise for communicants," are in startling propinquity with Ovid's Epistles, Cæsar's Commentaries, Cornelius Nepos and Ovid's Metamorphoses. But more vividly suggestive still are the items, "one hanger, one swivel, one hauberk and breastplate!"

What visions of plumed cavaliers and grisly round-heads cluster about the words of this old deed! Not very many years agone, and the father of this quiet country gentleman in the New World had defied " silent William," had kissed the hand of his exiled Stuart king, perhaps bent his knee in the presence of the *Grand Monarque.* That hauberk may have shown brightly in the morning rays on Marston's fatal moor, — the breastplate, dull and dented, have covered a sad heart as the sun set on Worcester's bloody field.

In 1741 Elizabeth, daughter of George Seaton, married "John West of York River, gentleman," a scion of a noble British house, being a direct descendant from father to son of Lord De la Warre, the gorgeous colonial governor of Virginia. The Wests are a family of great historical distinction. They have been Barons from the male line since the year 1342; their ancestor, Sir Thomas West, having for great valor in the wars been summoned to Parliament as Lord West, early in the reign of Edward III. His son, the second Baron, shared in the glories of Crecy. The ninth Baron, having no issue, adopted his nephew William, who, impatient to inherit, prepared poison for his uncle, which so enraged his Lordship that he complained to Parliament, and the over-hasty William was disabled from succeeding to the estates. The too fiery youth, however, served so gallantly in Picardy as to efface the stain of his ill-timed exploit; and by act of Parliament he was restored to the full honors of his House. It was his grandson, the Earl De la Warre, who in 1610 was appointed "governor for life" of Virginia, being accompanied by a number of stately nobles, his appointments far better fitted for a luxurious court than the wilds of the "plantations."

Upon the Earl's departure from America, his mission being relinquished by reason of ill-health, his second son, the Honorable John West, remained in the colony, having acquired possession of an immense tract of land, which was inherited by his eldest son and heir, John. This princely estate, situated in King William County, at the head of York River, received the name of West Point, in honor of the family; and is now well known in connection with General McClellan's peninsular campaign during our late civil war. Here also Mr. John West established a village called De la Warre,—no longer in existence. Two descendants of this gentleman, Sir Thomas and Sir Francis West, renewed their ancestral dignity, becoming in turn governors of Virginia; and thus intermarrying with the Dandridges, Claibornes, Byrds, Pegrams, and other great folk of that day, the family continued in high esteem. West Point, being strictly entailed, descended always to the eldest son, according to British law, until the revolt of the American colonies, at which period it was in the possession of Colonel John West of York, who married Miss Elizabeth Seaton, respecting which distinguished lady a descendant writes: " My grandmother, Mrs. West, the aunt of the late beloved Colonel Seaton, was born in the neighborhood of West Point, on her paternal estate. I remember her quite well, as very handsome, exceedingly

1 *

dignified and imposing in appearance, with a courteous demeanor like the stately Virginia ladies of the olden time." A magnificent silver urn and a rare India china bowl, the latter during many generations the christening chalice of the heirs apparent of the De la Warres, are now among the family relics in possession of Mrs. Walter Brooke of Washington, having been brought to this country by her great-great-grandfather, Sir Thomas West; and, so precious was the porcelain heirloom, that when broken, a hundred years ago, it was sent to England to be repaired with bands of silver. After the Revolution, the law of entail being set aside, the estate of West Point was divided among the several children of Mr. John West and Elizabeth Seaton, his wife. Their elder son, Thomas, married Miss Bolling, a direct descendant from the Princess Pocahontas, but left no issue. The younger son, Mr. John West of Norfolk, left two sons, one of whom, De la Warre Seaton West, died in the Confederate service in 1863; the other, Mr. Thomas Bolling West, being now the lineal male representative in this country of the great English Viceroy of Virginia.

In 1776 Mr. Augustine Seaton, son of George Seaton, married Mary, daughter of Samuel Winston, Esquire, of Louisa County, Virginia. Two hundred years ago, five brothers Winston, of Winston Hall, Yorkshire, England, gentlemen of fortune and family, emigrated to the colony in the spirit of adventure which led so many scions of good houses to accompany the early governors to the New World. These brothers, all men of great stature and uncommonly handsome, — so tradition and family portraits assert, —

and well endowed morally and intellectually, settled in Hanover County, stocking Virginia with a stalwart and prolific race, the offshoots founding fresh branches in Kentucky, Mississippi, and North Carolina, in which States at this day their representatives are noted for their fine personal presence. One fair Winston matron presented to the nation three sons at a birth, who each one attained to over six feet of superb manhood. But the name which most brilliantly illuminates the Winston family record is that of the immortal Patrick Henry.

Colonel John Henry, a native of Aberdeen, Scotland, and nephew of the historian Robertson, came to this country in quest of fortune, enjoying the patronage and friendship of Governor Dinwiddie of Virginia, by whom he was introduced to Colonel Syme of Hanover, whose wife was Miss Sarah Winston, in whose family he became domesticated, and whose widow he subsequently married, continuing to reside on the family estate of Studleigh, where their son Patrick Henry was born.

The great orator seems to have been another exemplification of the theory that genius is usually derived from the mother. "The family of Winston," says Mr. Sparks, "was among the most distinguished of the colony; and, so far as the eloquence of Patrick Henry may be supposed hereditary, it seems to have been transmitted through the female line." Wirt says: "She possessed in an eminent degree the mild, benevolent disposition, the undeviating probity, the correct understanding and easy elocution, by which that ancient family has so long been distinguished.

Her brother William, popularly called Langaloo, the father of the present Judge Winston, is said to have been highly endowed with that peculiar cast of eloquence for which his great nephew was celebrated." " I have often heard my father," says Mr. Nathaniel Pope, " who was intimately acquainted with William Winston, say that he was the greatest orator whom he had ever heard, Patrick Henry excepted: that during the French and Indian war, after Braddock's defeat, when the militia were marched to the frontier against the enemy, William Winston was lieutenant; that the men, indifferently clothed, without tents, and exposed to the rigor and inclemency of the weather, discovered great aversion to the service, and, clamoring to return to their families, were on the point of mutiny, when Winston, mounting a stump, — the rostrum of the field orator in Virginia, — addressed them with such keen invective, and declaimed with such eloquence on liberty and patriotism, that the troops cried out: " Lead us on! lead us against the enemy!"   Judge Winston, the son of this military Demosthenes who had thus opportunely proved his descent from a rhetorical race, at the death of his cousin Patrick Henry, intermarried with his widow, a daughter of Nathaniel Dandridge, Esq.

The fiery spirit, which, breathing through the burning words of Henry, lighted the flame of rebellion throughout the colonies, the love of liberty which glowed in his soul, were shared by others of his kindred, who also devoted " fortune and sacred honor " to their country's cause; his seven cousins, sons of Mr. Samuel Winston, being ardent patriots and actively prominent in the contest against Farmer George; one of them especially, Colonel Joseph Winston, winning great renown for his gallant services throughout the Revolution. Colonel John Campbell of Abingdon, in preparing his " Memoir of the Military Transactions of West Virginia," says : " In the unique affair of King's Mountain Colonel Winston played a very conspicuous part. He led the right wing of the American forces, and bore a distinguished part in this Bunker Hill of the South, contributing greatly to that momentous victory, of which the battles of Cowpens and Guilford were among the *consequences*. Mr. Jefferson, in a letter now before me, says that he remembered well the deep and grateful impression made by that memorable victory. It was the joyful enunciation of the first turn in the tide of success that terminated the war with the seal of our independence."

Mary, the youngest sister of these gallant Winston brothers, became the wife of Mr. Augustine Seaton, and the mother of William Winston Seaton, who was born January 11, 1785, and in whom were fitly concentred the mingled high qualities of the brave stock from which he sprang.

Chelsea, the ancestral home, — since passed into the sixth generation on the mother's side, — is one of the most ancient houses in Virginia, its brick having been imported from England; and it is still, despite the dilapidations of two revolutions, an imposing and stately residence. Here were the graves of young Seaton's forefathers ; and within the venerable mansion were gathered cherished Old-World family relics, with worm-eaten wills and musty parchments, while on the walls were the portraits of his progenitors of a century and a half. One of these, representing a superb cavalier in the elaborate scarlet hunting-garb of his day, gun in hand, leaning on his horse, his dogs crouched at his feet, his bugle raised as if to wind a " mote," had suffered damage during some Revolutionary skirmish, an unfortunate bullet having whistled through the canvas, destroying one of the blue eyes of the handsome Nimrod ; and this pictured hunter, captivating the boyish fancy of young Seaton, gave doubtless the first impulse to his well-known passion for field sports, which he continued to pursue with zest when nearly fourscore years of age.

Under the paternal roof passed young Seaton's childhood, in the happy companionship of brothers and sisters, his tastes refined by gentle maternal influences, his intelligence quickened by the noted society frequenting his father's hospitable home, which numbered among its cherished guests the illustrious Patrick Henry. Mr. Seaton ever retained a vivid remembrance of the fascinating speech, wonderful play of countenance, and commanding presence of his great kinsman, who, himself a devoted follower of the hounds, guided the first shot of his young relative, whose proverbial skill, thus acquired in chasing the deer through the wild woods on the Mattapony, received sixty years afterwards enthusiastic recognition among the " preserves " of England.

A domestic tutor directed the youth in the earlier paths of learning, until he reached in Richmond what was then the culminating academic polishing of Ogilvie the Scotchman, " whose Earldom of Finlater slept while its heir was playing pedagogue in America. . . . . A great enthusiast by nature, and a master of the whole art of discoursing finely of even those things which he knew not well, he dazzled much, pleased greatly, and obtained a high reputation ; . . . . infusing into his pupils by the glitter of his accomplishments a high admiration for learning and for letters." *   With young Seaton this was no difficult task ; for an absorbing delight in reading had been one of his earliest developed tastes ; and in his father's solid library his opening mind was nourished on wholesome pabulum, forming the foundation of the liberal, wide-embracing culture for which he was in after life distinguished. His father, a gentleman noted for his high-toned bearing, winning manners, and strong good sense, died suddenly at West Point, the residence of his sister, Mrs. John West of York.

At the early age of eighteen Mr. Seaton's mind was matured, his ambition aroused, his vocation decided, and he passed into the arena of public life, entering with manly earnestness upon the career of political journalism, of which he was one of the country's pioneers, and which his well-won fame and social distinction crowned with honor. Mr. Seaton made his first essay in the field of politics as assistant editor of a Richmond journal, having already acquired a practical knowledge of " the art preservative of all arts " in the same office with that master of Virginia journalism, Thomas Ritchie, the early personal friendship thus formed surviving forty years of wide divergence in political sentiment and action. Our youthful editor, by his

* Atlantic Monthly, 1860.

talent for ready expression, his force of character and fairness of discussion amid party heat, soon made his mark, and won an invitation to take charge of a more prominent journal in Petersburg, then edited by Colonel Yancey, who, "one of the most discerning men of the day, predicted a glorious future for young Seaton, advising him to strike for that fame he so nobly won and carried with him to an honored grave."

In the midst of unqualified success and personal popularity Mr. Seaton was called on a friendly errand to Raleigh, which chance visit proved to be the event by which his whole future life was influenced.

Little more than half a score of years had passed since Colonel Jack Lane of Halifax, on the Roanoke, had presented the site of the "City of Oaks" to the State. This gentleman had been a member of the Provisional Convention, which met at Hillsborough in 1775, in defiance of the proclamation of Governor Martin forbidding the assemblage "in the heart of the Province of a body of men with the purpose of extending more widely the traitorous and rebellious designs of the enemies of His Majesty"; and denouncing the address of the Mecklenburg Committee as "a publication the preposterous enormity of which cannot be adequately described and abhorred." To which the convention responded by a resolution, that the Governor's Proclamation should be burned by the common hangman, as "a false, scandalous, scurrilous, mischievous, and seditious libel." It was at the house of Colonel Lane that the General Assembly of this most rebellious of Provinces met, amidst the darkest hours of the Revolution. The corner-stone of the State House at Raleigh had been laid by this patriot in 1792 ; and now, in the spring of 1806, Mr. Seaton found in the young capital a society refined, intelligent, simple in manners, unaffected in worth, a few of its members with the halo of the achievements of "seventy-six" surrounding them, others, whose names, after a lapse of sixty years, would be among those whom their country will not let die.

The household of Joseph Gales, the editor of the " Raleigh Register," the most influential journal in the State, was presided over by a wife whose intellect and womanly charm, united to the inexhaustible benevolence of her husband, with the loveliness and talent of their children, made their home the centre of culture, hospitality, and refined gayety. To this circle Mr. Seaton brought the prestige of recent political success and distinguished family connection ; he had familiarly conversed with Jefferson, Marshall, Aaron Burr, and Patrick Henry ; possessing, moreover, an uncommon charm of manner and person, for which he had already been noted in Richmond, especially among the gentler portion of creation, by whom he was pronounced " the most elegant young man in Virginia."

It was, then, in this pleasant home circle of Mr. Gales that Mr. Seaton's public career was to be shaped, and his domestic happiness to receive its crowning grace, — the first result springing from the friendship with his colleague that was to be, Joseph Gales the younger, — the second auspicious realization being secured by his successful wooing of Miss Sarah Gales, the sister of his future associate.

In the spring of 1807 Mr. Seaton yielded to the

advantageous offers and persuasions of the retiring editor to assume the proprietary editorship of the " North Carolina Journal," in the interesting old town of Halifax, late the State capital. Diffident of his ability, and singularly modest in self-appreciation, he accepted with hesitation the post, — a responsible one at this party crisis ; for in the solid " Old North State," as in Virginia, politics at this period moved all men to unwonted passion, and the position of editor was one of personal danger, to maintain which required alike a stout arm and cool head. Especially was this the case at Halifax, at that time noted for the violence with which its political waves ran, as also for the desperate character of its partisan leaders. But Mr. Seaton soon showed himself master of the situation. To curb this fiery opposition, to obtain from his opponents a candid discussion of the political questions at issue, to charge valorously against the pure Federalism of which that region had been heretofore the stronghold, and to transfer its allegiance to Republicanism, were the fruits of the young editor's successful contest.

"There can be no doubt that he who made a change so radical conducted his paper with spirit. Yet he must have done so with that wise and winning moderation and fairness which have since distinguished him and his associate. William Seaton could never have fallen into anything of the temper or the taste, the morals or the manners, which are now so widely the shame of the American press ; he could never have written in the ill spirit of mere party, so as to wound or even offend the good men of an opposite way of thinking. The inference is a sure one from his whole character." *

Halifax, noted for the Constitutional Convention of 1776, is an ancient town, and was, many years ago, the seat of elegance, wealth, and refinement. Among its more distinguished citizens were Willie and Governor Allen Jones, sons of the Attorney-General under the Colonial Government, who had been educated at Eton and Oxford, England, and were men of uncommon social talent. Willie Jones, whose daughter married John Eppes, the first wife of whom was a daughter of Thomas Jefferson, was the leader of the great majority that declined to accept the Federal Constitution in 1780 at Hillsborough, and was regarded at the time as the exponent of Mr. Jefferson, whose disciple he was in religion as well as politics. He was buried on his estate near Raleigh, his coffin being by his direction placed with the head to the north. He was one of the earliest and most influential friends of Joseph Gales, and at his house in Halifax Mr. and Mrs. Gales paid a visit on their arrival in North Carolina. His style of living was English, his hospitality genuine, genial, and overflowing ; but " our army swore terribly in Flanders," and profanity at the close of the American and during the French Revolution was general and fearful, of which Willie Jones was a conspicuous example. Mrs. Gales had the moral courage, while thanking him for the kindness of their reception, to intimate that there was but one abatement in their gratification, — " that profanity was not usual or pleasant to the ears of an English lady." He received the

* Atlantic Monthly, 1860.

gentle reprimand in a proper spirit, and became ever after more guarded in expression.

In Stokes County Mr. Seaton's uncle, Colonel Joseph Winston, of Revolutionary celebrity, resided on his beautiful estate, hedged about with reverential pride by the old North State, whose adopted son he was, and which he was at that period representing in Congress. He was especially attached to his young nephew, who, in a letter to Miss Gales, thus speaks of a visit to his distinguished relative : —

"My uncle lives at the most magnificent place I have seen in this State; and is so obliging and attentive in his endeavors to make my visit agreeable that he almost distresses me. His mansion is near the mountains, and I am sitting enjoying a full view of them, — a sight so grand, so sublime, I never witnessed. It seems as if their 'cloud-capt' summits were within a squirrel's jump of Heaven." Mr. Seaton remembered his uncle as of stately, old-school manners, and commanding presence ; and the portrait of him in possession of the family proves him to have inherited the proverbial Winston gift of good looks.

A contemporary of Mr. Seaton during his residence at Halifax, still living at a very advanced age, thus speaks of him as he appeared in the bright flush of manhood.

"I remember perfectly Mr. Seaton's personal appearance at this period," writes the venerable lady ; "he was noble-looking, singularly handsome, with most prepossessing manners, of great dignity, his every act proving him worthy the regard of our best citizens. In his too brief editorial career among us he commanded the respect of his 'adversaries by his ability and high tone, while his urbanity and courtesy no less won their regard. But the sphere was too narrow for one of his talents, and he sought a wider field of action, to the regret of our community."

Combining such varied and attractive qualities, it may readily be supposed that he speedily eclipsed all rivals in the generous esteem of his own sex, and in the appreciation of the fair daughters of Halifax. No gathering, whether the object would be to lead a partner in " Sir Roger de Coverley," to follow the hounds, or to engage in whist and punch, was deemed complete unless brightened by his genial presence ; but the social habits of that day — still such as prevailed in colonial times among good King George's lieges, when conviviality not infrequently degenerated into excess — were ever repugnant to Mr. Seaton's tastes. Not that he ascetically held aloof from the amusements natural to his age and position, as may be inferred from the memorandum in his day-book, " A rubber and punch last evening," — the significant entry on the morrow being, " For medicine, twenty-five cents." The sequel of some similar occasion of good-fellowship is narrated in the following penitential extract from a letter to Miss Gales : " I am astonished when I reflect on my temerity in having written to you. Suffering under a headache, hypochondria, ennui, home or rather heart-sickness, I must have sent you a refreshing account of my recent perambulations and adventures. However, I might as well candidly attribute all my afflictions to the two primary causes, — wine and tobacco, — whose stupefying qualities had so entirely enervated

the powers of my Pegasus, that I could not, for my
life, have spurred him out of a jog-trot, although I
was writing in college, the seat of science and erudition, where I expected my pen would instinctively
trace the characters of the most refined and accom- —
plished language."

Replying to Miss Gales, who gently rallies him on
his enjoyment of society while absent from her, he
says: "So you are really apprehensive of a developed
and determined taste for dissipation? Although I
sincerely deprecate such a contingency, I think there
is some danger of it becoming inveterate. Moving
in the region where every propensity for pleasure may
be indulged, it would require all the philosophy of
Lady Magdaline Montmorell to resist the fascinating
amusements of the gay world. Still, I feel no dread
so long as *your heart* remains in the *right* place."
He further adds: "I am studying the parts of 'Captain Absolute' and 'Duremil,' and hope to acquit
myself with credit"; by which it will be seen that
among the profane amusements of the taste prevailing
with the youth of Halifax was the love of stage-plays,
in the enacting of which, we gather from contemporary
record, Mr. Seaton gained no slight reputation, having
indeed achieved histrionic triumphs previously in Raleigh, in conjunction with his future brother-in-law,
Joseph Gales the younger, their talent embracing
rather an ambitious range of character; for at that
primitive era ladies did not deign to tread the boards,
and Mr. Seaton was alternately "My Lord Duberly,"
"Young Mirabel," or "Donna Violante"; while Mr.
Gales personated "Lydia Languish," or "Miss Lu-

cretia McTab." Small was the stage, simple the accessories, yet among the auditors were those whose critical appreciation a Siddons or a Garrick might not have disdained to deserve.

There sat the learned, genial Judge Gaston, who was equally happy in sentimental song and convivial chorus, or in racy anecdote, following, perchance, on a profound· and elaborate "summing up" from the Bench. Unbending from his usual staid reserve was Nathaniel Macon, "whose name has stood as a sort of proverb for honesty." By his side, polished, insinuating, bewitching the hearts of gentle and simple, was that wily genius, Aaron Burr; while, greater still in his charming guilelessness, the wise and benevolent Chief Justice Marshall — whom, in Richmond, Mr. Seaton had often seen carrying in his hand from market the diurnal leg of mutton — undisguisedly wept over the woes of Jane Shore, or laughed with boyish glee until the tears fairly rolled down his cheeks, when, seated near the stage, he overheard the "asides" of Mr. Seaton, who, as "Frederick" in Colman's "Poor Gentleman," thus interpolated his apostrophe to the miniature of his absent love, with iterated threats to an obstreperous urchin perched near the footlights : —

"Give me those dear bewitching features " — (Bob, stop cracking those walnuts) — "where sweet expression always speaks and sometimes sparkles," — (Bob, do you hear me ?) — "Give me that dimpled beauty !" — (Bob, if you don't stop cracking those walnuts I 'll crack your d—d head !)

Although thus engaging in the pleasures natural to

his genial nature, and to which his presence lent such added spirit, Mr. Seaton's character and habit of thought were marked, even at that impulsive age, by a high sense of moral responsibility, a serious estimate of the duties of life, and a deeply-rooted reverence for all religious influences, which formed the sure foundation for the finished and gracious super-structure of his beneficent and rounded life. He thus writes of his first sorrow since manhood: —

"HALIFAX, 1808.

" . . . . I am confident that you participate in all my joys, and no less in my sorrows. You are acquainted with my heart, and know it to be susceptible of the keenest distress. Judge, then, what must be my feelings in learn-ing the loss of a much-loved brother. . . . . When death deprives us of a relative, however near, whose advanced years impress us with the daily expectation of the most certain of all events, we can bear the loss at least with proper resignation, if not with calmness; but to see a beloved brother snatched from us who had just started in the career of life, and whose amiable qualities had strengthened our natural love, adding respect to affec-tion, is more than our firmness can at first sustain. . . . . Yet I will not repine, but endeavor to think that Heaven wills the death of every being that falls, and submit to its dispensation. 'T is fruitless, I know, to mourn a loss which cannot be remedied; but what breast can smother its sor-row or repress the tear of affection at the departure of one so dearly and so deservedly beloved? He had just arrived at the age of manhood. Deprived of his father before he could profit by his virtuous counsel, and unassisted by that advice which could best instil into our minds correct prin-ciples, I feel proud that he advanced so far on his journey with honor to himself and credit to his connections. Thrown upon the ocean of life with no experienced friend to point out to him its rocks and quicksands, his reputation might have been wrecked ere he was aware of danger. . . . . My venerated mother is inconsolable. I have done all in my power to afford alleviation to her affliction, and I pray Heaven it may answer my wishes. . . . . God bless you."

"HALIFAX, July, 1808.

" . . . . You have heard of the death of Mr. John Gilmour, a man whom I respected very highly, my first friend here, and who always showed me the greatest attention. His funeral was attended by all the most respectable inhabitants of the town and neighboring country. At the request of Mr. Burt and others, I had consented to read the Service. After the body was deposited I approached the grave. Never did I feel so great a degree of agitation ; I was scarcely able to support myself, the power of utterance seemed suspended, and it was some time before I could command my voice sufficiently to proceed. The scene before me, and the solemn office I had undertaken to perform, impressed my mind with sensations of awe and reverence which I never before experienced. Never did I pray more fervently ; every word that fell from my lips was breathed in a spirit of the truest devotion. . . . . Why do you say that I consider the claims of religion in too light a manner ? Are you acquainted with any acts of moral depravity which manifest in me the want of a proper sense of religion ? or is it because I have ever condemned, as I shall ever reject, the precepts of bigotry and fanaticism ? Every man is endowed with reason by which to enable him to judge of right from wrong. Mine has always taught me to reject that with which I could not reconcile it ; and if it is too weak to point out a better course, the fault lies not with me, I am sure. Nature has implanted in my bosom, as in every other, a monitor, the dictates of which, guided by reason and reflection, I am content to follow; and, in so doing, am confident that I shall never err past forgiveness.

"If, however, the conclusion you draw, that 'the man with little religion must have as little affection,' were not inconsistent with the supposition, I should imagine you were led to the remark by the knowledge that at present the object of my idolatry is one who (though I offend against the rules of gallantry), I must confess, is not a deity of the celestial order, but one that I shall ever worship, and whose kindness and affection have confirmed my infidelity.

"My dearest life, let no doubts of my being fully impressed with a reverent sense of duty to my Maker, disturb your peace. The man whose heart is capable of entertaining the pure and exalted sentiment of love cannot, in my opinion, be destitute of religion; although, I will admit, his judgment may lead him into an improper conception of it."

"HALIFAX, 1808.

" . . . . I rejoice to learn that you are once more lodged in the peaceful bosom of your enviable family. Surrounded as you were by a crowd of adorers vying with each other in their devotion, and, I suppose, with their hearts in their hands, ready, at a smile, to cast them at your feet, I am surprised that yours is not reduced to a cinder, or perforated as a honey-comb. . . . . Add to all this, the stentorian eloquence of G. C., endeavoring to impress on your mind the charms of Georgia. I dare say, he wished to convince you that the croaking of frogs and the roaring of alligators, pouring forth their divine strains in heavenly concert, produce 'a concord of sweet sounds,' compared with which the music of the spheres is as far inferior as the light of a taper is to the blaze of a meridian sun. Had I known that you were driving with the Governor, I should have been doubly uneasy, as his confounded horses have before shown a disposition to thwart any gracious intentions towards his Excellency. I wish they were in Guinea, and that I were with Mrs. G., that we might unite in abusing their owner a little. . . . . I am much pleased with your intention of learning to paint, for several reasons : one, that I think it an elegant accomplishment, and in which I delight ; another, that I wish my wife to excel still more than she already greatly does, every other woman I ever saw. I wish you would add geography to it. . . . . I am glad that you are improving your French ; and so confident am I of your paying a visit to this place, at some time, that I am preserving a file of French papers for your amusement. Am I not very considerate to begin already to provide for your pleasures ? "

That Mr. Seaton's services in behalf of his party were most acceptably performed, we may judge from the evidence of Mr. Atlas Jones, a prominent politician of the day, who thus writes to the spirited young editor : —

" Your journal is very much approved in Deep River ; my copy is borrowed by many gentlemen who take other papers, and their sentiment agrees with my own, that it is the best edited gazette in the State ; more candid, more impartial, and less fermented by the spirit of party. The dignity and fairness of your editorials have a powerful influence over even prejudiced minds, and give a steadily increasing value to your journal."

Notwithstanding that this emphatic testimony to his ability and success inclined him to remain at his post, the specific object for which Mr. Seaton had assumed the editorial chair at Halifax having been satisfactorily achieved, he resolved to seek a wider sphere for his energies; and, returning to Raleigh, became associated with Joseph Gales in the " Register," being doubtless mainly impelled to this decision by the sweet influences moulding his career, and which were destined to crown with tender joy all the future days of his life.

A sketch of the history of Joseph Gales will best illustrate the source whence such abounding virtues drew their life, as were manifested in the lives of his children, whose ability and worth are an enduring monument to the excellence of their honored, stout-hearted father.

The family of Gales, until illustrated by the virtues and well-won eminence of Joseph Gales, was unknown out of the simple annals of the rural home of him who may be called its founder; owing the respect and consideration now investing the name to no fortuitous gifts of inheritance or remote ancestry. The name of *Gale* is a familiar one both in England and this country, notably in the State of North Carolina, in which " the county of Wake, erected in 1772, perpetuates the maiden name of the accomplished wife of Governor Tryon," whose mother, Lady Wake, was Penelope Gale. " The name of Tryon," says Governor Swain, " has been expunged from the map of the State, but not from the memory of men ; and the unenviable fame of the royal

Governor, and the good name of Penelope Gale Wake, are alike immortal."

But the patronymic with the final *s* can be retraced no further than to Richard Gales, who guided the youth of the ancient village of Eckington, Derbyshire, England, in the path of learning, and who was deemed a good classical scholar.

His son Timothy — who continued in his native village to vary his routine of labor with the lighter duties of Parish Clerk — married into the family of Clay, well known in the West of England as Iron-founders, and as possessing unusual mechanical skill; the ingenious Henry Clay, a nephew of Mrs. Timothy Gales, being noted as the first manufacturer of decorative articles in *papier maché;* his warerooms being at that time among the great attractions of Birmingham, the " toy-shop of Europe." Joseph Gales always thought that Henry Clay of Kentucky strikingly resembled his own relatives, the English Clays, some of whom had emigrated to this country ; and it is not improbable that they and the peerless Son of the West sprang originally from the same stock. Timothy Gales was drowned at the advanced age of eighty-three, while attempting to cross a stream by means of a fallen tree.

The excellent old man transmitted his virtues, accompanied with but little worldly store, to his son Thomas. Mrs. Winifred Gales, in her autobiography, addressing her children, says: " If Pope's axiom be true, that ' an honest man's the noblest work of God,' then were your paternal ancestors nobles of God's own making. In every relation of life they conducted themselves with an admirable propriety, and were governed

by an integrity that elicited the good-will and respect
of their compeers. Your grandfather, Thomas Gales,
was indeed an Israelite without guile; and his that
true nobility of soul to which wealth could add no
distinction, rank no lustre. Your grandmother Gales
was from Newport-Pagnell, Buckinghamshire; and of
this truly excellent woman I cannot deny myself the
pleasure, and her the justice, to say that she was worthy the ardent affection of her family, — and was, of
all persons I ever knew, the most disinterested and
candid; self was omitted from her vocabulary."

The oldest child of this estimable pair, Joseph, was
born at Eckington, in 1761. In 1809 his venerable
father went to rest, which event was communicated
to Joseph Gales, then residing in North Carolina, by
James Montgomery, in the following letter, which is
interesting as an expression of the undiminished affection cherished by the amiable poet, after a separation
of fifteen years, for his former patron and master.

"SHEFFIELD, October 20, 1809.

"DEAR SIR, — A letter from me is now such a rarity,
that the very appearance of my writing will be an omen of
mournful tidings. Such tidings indeed I have to communicate, but they are mingled and softened and sweetened
with so many consolations, not vain and imaginary, but
deep and unfailing, that you will think, with me, that there
is at least as much cause for gratitude as for grief, when I
inform you that your dear and venerable father departed
this life, most peacefully and piously, on Saturday last. . .
You will therefore be less shocked, though not less sorry to
learn, that he has had the privilege of going first to his eternal home.   For many months past I have with secret cou-

cern perceived his decline from that florid and hearty complexion of health and vigor which marked his green old age. . . . . On my return from Scarboro' and Harrowgate in September I saw him at Eckington, and then indeed I read on his meek emaciated face the sentence which is passed upon all the living. . . On the 14th he expired as quietly as an infant falling asleep. . . His mind seemed deeply engaged in meditation on those most awful concerns that ought to occupy more of our thoughts in health than they usually do. He was always sweetly and solemnly affected when his daughters prayed with him, or spoke gentle words of hope and faith in God. The expressions that fell from his dear dying lips were divinely consoling to us whom he has left behind. We have a confidence, which we would not relinquish for all the hopes that this life can offer, that he is at rest at the footstool of the Eternal Throne, and that we shall all meet him in everlasting felicity, and inseparable communion. Thus far of the honored and loved and lamented dead who is gone before us. Of the living, your mother is humbly and simply resigning herself to the will of the Lord. . . . No words that I could command would do justice to the filial piety of your sisters, and their unwearied attention to every word and look of their suffering but now sainted father. . . Your name was frequently in their hearts and on their lips. . . . I send most cordial and affectionate remembrances to dear Mrs. Gales and to all your beloved family. I shall write next week by the Packet, hoping that you will certainly receive one or both of these letters, from

" Your sincere friend,

" J. Montgomery.

" Mr. Joseph Gales."

It was then, with no patrimony save the indiscerptible one of probity, industry, and a good capacity, that

Joseph Gales entered upon the arena of life, achieving, by the unassisted force of these qualities, a just distinction in his native land, which was recognized and deepened into reverential love in that of his adoption. Alternating his hours of work — for in that frugal household toil was a necessity — with persistent and conscientious study, the stout-hearted boy had soon exhausted the educational resources of Eckington. Mr. Gales, in writing of this period of his life, says : " The inhabitants of our village were in moderate circumstances, and of good morals, and I have thought the latter merit in a great degree owing to the attention paid to the cultivation of music. Fortunately, there was a resident of Eckington of better fortune, and who had received greater advantages than the rest of the villagers, and who to a knowledge of music superadded the gift of a fine bass voice, singing well and playing on more than one instrument. This gentleman gladly instructed all who wished to join the village choir, where my father had charge of the violoncello and sang bass, while my brother and I sang treble." This love of the gentle art continued through life to be the favorite recreation of the hours of leisure snatched by Mr. Gales from his industrious career.

And now at the age of thirteen the stalwart lad began to heed the stirring of a moderately ambitious nature, prompting him to seek a more advanced post in the bivouac of life than the humble one occupied by his worthy forbears.

An advantageous opening soon offered in the city of Manchester, where the young Joseph was bound for a term of seven years to the bookbinding and printing business; and where, during three years, he applied himself with characteristic diligence to his specific duties, and the acquisition of all the extraneous knowledge within his circumscribed means.

The system of apprenticeship, as conducted and legally countenanced at that period, in England, was disgraced by a severity, a cruelty, little removed from the tyranny of the feudal ages. No Exeter-Hall fabled sufferings of slavery could surpass those to which respectable youths were subjected by their irresponsible master, who held almost unchecked power over the very life of the apprentice. The experience of young Gales did not differ from that of many of his fellow-bondsmen; but rather than afflict his parents with a knowledge of his situation, he bore in silence the humiliations, starvation, and personal inhumanity of his employer, continuing bravely to fulfil his duties and practice his craft, until a series of outrages culminated in an attempt on his life by his master's wife, "a notorious vixen," who in a fit of passion seized a knife and swore to run it through the heart of the mild, obedient boy. Escaping from the infuriated woman, his relatives appealed to a court of justice, and pending the decision, young Gales determined to place himself beyond the power of his evil taskmasters. "I therefore set out," he says, in recounting the occurrence, "with not more than half a crown in my pocket, to walk over fifty miles to my native village; and to show the state of my religious impressions at that time, I will mention, that, in a solitary spot on the mountainous moors over which I wended my way, I bent my knees in prayer to my God, thanking him for my release from a heavy bondage and praying for his future guidance and protection."

This incident is illustrative of the simple, firm trust in an overruling Providence which ever characterized Joseph Gales; who, indeed, in guileless purity, singleness of purpose, and stern uprightness, seemed framed in patriarchal mould, — "A just man, and walked with God."

Fortune smiled compensatingly on the next venture of the earnest young typographer, who, in the fine old town of Newark, entered into an apprenticeship with a generous, worthy gentleman, under whose guidance he became a master in his craft, and in whose home he found culture, refinement, and affection. He was now approaching man's estate, intelligent, robust, and bright-eyed, which passports to feminine favor were appreciated by a fair young creature, whom, after a wooing of five years, Mr. Gales won to be the partner of his checkered life; his joy in prosperity, his comfort and helpmeet in adversity. This young lady was Miss Winifred Marshall, daughter of John Marshall, of Newark-upon-Trent.

The family of Marshall had for many generations occupied a position of high respectability in Nottinghamshire, whence they sprang from an ancestry of gentle birth, possessing competent means, and noted for a love of letters. Mrs. Gales, in her autobiography, says: "Your grandfather Marshall's family, my dear children, were proud of their lineage, and though their claim to distinction on the score of wealth had passed away before my time, yet they were tenacious of their pretensions and loved to dwell upon the family descent.

Genealogical tree, seals, parchments setting forth hereditary family claims, were jealously cherished possessions, exciting my youthful interest; *now*, in this land
where honorable conduct is the only patent of true nobility, such distinctions seem puerile ; yet a degree of
tenderness pervades my feelings at this retrospective
view, and I am pleased to remember that my ancestors were persons of integrity, well-educated, and of no
mean intellect."

It will suffice for this sketch to retrace the family
history only to Gervase Marshall, a clergyman of the
English Church, and Rector of Whatton in Nottinghamshire, whose wife brought him the livings also of
Balderton and Farndon.

His eldest son, Gervase Marshall of Southwell, married Mary, daughter of William Burnett, — a great-
nephew of the celebrated Bishop Burnett, — whose
wife was Elizabeth, daughter of Mark Lamb. Through
this lady the Marshalls were nearly allied to the Melbourne family, having a common ancestor in Matthew
Peniston Lamb, of Brocket Hall, Hertfordshire. Sir
Matthew Lamb — an inmate of his cousin Elizabeth's
house while pursuing his legal studies — was the father of the first Lord Melbourne, whose family honors
and estates it was at one time supposed would devolve
on the son of Gervase Marshall ; but subsequently an
heir was born to the title, the late Viscount Melbourne,
the Premier and friend of Queen Victoria. The sister
of this second Lord Melbourne, the Countess Cowper,
afterwards Lady Palmerston, died in 1869, surviving
her husband, the great Premier, several years ; and
while he during half a century shaped the policy of

Europe, the beauty and fascination of Lady Palmerston held equal sway over English society during four reigns.

Gervase, the eldest son of Gervase and Mary Marshall, occupied in early life an honorable position in the royal household of King George II., but finding the duties of a court life incompatible with the prosecution of his favorite pursuits, he retired to the country, there to remain absorbed through a long life in the " Follies of Science," casting horoscopes and seeking the Philosopher's Stone.

His sister Mary married George Hodgkinson, Esq., a lawyer of eminence of Southwell, who was, says Mrs. Gales, "an elegant gentleman in appearance, manners, and acquirements, and related to the family of Pierrepont, Dukes of Kingston. I met frequently at my aunt's house Charles Pierrepont, who at the death of the Duke of Kingston, and the extinction of that title, succeeded his relative in the minor title of Earl Manvers."

John Marshall, of Newark, the youngest son, married, in the memorable year 1745, Elizabeth, daughter of Simeon Weston, of Carleton-upon-Trent. "My mother," writes Mrs. Gales, "was an only child, and her patrimonial inheritance was considered at that time quite large. According to the testimony of old friends, she was a very lovely girl, and at a later period was the handsomest woman of her age I ever saw. Her tastes were superior and her manners polished ; but, better still, she possessed the strength of a sensible mind and the piety of a Christian, living in the exercise of faith, and dying at the advanced age of eighty-three years."

John Marshall was a man of strong intellect, well improved by a liberal education, possessing a cultivated taste for science and letters, a too absorbed devotion to which, combined with an inert habit, lessened the practical usefulness of his life, and cut short his career at the age of fifty years. His children inherited his fine natural gifts, but the endowment of intellect, vivacity, sensibility and beauty, was conferred in especial measure upon the youngest daughter, Winifred, born in 1761.

"Well do I remember my honored father's countenance," writes Mrs. Gales sixty years after his death. "He was very handsome, had a dark, fine eye, with a very dignified manner. The best likeness of him I ever saw, strange to say, was a portrait of Dr. Markham, Archbishop of York, which hung in my uncle Hodgkinson's parlor, he being related to that Prelate, whom I also remember well, having when a little girl seen him during a visit he made to my uncle, with his wife and seven daughters. I was my father's favorite, on whom was showered every indulgence ; and although he carefully superintended the education of all his children, my love of reading, which I have from youth pursued with never-ceasing avidity, drew me more nearly to his side. Very often after the family had retired, in reading or conversation we wasted the midnight oil. I read to him all the political ephemeral works on the right (the Ministerial) side of the questions of the day. "Ah," said a gentleman to me subsequently, while Mr. Gales published the Sheffield Register, "what would your father say, could he now witness your political heresy !"

"Among my more solid literary food, I remember 'Longinus on the Sublime,' Adam Smith's 'Essays' and 'Wealth of Nations,' Burnett's and Clarendon's Histories, various Topographical works, Shakespeare, Milton, and the best poets. A favorite volume, generally carried by my father in his pocket, and which he pronounced the best extant on the subject, was Scougall's 'Life of God in the Soul of Man.'"

Here indeed was substantial mental pabulum for a girl of seventeen, but not calculated to satisfy the ardent poetical mind and sprightly imagination of the young Winifred, who, already a devotee at the shrine of the muses, writing graceful verse, sought still further relaxation and achieved no slight fame, in portraying the history of "Lady Emma Melcombe," "Matilda Berkeley," and other heroines of the sentimental or "Minerva Press" school. A not uninteresting coincidence, as quite in keeping with the romantic turn of Mrs. Gales's own taste, may be cited.

The heroine of one of her novels, written while still Miss Marshall, was styled the Lady Julia Seaton. Thirty years afterwards, having as Mrs. Gales sought a home in America's western wilds, her daughter married Mr. Seaton; and she saw perpetuated in their daughter the name of her own eldest English child of fiction.

"This day forty-eight years ago," writes Mrs. Gales, May 4, 1832, "I pledged my faith and best affections to the dear and honored companion of my joys and sorrows. It was a lovely spring morning, and the drive from Collingham to Newark, my native place, was delightful. We were married by my brother, an

Episcopal clergyman, in the venerable church which for more than six centuries has resisted the dilapidations of time and warfare, whence we drove thirty miles to Eckington, the residence of my newly acquired parents, who greeted us with the most affectionate salutations of welcome."

Mr. Gales had already established himself at Sheffield, Yorkshire, as Printer and Publisher; possessed of small fortune indeed, but, as he records with commendable pride, with what he " found to be more valuable than money, — the character of an upright, industrious business man." Characteristically, the first work undertaken by Mr. Gales was the publishing of a folio Bible, illustrated by plates, with annotations from the versatile pen of his clever wife.

In 1787 Mr. Gales issued the first number of the Sheffield Register, a weekly journal, which soon won its way to unprecedented esteem and circulation in the West Riding of Yorkshire, treating as it did of science and literature, foreign and domestic politics; the expression of its views being marked by good sense, high tone, and probity of purpose, — life-long characteristics of its founder. Mr. Gales continued to prosper; the happiness of his domestic circle being enhanced by the birth of several children, among whom were Joseph, born at Eckington, April 10, 1786, and Sarah, born at Sheffield, May 12, 1789.

In 1792 the subject of Parliamentary Reform awoke, after a number of years, like a giant refreshed with wine, and shook England to its centre. When in 1782 this question of Equal Representation of the people in the House of Commons had been agitated, meetings were held throughout the kingdom to discuss the rights of the unfranchised classes, and the best means of forcing from their legislators the recognition of their legitimate demands as freemen.   Delegates from the associations first assembled at the Thatched-House Tavern in London, some of the most prominent members being the Dukes of Norfolk and Richmond, William Pitt — then an opposition member, afterwards Premier of England — and Major John Cartwright, who, thirty-five years after the failure of these initiatory measures of Reform, was again active in arousing the people of England to a candid and peaceable mode of redressing their grievances.

The Resolutions were offered by William Pitt, and unanimously adopted, and, in the form of a Petition, were presented to the House of Commons for a Reform in Parliament, "without which," said the preamble, "neither the liberty of the nation can be preserved, nor the permanency of a wise and virtuous administration be secure."   Mr. Pitt's motion in Parliament was supported by Charles James Fox, and lost.   Sir George Saville said in debate, that "the House might as well call itself a representation of France as England."

The following incident, as related by Mrs. Gales, is of interest, as illustrative of the mode of carrying English elections, and of the influence exercised by the gentler sex over the ballot-box at that period, — an influence as powerful, if not so openly exerted, as that claimed by the friends of female suffrage to-day.

"I well remember hearing the bells ring a muffled peal for the death of the famous Marquis of Granby, the celebrated military commander, whose portrait still forms the weather-beaten sign of old English inns; a man of great worth, and whose general popularity among the English had not been equalled since the days of Marlborough. I was a young girl when the Marquis was a candidate for the borough of Newark, where my father lived, who held the office of 'Headborough' of the county, and who was anxious for the success of the ministerial candidates. The election was strongly contested, and the friends of the government, fearing defeat, were assembled for consultation, when Shelley and the Marquis joined them. 'How goes the poll?' 'Ah, we fear against you.' The Marquis thought a moment, then ordered his servants to go out and purchase several large baskets of oranges and take them to Appleton Close. 'I saw a number of females playing at ball in a beautiful green enclosure,' said he, 'and we will distribute the fruit among the fair.' The party accompanied him, and with a gay, captivating manner he said to a pretty girl, 'Play with me sweetheart, for oranges.' The game began, and in every orange he *stuck a guinea;* and every damsel had a game with the gallant Marquis, her orange and guinea.

"'Shelley and Manners'—the family name of the great ducal house of Rutland—was now the burden of the song. 'I am wearied and will go now to bed,' said the Marquis, 'but let me know when we are elected. Every one of these women will oblige father, brother, husband, and lover to vote for us.'

"The orange device succeeded, and at midnight it was announced that the Marquis and Shelley had triumphantly carried the day."

"Now again, ten years later," writes Mrs. Gales, "the people were once more awakened to the assertion of their political rights, and disturbed, alarmed, could see only tyranny and oppression on the one hand, reform on the other, while the rulers recognized in the movement only rebellion and revolution. To men capable of thought, neutrality of opinion in this crisis was impossible; and if their views passed into speech, or became visible on paper, they were ranked, according to the side embraced, as Disorganizers or as Royalists; the latter class comprising those whom hereditary possessions or official position rendered strictly conservative, their slogan being *Aris et focis*, which in their translation signified, *Our places, our pensions.*

"Honorable exceptions, however, to this spirit of caste were to be found in the phalanx of reformers, comprising men of talent, rank, and wealth; among whom were Earl Stanhope, Marquis of Lansdowne, Sir Charles Grey, Horne Tooke, Sheridan, and, in our own vicinity, the Duke of Norfolk, Lord of the Manor of Sheffield, the Shears — eminent bankers — and others of learning and integrity among our personal friends.

"*Constitutional Societies* were established in the country, breathing a spirit of peace. Mr. Erskine's speech at a meeting of the 'Friends of the Liberty of the Press,' expressed the true feeling of this momentous period. 'If,' said the eloquent jurist, 'in the legal and peaceable assertion of freedom we shall be calumniated and persecuted, we must be content to suffer in its cause, as our fathers before us; but we will, like our fathers, persevere until we prevail.

"Such was the original spirit actuating the public mind at the meetings inaugurating this movement."

Sprung from the yeomanry, Mr. Gales was naturally in sympathy with his order; and the 'Register' firmly, but moderately, espoused the liberal cause, being the only journal in the West Riding which, open to discussion, candidly avowed its sentiments on the question of the day. Mr. Gales had obtained great ascendency over the industrial classes of the community, to whom he became endeared by his unaffected goodness, urbanity of manner, and proverbial integrity; yet, while boldly upholding the popular demands, striking heavy and well-aimed blows with manly freedom at the ministerial paltering policy, he was temperate in language, and invariably prudent in counsel.

In the midst of this feverish perturbation of the public pulse, Mr. Gales received into his employment a prepossessing youth, "who quickly and progressively matured into his assistant editor, dearest friend, and finally successor in his journal." This youth was James Montgomery, the poet.

The first waves of the French Revolution, dashing against the shores of England, gave a fresh impetus to the hopes of reform; the destruction of the Bastile exciting general enthusiasm, "filling the heart with hope that the day-star of liberty had dawned over earth; for no one could foresee that this glorious upheaval of peoples would degenerate into a licentiousness which prostrated all order and violated every right." Montgomery, who threw himself with youthful ardor into the popular cause, says of this period: "The excitement of the most violent passions caused such a conflict of minds, such activity of the highest powers of the human soul, as had never been exhibited since Britain was an island. Every man, woman, and child in the kingdom was a politician."

No district was more agitated than Sheffield, one of the most important English centres of manufacturing interest, whose mechanics were a well-paid, intelligent, reading, and consequently liberal body of men. The "Test Law," by which Catholics and Dissenters from the Established Church of England were cut off from all governmental office, was also an irritating source of discontent to a large body of the most respectable and influential English subjects ; and not the least of the Duke of Wellington's claims to the gratitude of posterity, is in the abrogation of those puerile and odious laws during his Premiership. With the exception of the Duke of Norfolk, Lord of the Manor, the chief of whose great house has always been the leading Catholic of the realm, the residents of Sheffield were generally Dissenters, the majority being favorable to Reform ; the Unitarians, to which enlightened branch of the Christian Church Mr. and Mrs. Gales belonged, being earnestly so, although they did not manifest their opinions by constant attendance at the political meetings ; partly by reason of their domestic habits, and still more from prudential motives induced by the recent scenes of violence at Birmingham, and the disgraceful persecution of Dr. Priestley, the eminent convert to liberal Christianity.

The riots of Birmingham were occasioned by a handbill, attributed to Dr. Priestley, calling on the friends of liberty to celebrate the anniversary of the destruction of the Bastile ; and from this little spark the party of Church and State kindled the flame which consumed the houses of the wealthy Unitarians. Dr. Priestley's loss was irreparable in a valuable philosophical apparatus, his unpublished manuscripts, and a library which it had cost him forty years to collect. Dr. Priestley's claims to distinction in the annals of Christian piety and intellectual progress are too universally known to need any detailed history in this sketch. Goaded by party enmity, he was finally forced to seek an asylum in the United States, where Mr. and Mrs. Gales renewed with him the intimacy so valued in Sheffield. "A man of more genuine piety, simplicity of manners, and frank charm than Dr. Priestley never lived," writes Mrs. Gales. "Ardent in opinion, even his opponents honored him for his gentle urbanity; and the celebrated Dr. Parr, one of the most strenuous supporters of Church and State, avowed reverence for him in a letter to the inhabitants of Birmingham, which generous eulogium concludes thus : —

" ' Let Dr. Priestley be confuted where he is mistaken, exposed where he is superficial, repressed where dogmatical ; but let not his attainments be depreciated, because they are numerous, almost beyond parallel ; let not his talents be disparaged, for they are superlatively great ; let not his morals be vilified, for they present even to common observers the innocence of a hermit and the simplicity of a patriarch, and because a candid eye will discover in them the deep-fixed root of religious principle and the solid trunk of virtuous habits.' "

In theological science Dr. Priestley had conscientiously progressed from Calvinism to Unitarianism, and was, to his latest moment, one of the ablest foes to infidelity.

In the spring of 1793 the political cloud grew darker, every one looking with fear to the impending storm. The main object of the Reformers at this period was the abrogation of *Septennial* and the introduction of *Annual* Parliaments, granting free suffrage to all males. "William Pitt," writes Mrs. Gales, "as if to show how great, how mean, how versatile is man, now voted *against* Reform, alleging that he did not believe the people to be suffering any evil on that ground"; and in thus opposing the rights of the people Pitt made his professed patriotism a stepping-stone to the highest round of the political ladder. "Petitions addressed to the King and Commons poured in from all quarters; the press teemed with pamphlets from both sides, one of which, by Count Zenobia, a German patriot of distinction, and purporting to be written by an independent English country member, was a spirited, sensible rebuke of Pitt's tergiversation, procuring for its author the honor of being sent out of the country under the Alien and Sedition Law."

At this juncture Thomas Paine, already a celebrity in the American colonies, reappeared on the English political stage, aiding by powerful, if misdirected appeals, to widen the breach between the people and the government. The son of an English Quaker, he had been introduced in London to Benjamin Franklin, who, discerning his talent, advised him to seek America as a more promising field in which to work off superfluous energy. Paine, disembarking at Philadelphia in 1774, soon became noted for his outspoken heresies, editing with ability the Pennsylvania Magazine; and upon the declaration of hostilities between the rebellious colonies and the mother country, wrote his famous pamphlet, " Common Sense," the importance of which production the Pennsylvania Legislature recognized by voting its author the enormous sum of £ 500. His restless spirit carried him back to Europe at the moment when the English nation was seething in the turbulent waves of faction, and France convulsed by the disastrous outbreak of ferocious radicalism. Naturally, Paine with hot ardor threw himself into the contest, issuing his fiery " Rights of Man," in answer to Edmund Burke's " Reflections on the Revolution in France "; the latter one of the most celebrated pamphlets of modern times. Burke's Toryism on this stupendous question severed him from Fox, Sheridan, and other erewhile friends, rendering him the target for every species of invective from his quondam Whig associates. Yet Burke was no apologist for tyranny, — no man loved true freedom more; but his prescience descried, and his warning eloquence vividly depicted, the dangers of the quicksand into which French liberty was destined to be so fatally engulfed.

Paine proved to be the firebrand which, igniting the combustible elements of the opposing parties, caused an explosion involving the ruin of many eminent men, and tending directly also to a crisis in the fortunes of Mr. Gales.

Many respectable booksellers had been arrested and punished under an *ex post facto* law for selling Paine's

"Rights of Man," and other appeals obnoxious to the
Ministry.   Among the delinquents was Holt, a printer
of talent, who had learned his craft in Mr. Gales's office,
and who, for reprinting a letter from the Duke of Richmond in favor of Reform, was convicted of treason and
sentenced to four years' imprisonment, with a fine of
£ 200.   Richard Phillips, of Leïcester, received nearly
as severe a sentence, prosperously ending his subsequent career, however, by being knighted, when carrying up an address to the throne as Sheriff of London.
To an American was Mr. Gales indebted for exemp-
tion from a similar fate.   " This gentleman," writes Mrs.
Gales, " was Mr. Thomas Digges, who had come to
Sheffield on a visit to the Duke of Norfolk.   We were
delighted with his manners and conversation, frank,
manly, and polished, and he opened to us a new view
of America, giving the first impetus to our feelings respecting the present home of our adoption.   The casual
acquaintance ripened into intimate friendship, which
was proved in this way.   During an absence of Mr.
Gales in London, Mr. Digges one morning requested
to see me alone, asking me anxiously if we had any of
Paine's works.   ' Yes, a great many.'   He replied, ' Let
me then as a friend entreat you to put them carefully
aside, and if inquired for, to deny the possession of a
single copy.   I have indisputable authority for saying,
that to disregard my advice would be productive of
positive danger.'

" We had sold hundreds and printed thousands of
Paine's works, but now acted gratefully on the friendly
warning of Mr. Digges, whom we next met, twenty years
afterwards, on the banks of the Potomac."

The King now issued a Proclamation, forbidding his subjects to read " those dangerous Books," characterizing them as " wicked, seditious works," which prohibition naturally increased the general eagerness to obtain them, their sale, in Scotland especially, rising from three to seven hundred copies a week.

On the day of the Proclamation the Attorney-General entered upon the prosecution of Paine, who, while the trial was pending, escaped to France, where he was chosen a member of the atrocious Jacobin Convention. He voted, to his credit be it recorded, against the death of Louis Sixteenth, proposing, in lieu of the guillotine, that the King be imprisoned or banished; which humane alternative offending the *Bonnets Rouges*, Paine was sent to expiate his treasonable lenity in the Luxembourg. On the fall of Robespierre he was released, and once more sought America, where his subsequent career is a matter of history. Even in death he caused contention, the Quakers refusing, because of his aggressive atheism, to allow him burial in their cemetery. It is almost impossible at this distance of time to form an impartial estimate of a man execrated by one half of his contemporaries as a mischievous Infidel, and lauded by the opposing party as an apostle of liberty; but Mrs. Gales bore testimony, from friendly personal intercourse, to Paine's sincerity, the simplicity and sweetness of his nature, and the sprightly wit that charmed the social circle.

The following impromptu, thrown off in sportive vein at some suggestion by Mrs. Gales, is an interesting specimen of the famous agitator's versatility.

ME AND MY MUSE.

A TALE.

From the Castle in the Air to the Little Corner of the World.

'T WAS in the dog-star's raging days,
When all the heavens were in a blaze,
 And thought itself was tired ;
'T was then a lady laid on me,
The cruel task of Poesy,
 As if I was inspired.

I sought my muse ; I found the maid
Reclining in a myrtle shade,
 With slumber in her eye ;
She looked as dull as dull could be,
She scarcely cast a glance at me,
 And this is her reply : —

" The lady that you love to praise,
'T is she that must inspire your lays,
 And touch the spring of thought ;
She 's handsomer, you know, than me,
You like her better too, I see,
 Though I 'm without a fault.

" I 've been your muse for many years,
Sometimes in joy, sometimes in tears,
 But always with applause :
'T was I that passed the Stygian Gulf,
And brought to life your General Wolf,
 Against all Nature's laws.

"'T was I that taught you how to plan
Your *Common Sense*, your *Rights of Man,*
 Your *Age of Reason* too :
I led you to the source of thought,
From whence the heavenly flame was caught,
 That burns forever new.

" I taught you castles in the air,
And how to write to ladies fair,
    With whom you might be smitten ;
To hint a love you dare not tell,
And yet to hide that hint so well,
    In sonnets you have written.

" I 've been more constant than a wife ;
I never vexed you in my life,
    Nor thought a thought untrue ;
But since your fickle fancy chuse
To have a lady for a muse,
    I can be hard on you."

" Then, charmer of my life," said I,
The tear just standing in my eye,
    As when the heart is grieved ;
" Pray look again and you will see,
'T is you she courts, it is not me,
    So pray be undeceived.

" Besides, I 'm growing out of date,
At least, I 've fancied so of late,
    But she is still divine."
" Oh ! be it so," replied my muse,
" I 'll send her whatsoe'er she chuse,
    But be you ever mine."
                         T. P.

The royal proclamation was at once made a test of political principles. A public meeting was convened at Sheffield, at which Dr. Browne, a gentleman of standing in the " Church and State " party, offered resolutions of " Thanks to his Gracious Majesty for his interest in the welfare of his subjects, in prohibiting the circulation of Paine's writings "; which resolutions, after various spirited addresses, were negatived. Another meeting was called for the following evening, of persons favorable to addressing the King, which was not attended by the friends of liberty, among whom, of course, was Mr. Gales.

" While we were at tea," records Mrs. Gales, " alarming shouts were heard, and the appalling rumor spread that a furious mob was threatening Cutlers' Hall. Mr. Gales ran immediately, without his hat, to the scene of riot, and found the Vicar of Trinity Church haranguing the swaying crowd. He talked to the winds. In a moment the new-comer was discovered, and the cry arose, 'Mr. Gales in the chair!' It was repeated by a thousand voices, and without any personal volition he was carried to the chair rapidly vacated by the Vicar. There was no time to hesitate, and eloquence, had your father possessed the power of Tully, would have availed little at this crisis. A few plain words best suited the emergency, and in his usual quiet, composed way, he asked, ' Is this large assemblage of citizens before me, here in consequence of the handbills issued to-day ?'

" ' Yes.'

" ' Did you intend to sign a vote of thanks to the King ?'

" ' No ! No !'

" ' Then, my friends, you certainly have no business here. *You* expressed your sentiments yesterday, and surely would not deprive your neighbors of the same privilege. Sheffield has hitherto been celebrated for the orderly conduct of the manufacturing part of the community ; do not forfeit your claim to this honorable distinction.'

" ' Speak on, Mr. Gales ; you are a good man, we will hear what you say.'

"'If you rely on my advice because you believe me to be your friend, I will prove it by recommending that every one depart peaceably home. Oblige even your enemies to respect you by respecting yourselves.'

"'Home, home!' was the general cry. And in twenty minutes not one of the angry thousands assembled was to be seen.

"'See,' said an Anti-Reformer, 'what influence Gales has over the populace. By what art has he attained this power?'

"'By pleading the poor man's cause, by advocating equal representation, by treating them as brethren. Gales is a friend to the oppressed, an admirable man in every relation of life.'

"'Yes, yes; we know all that, and there's the rub; he could lead ten thousand men by the crook of his finger; and if French principles should take root, what might not be the result of his popularity!'

"This occurrence called forth praise from all sides, raising your father still higher in the esteem of the popular party, and increasing the respect even of our opponents.

"About the close of 1792 a new meteor blazed in the political horizon in the person of Henry Redhead Yorke. He was the son of a Governor of one of the West India Islands, by whom he had been sent to England for education and placed under the superintendence of Edmund Burke, whose favorite *protégé* he soon became. At the beginning of the French Revolution he was an ardent aristocrat, having imbibed the sentiments of his high-minded friend and patron; but

chancing to be at Paris during the sittings of the Jacobin Club, and carried away by the specious programme
of that infamous body, he flung aside his conservative
principles, becoming a sudden proselyte and flaming
stickler for the rights of man. This defection naturally
severed all friendship or intercourse with Burke.

" The first notice Mr. Gales had of this extraordinary
man was through two pamphlets : ' Reasons against
the Abolition of the Slave Trade, by Henry Redhead
Yorke.' 'Answered and Refuted by Himself.' The
first one he had written before he left England; the latter, after his return. He came to Sheffield as a dele-
gate from the Derby Society, fascinating by his charming manners, wit, and unusual attainments all who
came within the sphere of his influence, while his discussion of the all-absorbing national question, in throw-
ing new light on the subject, rendered him a powerful
auxiliary in the Reform movement. Few men could
withstand his eloquent boldness of assertion and flattering prognostication ; and several powerful appeals,
'The Times that try Men's Souls,' quoting from Locke
and Milton, largely increased his popularity."

A deep-seated alarm now pervaded all classes, public
indignation being still further excited by the employment of Hessian and Hanoverian troops, and the forma-
tion of volunteer companies by the Court party, for the
purpose of overawing the " seditious populace." A public meeting held at Chalk Farm near London, for the
purpose of denouncing this aggression upon the rights
of Englishmen, and one convened in a similar spirit at
Castle Hill, in Sheffield, precipitated events to a crisis.
The resolutions offered and advocated by Yorke on the

latter occasion created such wild enthusiasm that the multitude drew him in a carriage through the streets. " I had the honor to be drawn along with Yorke amidst excited thousands," writes Mr. Gales.

This protest was, however, disastrous in its results, as forming a pretext for the arrest by Government of many of the obnoxious participants. At the first note of alarm Yorke left Sheffield, being, however, after many ineffectual attempts for his apprehension, arrested in a singular and characteristic manner. Secreting himself on the banks of the Humber, he used to amuse himself by sailing about the coast in a skiff. On one of his excursions he saw a boat approach which he could not avoid, and the oarsmen bearing down, hailed him : " What is your name ? "

" Melville. Why do you ask ? "

" No. You are Redhead Yorke. I know you by your eyes, which a lady so well described that they cannot be mistaken."

Instead of being alarmed at his discovery and its sure consequences, he coolly replied, " Who was the dear creature who so sweetly observed me ? I hope she was young and beautiful."

The fascinating " conspirator " was committed to Doncaster jail, and finally sentenced to four years in York Castle, for misprision of treason.

" There he was incarcerated," writes Mrs. Gales, " when we left England, his efforts in the cause of Reform terminating in a manner befitting his romantic career. The beautiful daughter of Mr. Clayton, the Governor of the Castle, became attached to this extraordinary young man, and at the expiration of his term of imprisonment they were married. He published a volume called 'Mural Hours,' composed in prison, taking its idea perhaps from the 'Attic Nights' of Aulius Gellius. He subsequently edited a ministerial paper, and became one of the most strenuous opponents of Reform."

The thunder that had so long rolled at a distance at length burst, and the bolt that struck many distinguished victims, also shattered the more humble fortunes of Mr. Gales.

"Gerald, and other eminent patriots," writes Mrs. Gales, "were arrested, and sentenced to Botany Bay; two more were executed for treason whose crime lay in attending patriotic meetings; two dissenting. clergymen were transported to New South Wales; while Mr. Muir, a Scotchman of high standing, underwent the same severe sentence, being convicted, on the evidence of his servant, of lending seditious books to his neighbors. Hamilton Rowan, a distinguished man and good friend of ours, who had a beautiful seat near Newark, was implicated, but escaped to America, where, with other refugees from the injustice of our native land, we met him in later years. The dreadful fate of the brothers Sheares, and of the young and gifted Robert Emmett, has been wept over wherever freedom is loved."

Horne Tooke, Thelwell, and Hardy were apprehended in London, the last-named being Secretary of the London Society, and among whose papers was found an account of an enthusiastic Reform meeting at Sheffield, at which a hymn written for the occasion by Montgomery was sung in full chorus; "and thus," as the poet said, " one of my first hymns ever sung, found its way into Billy Pitt's green bag."

But material more inflammatory, and more moment-ous in its effect on the fortunes of Mr. Gales had also found its way into the Premier's hands. A capable, clever printer in the Register office had rashly indited an insurrectionary letter to the London Club, detailing very formidable revolutionary plans as to arms and troops, which sage epistle, seized with Hardy's papers, was dated " Gales's printing-office."

Mrs. Gales was now seriously alarmed, and tried to dissuade her husband from printing for these societies, or having any connection with them; but he replied, that "so long as their object continued to be none other than the one avowed, — Parliamentary Reform, — it was his duty to stand by them." But the blow now fell, from which Mr. Gales was only saved by his timely absence in Derbyshire.

The alarming rumor one morning flew through Sheffield that King's Messengers — names of terror in those days — armed with a Secretary of State's warrant, were on their way to arrest Redhead Yorke, Mr. Gales, and his spirited but indiscreet printer. The extreme measure of the suspension of the Habeas Corpus Act, cutting off victims of suspicion from legal redress, the severity of sentence in the cases of mere sympathy with Reform, and the knowledge that certain impris-onment and probable conviction awaited his return, combined to induce Mr. Gales to yield to the represen-tations of influential friends — conveyed to him by Montgomery — and to place the German Ocean between himself and prosecution.

3 *

"A few days passed in extreme inquietude," writes Mrs. Gales, "when early one morning I was awakened by a message from the men in the office informing me that the 'King's Messengers' were in town. Calling up my sister-in-law and Montgomery, we were listening with trembling anxiety to the account of the atrocious conduct of Ross and Diggs, whose very names carried terror, when Justice Althorpe and some strangers entered.

"'You are Mrs. Gales I presume,' said a well-looking man.

"I bowed with a swelling heart, but could not speak.

"'It is with great concern, madam,' said Colonel Althorpe, 'that by duty I am included in so painful a business; but the exigency of the times calls for extreme vigilance, and I am sorry to add that Mr. Gales is implicated as printer of seditious works, and we are authorized to search for the authors.'

"I cheerfully accompanied them through the house, opening each door, but they only bowed and passed on; but they were answered very cavalierly by the indignant printers at work in the office.

"'You have a very extensive establishment, madam, and I am informed that you are fully competent to carry it on in all its branches.'

"'I endeavor to do my duty, sir. But when is this persecuting spirit to cease? Where will it end, if an Englishman cannot discuss public measures, and inform the people through the press, of what so nearly concerns their interest?'

"'I hope at least, madam, that Mr. Gales may no longer be involved in the dangers of this period; and knowing the opinion entertained of him by his political opponents, I shall rejoice to learn that he remain absent until the present state of feeling shall subside.'

" They courteously took leave, and I mention their civility as being in such contrast with their usual cruelty in these domiciliary visits. A lady eighty years of age was rudely taken from bed, while her room was searched. And in London, when Thomas Hardy was arrested, they brutally insulted his wife, by telling her that she might see her husband hanged if she wished. She sank under her fears, her infant and herself dying during her husband's imprisonment."

The good sense, cleverness, and energy of Mrs. Gales were severely tested at this trying moment ; but her latent force of character was called forth, and her resolution strengthened as the difficulties increased. " My husband gone, a large printing establishment in full business, a paper to edit, and a young family claiming my care." From every rank of the community now flowed in evidences of the respect and personal love entertained for Mrs. Gales and her absent husband, in generous and delicate proffers of service from the lowly as well as affluent citizens. Mrs. Gales was especially touched by the expression of feeling on the part of the workingmen, who regarded Mr. Gales as their exemplar and protector. During one of the riots, frequent at this disturbed period, a volunteer guard kept watch around her sleeping family, shielded for the remainder of their stay in Sheffield by these unknown friends.

A deputation of mechanics waited on Mrs. Gales to present a paper signed by the head workman of every craft in Sheffield, stating that they "had sworn to protect her and her children, and if it was her husband's wish to return, thousands stood pledged to guard him." "My feelings," says Mrs. Gales, " overcame me at this demonstration of devotion; but when composed, I pointed out that this proof of attachment would bring ruin on them from civil authority, and I would give them the advice which my husband would approve: that they return home, and continue to be orderly, industrious, temperate citizens. After asking to shake my hand in farewell, they gravely went their way. Worthy men of Sheffield! never shall this kindness be effaced from my memory."

Mr. Gales had safely reached Amsterdam, thence making his way to Hamburg. To return to England would be to risk the tender mercies of a packed jury and prejudiced judges; and the turn of events hastened to a decision the project long entertained by Mr. Gales, to try his fortunes in the more congenial political clime of the new Western Republic. A sentence or two from the letter instructing his wife and children to join him in Germany prove that no storm of adversity, as no temptation of poverty, could swerve the rigid integrity of this upright man.

"Bring nothing with you, my dear Winifred, but what the strictest justice warrants. Let us meet in peace, with a clear conscience, and my trust is in God, that he will help us. We are young, healthy, and able to struggle for a support for our dear children; and leaving no one behind us who can with truth say that we have wronged him, fear not but that He who feeds the young ravens will feed us."

Mrs. Gales now made all arrangements, and offered the establishment for sale. Very liberal proposals were made for the 'Register' by an agent for Government, which would gladly have suppressed so obnoxious a medium of free discussion; but Mrs. Gales rejected the offer with spirit, and had the satisfaction of placing the paper in the hands of one who would manfully uphold the principles so vigorously advocated by its conscientious founder.

The moment of parting came; and amidst the tears of friends, and the ardent blessings of the humbler crowd that filled the street, Mrs. Gales bade farewell to the endeared scenes and loved relatives whom she was to behold no more on earth; and sailing from Hull, her native land set upon her sight forever.

"The torchlike blaze of the 'Register' being thus quenched, it soon afterwards, in the hands of Montgomery, revived under the milder light of the 'Iris.' The young poet-editor inherited the political odium attaching to his predecessor in the eyes of the government; and, watched with vigilance, was marked out as the victim of that bolt of vengeance which had missed his patriotic master." Under the most paltry pretext of writing and printing seditious songs, he suffered a state prosecution at the hands of Sir John Scott, subsequently Lord Eldon, and was twice imprisoned in York Castle.

The incidents and labors of Montgomery's career, as journalist, politician, and philanthropist, are too familiar to the public to be here recited. As a poet, his name is indelibly inscribed in the ranks of England's most cherished sons; while his memory is endeared to thousands of Christians, who find in the fervor and poetic fire of the unsurpassed hymns of this "sweet singer in Israel" the truest expression of their soul's worship.

In 1825, on the occasion of Montgomery's retirement from public life, he was complimented by a dinner, offered by gentlemen of every shade of political opinion, presided over by Earl Fitzwilliam, whose father had been the poet's first patron. The runaway youth with his cherished manuscript in his pocket, his sole wealth, had the good fortune to meet the Earl riding in his park at Wentworth; and pulling out the poem, presented it to the kindly nobleman, who, reading it on the spot, gave the elated author his first golden guinea.

In replying to a toast at this banquet, Montgomery spoke of Mr. Gales and the cause he had so nobly defended.

"With all the enthusiasm of youth I entered into the feelings of those who called themselves the friends of freedom and humanity. Those with whom I was immediately connected, verily were such; and had all the Reformers of that era been generous, upright, and disinterested like the noble-minded editor of the Sheffield Register, the cause which they espoused would never have been disgraced, and might have prevailed at that time; since there could have been nothing to fear from the patriotic measure of patriotic men."

Strongly attached to the family of Mr. Gales, Montgomery passed into his remaining household, consisting of three sisters, to whom, until the circle was broken by death, he supplied the place of a brother. The ill-health of the eldest Miss Gales alone prevented the

cementing of this fraternal association by a more tender
tie, her virtues being commemorated by Montgomery
at the period of her death, by the following hitherto
unpublished lines : —

> " She went as calmly as at eve
>   A cloud in sunset melts away,
>   While blending nights and shadows weave
>   The winding-sheet of dying day.

> " No : — the day dies not : — round the globe
>   It holds its flight o'er land and main ;
>   Morn, noon, and evening are its robe,
>   And solemn night its flowing train.

> " So when to us she seemed to die,
>   And leave a shadow in her shroud,
>   'T was but the glory passing by,
>   And darkness gathering round a cloud.

> " Such words as angel-lips conveyed
>   To Mary at the sepulchre,
>   Where she had seen her Saviour laid,
>   Seemed for a moment true of her.

> " For she had risen, and cast away
>   The vestments which her spirit wore ;
>   ' The linen clothes and napkin ' lay,
>   But she, our friend, was there no more.

> " Yes, she was risen, and whither flown
>   The mind of man might not conceive ;
>   Yet, that she stood before the Throne,
>   Faith, though it saw not, could believe.

> " For by no sophistry beguiled,
>   She loved the Gospel's joyful sound,
>   Received it like a little child,
>   And in her heart its sweetness found.

> " Farewell, a brief farewell, dear friend !
>   Dear sister ! — we are following fast ;

> O for endurance to the end,
> And home in Heaven when toils are past !
>
> " Ashes to ashes, dust to dust,
>   We laid thee where thy fathers sleep :
>   There, till the rising of the just,
>   Watch o'er thy bed the stars will keep.
>
> " ' Good night !' once more: — when next we meet
>   May this our salutation be,
>   ' Good morrow!' at the judgment-seat ;
>   ' Good morrow !' to eternity.
>   " J. MONTGOMERY.
> " THE MOUNT, SHEFFIELD,
>   February 24, 1838."

A member of Mr. Seaton's family thus describes, in 1848, a visit to the " Mount " in Sheffield, where the venerable poet, then seventy-seven years of age, was happily passing the placid evening of a somewhat stormy life, in the faithful companionship of the survivor of the Gales sisters : —

" Who says that Montgomery is morose ? He is a trump, a delightful old man, whom I could reverence and love in a week, so unsophisticated and pure in his tastes and habits is he. I have seen him and Aunt Sarah every day, and they are cordial and affectionate as possible ; and in the dinner at their house I enjoyed the meeting exceedingly ; Montgomery took his pipe, and chatted in the most charming, easy, and winning manner."

At the close of a spring day in 1854 the aged poet surprised Miss Gales at family worship by handing her the Bible, saying, " Sarah, you must read " ; after which he prayed with a peculiar pathos, exciting his friend's attention, conversing cheerfully, however, while smoking his customary pipe. But the end of earth had come ; and a few hours later, while speaking with Miss Gales, "he fell on sleep."

The transit of Mrs. Gales, from Hull to Hamburg, was not without danger, from a severe gale threatening instant destruction ; but all suffering was forgotten in the joyful reunion with the exile at Altona. In September they embarked for America, but the manners of the captain, and the whole discipline of the vessel, were so offensive as to excite disgust and uneasiness among the passengers ; and a prolonged calm succeeding to a terrific storm, adding to the discomfort, induced Mr. Gales to forfeit his passage. Hailing a passing pilot-boat, the wandering family once more safely landed on German soil.

This incident, apparently affecting only the personal comfort of Mrs. Gales, was a providential link in the chain of events shaping the future fortune of Mr. Gales, and that of his descendants in the New World. With characteristic industry, during the winter he set himself the task of mastering the German tongue and the art of short-hand ; and it was his skill in the latter chance acquisition that virtually founded the National Intelligencer, and gave to fame its brother editors.

Altona, in the Duchy of Holstein, the claim to whose allegiance was so recently *casus belli* between gallant little Denmark and the great German powers, is a quaint, pretty town on the banks of the Elbe, separated only by ancient, picturesque gates from the beautiful free city of Hamburg ; and it would be interesting to present the details of continental life during a residence there seventy-four years ago, as noted

by the graphic and sprightly pen of Mrs. Gales ; but
the limits of this sketch preclude more than a passing
glance at a few of the persons and incidents described
in her autobiography.

"The season set in with intense rigor, and persons
in America recollect the bitter severity of the winter
of 1794. The rivers became solidly frozen to a great
thickness, insomuch that hundreds of persons assembled on the Elbe, lighting large fires, eating, dancing,
skating, and roasting oxen whole on the ice. Early
in January, 1795, General Pichegru and his victorious
army having expelled the Austrians from the Nether-
lands, drove the Dutch and British before them, and
passing over the frozen Meuse, literally conquered the
country on skates.

"This unlooked-for event in a manner affected our
humble fortunes, bringing as it did to Altona an influx
of several thousand French emigrants, among whom we
renewed old and formed fresh friendships. The French
royalists had escaped in vast numbers from Jacobin-
ical atrocities to England and Holland, and on the advance of Pichegru they fled dismayed from their asylum, the females shrieking, 'They are come, the French
are come ; we are lost !' But Pichegru possessed the
spirit of humanity always accompanying true bravery,
and on his entrance into Amsterdam performed a most
gracious action. Whilst the affrighted French were
flying in all directions, a small number of them, maddened by conflicting feelings, rushed into the victorious general's presence, demanding instant death ! To
their impassioned supplications Pichegru replied, with
averted face, 'I know you not,' motioning as he left

the room to one of his aides, who, conducting the reckless creatures into another apartment, drew their attention to a table covered with *rouleaux* of gold. A few, yielding to the pressure of the moment, availed themselves of this noble, delicate liberality; others, from honorable but mistaken feeling, turned silently away. One of the latter, a gifted man of high rank at home, related this anecdote to us, with expressions of gratitude for the kindly victor.

"Reduced to utter penury, it was no unusual thing for us to see in the streets of Altona the cherished Cross of St. Louis glittering beneath the threadbare vestments of these *emigrés;* and ladies who had graced the circles of a court cheerfully submitted to menial employments.

"We were surprised one morning by a visit from Citizen, *ci-devant* Count, Zenobia, whom we had known in Sheffield, where Mr. Gales published for him the spirited pamphlets advocating the liberal cause, which had rendered him so obnoxious to the Ministry; and while waiting to correct his proofs he had passed many hours in my drawing-room. He was a novel character to me, very entertaining, having for some years been Envoy from Venice to England, where he remained after his embassy had ceased. Speaking English fluently, he was now, in Germany, a welcome guest at our humble board, his wife also being a pleasant acquisition to our circle, a beautiful woman, with a superb suit of brown hair that swept the floor.

"He presented to us General Clarke, of the Irish Brigade in France, a most charming man, who afterwards, such are Fortune's caprices, was created by Napoleon a peer of France, Duc de Dantzic, and accompanied Madame Lafayette to Olmutz.

"Among other notables of our little coterie may be mentioned General Dumouriez, who there wrote his memoirs ; and Mr. Dutton, proscribed in England as the author of essays under the signature of *Junius Redivivus*, for whose apprehension a large reward was offered.

"Citizen and Citizeness Zenobia were pleased with my children, and frequently begged that they be allowed to accompany them to dessert at the celebrated *table d'hôte* in Altona, where my little girls were always received with enthusiasm, returning to me full of admiration at the beauty of the ladies, their lovely red cheeks, and grand gowns.

"Among the emigrants whom we came to know well was the celebrated Madame de Genlis, whose husband, Sillery-Brulart, had been a victim of the guillotine. She retained in full her great beauty and fascination, was witty, perhaps a little frivolous, and unsubdued by the fearful scenes that had banished her from the brilliant society of a luxurious court. She often spoke with devoted affection of her former pupil, the Duc de Chartres — afterwards King Louis Philippe — and I was surprised in after-years to learn that she had transferred her allegiance ardently to the Imperial Corsican, by whom she was allowed a pension and handsome apartment at the Tuileries, playing again a conspicuous *rôle* at the court of St. Cloud. Estranged from the Orleans family by this defection, the accession of Louis Philippe brought her no increase of honor, and this once-cherished favorite of princes sank into poverty and obscurity. She was engaged in literary pursuits while at Altona, writing there her 'Knights of the Swan.' My little Sarah — afterwards Mrs. Seaton — was her special pet, and so much did the child win upon her affection, that she urged us to let her fill the empty place in her heart ; but we could not part with our daughter, even to bestow upon her all the worldly advantages attending the rank and fame of Madame de Genlis."

In the diverse circle thus strangely resolved into social harmony was the philanthropic Joel Barlow with his wife, whose acquaintance with Mr. and Mrs. Gales ripened into intimacy. This gifted man had already played a prominent part in the revolutionary dramas of the rebellious American Colonies, and of republican France, having left college to participate in the victory of White Plains. Returning to the prosecution of his studies, the youthful patriot's graduating poem was on the "Prospect of Peace," and still fired by rebellious ardor, he prepared himself, after *six weeks'* devotion to theology, for the post of army chaplain, one of the unusual duties of which spiritual office he assumed to be the composition of spirited odes, by which to animate the soldiers. His "Vision of Columbus," afterwards elaborated into his *magnum opus* the "Columbiad," met with great success both in London and Paris ; and Miss Berry, the beautiful friend of Horace Walpole, speaks of it as a work of genius.

This enthusiastic nature naturally led its possessor to the van, in the cry of liberty then shaking thrones and peoples, and Joel Barlow precipitated himself into the maelstrom of French anarchy, becoming involved in the intrigues of the Girondists; and in a poem entitled " The Conspiracy of Kings " launched a furious denunciation at the devoted head of Edmund Burke as the author of the calamities of the times. Being sent on a diplomatic mission to Savoy, he made stirring appeals to the Piedmontese to embrace the alluring principles of Revolution, composing meanwhile his humorous poem, " The Hasty Pudding."

He now formed one of the most brilliant members of the little community of *proscrits*, united by the sympathetic tie of persecution in this hospitable German town. " Once more," writes Mrs. Gales, " were we tempted to part with our little daughter Sarah. Our kind friends the Barlows earnestly plead with us to resign her to them, if only for a year. ' We will take her to France, and give her again to your arms in America,' said they ; but we firmly resisted the entreaty, and happily so, for Mr. Barlow was appointed Consul at Algiers — where he released the prisoners held as slaves by the Barbary Powers — and to various other missions; so that we only met in America after an interval of fourteen years."

During the winter the domestic content of Mr. and Mrs. Gales was enhanced by the birth of a daughter, named, in commemoration of their city of refuge, Altona Holstein.

The moment now arrived in which these English wanderers were once more to leave kind friends and pleasant scenes, and in July, 1795, they sailed for Philadelphia. The ship skimmed lightly over the summer seas in uninterrupted safety, except from an incident that afforded the facile pen of Mrs. Gales subject-matter for frequent romantic after-sketches.

"When about four hundred miles from the Delaware Capes, one morning the lookout called, 'A sail, a sail ahead.' 'A pilot-boat,' said one. 'How curiously rigged, and what a cloud of canvas she carries!' said another. 'But,' said I, placing the telescope to my eye, 'the people on her deck are dancing like wild men'; and at these words a shot whizzed across our bow from the privateer, to bring us to.

"All was now hurry and consternation. England, France, and the Barbary Powers were at war, and the Algerine pirates were spreading terror over every sea. In a moment it was determined that some of the passengers were to be Spaniards, — ourselves, an American family returning from Hamburg, — the Germans to remain *in statu quo*. Within half an hour the privateer had boarded us, put our crew under hatches, and carried off our captain, leaving a lieutenant and prize-master in charge of our vessel.

"Shielded by my clinging children, and fearing no insult, I went on deck, when the lieutenant, bowing, said, 'An American family from Hamburg, madam?' I merely bowed. 'Your husband may be an American, but you surely are an Englishwoman, and these children,' patting the heads of Joseph and Sarah, 'were born on British soil.'

"'Can you, then, draw such nice distinctions between those who, though living in different hemispheres, claim a common origin and speak the same language?' I replied.

"'Yes, madam, for I am an Englishman.'

"I instantly made up my mind, and held out my hand to my countryman. At the same moment the bluff prize-master came up, saying, 'You are a York-shire woman too, madam, and blessed is the sound of your voice, for it is thirteen years since I heard my native dialect.' I shook hands also with him cordially, and then expatiated on the hardship of being carried to Bermuda. Lieutenant Bethel tried to console me; his house, the prettiest on the island, should be at my service, and we should be honored guests.

"In quite a prolonged conversation I adjured him to abandon a profession in which every man's hand was against his own.

"Late at night the captain returned, and came to our cabin, where I sat reading. 'Well, where is this lady passenger and her children, who are like angels in green and gold?'

"His voice made me tremble, but I calmly returned his salutation. He insisted on seeing the children, and I lighted him to their cots, when he passed his hand gently over their sleeping faces, and, stooping, kissed my little girls. From that moment I was assured of our safety.

"The letter-bag was handed to him by his orders, and as he opened and deliberately read its contents, I smiled. 'What amuses you, madam?'

"'Your honorable profession, sir, which rises every moment in my estimation.'

"He crimsoned, saying, 'Do you remember that you are a captive?'

"'Yes, but if we had had but one stern-chaser, you could not have called me so.'"

A lengthened colloquy ensued, in which the tact and spirit of Mrs. Gales, pleading for husband and children,

won the day ; and the privateer relinquished his prize,
parting with his late prisoner even cordially, his last
words being : " Until your reputation for personal ve-
racity shall be established in Philadelphia, do not say
that this vessel had been during many hours in possession of, and was voluntarily surrendered by, Hutch-
ins and Bethel. To you alone, madam, it is relinquished."

Good cause indeed had the souls on board that ship
to be grateful to Mrs. Gales for deliverance from the
clutches of the captain of this privateer, — a bad man,
already notorious for every violation of honor and humanity.

Immediately on his arrival at Philadelphia Mr. Gales
sought employment as a printer, his skill as a crafts-
man and his merit as a man commanding speedy recognition. The reports by the press, of the congressional
debates were at this period few and meagre, the art
of short-hand being in its infancy even in the British
Parliament ; and when a faithful transcript by Mr. Gales
of a day's debate in Congress appeared in full in the
succeeding morning's paper of his employer, the sensation was immense among the reading public of the city.
This stenographic skill proved a ready stepping-stone
to better fortune, and Mr. Gales soon purchased the
Independent Gazetteer from the widow of Colonel
John Oswald of Revolutionary fame.

Several years now passed in prosperity, the social
pleasure of the family being greatly increased by the
renewal of several home friendships among the refugees who had here gathered to seek safety from the
storm evoked by English Reform, among them being

4

the learned and pious Priestley, who here baptized several of Mrs. Gales's children.

" A number of our English friends," says Mrs. Gales, " were, like ourselves, Unitarians ; and there being no church for this denomination of Christians in Philadelphia, it was resolved to form a society of those of our faith ; and a room was engaged in the University Buildings in South 4th Street, where our first meeting was held June 12, 1796. This little flock consisted at first of only thirteen individuals and their respective families. Six persons were appointed to officiate as lay readers, Dr. Priestley's forms of prayer being used, each reader selecting such sermon as he thought proper, Mr. Gales being the first reader who officiated. After we left Philadelphia in 1799, the number of the society largely increasing, a place of worship was erected in 1816 ; and in 1828, the congregation being greatly multiplied, the present church was built and consecrated to the worship of the One True God, — ' for there is one Jehovah, one God.' "

The yellow-fever during several seasons had devastated Philadelphia, and Mrs. Gales was among the sufferers from this terrible visitation. In 1799, the scourge again appearing, threatening now to become an annual calamity, Mr. Gales yielded to the advantageous inducements urgently offered him by some warm friends among the North Carolina Delegation, and decided to remove to the recently established capital of that State, Raleigh. He disposed of his paper to Mr. Samuel Harrison Smith, who in 1800 accompanied the government to Washington, where his journal was rebaptized as the National Intelligencer.

A third time, then, Mr. and Mrs. Gales left a comfortable home and agreeable social surroundings for untried scenes in a foreign land; but in the hospitable little Southern community to which they now directed their almost pioneer steps, the open hand of kind welcome was extended to the new-comers. Mr. Gales at once established a journal, reviving the name and motto of the one that had fought so good a fight in stanch old Sheffield, — The Raleigh Register.

" By the constant merit and sober sense of his paper," says the Atlantic Monthly, " its moderation and its integrity, Mr. Gales won and maintained the confidence of all on that side of politics with which he concurred, — the old Republican, — and not less conciliated the respect of his opponents. In the just and kindly old commonwealth which he so long served, it would have been hard for any party to move anything for his injury; and the good North State honored and cherished no son of her own loins more than she did Joseph Gales. In Raleigh there was no figure that, as it passed, was greeted so much by the signs of a peculiar veneration as that great, stalwart one of his, with a sort of nobleness in its very simplicity, an inborn goodness and courtesy in all its roughness of frame, — a countenance mild, commanding yet pleasant, betokening a bosom that no low thought had ever entered. You had in him, indeed, the highest image of that stanch old order from which he was sprung."

Thirty-four years now passed tranquilly and happily, cheered by constant evidences of regard from the community, and surrounded by a band of dutiful, affectionate, and gifted children. · But the time had now come for repose from the labors of this prolonged life, and Mr. Gales decided to remove to Washington to pass the remainder of his days near his two children, Joseph and Mrs. Seaton. This intention being publicly announced, produced a considerable excitement in the little city of which, during one third of a century, Mr. and Mrs. Gales had been active members. They could not be parted from silently. A public dinner was given in this good man's honor, presided over by Governor Swain, on which occasion every respectable citizen of the community, and many friends from a distance, — among whom were Judge Gaston and Chief-Justice Marshall, — assembled to pay tribute in warmest expressions of respect and love, and with full hearts to bid farewell to their venerable parting friend.

The Register was transferred to his third son, Weston Raleigh Gales, who was endowed in full measure with the intellectual activity, editorial facility, and a nature brimming over with every generous and kindly impulse that characterized his parents, and whose premature death was mourned by his State and city as a public and personal loss.

Passing, then, into the hands of Mr. Weston Gales's youthful son, Seaton Gales, the Register, thus in the third generation of its founder's family, continued to be conducted with the ability which had won for it so prominent a position among the journals of the South.

It was not possible for Mr. Gales, even at his advanced age, to cast off completely the harness of toil; and in the chief management of the affairs of the African Colonization Society at Washington he found, until his final return to Raleigh, congenial occupation for his benevolent nature.

The close of Joseph Gales's career now drew near; but he was preceded to the abode of "just men made perfect" by his honored life-companion, whose poetic and buoyant temperament, conversational gift, and gay intelligence had brightened his leisure hours, as her womanly tenderness and self-sacrifices had chased many shadows from his laborious existence.

Within two years of her death he fell quietly asleep, in the sustaining faith which had guided his useful, blameless Christian life.

It was, then, under the auspices of a man whose nobility of nature was so kindred to his own that Mr. Seaton made his next step in political journalism. In the same year, 1809, the relationship was yet more closely cemented by his union with Miss Sarah Gales, who had shared with her brothers and sisters a careful training by her father, being schooled in Latin and English classics, well versed in French and Spanish, with a taste for general literature critically cultivated; acquiring also from her father a rare accomplishment for a lady, that of stenography. Inheriting with the excellent judgment of her father the conversational talent and the generous nature of her mother, she had formed the delight of her parents' home, where, surrounded by intellectual influences, and in the companionship of cultured minds, she had acquired the accomplishments, and developed the virtues, which subsequently adorned her husband's home with gentle goodness and social distinction.

Meanwhile Joseph Gales the younger, bred to the paternal art, and matured in profession and character, had entered upon the career of journalism in which he was destined to attain unusual eminence.

" His boyhood, as usual, prefigured the man ; it was diligent in study, hilarious at play; his mind bent upon solid things, not showy. For all good, just, generous, and kindly things he had the warmest impulse and the truest perception. Quick to learn and to feel, he was slow only of resentment. Of the classic tongues he can be said to have learnt only the Latin. For the positive sciences he had much inclination, since it is told that he constructed instruments for himself, such as an electrical machine, with the performances of which he amazed the good people of Raleigh. Meantime, he was forming at home, under the good guidance there, a solid knowledge of those fine old authors, whose works make the undegenerate literature of our · language, and then constituted what they called Polite Letters." *

Graduating at the State University, this young printer, to obtain a more thorough knowledge of his craft, was sent to his father's old English friend, William Birch, of Philadelphia, where he speedily became skilled in his art. The chance acquirement by Joseph Gales of the art of stenography again led, at this juncture, to important results, in its bearing on the fortunes of his son, whom he had already instructed in this adjunct of his intended profession.

Mr. Samuel Harrison Smith, having transferred, with the removal of the seat of government, the paper purchased of Joseph Gales to Washington, there reissued it on the 31st of October, 1800, under the double title

* Atlantic Monthly, 1860.

of "The National Intelligencer and Washington Advertiser."

"During the whole of Mr. Jefferson's administration, the most confidential personal and editorial relations existed between the President and Mr. Smith, who ably supported his administration, as he continued to do that of Mr. Madison, who, as Secretary of State, and subsequently as Chief Magistrate, manifested the utmost respect and confidence for Mr. Smith's intellectual ability, patriotism, and moral purity."

In 1807 Mr. Gales offered his son Joseph, then just of age, as an assistant to Mr. Smith in the business of the "Intelligencer," with an especial view to his employment as a reporter, and himself attended the ensuing session of Congress for the purpose of initiating his son in the difficulties of reporting the debates.

His pupil soon became noted for his stenographic accuracy, and eventually one of the best reporters known at that day. "To the 'Intelligencer' young Mr. Gales brought such vigor, such talent in every department, that within two years of their association he was admitted by Mr. Smith into partnership." In 1810 Mr. Smith withdrew from his laborious occupation as editor, wishing to pass the remainder of his life in the literary and philosophical pursuits for which his love of letters and liberal culture so signally fitted him. " . . . . The evening of his life of blameless purity found him conscious, prepared, and tranquil; and having lived the life of a philosopher, he gave to the friends who surrounded him a lesson how to die as a Christian." *

* National Intelligencer.

"Of the administrations of Mr. Jefferson and Mr. Madison the Intelligencer had been the supporter, only following in that regard the transmitted politics of its original, the 'Gazetteer,' derived from the elder Mr. Gales. Bred in these, the son had learnt them of his sire, as he had adopted his religion or his morals. Sprung from one who had been educated in England as a republican, it was natural that the son should love the faith for which an honored parent had suffered." *

In October, 1812, Mr. Seaton united his fortunes with those of his brother-in-law, which association transferred the names of Gales and Seaton from the head of the Register to that of the Intelligencer, and the former journal reverted to its original status, with Joseph Gales, senior, as editor.

"Raleigh, in this instance, gave to Washington a brace of editors trained in the office of the Raleigh Register, who, during half a century, published a paper that for ability, fairness, courtesy, dignity, purity, and elegance of style, obtained a reputation equalled by few Gazettes in any part of the world."

"The early tie of youthful friendship which had grown between Mr. Seaton and Mr. Gales at Raleigh, and which the new brotherly relation had drawn still closer, gradually matured into that more than friendship or brotherhood, that oneness and identity of all purposes, opinions, and interests, which ever after existed between them without a moment's interruption, and was long, to those who understood it, a rare spectacle of that concord and affection so seldom

* Atlantic Monthly, 1860.

witnessed, and which could never have come about except between men of singular virtues." *

The wings of the capitol, the President's mansion, a few public buildings, and a score or so of private dwellings stranded among the marshes, scattered from Greenleaf's Point to Georgetown, over rural hills and along the banks of " Goose Creek once and Tiber now," then constituted the main features of the infant metropolis, — the " Federal City," as General Washington modestly addressed a letter, franked by his own great name, now in the writer's possession. The increase or improvement of the city had not made many strides since the removal thither of the government, " which," as Mr. Wolcott expressed it, " left the comforts of Philadelphia to go to the Indian place with the long name, in the woods on the Potomac." Contemporary accounts represent it as desolate in the extreme, with its unopened streets and avenues, its deep morasses, and its vast area covered with trees instead of houses."

" The ridge of hills," says Mrs. Harrison Smith, " of which Capitol Hill forms a part, was covered with a growth of fine, wide-spreading forest trees, natives of the soil, which, if properly managed, would have formed a noble park; but in purchasing the ground no right to these majestic trees had been reserved by the government, and they were felled and sold by their original owners for fuel."

" I wish I were a despot," cried Mr. Jefferson, " that I might save those noble trees."

Many a snipe has fallen before Mr. Seaton's unerring aim where his old homestead stands, and many a

* Atlantic Monthly, 1860.

4 *   F

covey of partridges has his pointer flushed among the woods of our now broad avenues. Notwithstanding the desolate surroundings of the inchoate city, its society had already attained the cosmopolitan features characterizing a political capital. " The literary and philosophical, as well as political reputation of Mr. Jefferson, had made it the resort of foreigners, of men of science, and of all European travellers "; and upon the accession of Mr. Madison, and notably of his charming wife to the honors of the executive mansion, a refined ease and polished gayety pervaded the circles graced by the winning presence of the new Presidentess.

Mr. and Mrs. Seaton, upon their entrance on the more enlarged sphere of their new home, were welcomed with the hospitality characteristic of that day; the consideration evinced towards them as strangers, speedily warming in the community to the respect and personal affection due to their virtues and rare attractive qualities. Few are the survivors, and fewer still the records of that era of a courtly tone and stately grace of society, marked by the simplicity of high breeding, and the absence of tawdry display; when the flavor of royalty still clung to habits and modes of speech; when Mrs. Madison was approached as a Queen, and the President's mansion was designated as the " Palace."

Mrs. Seaton's family correspondence depicts many interesting persons and incidents prominent during this period; various extracts from which will best illustrate the position of herself and husband, their domestic happiness, and the intelligent perception which seized and graphically portrayed the living manners as they rose; while it will be matter for regret that family reserve should deprive the public of these entire ana, which have now crystallized into valuable social history.

Mrs. Seaton humorously describes the difficulties attending her housekeeping researches, the young metropolis being entirely supplied with such requisites by Georgetown, at that period the emporium of fashion, and thus continues her diary: —

"October, 1812.

"Yesterday was a day of all days in Washington, — hundreds of strangers from Maryland and Virginia, in their grand equipages, to see a race! Gov. Wright with his horses to run, Col. Holmes with his, and people of every condition straining at full speed. Mr. and Mrs. Madison, the departments of government, all, all for the race! Major L——, who is hand and glove with every grandee, and perfectly in his element, called for William (Mr. Seaton), while I accompanied Dr. and Mrs. Blake, and old Governor Wright of Maryland, in their handsome carriage to the field. It was an exhilarating spectacle, even if one took no interest in the main event of the day; and such an assemblage of stylish equipages I never before witnessed. A large number of agreeable persons, residents and strangers, were introduced to us. . . . . .

"Yesterday the first drawing-room of the season was held. Joseph (Mr. Gales) and R. started in fine style, the latter sporting *five* cravats, Joseph contenting himself with *three*. William was much solicited to accompany them, but as I have not yet been presented to her majesty, and it not being etiquette to appear in public until that ceremony be performed, he preferred remaining with me. Mrs.

Madison told Joseph, that she 'anticipated much pleasure in my acquaintance.' . . . . I shall not fail to enumerate every instance of attention exhibited towards us, as I know that your maternal tenderness is ever awake on our account."

"November 12, 1812.

". . . . On Tuesday, William and I repaired to the palace between four and five o'clock, our carriage setting us down *after* the first comers, and *before* the last. It is customary, on whatever occasion, to advance to the upper end of the room, pay your obeisance to Mrs. Madison, courtesy to his Highness, and take a seat; after this ceremony being at liberty to speak to acquaintances, or amuse yourself as at another party. The party already assembled consisted of the Treasurer of the United States; Mr. Russell, the American Minister to England; Mr. Cutts, brother-in-law to Mrs. Madison; Gen. Van Ness and family; Gen. Smith and daughter from New York; Patrick Magruder's family; Col. Goodwyn and daughter; Mr. Coles, the Private Secretary; Washington Irving, the author of Knickerbocker and Salmagundi; Mr. Thomas, an European; a young Russian, Mr. Poindexter, William R. King and two other gentlemen; and these, with Mr. and Mrs. Madison, and Payne Todd, their son, completed the select company.

" Mrs. Madison very handsomely came to me and led me nearest the fire, introduced Mrs. Magruder, and sat down between us, politely conversing on familiar subjects, and by her own ease of manner making her guests feel at home. Mr. King came to our side *sans cérémonie*, and gayly chatted with us until dinner was announced. Mrs. Magruder, by priority of age, was entitled to the right hand of her Hostess; and I, in virtue of being a stranger, to the next seat, Mr. Russell to her left, Mr. Coles at the foot of the table, the President in the middle, which relieves him from the trouble of serving guests, drinking wine, etc. The dinner was certainly very fine ; but still I was rather surprised, as it did not surpass some I have eaten in Carolina. There were many French dishes, and exquisite wines, I presume, by the praises bestowed on them ; but I have been so little accustomed to drink, that I could not discern the difference between Sherry and rare old Burgundy Madeira. Comment on the quality of the wine seems to form the chief topic after the removal of the cloth, and during the dessert, at which, by the way, no pastry is countenanced. Ice-creams, maccaroons, preserves and various cakes are placed on the table, which are removed for almonds, raisins, pecan-nuts, apples, pears, etc. Candles were introduced before the ladies left the table ; and the gentlemen continued half an hour longer to drink a social glass. Meantime Mrs. Madison insisted on my playing on her elegant grand piano a waltz for Miss Smith and Miss Magruder to dance, the figure of which she instructed them in. By this time the gentlemen came in, and we adjourned to the tea-room, and here in the most delightful manner imaginable I shared with Miss Smith, who is remarkably intelligent, the pleasure of Mrs. Madison's conversation on books, men and manners, literature in general, and many special branches of knowledge. I never spent a more rational or pleasing half hour than that which preceded our return home. On paying our compliments at parting, we were politely and particularly invited to attend the levee the next evening. . . . . . I would describe the dignified appearance of Mrs. Madison, but I could not do her justice. 'T is not her form, 't is not her face, it is the woman altogether, whom I should wish you to see. She wears a crimson cap that almost hides her forehead, but which becomes her extremely, and reminds

one of a crown from its brilliant appearance, contrasted
with the white satin folds and her jet black curls ; but her
demeanor is so far removed from the hauteur generally
attendant on royalty, that your fancy can carry the resemblance no further than the head-dress. . . . . In a
conspicuous position every fault is rendered more discern-
ible to common eyes, and more liable to censure; and the
same rule certainly enables every virtue to shine with
more brilliancy than when confined to an inferior station in
society; but *I*, and I am by no means singular in the
opinion, believe that Mrs. Madison's conduct would be
graced by propriety were she placed in the most adverse
circumstances in life.

"Mr. Madison had no leisure for the ladies : every
moment of his time is engrossed by the crowd of male
visitors who court his notice, and after passing the first
complimentary salutations, his attention is unavoidably
withdrawn to more important objects. . . . . Some days
ago invitations were issued to two or three hundred
ladies and gentlemen, to dine and spend the day with Col.
Wharton and Capt. Stewart, on board the Constellation, —
an immense ship of war. This, of all the sights I have
ever witnessed, was the most interesting, grand and novel.
William, Joseph, R. and I, went together, and as the
vessel lay in the stream off the Point, there were several
beautiful little yachts to convey the guests to the scene of
festivity. On reaching the deck we were ushered immediately under the awning composed of many flags, and found
ourselves in the presence of hundreds of ladies and gentlemen. The effect was astonishing : every color of the rainbow, every form and fashion, nature and art ransacked to
furnish gay and suitable habiliments for the belles, who
with the beaux, in their court dresses, were gayly dancing to
the inspiring strains of a magnificent band. The ladies

had assumed youth and beauty in their persons, taste and splendor in their dress; thousands of dollars having been expended by dashing fair ones in preparation of this *fête*. . . . .

"At the upper end of the quarter-deck sat Mrs. Madison, to whom we paid our respects, and then participated in the conversation and amusements with our friends, among whom were Mrs. Monroe, Mrs. Gallatin, etc. I did not dance (though ''t was not for want of asking'), being totally unacquainted with the present style of cotillons, which were danced in the interstices, that is, on a space of four feet square. There was more opportunity to display agility than grace, as an iron ring, coil of rope, or gun-carriage would prostrate a beau or belle. A number of gentlemen were introduced to me, among others Mr. Johnstone, of Kentucky, a pleasant, sensible man, from whose conversation I derived much satisfaction, and who presented to me the gallant Captain Hull and Lieutenant Morris, who so 'nobly fought the foe' on board the Constitution.

"We naturally, in imagination, frame the figure of any character of celebrity; and I must confess to being considerably disenchanted in my fancied hero's appearance. A little sturdy, fat-looking fellow, with a pair of good black eyes, but not 'like Mars to threaten and command,' I should never have suspected the gallant Captain Hull and the jolly little man to be one and the same person. Lieutenant Morris has a more interesting appearance; is pale and thin. . . . . The banquet consisted of every delicacy that the District could produce, — claret, Burgundy, and every vintage that could be wished for by connoisseurs. Mr. Payne Todd and Colonel Goodwyn were my cavaliers for the nonce. We rose from table at dark, and returned home with an interest in the fate of every brave sailor on board ; and whatever good or ill fortune may befall Captain Stewart, he will ever have the sympathy and good-will of our inhabitants ; for, independent of his endeavors to contribute to the pleasure of his friends by incurring the expense of this party, his general amiability of deportment has interested them in himself and crew. . . . . .

"It is customary to breakfast at nine o'clock, dine at four, and drink tea at eight, which division of time I do not like, but am compelled to submit.   I am more surprised at the method of taking tea here than any other meal.   In private families, if you step in of an evening, they give you tea and crackers, or cold bread ; and if by invitation, unless the party is very splendid, you have a few sweet-cakes, — maccaroons from the confectioner's.   This is the extent. Once I saw a ceremony of preserves at tea ; but the deficiency is made up by the style at dinner, with extravagant wines, etc.   Pastry and puddings going out of date and wine and ice-creams coming in, does not suit my taste, and I confess to preferring Raleigh hospitality.   I have never even *heard* of warm bread at breakfast. . . . . .

"On Tuesday last was the grand naval ball, given in honor of Captains Hull, Morris, and Stewart, of which I must say a few words. . . . . . The assembly was crowded with a more than usual portion of the youth and beauty of the city, and was the scene of an unprecedented event, — two British flags unfurled and hung as trophies, in an American assembly, by American sailors. *Io triumphe!* Before we started our house had been illuminated, in token of our cheerful accordance with the general joy which pervaded the city, manifested by nearly every window being more or less lighted.   This was inspiring, and calculated to give every patriot and old officer in Washington an inclination to join in the festivities of an evening devoted to the pleasing task of paying homage to the bravery and politeness of the naval heroes.

" The countenances of the old and young were bright and unclouded on our entrance, and cheerfulness was the order of the night, when suddenly a loud noise and huzzaing were heard from below, and such running and confusion as I cannot describe. Some thought it fire, others that the unusual weight had caused the dancing-room to give way; but all were relieved from terror by a wildfire rumor that Lieutenant Hamilton had arrived with the Flags. My first dancing essay was checked, every man deserted his partner, and in a few minutes those who hoped the news to be true were gratified by ocular evidence of its certainty, while those sceptics who make it a point never to allow ' McDonald's army to prosper, right or wrong,' were convinced, apparently against their will, that for once American seamen were *equal* to Britons on the ocean.

" Young Hamilton appeared, preceded by General Cushing, Hull, Morris, his father, and many old naval and field officers, and in a moment was encircled in the arms of his mother and sisters, who have never seen him since his providential escape from the Richmond Theatre, where he went with young Gibbon, who met with such a tragic fate. I cried excessively, and could not check my tears, at which I was considerably abashed; but, on looking around, I recovered, in the conviction that I was far from being singular.

" After half an hour's congratulation and chat about our young officer's adventures, and a description of the seventeen-minutes engagement with the Macedonian (which was never nearer than half a mile), I finished my cotillon, and, after dancing till midnight, retired from the exciting and gratifying scene. . . . . Last night William had a supper, among our guests being Hull, Morris, Stewart, Hamilton, the Laws, and *all* the young officers. . . . . "

"January 2, 1813.

"Soon after our arrival here I received a very polite message from Mrs. Gallatin, to the effect that 'as soon as I was established in my own house she would do herself the pleasure to wait on me.' Yesterday, however, I discovered that it is a point of etiquette for all new settlers in the city to make the first visit to the families of the Secretaries. This ceremony I knew was indispensable towards Mrs. Madison; but as Dr. Eustis and Mr. Hamilton have resigned, it is now unnecessary in their case. Mrs. Gallatin's civility in calling on me prevented my suspecting that I had failed in politeness to the other officers of the Government; and this leads me to describe the brilliancy of her first ball.

"The assembly was more numerous at the Secretary of the Treasury's, — more select, more elegant, than I have yet seen in the city. Ladies of fifty years of age were decked with lace and ribbons, wreaths of roses and gold leaves in their false hair, wreaths of jasmine across their bosom, and no kerchiefs! Indeed, dear mother, I cannot reconcile this fashion to myself, and though the splendid dress of these antiquated dames of the *beau monde* adds to the general grandeur, it certainly only tends to make the contrast still more striking between them and the young and beautiful. Do you remember a frontispiece to one of the plays in the 'British Theatre,' — Bridget in the 'Chapter of Accidents?' I can only think of this picture in beholding such incongruity of dress; while that of young girls is equally incompatible with general propriety. . . . . . Madame Bonaparte is a model of fashion, and many of our belles strive to imitate her; . . . . but without equal *éclat*, as Madame Bonaparte has certainly the most transcendently beautiful back and shoulders that ever were seen. . . . . It is the fashion for most of the ladies a little advanced in age to rouge and *pearl*, which is spoken of with as much *sang froid* as putting on their bonnets. Mrs. Monroe paints very much, and has, besides, an appearance of youth which would induce a stranger to suppose her age to be thirty: in lieu of which, she introduces them to her *granddaughter*, eighteen or nineteen years old, and to her own daughter, Mrs. Hay, of Richmond. Mrs. Madison is said to rouge; but not evident to my eyes, and I do not think it true, as I am well assured I saw her color come and go at the naval ball, when the Macedonian flag was presented to her by young Hamilton. Mrs. C. and Mrs. G. paint excessively, and think it becoming; but with them it is no deception, only folly, and they speak of it as indispensable to a *decent* appearance.

"But I have digressed from the entertainment. I am sure not ten minutes elapsed without refreshments being handed. 1st, coffee, tea, all kinds of toasts and warm cakes; 2d, ice-creams; 3d, lemonade, punch, burgundy, claret, curaçoa, champagne; 4th, bonbons, cakes of all sorts and sizes; 5th, apples, oranges; 6th, confectionery, denomination *divers*; 7th, nuts, almonds, raisins; 8th, set supper, composed of tempting solid dishes, meats, savory pasties garnished with lemon; 9th, drinkables of every species; 10th, boiling chocolate. The most profuse ball ever given in Washington. . . . . I was engaged to John Law as a partner for cotillons the day before. This gentleman ranks high in William's estimation, and I am always pleased by his polite attentions in company. Governor Turner invited me to dance when I first entered the room, and I was glad of an excuse to plead a prior engagement, as I know the offer proceeded from goodness of heart which manifests itself in kindness to a good Carolinian, and not from a desire to dance in a crowd where *I* could hardly preserve my equilibrium. I danced also with Mr. Black-

ledge.   Mr. Pickens was not there, on account of his mother's death.   Mr. Macon was very polite and lively, likewise
William King, who, though not so solid or amiable as Pickens, in my opinion, is a very pleasant companion.   Young
Swartout, who was so unfortunately entangled in Burr's
web, was introduced to me, and I like him much.   He
was in town on Christmas Day, and William wished to invite him to dinner, but apprehensive that it would not be
congenial to the other guests, postponed it ; though he
esteems him highly, and he is universally admired by old
and young. . . .

"The issue of the Daily Paper gives us now *every* evening the duties of Proof Night, but Joseph and William
divide their labors and cheerfully put their shoulders to
the wheel, which makes everything smooth and agreeable.   The President admires it, and indeed every one
who has seen it, with this remark : 'But I am afraid it
cannot be supported in such handsome style.'   However,
William and Joseph are both sanguine as to its success,
and anticipate as many as five hundred subscribers before
the conclusion of the year. . . . . Miss M—— played at
the drawing-room in 'high style,' but I think our D. G.
could have excelled her.   I played once at Mr. Madison's
at a private party, but declined exhibiting at the drawing-
room. . . . . On New Year's Day we went to greet Mr.
Madison, which ceremony is generally deemed a test of
loyalty, and of course the terrace was thronged with
carriages from 12 till 3 o'clock, with constant streams of
visitors.   Daschkoff, the Russian Minister, was there, and
Serrurier, the French, both apparently uninteresting men,
but most splendid in uniform and equipage.   The good
wishes for the New Year resounded from all quarters, and
the Carolinians were very earnest in paying the compliments
of the season to us.   Indeed, I think that *our* members

appear very well here generally. There is a most interesting, venerable revolutionary officer, Colonel Cushing, with whom I am well acquainted, and who reminds me of Colonel Ingle ; and I cannot help wishing I could see them together ' shoulder their crutch, and show how fields were won.' "

Madame Patterson Bonaparte, the divorced wife and widow of Jerome Bonaparte, King of Westphalia, still survives her weak and selfish husband, and has recently followed to the grave their son, Jerome Napoleon Bonaparte. She has long outlived the despot whose decree invalidating her marriage enlisted in her behalf the sympathy of Europe, the indignation of her own countrymen, and the reprobation of France. With intellect, tact, courage, and energy as her only weapons, she resisted the imperial brother, who sought to degrade her wifehood ; and spurned the unmanly poltroon who, at the dictate of ambition, avarice, and fear, falsified the vows so solemnly pledged to the young wife, forswore the tender, passionate letters to his " beloved Eliza," and, summit of stony heartlessness, sought to wrest their child from its mother's arms. When, judging her by his own dwarfed nature, King Jerome, after his *soi-disant* marriage with the amiable Princess Katherine, insulted the dignity of his true wife by offering to her acceptance the principality of Smalcand, she replied with spirit, that " Westphalia no doubt was a considerable kingdom, but not large enough to hold two queens." His malignity could devise no more worthy revenge than in his will to ignore her existence and that of her son, whose rights she personally contested in Paris with unabated vigor and resolution; but her son stood too near the throne, and her grandson, the handsome, gallant young officer, was too deeply seated in the affections of the French army, to render possible a verdict in their favor; which, in legalizing their claims, might have rendered them formidable rivals, in the Napoleonic succession, to their young kinsman the Prince Imperial. During this trial, conducted on behalf of Madame Bonaparte with admirable skill by the renowned Berryer, Prince Napoleon, while disgracefully and successfully striving to defraud his father's son of his legitimate inheritance, cleverly characterized the brave woman battling for her son's birthright and her own wifely fame: "*Ambitieuse, un tact merveilleux, un esprit indomptable, et pour le reste, une réputation sans tâche.*"

Emile de Girardin, the brilliant *littérateur* and journalist, an ardent supporter of Madame Bonaparte's opposing litigant, Prince Napoleon, asked her for a true estimate of King Jerome. "*C'est un liard qui s'est glissé par hazard entre deux Napoleons,*" was the witty reply,— a *mot* keenly relished by the appreciative Parisians.

Madame Bonaparte retains in marvellous force the well-stored memory, the grace and strength of phrase that distinguished her even amid the hosts of celebrities who make for us the history of their day,— a society irradiated by the brilliant if somewhat fatiguing monologues of Madame de Staël, the Russian *finesse* of Gortschakoff,— then young, subtle, handsome, and irresistible,— the masterly and tender eloquence of Le Maîstre, and the lightning epigrams of Talleyrand, whose Damascene thrusts Madame Bonaparte parried

with a blade nearly as keenly tempered as his own.
To these mental gifts was added a beauty of a Greek
yet glowing type, which not even the pencil of Stuart adequately portrayed in the exquisite portrait that
he wished might be buried with him; nor yet on his
other canvas, which, with its dainty head in triple
pose of loveliness, still smiles in unfading witchery, —
a beauty which equalled that of her friends, Lady Jersey, the cynosure of the Regent's Court, and the fair
Lady Ellenborough, who eloped with Prince Swartzen-
burg, and then, in emulation of the eccentric niece of
Pitt, the Lady Hester Stanhope, fled to the desert to
reign as queen of the Bedawêe. Madame Bonaparte's
charms did not pale even in the presence of Madame
Récamier and Princess Pauline Borghese, Napoleon's
favorite but frivolous, heartless sister, whose beauty
was the wonder of the day, and whose statue by Canova, now one of Rome's treasures, fairly rivals that
of her sister Venus, which, in the Pitti Palace, " en-
chants the world." Madame Récamier's empire over
the hearts of men was due not more, perhaps, to her
beauty — bewildering as it was with her soft eyes, se-
ductive smile, dazzling skin, and shoulders of a god-
dess — than to her subtle flattery, and the amiable tact
that allowed her to recognize the lustre of neighboring planets. " *Vous êtes la plus belle femme au monde,*"
she said to Madame Bonaparte, "*plus belle même que
la parfaite Pauline Borghese.*"

" *Mais ça est bien impossible, vu que ma belle sœur est
parfaitement belle,*" was the deprecating reply.

It was Madame Bonaparte's triumph, that in an era
of society free to license, though its laxity was grace-

fully veiled by the lingering refined elegance of ante-Imperial *salons*, her name should have remained unsullied. Her romantic story, her anomalous position, her wit and beauty, made her a shining mark for the homage of the one sex, the envy of her own; but her undeviating propriety and acknowledged discretion shielded her from even the whisper of detraction.

"*Chère Madame*," said her good friend, the Grand Duke of Florence, — the Sovereign Prince recently dead, who was at that period the charm of his Court, as conspicuous for his rigid principle as for the elegance of his person and captivating courtesy, — "*chère Madame, savez vous que nous sommes d'une singulière moralité, vous et moi? Nous seuls, dans ma belle et morale capitale, nous trouvous sans amant.*"

It was Madame Bonaparte's misfortune not to have met the Emperor Napoleon, to whose greatness she ever paid willing and ardent tribute. Her rigorous exclusion from the shores of France would almost indicate that he feared the power of his new sister's attractions; and with his actual sensibility to womanly charm, subordinate as it seemed to his cold, selfish ambition, it can hardly be doubted that she would have disarmed his anger, conquered his prejudice, regained her husband, and it may even be have changed the destiny of France, — have lived to see her son, an American Bonaparte, bequeath to his son and successor the Imperial Throne.

"January, 1813.

".... A few days since we were invited to Dr. Ewell's to a christening. This gentleman is a brother to the Dr. Ewell who was in Raleigh, and who speaks of your kind hospitality. Gratitude would seem to be a characteristic feature in this family. Having in the beginning of Hamilton's prosperity received some kindness from him, Dr. Ewell invited some fifty persons to celebrate the baptism of his son Paul Hamilton. Everything was conducted in much style, Mr. and Mrs. Hamilton occupying the head of the table at supper. Jones, the new Secretary, was not there, and at the conclusion of supper, Dr. Ewell, called on for a toast, made a graceful little speech, and bowing to the ex-Secretary, said emphatically,

> ' Let others hail the rising sun,
> *I* bow to him whose race is run.'

" We saw a letter the other day from General Jackson to Mr. Monroe, in which he mentions having sent Major Gales into the town of Pensacola to demand the capitulation of the fort. We have since received a letter from Judge Toulmin, in which he mentions Thomas staying a day at his house with General Jackson. I long to hear again from New Orleans, though the last accounts are very favorable, stating the army to be perfectly prepared. Crooks, editor of the Mercantile Advertiser, has sent us a London paper, in which is contained an extract from the Iris, from the pen of Montgomery, in answer to an abusive paragraph in a government paper edited by Canning. It is warm from Montgomery's heart, and exposes the ignorance and malice in regard to American affairs."

Thomas Gales, the brother of Mrs. Seaton, was a man of brilliant promise, cut off in the flush of successful and vigorous manhood. He had followed the footsteps of his brother Joseph, in preparing himself as a practical printer in Philadelphia, but preferring the profession of law, studied under General Walter Jones of

Washington, the eminent lawyer. Being captivated by the representations of friends as to the promising field for his profession in Louisiana, he removed thither, and married the daughter of Alfred Hennen, Esq., of New Orleans, a lady beautiful in person and of superior powers of mind. In a few months he was appointed by General Wilkinson, then commander-in-chief, Judge-Advocate-General of the Southern Department, and Justice of Faubourg St. Marie, which arduous position he filled well, being held in high esteem. He took an active part during the war, being on General Jackson's staff at Pensacola, where, at the surrender of the fort, he with his own hands hauled down the Union Jack and ran up the American flag. He possessed in a remarkable degree varied social powers, a generous nature, with a cultivated, energetic mind.

" March 5, 1813.

." . . . . Mrs. Madison called on me last week, and very politely invited me to attend the drawing-room of Wednesday, and 'not to desert the standard altogether,' which, promising to do, I prevailed on William to accede to my wishes. Judge Johnson pushed his way through the crowd to speak to me, saying, with his usual gallantry, that 'he had been examining every group of Youth and Beauty in expectation of identifying Mrs. Seaton.' Immediately afterwards a gentleman came up with Judge Marshall, who had inquired for me, and wished to pay his compliments, he said. You may remember, perhaps, that I always stood high in his good graces. . . . . Our dinner-party on Saturday consisted of Judge Johnson, Colonel Swift, Major William Hamilton, Mr. Bolling Robinson, from New Orleans, and a few other strangers. . . . . . Mr. Robinson is a young man, extremely prepossessing in his appearance and manners, originally from Petersburg, and exceedingly popular. I should like you to be acquainted with him, as he is a fine, noble, independent man, whose genius and benevolence are reflected in his countenance, and whose brilliant intrinsic merit renders him a favorite visitor at our house. . . . . .

"Yesterday the most crowded and interesting sight we ever witnessed was presented to our view in the inauguration of Mr. Madison. Escorted by the Alexandria, Georgetown and city companies, the President proceeded to the Capitol. Judge Marshall, and the associate Judges, preceded him and placed themselves in front of the Speaker's chair, from whence the Chief Magistrate delivered his inaugural address; but his voice was so low, and the audience so very great, that scarcely a word could be distinguished. / On concluding, the oath of office was administered by the Chief Justice, and the little man was accompanied on his return to the palace by the multitude; for every creature that could afford twenty-five cents for hack-hire was present. The major part of the respectable citizens offered their congratulations, ate his ice-creams and bonbons, drank his Madeira, made their bow and retired, leaving him fatigued beyond measure with the incessant bending to which his politeness urged him, and in which he never allows himself to be eclipsed, returning bow for bow, even to those *ad infinitum* of Serrurier and other foreigners. . . . . .

"You will regret to hear that your good friend Joel Barlow is dead. I send the notice of the event from foreign papers. Although of too tender an age to appreciate the generous and brilliant qualities of this eminent man when the recipient of his kindness in Germany, I still retain a vivid remembrance of his appearance and manners. The place and circumstances attending his death seemed a fitting close to his volcanic and eccentric career."

Joel Barlow exercised a very uncommon influence over men through his personal eloquence, and it was doubtless to employ him in the furtherance of some project by which to win the popular good-will, that the Emperor Napoleon, who judged highly of his ability, requested his presence at Wilna, where, overcome by excitement and a forced journey, Mr. Barlow was attacked by his fatal illness. The unfavorable feeling excited against him in America in consequence of his reputed atheism — a mistaken charge, for he was a deist — was founded chiefly upon his intimacy with Tom Paine, who, when imprisoned in France by the Jacobins, had intrusted his " Age of Reason " to Mr. Barlow's care for publication ; but the prejudice, although diminished, still existed and formed one count in the indictment against him on the occasion of his nomination as Minister to France. The vote of Timothy Pickering in his favor having at the time excited invidious comment, Colonel John Lee, a distinguished citizen of Maryland, obtained from Mr. Pickering the following valuable memorandum of the debate in secret session on Mr. Barlow's appointment, which has not hitherto been made public : —

" Against the nomination it was said, —

" 1. That Mr. Barlow stood on the books of the Treasury a debtor to the United States.

" 2. That he went to France poor and returned rich, without any known means of acquiring wealth ; hence it was inferred that he had acquired his wealth by improper means, and the speculations in American claims under the Louisiana Treaty were mentioned as a possible mode.

" 3. That having lived in France many years, *there* must be his predilection and attachments, and that he was also a French citizen.

" 4. That Mr. Barlow was a poet, and poets dealing in visions were ill qualified for the business of the world. Addison and Prior were mentioned as instances. And an opinion (by General Smith) was explicitly given, that Mr. Barlow was not qualified for the mission.

" 5. That he had no mercantile knowledge, which would be very important in enforcing claims for the restitution of American property in France."

" To the first objection, Mr. Clay produced a letter from the Comptroller of the Treasury to Mr. Barlow, stating that his accounts of moneys expended in negotiating treaties with the Barbary powers had been finally closed at the treasury ; and with respect to his being a French citizen, Mr. Clay stated that this citizenship was merely honorary, and that the title of French citizenship was by the same act conferred on General Washington and General Hamilton. Mr. Pickering stated that he knew Mr. Barlow when a chaplain in the Revolutionary war, that he maintained a good character until he went to France, — that whore of Babylon which had polluted the world ; that it was understood that Mr. Barlow, in France, had renounced his belief in the Christian religion, but not that he had become an atheist, though at one period of the French revolution it had been formally proclaimed in their national Assembly that there was no God, and that afterwards Robespierre claimed much merit for causing a counter declaration to be made in favor of God; that Mr. Barlow possessed an understanding superior to such an opinion, which only fools could entertain; that his being a deist could not be a serious objection with the party now in power, nor with a majority of the people of the United States, who had raised to higher offices — the highest in the nation — men whose faith was doubtless the same with Mr. Barlow's. . . . . That it was true that Mr. Barlow was a poet, but certainly not a mere poet, for it had been objected against him that he had become rich, — a proof that he understood the world as well as poetry; that his abilities and general literature were well known, and in his reading it was most probable that he had made the law of nations a part of his studies. That in the early period of the French Revolution he had written some pamphlets which gained him considerable distinction; and it was also true that he had written some things that were extravagant. There was at the time a political frenzy, and Mr. Barlow appears to have been within its vortex. This fanaticism pervaded the United States; and Mr. Pickering confessed that he had himself partaken of the general enthusiasm of his country in favor of the revolution, and entertained the hope that a new government was to be established in France, — a hope frustrated by the atrocious conduct of its successive rulers. . . . . . That, for his own part, Mr. Pickering had no reason to be pleased with Mr. Barlow; on the contrary, his conduct at the time when the French Directory most grossly insulted the government of the United States, appeared to be very reprehensible. That the sentiments expressed by Mr.

Barlow in a letter to his brother-in-law, Mr. Baldwin, concerning our government, were so exceptionable as to attract Mr. Pickering's notice, in a report he made to President Adams on French affairs and Mr. Gerry's negotiations at Paris, which the President communicated to Congress, and in which Mr. Pickering had pointedly reprobated the conduct of Mr. Barlow. That this very conduct of Mr. Barlow was acceptable to the party then in opposition, and now in power. That Mr. Barlow now entertained very different sentiments respecting the French. That he had an intimate knowledge of the language, — a consideration of some consequence to a Minister to that government. That although Mr. Barlow would be a most improper Minister to send to the Court of London, yet he possessed so many qualifications suited to that of Paris, that Mr. Pickering was disposed to vote in favor of the nomination. In answer to the objection that Mr. Barlow was not qualified to enforce the claims for restitution of American property seized and sequestered by the French Emperor, Mr. Pickering remarked, that if the objection were well founded, he really thought it of little consequence, because there was no ground to expect that even one cent would ever be restored. The French Emperor took, and held, that property as a pledge that our government would conform to his views in respect to Great Britain. But Mr. Pickering considered the measure now agitated in the other House to be so far from a compliance with the Emperor's expectations, that if it should be adopted, Bonaparte would make it a cause for confiscating the whole of the American property at once. We know, too, that if Bonaparte is not furnished with a pretext, he can easily fabricate one.   Witness his making the non-intercourse law a ground for confiscating American vessels and cargoes, on the principle of retaliation for the confiscation of French vessels in the ports of the United States, when not one such vessel had been touched !   We should also recollect the information given by General Armstrong respecting the neutral property seized and then under sequestration in France, amounting to twenty million of livres : 'that the very magnitude of the sum was a decisive reason why the Emperor would not release it.'   But the American property in his hands now amounted to a much larger sum,—probably to twenty millions of dollars,—which proportionably strengthened his motives never to let go."

Mr. Barlow's distinction, and extended fame in two hemispheres, render every memento of so brilliant a man valuable; and the subjoined notes from the autographs are interesting, as bearing trace of the great men and events with whom he was familiarly associated : —

"À MONSIEUR, MONSIEUR BARLOW,

   HOTEL DE LANGUEDOC, Rue Grenelle, St. Honoré.

" Mr. Jefferson presents his compliments to Mr. Barlow. He wished yesterday to have had more particular conversation with him, but the circumstances of the moment did not permit it.   He should be very happy to see Mr. Barlow at a family dinner to-day, where he will be more at liberty in his inquiries, and have a better opportunity to show his respect for him.   Mr. Barlow will be so good as to bring with him his young charge, Master Greene.

 " Saturday, July 5, 1788."

"Thomas Jefferson, President of the United States,
Washington.

"Dear Sir, — The bearers of this, the two Mr. Emmets, from Ireland, have been particularly and grievously persecuted by the English government for their political opinions; that is, for their inflexible and enlightened attachment to those principles of liberty which they, and we, think ought to prevail in all societies.

"The elder Mr. Emmet was an eminent counsellor in Dublin. He was imprisoned and detained there after the peace. His brother took refuge in Paris, where he has occupied himself in pursuit of the sciences, with good· proficiency. They have now chosen America for their second country, — a movement which, if our fathers had not made it for us, you and I might be making at this moment. May I beg you, dear sir, to favor them with your good advice, as well as other acts of friendship and protection which may be useful to them. I know not what fortune they carry, except that of fair and honorable reputations and good talents.

"Your obedient servant,

"Joel Barlow.

"Paris, 29 July, 1802.
"To Mr. Jefferson."

"To Mrs. Swan, Boston.

"Dear Mrs. Swan, — The continuance of your grief for the loss of our excellent friend, General Jackson, awakens all my sympathy, and has induced me, at last, to give utterance to those feelings which I had hitherto suppressed. It is, indeed, a heavy loss — a wide breach in the circle of my friends as well as in that of yours; and since you could not doubt of my most cordial condolence, it seemed to me that my silence would be more efficacious than my language in obtaining for you that relief which your own habitual

5 *

reflections on the frailty of human dependencies could not fail to furnish. But as you call for a communication of sentiment on the virtues and character of our friend, let us indulge a moment in the melancholy recital. To dwell on the amiable qualities of those we love, is to strengthen such qualities in ourselves.

"The place of his birth and education being distant from mine, many of his surviving friends must have known him longer than I did, though few have known him better. I knew him an early and zealous military volunteer in the service of our country in its revolutionary war. I knew him always at the post of duty, frequently at that of danger. He raised a regiment in 1776, which he continued to conduct, with skill and bravery, through all the vicissitudes of fatigue and privation, through battles, defeats, and victories, till the object was attained for which he drew his sword, — the liberty of his country. At the peace of 1783 — not so much in imitation of the Roman Cincinnatus as in obedience to the call of honest industry — he retired with the other illustrious relics of our armies to the pursuits of civil life. These pursuits, though less brilliant than those of war, are sometimes more difficult to follow with consistency, as the history of our country has abundantly proved. How many of his former fellow-laborers in the arduous toils of independence have forgotten the principles they once taught us to revere; and, as if disgusted with their own good fame, are striving to destroy the institutions with which that fame was united! Our departed friend never deviated from himself in this unhappy manner. Henry Jackson continued firmly to support the republican system which General Jackson had assisted to establish.

"If it was this adhesion to principle that lost him the affections of some of his few companions in arms who survive him in his native city of Boston, — if it was really for this reason, as I have understood, that they suffered his body to be committed to the ground without the accustomed pomp of military honors (vain pomp indeed, but sufficiently important in their view to be withheld, as a mark of disapprobation), let us pity them : it is n t upon our friend that this dishonor falls. No ! the stain of dishonor never touched him when alive, and death has now placed him forever beyond its reach.

"But as you may intend this letter for publication, it is not so important to dwell upon public character and political principles, which are well known to his country, as to bring into view the less conspicuous, but more endearing traits that distinguish him from most of those who have been dear to us in life. A purer heart, or a finer sense of duty than his, never guided the actions of a human being. His natural desire of doing good was strengthened by constant exercise ; and beneficent actions became so habitual as to be almost indispensable among his daily enjoyments.

" His private fortune, though ample for himself and for charity, was made so by a virtuous attention to frugality, by moderating his expenses and avoiding extravagant spec-. ulations. He seemed to consider himself only as the steward of his own estate ; as if the property of it belonged to his friends who were less fortunate than he, or less regular in their habits of life. To mention particular instances that may have come to our knowledge would betray his confidence ; and though the cause of morals would often gain by a less scrupulous concealment of good actions than their authors observe, yet secrets of this kind are a property to which the public has no right until the proprietors choose to give it up.

" If, my dear madam, these feeble expressions of my

regret should afford you any consolation for the loss of our incomparable friend, it will be from the assurance that I knew his worth, and that my attachment was founded on the same moral qualities in him which gave rise to your own. My consolation must arise from the continuance of your friendship to me and my wife; and from the confidence that your excellent heart, so nearly resembling his, will induce you, not only to continue your usual course of charities, but adopt in some measure the objects of his own; and do much of the good that he would have done had not a wiser dispensation arrested his career.

"Accept our best affections,

"JOEL BARLOW.

"KALORAMA, March 7, 1809.

At the period of Mr. Seaton's arrival in Washington, hostilities had already been declared against Great Britain. The country was roused to a spirit of patriotic fervor, although party feeling ran so high as to imperil the necessary measures of policy adopted by President Madison, to whose Administration the Intelligencer stood in the most intimate and faithful relations. "During the entire course of the war that journal sustained most vigorously all the measures needful for carrying it on with efficiency; and it did equally good service in reanimating, whenever it had slackened at any disaster, the drooping spirit of our people. Nor did its editors, when there were two, stop at these proofs of sincerity, nor shrink when danger drew near, from that hazard of their own persons to which they had stirred up the country." *

The metropolis, from its exposed and ill-prepared condition, seemed to invite the enemy's assault; and

* Atlantic Monthly, 1860.

each day the public ear was strained to catch the boom of the first gun that should announce the advance of the British squadron up the Potomac, or the descent upon the city by Ross.

Mrs. Seaton writes under date of March, 1813 : —

"Your fears, my dear mother, were not entirely without foundation, though we laughed you out of them when they were mentioned. When our removal to Washington was in contemplation, you expressed apprehension lest we should be exposed to British invasion and consequent cruelty. You will see by the Federal Republican, that the plan might be carried into execution without a miracle, of seizing the President and Secretaries with fifty or a hundred men ; and rendering this nation a laughing-stock to every other in the world. I did not think much of these possibilities until hearing them discussed by General Van Ness and others, who, far from wishing a parade of guards or ridiculous apprehensions to be entertained, were yet anxious that the city should not be unprepared for a contingency the danger of which did certainly exist. Col. Swift since his arrival here has sent an officer to Norfolk to inspect and make proper arrangements, and appears anxious to receive news of the results."

At the first call of danger Mr. Seaton and Mr. Gales enrolled themselves as privates in a volunteer infantry company, commanded by the gallant Captain John Davidson, encamped at Fort Warburton, the present site of Fort Washington; and served with this corps on the various expeditions on which it was detached during the war. Mrs. Seaton continues to depict the uneasiness of the inhabitants at this imminent danger of invasion.

"July 20, 1813.

" . . . . We still remain passive sufferers under the almost intolerably distressing state of suspense. Joseph has been home twice to attend to the paper, riding all night and returning the next day. William has never been home, but has removed six miles below Warburton with his company to intercept the enemy's scouting-parties and prevent their landing in small bodies. There are a sufficient number of troops at the fort and near it, it is generally allowed, but some fears are entertained of the enemy's approach in another direction; and though every precaution and preparation have been made, the citizens are in a cruel state of alarm. You will see that Congress has reported that we are in a securely defended position, nevertheless it is not to be expected that our fears can be so easily calmed after an excessive fright. I have no personal fears, being with my children in the abode of safety, at Mr. Smith's house. The British, peradventure they reach the city, would be in too violent a hurry to make good their retreat after the perpetration of all the mischief they might be able to effect, to stop for a moment in the interior of the country. Many families from the navy-yard and Capitol Hill have proposed to stay here during the continuance of the British in our waters, but Mrs. Henry Clay, Mrs. Cutting, and my family are all who are pressingly, tenderly urged to stay during this tempestuous season of disturbance. No uneasiness, therefore, is experienced here personally, but the possibility of either of our dear protectors being injured at Warburton, fills us with inexpressible anguish, you will readily conceive. Joseph assures us most solemnly that he does not believe they will dare attempt to land or pass the numerous and brave force of volunteers and regulars who are assembled, and positively believes that there will be no fighting. William and he are both perfectly well and in excellent spirits, which augurs well for victory if engaged, or a peaceable return. They have an express engaged to let us know every morning of their welfare. Nine of the office men are volunteers, and there are only three men and three boys left to get the paper out. Joseph will apply to General Armstrong for a furlough for William to come up from below, attend to the paper, and return the following day; so I shall go to the city to see my beloved, my devoted husband. Be perfectly at ease, I entreat you, as in case of an absolute attack on the city we should be still secure; and our protectors at Warburton would not be exposed to danger either, as the British would come up another way without exposing themselves to the fire of the fort. . . . . "

"July 22, 1813.

" . . . . William came from the camp yesterday, and after arranging the paper will return by daylight. He and Joseph will now come alternately during the time it may be thought necessary that the troops should remain on duty. Their friends think it out of reason that the paper should be neglected, and are of opinion that the proper and continual direction of the public record printed in their office is of infinitely more importance than any individual exertion they could possibly make in the camp; but this arrangement of one staying and one going would be very unpleasant, and they appear more disposed to encounter danger, or rather exertion, together, than separate. Joseph would more naturally incur the imputation of disinclination to defend his country from enemies than William, from the accident of being a foreigner, and therefore I should like him to prove the contrary, if he has indeed a political enemy who would be so ungenerous as to asperse his actions and motives. William, on the other hand, has been more accustomed to military duty, always belonging to a company in Richmond from boyhood, and being also a sportsman skilled in the free use of fire-arms. But for the necessity of one or the other being here, I should be unwilling for them to leave their companies even for a day, as they are a brave, handsomely disciplined corps as any in the District, and appear united as a band of brothers, encouraging each other in activity and good spirits. There is not a single instance of sickness in the whole number of 3,000 men. . . . . There were only two pressmen left in the office, and one of them ill this evening, so that the paper will be published with great difficulty. . . . . The House is sitting with closed doors to-day on a confidential message from the President, which is very well, as there would be no one to attend the debates or to take any note of their business. You will see that prejudice exists as strongly here against foreigners as anywhere, the Senate refusing to confirm Mr. Gallatin's appointment !"

In December, 1813, Mr. Gales married Miss Juliana Lee, the beautiful and accomplished daughter of Mr. Theodoric Lee of Westmoreland, Virginia.

"January 2, 1814.

" . . . . Yesterday being New Year's day, *every*body, affected or disaffected towards the government, attended to pay Mrs. Madison the compliments of the season. Between one and two o'clock we drove to the President's, where it was with much difficuly we made good our entrance, though all of our acquaintances endeavored with the utmost civility to compress themselves as small as they could for our accommodation. The marine band, stationed in the ante-room, continued playing in spite of the crowd pressing on their very heads. But if our pity was excited for these hapless musicians, what must we not have experienced for some members of our own sex, who, not foreseeing the excessive heat of the apartments, had more reason to apprehend the efforts of nature to relieve herself from the effects of the confined atmosphere. You perhaps will not understand that I allude to the rouge which some of our fashionables had unfortunately laid on with an unsparing hand, and which assimilating with the pearl-powder, dust and perspiration, made them altogether unlovely to soul and to eye.

"Her majesty's appearance was truly regal, — dressed in a robe of pink satin, trimmed elaborately with ermine, a white velvet and satin turban, with nodding ostrich-plumes and a crescent in front, gold chain and clasps around the waist and wrists. 'T is here the woman who adorns the dress, and not the dress that beautifies the woman. I cannot conceive a female better calculated to dignify the station which she occupies in society than Mrs. Madison, — amiable in private life and affable in public, she is admired and esteemed by the rich and beloved by the poor. You are aware that she snuffs; but in her hands the snuff-box seems only a gracious implement with which to charm. Her frank cordiality to all guests is in contrast to the manner of the President, who is very formal, reserved and precise, yet not wanting in a certain dignity. Being so low of stature, he was in imminent danger of being confounded with the plebeian crowd ; and was pushed and jostled about like a common citizen, — but not so with her ladyship ! The towering feathers and excessive throng distinctly pointed out her station wherever she moved.

"After partaking of some ice-creams and a glass of Madeira, shaking hands with the President and tendering our good wishes, we were preparing to leave the rooms, when our attention was attracted through the window towards what we conceived to be a rolling ball of burnished gold, carried with swiftness through the air by two gilt wings. Our anxiety increased the nearer it approached, until it actually stopped before the door ; and from it alighted, weighted with gold lace, the French Minister and suite. We now also perceived that what we had supposed to be wings, were nothing more than gorgeous footmen with *chapeaux bras,* gilt braided skirts and splendid swords. Nothing ever was witnessed in Washington so brilliant and dazzling, — a meridian sun blazing full on this carriage filled with diamonds and glittering orders, and gilt to the edge of the wheels, — you may well imagine how the natives stared and rubbed their eyes to be convinced 't was no fairy dream. . . . .

" I have just had a most delightful conversation with Mr. Wirt of Richmond, who called to see me, and prolonged his visit, finding me alone, very much to my gratification. He is one of the most elegant *belles lettres* scholars I ever met ; and excels in colloquial talent as much as he does in descriptive prose. I wish you knew him, as he is a being of the first order."

"June 27, 1814.

" . . . . Joseph has returned within an hour from a fatiguing and really dangerous expedition, without any other injury than excessive weariness, after being exposed to the fire of the British on an open plain, where the balls whistled round his ears for the first time. The scene was novel to him, but unlike most other novelties, it was not pleasing. He volunteered his services while absent, on every occasion of fatigue or hazard which occurred ; and was always ' to the fore ' when they expected attack. . . . . William has held himself in readiness to be called out with his company at a moment's warning ; but I trust they will have no further occasion for their services, as Gen. Armstrong has issued orders for the return of those who are at Benedict. Sunday, the day on which the cavalry, riflemen and infantry from Georgetown and Washington started to Nottingham, was a distressing period. Seeing Joseph go, and expecting William to be ordered off every moment, rendered the parade which took place before our door previous to starting extremely painful. . . . . False reports reached us from the scene of action, it being confidently asserted that six of Capt. Caldwell's troopers were killed; and you may imagine that each individual having relatives in the troop trembled and conceived the loss theirs. There was something very awful at the sight of cannon rattling through the streets, surrounded by soldiers, chiefly friends. I had never seen these dreadful implements of war associated with the idea of their immediate destination and probable use. The present danger has passed; yet we are kept in a perpetual state of alarm. Capt. Davidson's volunteers, among whom is William, were left in the city as our safeguard. . . . ."

Mr. Gales was absent on furlough for the purpose of placing his wife and Mrs. Seaton and family in safety at Raleigh; and Mr. Seaton was at the editorial post on the memorable morning of August 24, 1814, when the sound of the distant gun brought dismayed conviction to the affrighted and ill-prepared city, that the British were in truth advancing in force on the Capital. Dismissing the workmen to their respective corps, and closing the office, Mr. Seaton hastened to join his company, then at the Eastern Branch, which at once proceeded to the front, meeting the enemy at Bladensburg, where, placed in the advance, it acted a conspicuous part in the sharp engagement that ensued. Mr. Seaton always deprecated the injustice which this really spirited skirmish received at the hands of history;

and was glad when the incidents of the action were placed in their true light by the late Colonel John S. Williams, a nephew of the gallant Revolutionary patriot, General Otho Williams of Maryland, and a participator in the events he impartially narrates in his "Invasion of Washington."

The editors of the Intelligencer, in upholding their country's rights, in animating the public by their ardent and effective appeals to patriotism, had in an especial manner excited the ire of the valorous invaders; and no surer attestation of the value of their labors could have been offered than in the inglorious act of Admiral Cockburn, who caused the Intelligencer office to be sacked; and ordering the books and other property of the establishment to be piled on the banks of the canal, set fire to and destroyed them, himself urging the mariners to the pitiful work. The building was spared, however, at the intercession of the women of the neighborhood, who alone remained to guard the premises, there having been a *levy en masse* of the men. Sala, the brilliant English author, when in this country, in commenting on Cockburn's petty revenge on the editors, says: "The National Intelligencer still lives, and, what is more, the editor is living too. I had the honor of seeing Colonel Seaton one night, — a hale gentleman of eighty, very much resembling Lord Brougham in appearance, in full possession of his powers, editing his Intelligencer as fearlessly under the sway of Abraham Lincoln as he was wont to do under James Madison, — revered for his blameless character, and, as the Nestor of American journalism of the higher class, universally esteemed, not only by the great of his own country, but by all the diplomatic corps of Washington. But there is no doubt about our having thrown his types out of the window."

These types fortunately were partly saved by the energy of an Englishwoman attached to the family, who has also additional claim to mention, as having in her youth known Dr. Samuel Johnson, — the burly lexicographer having at one period lived in her village, — on whose knee she had often sat, and who had given her a sacredly.treasured pair of silver shoe-buckles.

It would be an injustice to include in censure all the British officers under Cockburn's command in this invasion, his inglorious deeds having been, in .truth, checked by a gallant Guardsman, to whom reference is made in the following letter from General George H. Stewart, a gallant Marylander, conspicuous in the skirmish of Bladensburg and the defence of Baltimore. Major, now Sir Norman Pringle, often, in later years, spoke to Americans of the mortification felt by himself and comrades at the vandalism disgracing the capture of Washington. He is a high-toned, well-bred, soldierly gentleman, of an ancient Scotch house, doing honor to the baronetcy to which he has recently succeeded.

"I do not remember to have mentioned to you that I wrote to our friend Major Pringle, at Stockholm, advising him to apply for one of the vacant consulates in this country, which I presume are more desirable than the one he now fills in Sweden. Pringle replied, that perhaps his presence here would not be acceptable, as he had been with the army in the capture of Washington, and consequently might have incurred some odium on that account. I rejoined that no one here would feel any the slightest objection to him on that score ; and when it should be explained that *he* was detailed with his Grenadier company to *protect private property on Pennsylvania Avenue* (which duty he performed faithfully and successfully, during the night, to the satisfaction of General Ross, and also of the citizens of that locality), I thought his appointment to any consulate here *would be acceptable.* . . . .

" Yours faithfully,

" G. H. Stewart."

"Colonel W. W. Seaton."

One of the most notable of Mr. Seaton's circle of friends, and chief, indeed, among the social celebrities of Washington at that period, was Mr. Thomas Law, of whom few persons then living had not some anecdote to relate, as well respecting his eccentricities as his brilliant talent. This distinguished gentleman was a younger brother of Lord Ellenborough, who had succeeded Lord Kenyon as Lord Chief Justice of the King's Bench, being raised to the peerage on his accession to the dignity of Lord Chancellor of England ; a second brother being Bishop of Bath and Wells. Mr. Law's early life was passed in India with Lord Cornwallis, holding there a high civil trust which he discharged with signal ability, receiving, on the resignation of his office, many gratifying testimonials to the beneficence of his rule. Infected by the spirit of liberty then moving all nations to violent upheaval, Mr. Law's enthusiasm was roused in favor of Republican institutions, and, inspired with ardent admiration for the character of Washington, he came to America; having, however, no political affinities whatever in this country. He attracted much attention from his fine person, aristocratic connections, and undoubted genius, and also from his wealth, which, accumulated in the golden days of India, was dissipated chiefly through building speculations, for which he had a mania; while he was also generous, prodigal indeed, in good works, as in the hospitalities dispensed at his country-seat near Washington. Mr. Law married Miss Anne Custis, sister of the well-known George Washington Parke Custis, of Arlington, the adopted son of Washington; but his numerous peculiarities unfitted him for domestic life. His eccentricities were many; one of his habits being to carry in his hand a piece of dough, which he constantly manipulated, the loss of which would cause him to lose the thread of his story. His absence of mind was at times inconvenient, being obliged, when asking on one occasion at the post-office for his letters, to confess that he did not remember his name; but a few moments afterwards, meeting a friend who saluted him as Mr. Law, he hurried back, gave his address, and received his mail. Another more embarrassing instance of his distrait faculties occurred at Berkeley Springs, where, after a bath, forgetting to dress, he appeared in the crowded grove *in puris naturalibus*, scattering consternation among the promenaders. A note from a lady residing in his house for some time winds up the enumeration of his oddities by saying, " What an uncomfortable, extraordinary old man he is, with his ' instinctive impulses !' on which theme he theorizes, as upon ' elective affinities.' "

Mr. Law was an enthusiast, and regarded by less sanguine mortals as more than visionary, especially when riding his hobby, the currency question, reams of discussion on this his favorite topic being in Mr. Seaton's library. In religious views he was a deist; and although he subscribed to the building of the Unitarian church, and went often to enjoy the simple, touching eloquence of Robert Little, its first pastor, he remarked on the first occasion of hearing him: "To think that Little was talking about Jesus Christ, and that I did not know he believed in that sort of thing!" Mr. Law was also quite a graceful poet, his *Vers de Société* being highly prized in the bright circle, the incidents and personages of which he cleverly commemorated. Mrs. Seaton writes in November, 1814: —

"Mr. Law yesterday brought me some lines applicable and striking, to us who are spectators of the ruins of the Capitol, and listeners to the constant disputation concerning a removal of the seat of government, or a rebuilding of the public offices. You can only half appreciate his effusions when deprived of the advantage of hearing him read them himself, as he is an energetic declaimer, and possessed of a full-toned, melodious voice. We see much of him and his sons, John and Edmund, who are both perfectly unexceptionable as regards either their manners, principles, or acquirements."

"A DREAM.

The scene of conflagration which by day
Excited feelings painful to convey,
Appeared in sleep; and faintly I disclose
The pleasing vision which in dreams arose.
High on the Capitol's smeared, smoky wall,
Midst fractured pillars of the Congress Hall

Columbia sat : full frequent heaved the sigh,
And grief's dull languor floated in her eye.
With wild emotion every feature wrought,
Her air was sorrow, and her look was thought.
Lo ! smiling Liberty, with heavenly grace,
And form angelic, gives a warm embrace ;
" Mourn not," she said, " the vandal's savage flame, —
A lasting tarnish to the invader's fame ;
To just revenge thy children it inspires,
And makes them emulate their sainted sires !
Extend your view o'er lakes, o'er seas, o'er lands,
Triumphant everywhere behold your bands ;
Whole fleets are taken and whole armies yield ;
Before your sons e'en veterans fly the field.
Even in sight of Albion's cliffs your fleet
Seeks the proud ruler of the waves to meet.
My spirit gives an energy divine,
And makes your sons all former deeds outshine."
Now an effulgent burst of western light,
And gilded clouds, wide spreading, struck my sight.
Justice descends ! but as she nearer drew
A blaze of glory hid her from my view.
I heard a voice, though solemn, full of love,
Pronounce she came commissioned from above.
" Droop not, Columbia," she exclaimed, "but trust
In power Almighty, as your cause is just ;
The machinations of the bad shall fail,
The force of numbers be of no avail.
Our God shall shield thy chosen land from harm, —
Our God protects thee with his outstretched arm !"
At this, methought a peal of victory rung,
And a new edifice in splendor sprung,
Like Phœnix from its ashes, and a sound
Of triumph and rejoicing rose around.
Sudden I woke, all glowing with delight,
And full of faith in all that passed by night.
One dove to Noah in the deluge bore
The welcome tidings of appearing shore :
Two harbingers from heaven methought appeared,
That sorrowful Columbia might be cheered.
O, may it be the Almighty's gracious will,
This welcome vision quickly to fulfil !"

"MY DEAR SIR, — I am to deliver an address on Saturday in lieu of Edmund, and in it I shall demonstrate, from important facts, the ruin which must ensue if it be attempted to liquidate our debt of 3,900,000 six per cent before the 1st January, 1830, and the benefits which will be obtained if all the surplus revenue be applied to public improvements. I have much to communicate. A meeting must be called to consider how we can extricate ourselves from our dilemma. Mr. Mercer would, I think, co-operate if he knew the objections to a canal which will cost $ 5,000,000, and which will never be used if accomplished.

"Bonaparte, by giving three hundred monasteries to manufacturers, and by lending money without interest for nine years, has elevated France more than he did by all his vainglorious conquests. If every slave State had a cotton manufacture in which only free persons would be employed, a town would spring up, containing say fifty thousand in each State, — here would be in twelve States six hundred thousand. The mulattoes, now a dangerous class, might be purchased and made free after six or eight years, and they would become tradesmen and shopkeepers. Irishmen and other foreigners would become weavers, etc. ; hay, fruit, vegetables, meat, would become valuable, land would rise in price, increased exports would produce wealth. The more whites and free persons having a common interest, the more safety and the more prosperity, for free labor is proved to be more advantageous. If the general government could give back to the States surplus revenue for such works, what a scene of advancement would be exhibited. The great object of statesmen should be to multiply whites and freemen in slave States.

"I rejoice at the vote for the 'dismal swamp' canal. Every day the advocates for public improvements increase.

The middle class is always adverse to despotism and party spirit; they wish for peace and quiet. Money only is wanted to make this country most prosperous; our Potomac canal, the Louisville canal on the Ohio, the Florida canal and many others, would yield 100 per cent to the nation. If also cotton were manufactured where it is produced, foreign competitors would be undersold.

"Think not I mean to bore you; this perhaps is the last letter I shall ever write on public affairs. When you have a spare half-hour, let your zeal induce you to come from the Capitol to me. The crisis is favorable; we only want concurrence among ourselves. I wish to unburthen myself to you, who have been so active and distributed letters and pamphlets so liberally. Bernard cannot report in time, and, be his report ever so favorable, it will be useless.

"I shall soon retire to the country, and swear never more to harass myself with finance; the charms of nature, too much overlooked hitherto, I will more dwell upon. On this subject I will show you some good lines. Consider my suggestion.

"That I know how to improve a country is shown by the accompanying letter from the man Johnson applauds in his tour to the Hebrides, and who went to India.

"Yours sincerely,

"T. LAW.

"To WILLIAM W. SEATON, ESQ.
 March 14, 1826."

"MEDDENPORE, March.

"DEAR SIR, — I cannot leave this part of the country, which is so happy under your care, without thanking you for myself and the party for the very great kindness and hospitality which you showed us, and for the pleasure of a higher nature for which we are indebted to you. Since we parted with you we have not rode a step without perceiving the beneficial effects which your wise as well as humane treatment of the peasants has produced in the country; large tracts, evidently newly rescued from the desert jungles, converted into corn-fields; houses, villages everywhere rising, and, above all, happy faces. I have often thought when riding formerly through different parts of India, that the poor people said in their hearts, ' There goes one of our tyrants, there is our oppressor, or the supporter of our oppressors'; a different idea has lately pleased me. I have imagined that ryots called out to their children, ' There is a countryman of our father, our benefactor,' etc., etc.

(Signed) "NORMAN MCLEOD."

"MONTICELLO, Dec. 12, 1822.

"Thomas Jefferson salutes Mr. Law with ancient and friendly recollections, and with a mind which does not easily part with early impressions. He hopes the years which intervened since they last saw each other have been to Mr. Law years of health and pleasantness, and that he yet has many such to come.

"Marching abreast with Mr. Law in the calendar of time, it is his particular lot to suffer by two dislocated wrists, now stiffened by age, and rendering writing slow, painful, and all but impossible. He is happy to find by the pamphlet Mr. Law has so kindly sent him, that *his* mind is still equal to the continuation of his useful labors, and that his zeal for the general good is unabated. Where they are next to meet, in this or some other untried state of being, he knows not. But if we carry with us the affections of this world, he shall thence greet Mr. Law with unchanged esteem and respect.

"To THOMAS LAW, ESQ."

"January 11, 1815.

"In twenty-four hours, dearest mother, we shall hear whether the British are repulsed from the shores of the

Mississippi, or in possession of New Orleans. We aro excessively uneasy about dear Tom. He would, we know, be in the very front of danger in any event; and General Jackson's bravery approaches to hardihood, it being well known that he will never desist from fighting while one of his men shall remain. The British are several thousand strong, superior in number, many of them well-tried veterans; while our force is said to consist of a proportion of one thousand regulars to three thousand militia, — add to which, the Spanish population are entirely disaffected, and inclined to the invaders. The general opinion here entertained is, that nothing short of a miracle can save that devoted city. These facts are from Senators Brown and Bolling Robinson, who are too well convinced of their truth to entertain a hope of the salvation of their country. Mr. Eppes and Colonel Johnson came in to tea this evening, who have put me in a little heart by assuring me, that if our arms be victorious, the contest decided in our favor when so unequally urged, a wreath of honor and glory will crown the survivors, and the gratitude of their fellow-citizens immortalize their worthy deeds. Colonel Johnson places the most implicit confidence in Jackson; and says that his soldiers *must* be successful under a commander whose skill equals his bravery. Heaven grant success! both for our individual happiness and the interests of our adopted country; to restore my brother to the bosom of his family, and to induce our implacable enemy to consult their interest in a speedy and honorable termination of the war, which would doubtless be accelerated by discomfiture in attack. What do father and yourself think of America now, without men or money to meet the immense armament prepared by the English for our coasts? The members of Congress are mad enough to bite off their own heads at their own proceedings, and still continue to act inconsistently, to disgrace their country in the estimation of their own and other nations."

"February 4, 1815.

" Let us join with you in present gratitude and joy, dear mother, in being permitted once more to welcome the anniversary of our beloved father's birthday. May this day find him still healthful and serene, dispensing happiness to all around him. We shall celebrate this festival of the heart in domestic quiet and loving content. The 4th of February will ever be distinguished by the inhabitants of Washington, as giving them the first authentic account of the most decided victory over our enemies that ever was obtained by America, with the loss of five men killed and twelve wounded on our side. The bravery, the daring intrepidity displayed by the poor English fellows, who persisted in advancing to the very mouth of the cannon, though mowed down by hundreds, render even the triumph obtained over them painful. We are still uncertain and anxious for the eventual fate of Orleans; but are entirely roused from the state of despondency which the prospect of inevitable destruction to so valuable a portion of the United States had occasioned."

"November, 1815.

" . . . . *On dit* that the winter will be extremely gay, and decked with all the splendor of polished manners, brilliant talent and transcendent beauty, and the drawing-rooms will sparkle with scintillations of wit and fire of genius. Mr. Jefferson's granddaughter, Miss Randolph, will lead the van in accomplishments and beauty; Miss Law, Miss Harrison of Philadelphia, and Miss Livingston will fill an elevated place in the admiration of every observer, while daughters and nieces of the members will fill up the interstices. There is every reason to expect a crowded and interesting winter, as it will be the first meeting of Congress since the peace. Mrs. Madison tells me that there will be a great many foreigners of distinction here. . . . . There was a document received some time since at the State Department, in Spanish, which frustrated the talent of all the city to translate. Estimating highly Mr. Jefferson's knowledge as a linguist, it was sent to him by the President. He called Miss Randolph, and gave her the manuscript for her morning task, and long before the appointed hour she placed in his hands an elegant and correct translation, which was at once transmitted to the department; and being an important state paper, it has paved the way very handsomely for Miss Randolph. She will stay with Mrs. Madison, and will no doubt be very attractive to the various well-informed visitors at the palace. . . . . At the first drawing-room, old Mr. Digges was very attentive to me, inviting me pressingly to visit Warburton and bring any party with me, and thence to go to Mount Vernon, return and stay a day with him, to view the charming scenery which he 'should delight to point out to the amiable daughter of his old friends.' He spent a couple of hours with me yesterday, — most agreeably on my part. This recalls our late trip to Mount Vernon, the occasion being an entertainment given by Major Miller and the officers of the Marine Corps, to a party of our friends. The band accompanied us; and after visiting the tomb, and seeing every object of note on the hallowed ground, we adjourned to the boat, where an elegant collation awaited us. We were invited with much politeness and earnestness by Judge Bushrod Washington to remain and partake of refreshments, but declined his hospitality. I, however, accepted his offer to walk over the house and see the various pictures of the former possessor. It is singular, that of all the likenesses preserved of Gen. Washington, the one held in greatest estimation as a striking resemblance was cut from a common water pitcher made in England. This piece of crockery is framed, and holds a place of honor in the drawing-room. An elegant organ was open, upon the desk of which was one of Handel's masterpieces ; but Mrs. Washington unfortunately was indisposed, or we should have enjoyed the pleasure of hearing her play. The Judge is passionately fond of music, and appeared much pleased with the skill of the band, which performed admirably in the grove. . . . . The gardener was a German, and whether it was my enthusiasm for his old master, the mysteries of horticulture which we discussed, or something winning in my ways, I know not ; but he took a fancy to me, and offered me plants of any kind I wished, which, however, I of course declined. While we were standing on the lawn with Judge Washington listening to the music, the old German walked up very formally through the assembled party, and presented me with a bouquet of great fragrance, with a bow and approving smile. The company congratulated me on my conquest ; and Judge Washington assured me that the favor was totally unprecedented and astonishing, as during his whole knowledge of him he had never given away a flower before."

Mr. Thomas A. Digges, whose acquaintance with Mr. and Mrs. Gales in England had given the first impulse to their subsequent removal to America, was a Maryland gentleman of ancient colonial family, and noteworthy English descent. One of his ancestors, Sir Dudley Digges, having unfortunately incurred the ire of Queen Elizabeth, he was condemned by the implacable sovereign to be first disembowelled, and then beheaded. He sent for Essex to use his powerful influence in interceding with the queen for a mitigation of the sentence, so far as to reverse the order of punishment, and permit him to be beheaded *first*. But to the petition of Essex the gentle virgin answered, " Why, that is the very beauty of it ! " During our Revolutionary struggle Mr. Digges visited England, where he remained during many years, being a welcome guest in the most distinguished circles of society, and maintaining intimate relations especially with the Whigs or Liberals, whose leader, the Prince of Wales, favored the rebels or American party, as opposed to the Tories, who sided with King George. Mr. Digges was a bachelor, a well-bred man, and charming companion, his conversation replete with thrilling memories of the French Revolution, the horrors of which he had witnessed, and sparkling with anecdotes of Fox, Sheridan, and other celebrities of the brilliant and famous Carlton House coterie. He was a man of many eccentricities of habit, but a generous heart withal, capable of kind deeds. Major L'Enfant, the engineer brought from France by Count Rochambeau, — who accompanied Lafayette to aid the Colonies, — was subsequently employed under General Washington to lay out the Federal City, in the growth of which the beauty and magnificence of his designs are daily developed. Feeling aggrieved at some unjust treatment from the government, he used to appear invariably at the Capitol each day, with a *bâton* under his arm, to prosecute his claim before Congress ; but being disappointed in his hopes, he retired to Warburton Manor, where for ten years previous to his death he enjoyed, from the generosity of Mr. Digges, a comfortable home.

The hospitalities of this charming seat, long years ago
passed away, were proverbial; and it was on the occasion of a visit to Mr. Digges, their former friendship being warmly renewed, that Mrs. Gales wrote the following *impromptu*, discovered by her host on her dressing-
table the morning of her departure from the manor: —

    " O, what a goodly scene mine eyes embrace !
        Mingling with Flora's tincts of varied dye,
      Painted on Nature's sweet and pleasant face,
        Woods, vales, and streams in sweet confusion lie.

     .   .   .   .   .

    "Let poets boast of Arno's ' shelvy side,'
        And sing the beauties of the classic Po,
      Give *me* Potomac's grand, majestic tide,
        Sparkling beneath the sun's effulgent glow !

    " Yet *one regret* must mingle with the pride
        Which erst enkindled at thy ' fair mild ' name ;
      Here Britain's navy dared *unchecked* to ride,
        And history will the monstrous fact proclaim.

    " Ah ! could the sainted Washington have seen
        The vandal hordes, with desolating rage,
      Pour dire destruction o'er the once-loved scene,
        And more than Gothic warfare rudely wage, —

    " E'en from those scenes of glory, where on high
        He sits enthroned amidst celestial choirs,
      E'en there he would have breathed a mournful sigh
        As rose the devastating monsters' fires.

    " But let not *one* foul stain eclipse the rays
        Diverging from a thousand gallant deeds;
      All else has been a glorious, splendid blaze,
        Worthy the poet's song, the historian's meed.

    " Let Plattsburg, Chippewa, and Orleans tell,
        There the proud triumph of our arms were shown ;
      While Erie, Champlain, and Ontario swell
        The note which Fame through every land hath blown !

     .   .   .   .   .

> " Farewell, Potomac ! o'er thy waters wide
> I take a lingering but delightful view ;
> Whilst the gay vessel dances on the tide,
> I bid thee, Warburton, a last adieu.
>
> " Perhaps no more to see my early friend, —
> No more his hospitable smile to meet,
> Where true politeness and kind friendship blend,
> The ever-welcome, grateful guest to greet.
>
>   " WINIFRED GALES."

The " one foul stain " to which the verses allude was, doubtless, the desertion of his post by the young officer in command, Fort Warburton being captured by the British in consequence of his running away. The fort was on the domain of Mr. Digges, the present Fort Washington being erected on its site.

"November, 1815.

" . . . . About fifty members have arrived and marked their seats in the new building on Capitol Hill, erected for their temporary accommodation by old Mr Law, Carroll, and others, who wished to enhance the value of their property. You will perceive by the papers that General Jackson's visit here has excited a great commotion. Dinners, plays, balls, throughout the District. I wish much that some little aerial machine, uniting expedition and safety, could be invented, that you could take wing and remain a day, or an hour even, with us, and participate in the pleasure which every true lover of their country must feel in conversing with so distinguished a warrior as Jackson. Immediately on Mrs. Jackson's arrival a dilemma was presented, and a grand debate ensued as to whether the ladies would visit her. . . . . Colonel Reid and Dr. Goodlet, the friends of years of General Jackson, having settled the question of propriety satisfactorily, all doubts were laid aside. . . . . I have seen a good deal of General Jackson and his wife, who both received me with great attention and civility. He is not striking in appearance ; his features are hard-favored (as our Carolinians say), his complexion sallow, and his person small. Mrs. Jackson is a totally uninformed woman in mind and manners, but extremely civil, in her way. . . . . I suppose there have never been in the city so many plain women, in every sense of the word, as are now here among the families of official personages. I have always heard it asserted without contradiction, that nothing was easier than to learn to be a fine lady ; but I begin to think differently, being morally certain that many among the new-comers will never achieve that distinction.   Among the most amiable and refined of my acquaintances is Mrs. Crawford, of whom, being introduced to me by my intimate friends Mrs. Meigs and Mrs. Forsyth, who are also *her* old friends, I shall probably see a good deal. She has received by Mr. Crawford, from Paris, the most elegant furniture ; but she has no disposition for gayety, and thinks her husband's appointment as Secretary of War the most unfortunate circumstance, inasmuch as it will require her to forsake, in a good degree, those domestic habits which have heretofore constituted her sole happiness. . . . . You may be sure, however, dear mother, that these homespun propensities of our great folk cannot diminish my respect for their intrinsic merit and many excellent qualities. . . . .

"May, 1816.

"This day, for the first time this year, we recognize spring.

> 'Burst are the chains which lately bound,
>   And, lo ! the emancipated ground
>   Her independence feels.
>   The liberated rivers flow,
>   And conscious forests laugh to know

> Their species are set free
> From tyrant Winter : — and again
> Bounds the white blood through every vein
> Of every joyous tree.'

Never here was this genial season so long retarded ; and even now we present the phenomenon of eating strawberries and cream by a bright fire. . . . . We have been on a jaunt to Annapolis, to visit the 'Seventy-four,' about to carry Mr. Pinckney on his mission. It is one of the oldest towns in the Union, and though exhibiting every symptom of decay, is the most lovely spot you can conceive. On our way we met Judge Duvall, who pressed us to dine at his house, about fifteen miles from Washington, on the roadside, where we spent a few hours most delightfully in the society of this venerable, patriarchal man and hospitable, loquacious, kind old lady, who displayed on her table every luxury in and out of season. The President and family had stayed a day and night just before, being much gratified in their visit. The evening we reached Annapolis there was a great ball in honor of the President, and half an hour after our arrival we received invitations. Every one was there. Among other families in Annapolis, we were glad to meet our friends Mrs. Rush, Mrs. Lowndes, General Scott, Rogers, Porter, etc., who all fraternized very cordially. Mrs. Madison was very polite, expressing herself surprised and delighted at our arrival, introducing me very handsomely to Mrs. Pinckney, — her husband I knew very well before, — Governor and Mrs. Ridgely, of Maryland, and other notabilities, which, in a strange land, was very kind and acceptable. Commodore Chauncy and wife treated us with great respect and attention, and Captain Creighton, the commander, was an old acquaintance, to see whom, indeed, was one inducement of our trip. The Seventy-four was the ostensible cause of the jaunt, but the beautiful country and scenery had by far the greater portion of our time. A description of the interior of such a magnificent man-of-war transcends my power; suffice it that the clock-work regularity, the rigid discipline reigning throughout, and the delicate neatness pervading every nook of the vast monarch of the seas, received my full meed of admiration. The little President was as gay as a lark, and jested very humorously on the incidents of their journey; the cares of state thrown off his shoulders completely metamorphosed him, and relaxed his frigidity amazingly. . . . . I called to see your old friend, Mr. Law, yesterday, and found him employed in the most delightful and edifying occupation, — whistling variations to an operatic air to his son and heir, aged five weeks !

" I enjoyed a treat last week, my dear sister, which, great as it was, I would have willingly transferred to you, from the consideration that you were enabled both by nature and education to enjoy it more exquisitely than I could without your advantages, — and this was a view of some of the finest paintings ever in America. Mr. Calvert of Bladensburg went to Antwerp, where he married a Miss Steers, whose father, a descendant of Reubens, and an enthusiastic devotee of art, became possessed of several masterpieces to the great Fleming, to which were added Titians, Vanderlyns, and other undoubted originals, — in all about forty specimens of the old masters. During Bonaparte's absolute sway in France, and his lawless thirst for the acquisition of paintings with which to adorn the Louvre, he instituted a search for these same gems, well known in the art world, which Mr. Steers apprehending, he secreted and subsequently brought his treasures to his daughter in America, for safe keeping. The Bourbons being now reinstated, without, as Mr. Steers thinks, any danger of a reverse of fortune, he has reclaimed the paintings; and

Mr. Calvert, inasmuch as such an opportunity might never again occur to the citizens of Washington, invited all connoisseurs and amateurs to come for five days and gratify their taste and curiosity. Peale from Philadelphia, King and Wood from Baltimore, were transported with admiration. The Grecian Daughter, as it is called, Euphrasia, by Reubens, excited the most lively emotions of admiration; but 'The unbelieving Priest,' by Titian, was decided by them to be incomparably the most splendid effort of genius in that superb collection. Although convinced that my emotions of delight were inferior to those which animated the countenances of many connoisseurs present, I have felt ever since as if I had gained an idea, as if another ray of intellect had been given me by which to estimate the productions of other artists, by comparing them with these imprinted on my memory."

"March, 1818.

" . . . . I have mentioned the very agreeable accession to our neighborhood in the Calhouns. You could not fail to love and appreciate, as I do, her charming qualities; a devoted mother, tender wife, industrious, cheerful, intelligent, with the most perfectly equable temper. Mr. Calhoun is a profound statesman and elegant scholar, you know by public report; but his manners in a private circle are endearing, as well as captivating; and it is as much impossible not to love him at home as it would be to refuse your admiration of his oratorical powers in the Hall of Representatives. Since his absence in Carolina his wife has spent much time with me, coming down at nine in the morning and stopping till ten at night, and we generally go to church together on Sunday. . . . . I returned last week the visit of Mrs. W., accompanied by Mrs. Calhoun, thinking it would gratify our old friend to give her the benefit of any acquaintance who might be thought by the mass of the people to confer honor by paying the first visit. But I do not fancy being pressed into such service, as has been recently the case with Mrs. M., whose husband having no acquaintance with whom he could take the liberty except myself, earnestly requested the favor of my introducing his wife to the President's family, foreign ministers, secretaries, etc. Decline I could not ; the respectability of the lady, as the wife of a member of Congress, being a sufficient passport into any society here. They were gratified in having the visits returned, and on being invited consequently to dine with Monsieur de Neuville, and to meet us and a few other acquaintances at Mr. Calhoun's. So far, so well ; but it is an office that neither William nor I are fond of, as it seems almost a demand for civility to our acquaintances, in addition to that voluntarily bestowed on ourselves. . . . . It is said that the dinner-parties of Mrs. Monroe will be very select. Mrs. Hay, daughter of Mrs. Monroe, returns the visits paid to her mother, making assurances, in the most pointedly polite manner, that Mrs. Monroe will be happy to see her friends morning or evening, but that her health is totally inadequate to visiting at present ! Mrs. Hay is understood to be her proxy, and there this much-agitated and important question ends ; and as there is no distinction made, but all treated alike, I suppose it will eventually go down, though this alteration in the old *régime* was bitter to the palates of all our citizens, especially so to foreign ministers and strangers."

Previous to the accession of Mr. Monroe to the Presidency, the lady of the executive mansion had followed the rules of etiquette in regard to social visiting usually accepted in the conventional world. Mrs. Madison, with her frank, cordial, unassuming manner, had shown no distinction in individual or political position, when reciprocating the respect and attention so universally accorded to her personally. But with the growth of the city it became fitting to draw the line of demarcation more stringently; and the question as to the propriety of indiscriminate visiting on the part of the ladies of the President's family, or indeed of the head of his house returning any visits whatsoever, was hotly debated; this social revolution creating no little heart-burning among those left in the shade of non-recognition. This apparently trivial subject assumed such important shape, as subsequently to involve diplomatic and state correspondence, being finally adjusted by John Quincy Adams, who drew up the formula which has since regulated social etiquette between Washington officials.

Mrs. Seaton writing on this subject at a later period, says: "I have a letter from J. Q. Adams to the President of the United States on the question of etiquette. Do not mention it, but I will forward it to you as a curious document, which will display the character of the man who *may* be our future President, in stronger light than all the public papers he has written, and proves him to be more of a bookworm and abstracted student than a man of the world."

The following extracts from this voluminous exposition of etiquette, are characteristic of the earnestness and clearness with which Mr. Adams treated even the apparently trivial details of this social question.

"To the President of the United States.

"Washington, December 25, 1819.

"Sir: The meeting held yesterday having terminated without any arrangement relative to the subject upon which it had, at your desire, been convened, to avoid being misunderstood in the course of conduct which I have hitherto pursued, and to manifest my wish to pursue in the future any other which you will please to direct, I have thought it necessary to submit the following observations to your candor and indulgence.

" It has, I understand from you, been made a subject of complaint to you, as a neglect of duty on the part of the Secretary of State, that he omits paying at every session of Congress a first visit of form to every member of the Senate ; and that his wife is equally negligent of her supposed duty, in omitting similar attention to the ladies of every member of either house, who visit the city during the session. . . . . I must premise, that having been five years a member of the Senate, and having during four of the five sessions been accompanied at the seat of government by my wife, I have never received a first visit from any one of the heads of department, nor did Mrs. Adams ever receive a first visit from any of their ladies. . . . . . Visiting of form was considered as not forming a part either of official right, or official duty.

" I never heard a suggestion that it was due in courtesy, from a head of department, to pay a first visit to senators, or from his wife to visit the wife of any member of Congress. . . . . Entertaining the profoundest respect for the senate as a body, and a high regard for every individual member of it, I am yet not aware of any usage which required formal visits from me, as a member of the administration, to them as senators. The Senate of the United States, independent of its importance and dignity, is of all the associations of men upon earth, that to which I am bound by the most sacred and indissoluble ties of gratitude. . . . . Unworthy, indeed, should I be of such confidence, if I had a heart insensible to those obligations. Base indeed should I feel myself, if inflated by the dignity of the stations to which their frequently repeated kindness has contributed to raise me, I were capable of withholding from them collectively or individually, one particle of the reverence and honor due from me. . . . . When I learnt that there was such an *expectation* entertained by the senators in general, I quickly learnt from other quarters, that, if complied with, it would give great offence to the members of the House of Representatives unless extended also to them. These visits of ceremony would not only be a very useless waste of time, but incompatible with the discharge of the real and important duties of the departments. . . . . Neither did the introduction of a system of formality appear to me congenial to the Republican simplicity of our institutions. . . . . In paying the first visit to ladies coming to this place as strangers, Mrs. Adams could draw no discrimination; to visit all would be impossible; to visit only the ladies of members of Congress would be a distinction offensive to many other ladies of respectability; it would have applied even to the married daughter of the President. . . . . Above all, we wish it understood, that, while we are happy to receive any respectable stranger who pleases to call upon us, we have no claim or pretension to claim it of any one. . . . . . I am entirely disposed to conform to any other course which you may have the goodness to advise.

"With perfect respect, I remain, sir,

"Your very obedient servant,

"J. Q. ADAMS."

"March, 1818.

". . . . Old Mr. Digges lives in the city at present, and brought me a letter yesterday addressed to him by Thomas Jefferson, which bears the imprint of a mind unimpaired by continual intellectual exertion, and characterized by a vivacity astonishing at the age of seventy years. Mr. Digges is perfectly at home here, one day dining *en famille* with the President, spending the next with Mr. Bagot, and frequently alternating between these great folk with us, equally easy and agreeable to all. Mr. Bagot told me that Mr. Digges knew circumstances and people in his (Bagot's) neighborhood better than himself, and there is no part of England, nor few prominent persons there, with whom he is not perfectly acquainted. This reminds me of the unprecedented entertainment that has just taken place in the city, — a ball given to a British Minister by American citizens. A more festive or brilliant assembly I never attended. The occasion was honored by all the officials and most of the strangers of distinction in town. Mr. Bagot acted, as he has done on every occasion since his residence here, the perfect gentleman, and she 'looked an empress.' They were both very much excited, and expressed gratitude in unbounded and apparently sincere terms. They will carry with them the admiration 'and good wishes of all who knew them here, as their private character is as much esteemed as their public deportment. William looked uncommonly handsome, and as it was a subject of general remark, you will not accuse me of wifely partiality, when I say that, as he waltzed the Spanish dance with Mrs. J. Q. Adams, he was the most elegant man in the assembly, not excepting the guest of the evening."

The Right Honorable Sir Charles Bagot, G. C. B., and Privy Councillor, was a son of Lord Bagot, of Bagot's Bromley, an ancient family connected with such historic houses as those of Suffolk and Fulke-Greville, while his mother was a daughter of Lord Bolingbroke. Sir Charles rose rapidly in the diplomatic service, a career for which his personal gifts especially fitted

him ; one of his first missions being that of Washington, where he was during some years the very popular
British Envoy, winning golden opinions by his handsome presence and engaging manners.   He was ably
supported in these diplomatic requirements by Lady
Bagot, who was the Honorable Miss Wellesley, a daughter of Lord Maryborough, late Earl of Mornington, the
eldest brother of the Duke of Wellington.   From her
father she inherited her uncommon beauty, he being
notably one of the handsomest men of his day, as was also
his brother, the late Lord Cowley, whose exquisite portrait by Lawrence was one of the gems of the Duke of
Wellington's famous gallery.   The amiability and good
breeding by which Mrs. Bagot attracted the regards of
the citizens were the more admirable, as it was whispered
that she found society in the New World a great bore,
and deplored "the necessity of sticking pins in herself
to keep awake at the stupid balls."   Sir Charles Bagot
subsequently succeeded Lord Sydenham in the distinguished post of Governor-General of Canada, where he
died in 1843.   His daughter married the present Marquis of Anglesey, son of the famous companion-in-arms
of Wellington, and one of the heroes of Waterloo.

"May, 1819.

" . . . . We heard to-day in Blagden's church a most
confused declamatory discourse, without method or matter,
· from Mr. Breckenridge, who is the Presbyterian Atlas of
the District.   The church is very commodious, and the
congregation highly respectable and intelligent ; but really
the illiterate and weak delivery of the speaker renders it
astonishing that so many well-informed people should
have selected a pastor so little likely to benefit his flock.

In Raleigh, where a good rational preacher can be heard every Sabbath, it would be deemed strange to give encouragement to any man, however amiable in private life, who had no single requisite for an orator, which is the case of the gentleman I mention. . . . . .

"General Jackson has attended several private balls since the decision of Congress, and has received universal homage from male and female, a circle constantly around him waiting for an introduction, and ambitious of exchanging a few words with the greatest of American generals. Such is the prevailing sentiment among the inhabitants and congregated strangers here. . . . . .

"Our dear father will hardly think it credible that a rational, intelligent human being in full possession of his mental faculties, should madly rush into eternity. You will have seen by the Intelligencer that General Mason has fallen a victim to his own and antagonist's vindictive passions; and the feelings of disgust and horror at the *mode* adopted by the duellists has occasioned as much sensation here as the murder of poor Conway did in Raleigh. It was the mildest of three propositions which were made to rid each other of existence; the first, being to sit on a barrel of gunpowder together; the second, to hold hands and jump from the top of the Capitol; and the third scarcely less impious, to shoot at each other within ten paces with three musket-balls! The antagonists were first cousins. McCarty's brother is the husband of Mason's sister. The deceased has cast a stain upon his memory, and involved a very large and honorable family in his disgrace, which no previous act of his life had allowed them to anticipate. He was universally beloved. Unfortunately for Mason, he selected some young officers in Jackson's suite as counsellors and seconds. Had he advised with any of his old friends in Congress, or here, the catastrophe might have been averted. . . . . .

" There has been more gayety than I have ever known here in the summer, caused by the farewell dinners, the private and public balls, given to Monsieur and Madame de Neuville, who have by their unaffected kindness to their equals and their munificence to the poor won upon the popular esteem and gratitude. They do not possess the external advantages of address and person for which Mr. and Mrs. Bagot were admired, and we shall never again, I imagine, witness so much style and splendor as the entertainments of the British Envoy presented. The public ball was a great success, Monsieur de Neuville making a very impressive little speech of thanks to the citizens. William, with five other married men, officiated as master of ceremonies, and I was pleased that he had an opportunity of testifying respect for the worthy old couple, as we have spent many agreeable hours in their hospitable house. They are uncertain if their master will send them here again, but profess a desire to represent their nation at this republican capital rather than at any of the splendid courts of Europe, not excepting St. Petersburg, considered by far the most magnificent in the world. They came, the morning they started, to see us, bringing remembrances for the children. The French, more than any other people, study these graceful attentions, slight in themselves, but the sure avenue to a mother's heart. . . . ."

The " Intelligencer," as an independent and national expositor, and indeed it may be said controller of public sentiment, was now a power in the land, while Mr. Seaton's commanding personal qualities and rare social gifts could not fail to establish a peculiar influence over his fellow-citizens. These slight sketches of a few of the prominent friends and events distinguishing Mr. Seaton's familiar circle indicate the marked consideration enjoyed by him, even at his early age, among the good and great of our golden era, and which, as time went on, matured into a reverential regard and appreciation of his character and attainments by the community. Under the public law, the citizens of Washington are privileged to bestow but meagre testimonials of respect and popularity, the municipal office being the highest in their power to confer on those who win their favor; and the first step in the progressive evidence of their esteem Mr. Seaton was at last persuaded to accept, as we see by Mrs. Seaton's mention.

"December, 1819.

" You will perceive by the paper that William's blushing honors crowd thick upon him, which, however, he bears with singular meekness, not having given himself a single air since his exaltation as alderman, for which office he has become increasingly eligible by his *embonpoint*.   There is greater commotion existing in the city than was ever known before about the election of Lord Mayor, the contest lying between Colonel Orr, Roger Weightman, Richard Lee, and General Van Ness. . . . . The drawing-room of the President was opened last night to a ' beggarly row of empty chairs.' Only five females attended, three of whom were foreigners. Mrs. Adams, the previous week, *invited* a large party, which we attended, at which there were not more than three ladies. In a familiar, pleasing manner, the sprightly hostess made known to each of her visitors that every Tuesday evening during the winter, when they had nothing better to do with themselves, it would give her great pleasure to receive them. The evening arrived, and with it two other guests besides her sisters ! Don't you think we must be reforming ? Some wise distinctions in etiquette were, however, probably the cause of the defalcation. There is to be a splendid party at Madame de Neuville's, who enlists all varieties of character under her banner. Since her return she has resigned herself to be poorly lodged in the attic, so as to afford more room below for constant hospitalities. Madame Van Greuhm, formerly governess to Governor Middleton's daughters, resides at Kalorama, and intends entertaining all citizens who have sufficient leisure to honor her invitations. The diplomatic corps are very much chagrined at the descent made by the Prussian Minister, considering it a degradation ; but inasmuch as he is a sensible, amiable man, and a *noble*, they magnanimously agree to forgive him. At the drawing-room, Madame de Neuville was exquisitely dressed in a white satin under-slip, with silver lace tunic, head-dress of superb pearls and lace."

" February, 1820.

" Congress has been occupied during three weeks in the discussion of the Missouri bill, — the right to prohibit the admission of slaves in the new State of Missouri ; or rather the question is, Shall Missouri be a State, or not ? for it is well understood that she does not wish to enter the confederation, except on an equal footing with other States which have been permitted to form their own constitutions without interference from Congress. The excitement during this protracted debate has been intense. The galleries are now crowded with colored persons, almost to the exclusion of whites. They hear all, but understand much less than half They know it to be a question of servitude or freedom, and imagine that the result will immediately affect their condition ; so, as one side or other of the question preponderates, they rejoice or are depressed. When the slaves of the Southerners, now here, return home with mutilated and exaggerated accounts of what they have

7   J

heard, I fear that many deluded creatures will fall sacri-
fices to their misapprehension of the question. Mr. Meade,
the Colonization Society, have all grasped at that which
was too mighty for individual hands, and have, with good
intentions, raised a flame which their united efforts at
counteraction will scarcely quench. If ever the abolition
of slavery be attempted, it must be by the government of
the United States; it cannot, it ought not to be touched
without awful consideration. Already does Maryland feel
the effects of this unfortunate discussion. The consequences of this ill-judged indulgence in public curiosity can
hardly be calculated. Had Congress sat with closed doors,
these evils would have been avoided. There is no *guessing*
when the question will be decided, as many members have
long speeches prepared for the benefit of an admiring world.
The Senators and members generally are so excited, that
unless their angry passions are allowed to effervesce in
speaking, the most terrible consequences are apprehended
even by experienced statesmen. This subject being made
subservient to political views, and having in perspective
the Presidential election, is bandied from one to the other
speaker alternately. Rufus King enkindled a flame in the
Senate by a factious speech which required the combined
efforts of all his contemporaries to moderate. I prefer Mr.
King's *oratory* to any I have heard, his manner so grave
and dignified, chaste language, disdaining flowers, orna-
mental tropes or figures, or the studied grace of gesture.
In this opinion I am singular, perhaps unique, as the palm
is unanimously awarded to Pinckney. Indeed, you may
have seen comparisons made between this celebrated modern and the ancients, Demosthenes and Cicero, in which
the latter are evidently in the background of the picture.
There have been not less than a hundred ladies on the floor
of the Senate every day on which it was anticipated that

Mr. Pinckney would speak, encompassing the Senators, and absolutely excluding Representatives, foreign Ministers, etc. Governor Tompkins, a very gallant man, had invited a party of ladies whom he met at Senator Brown's, to take seats on the floor of the Senate, having, as President of the Senate, unlimited power, and thinking proper to use it, contrary to all former precedent. I was one of the select, and gladly availed myself of the invitation, with my good friend Mrs. Lowndes, of South Carolina, and half a dozen others. The company in the gallery seeing a *few* ladies very comfortably seated on the sofas, with warm foot-stools and other luxuries, did as they had a right to do, — deserted the gallery; and every one, old and young, flocked into the Senate. 'T was then that our Vice-President began to look alarmed, and did not attend strictly to the member addressing the chair. The Senators (some of them) frowned indignantly, and were heard to mutter audibly, ' Too many women here for business to be transacted properly ! ' Governor Tompkins found it necessary the next morning to affix a note to the door, excluding all ladies not introduced by one of the Senators. Having so many polite friends among them, I shall probably attend the whole debate. . . . .

" On Sunday last I went to the Capitol, and listened with great interest to one of the purest strains of eloquence that ever issued from the pulpit in my hearing, — a young man named Everett, an Unitarian preacher from Boston, of rare talents and profound learning, professor of Greek and Hebrew at Cambridge. He has just returned from Europe, where he has been perfecting himself in languages, particularly Oriental knowledge. He left Constantinople and returned home at the same time as Mr. Lowndes. It is supposed that he will accept the post of chaplain to Congress next year. Jonathan Mason promises to procure for me Everett's sermon, which I wish dear father to read, especially that portion drawing an advantageous comparison between America and every other country, ancient and modern. . . .

"Maria Monroe is to be married on Tuesday to her cousin, young Gouverneur. The following day a brilliant drawing-room will be held, and the immense ball-room opened. The marriage to be entirely private."

"March 28, 1820.

" . . . . The New York style was adopted at Maria Monroe's wedding. Only the attendants, the relations, and a few old friends of the bride and groom witnessed the ceremony, and the bridesmaids were told that their company and services would be dispensed with until the following Tuesday, when the bride would receive visitors. Accordingly all who visit at the President's paid their respects to Mrs. Gouverneur, who presided in her mother's place on this evening, while Mrs. Monroe mingled with the other citizens. Every visitor was led to the bride and introduced in all form. But the bridal festivities have received a check which will prevent any further attentions to the President's family, in the *murder* of Decatur! The first ball, and which we attended, consequent on the wedding, was given by the Decaturs! Invitations were out from Van Ness, Commodore Porter, etc., all of which were remanded on so fatal a catastrophe to the man identified with the glorious success of his country in the late war. In the event of another war, *he* would have been the first one to whom his country would have turned for a repetition of services so hazardous and valuable. Commodore Barron lies ill, but not dangerously wounded. The explanation which took place *after* the rencontre, and before they were removed from the ground, would have prevented it. They repeated to each other that they harbored no enmity, and hoped to meet, better friends, in another world. Commodore Decatur suffered excruciating agony for several hours after arriving at his home, and his chief surgeon, Dr. Lovell, told me that he said only: ' If it were in the cause of my country it would be nothing.' He has left the whole of his property, which is very large, to his wife, with the exception of legacies to his two nieces, the Misses Mc-Knight, who reside with him. So *many* friends were privy to this intended duel, that it appears most extraordinary it should not have reached the ears of the President, who alone could have averted it. Mr. Wirt, Bomford, Rogers, Porter, Bainbridge, General Harper, his father-in-law, Mr. Wheeler, all, all kept the secret, though they did everything else to prevent it. Mrs. Decatur never saw her husband, not even after death. She still lies in a lethargic stupor, her physicians fearing apoplexy, and unable to bleed her. No child, no relative except her father, an old man, what must be her situation when her sense of feeling shall return with all its poignancy. Commodore Barron has a wife and eleven children. If he recover, he will be an object of execration to his enemies, and scarcely of pity to his friends. . . . . We attended, a few days since, a grand mass for the repose of the soul of the *Duc de Berri*, a most imposing ceremony, and interesting from the sympathy universally excited by the sad fate of so amiable a prince. . . . . William has been applied to by all his own friends and very many of the citizens, to know if he will consent to serve as mayor ; but he has uniformly declined the proposition, flattering as he feels it to be, viewing it as both unneighborly and unfriendly to oppose the known wishes of ——, who has always had this elective honor at heart, and who is conscious that he could not be elected if William were to allow his own name to be mentioned for the dignity. There are only eight candidates !

" You see that John Randolph did not have much en-couragement for his crazy proposition. It is the universal opinion that he is deranged, and he affords, certainly, con-firmation of this idea every day of his life by his *outré* conduct. He is chock-full of fight ever since the late duel, and endeavors to provoke a quarrel with everybody he meets, makes speeches in favor of this mode of settling disputes, and seems entirely to have forgotten the excuse he made to Bolling Robinson ! "

The celebrated, eccentric John Randolph, as is well known, vehemently opposed the Missouri Compromise, not so much probably from any principle involved in that important question, as from his innate aversion to be led by the arguments of a majority, and from his Ishmaelitish nature, which delighted in provoking every man's hand against his own, — an inborn aris- tocrat, and yet from mere perversity of temper uphold-ing every levelling project. It was during these acri-monious compromise debates that he stigmatized the Northerners who voted for that pacificatory measure as " doughfaces," which cognomen was long a slogan in party warfare ; and it was on this occasion also that he allowed his peevish antagonism to overpower his gallantry. The floor and gallery of the House were crowded by eager listeners among the fair sex, when Randolph rose, and all looks fastened on his weird figure, as, pointing that long skeleton index-finger toward the ladies, and in his peculiar, shrill, squeaking voice, he said : " Mr. Speaker, what pray are all these women doing here, so out of place in this arena ? Sir, they had much better be at home attend-ing to their knitting !" The reproof, though undeserved, was accepted, and for a few days following the congressional gladiators received no inspiration from bright eyes.

Randolph's hostility to Clay — whose acceptance of the position of Secretary of State in the Adams cabinet had induced the cry of " bargain and corruption," and greatly impaired the popularity of the great Commoner — culminating in his insulting denunciation of Adams's election as a " coalition of Puritan and black-leg," and for which characteristic epigram Clay demanded satisfaction on the field of honor, had existed from their first meeting in public life. Of that famous duel between the fiery Virginian and the peerless Kentuckian Mr. Seaton was known to have an inside history ; but, unfortunately, the authentic version of this, as of so many of the great events, and the inexhaustible anecdotes of the compeers of Mr. Seaton's exceptional career, with which his memory teemed, are without written record, and lost to history. Especially of Randolph's inner life, the true man underlying that crust of eccentricity and infirm temper, Mr. Seaton seemed to hold the key, his relations with him being of a nature that brought him very near the singular and gifted man. During several years Mr. Seaton and Mr. Gales were exclusively their own reporters in the Senate and House 'of Representatives, where they respectively had appropriated to them a seat at the side of the Vice-President and the Speaker. This privilege, with its concomitant of the daily exchange of the snuff-box and friendly sentiment with the members, giving the brother-editors a rare insight into the secret springs of debate, the actual force and individuality of the giants of that day. Mr. Randolph sat near Mr. Seaton, and on one occasion when Mr. Clay, speaking in his not unusual personal and self-sufficient strain, said, among other things, that "his parents had left him nothing but *indigence* and *ignorance*," Randolph, turning to Mr. Seaton, said, in a stage whisper to be heard by the House: "The gentleman might continue the alliteration, and add *insolence*." It was said that Clay was somewhat afraid of his antagonist's caustic wit, and on this occasion at least it was not resented by the "Rupert of debate."

A member of Mr. Seaton's family, writing from Virginia early in 1833, says: "Mr. Randolph has been staying with us, but so feeble that he could not leave his room. He talks as much and as wonderfully as usual; and is, if possible, more witty and eccentric than ever. Cousin J. remarked to him that he was surprised to see him persist in the exploded fashion of wearing round-toed shoes. 'O,' replied Mr. Randolph, 'I am like Ritchie, — I neither track one way nor the other.' He spoke with great regard of Gales and Seaton, and their talent, and wishes to be kindly remembered."

"February, 1821.

" . . . . The city is unusually gay, and crowded with agreeable and distinguished visitors. Mr. Canning's initiatory ball seemed to rouse the emulation of his neighbors, and we have had a succession of *fêtes*. The British Minister's rout was unique. The English are half a century before us in style. Handsome pictures, books, and all sorts of 'elegant litter' distinguish his rooms, the mansion being decorated with peculiar taste and propriety.

"Mr. Canning is himself a most unpretending man in appearance and manners; modesty appears to be his peculiar characteristic, which for a foreign minister is no negative praise. . . . . The birthnight ball was brilliant. The contrast between the plain attire of President Monroe and Mr. Adams, and the splendid uniforms of the diplomatic corps, was very striking; the gold, silver, and jewels donned by the foreigners in compliment to the anniversary festival of our patriot and hero certainly adding splendor to the scene. The captivating D'Asprament made his *début* in brilliant crimson indispensables laced with gold, an embroidered coat, stars and orders, golden scabbard and golden spurs. Poor girls! perfectly irresistible in person, he besieged their hearts; and, not content with his triumphs there, his sword entangled their gowns, his spurs demolished their flounces in the most attractive manner possible, — altogether he was proclaimed invincibly charming. Mons. de Neuville has adopted a new course since his return. Formerly, his secretaries were remarkably small and insignificant in appearance, and he now appears to have selected his legation by their inches. The most cultivated Frenchman whom I have ever met is now in Mons. de Neuville's family, — the Chevalier du Menu. He has resided ten years in America, and is a poet, orator, and scientific man, though still young. . . . ."

Mr. Stratford Canning, the son of a London merchant, and a cousin of the eminent statesman George Canning, who died in 1827 while Prime Minister of England, filled very acceptably during three years the post of British Envoy to Washington; and although not possessing the popular manners of his predecessor Mr. Bagot, he was remarkable for exquisite high breeding, refinement, and the best attributes of an

English gentleman, which won the appreciation of the government and warm good-will of the community. He was tall, slender, and somewhat out of health, a consequence of which delicate state created some animadversion among the genial *convives* of the day. The fashion then prevailing of drinking wine with each guest, Mr. Canning, instead of a decanter of generous Burgundy, always had one of toast-and-water placed at his plate, in which innocuous beverage he pledged the health of all; but his *ruse* was discovered, and subjected him to some ill-natured criticism.

Although of a perfect and captivating courtesy, he was reserved in manner, and it is said sometimes allowed his diplomatic suavity to be overcome by a certain impatience and even asperity of temper, which subsequently, on a grander stage and while adjusting the most delicate and momentous negotiations, unfortunately developed into an acrimony which, irritating Prince Gortschakoff, incited the famous Russian "ultimatum," and precipitated the great powers into the Crimean war. In 1841 Mr. — then Sir Stratford — Canning was appointed Ambassador at the Porte, where he remained until the close of the war; his prolonged study of Eastern politics, his diplomatic sagacity, and his unequalled influence over the Sultan enabling him to perform very important services for his country, especially as connected with the status of Christians in Turkey. He also showed acceptable kindness, politically and socially, to Americans, on various occasions while in Constantinople. In 1852 he was raised to the peerage, under the title of Viscount Stratford de Redclyffe.

" 1822.

" . . . . You will perceive that among the new members there are as many speakers as usual, and that consequently your sons are sufficiently occupied, notwithstanding their acquisition of a stenographer at $1,000 per session. I think, dear father, you would have thought this handsome compensation when you pursued the same avocation with more indefatigable intensity in Philadelphia. You will perceive by the debates that truly the course of editors never does run smooth. In truth, 't is a thankless task in most instances, considering too that the labor is voluntary and of no pecuniary value, unless enhancing the interest of the paper may be considered an equivalent for querulous carping and fault-finding from dissatisfied members, who feel themselves slighted in not finding their wisdom displayed to their constituents in two or three columns of the Intelligencer. Joseph writhes under these attacks, being never very tolerant of censure, but William bears them with rather amused patience. Some of the friends of the editors begin to be extremely anxious to know under what colors the Intelligencer will sail during the next three years' voyage, and urge them to declare immediately in favor of the only man fit to guide the government bark, each individual probably having a different man in view. Encompassed as they are by friends in the shape of presidential candidates, the choice will be unpleasant, come when it may, and they feel no anxiety to anticipate the free and full expression of the Republican majority. Meantime, the present incumbent is treated with very little ceremony, while casting about for his successor ; and there was some humor in Colvin's proposition, that "a committee be appointed to wait on the President and ask him to have the goodness to resign, inasmuch as gentlemen were in a hurry and did not like to wait. . . . . . ."

" The Unitarian church has been dedicated with all the solemnity and simplicity characterizing the profession of its members. Mr. Little's discourse on the occasion was irresistibly forcible and pathetic, his impressive manner adding to its exceeding interest. The performance of the choir created pleasure and surprise in all the audience, who were not aware of the harmonious treat prepared for them. How we wished that you, dear father, could have been present to join in every part of the day's services. There were upwards of four hundred persons present, which, considering that the Bishop preached and administered the rite of confirmation at the Episcopal church, was a very large congregation. If you will now come to us, you may worship God according to the mode you prefer, and under the voice of a man after your own heart, for so I think Mr. Little will prove. So patriarchal in appearance, mild and truthful, yet so energetic in his appeals to the reason and the heart, that the most indifferent auditor finds himself imperceptibly engaged in self-examination. The closing sentences of his beautiful effort were thus : " All is torpidity in the grave. ' Shall it be said that we have left no useful memorial behind us? What ! not a handful of grass which the mower may regard as the fruit of our labor? Forbid it, Gracious Father! These walls I trust will bear witness that our lives have not been altogether useless to mankind. Some I hope may be better and wiser for our exertions in the cause of truth. If not in an obvious and direct manner, yet in some effectual way may we have served our generation, and promoted the knowledge, the service, and the will of the *one true God.*"

As has been seen, Joseph Gales had been mainly instrumental in the dissemination of his religious faith in Philadelphia, by his successful efforts in the establishment of the first church erected there for the worship of Unitarian Christians, while his name will be held in grateful memory as being in truth the founder of Unitarianism in Charleston and Washington. His daughter married the Rev. Anthony Forster, an esteemed Presbyterian divine of the former city, who, a year afterwards, announced to Mr. Gales his renunciation of Calvinism, saying : " In reading all the most eminent works on divinity in order to convince you of *your* error, the issue has been that I am convinced of *my own.*" Mr. Forster was ordained pastor of the first Unitarian Church of South Carolina, being at his death succeeded in the pastorate by Rev. Mr. Gilman, of Massachusetts. Mrs. Seaton thus writes of her relative's change of views : —

"That he whom I have been accustomed to consider most tenacious, bigoted even, in adherence to the Athanasian creed, should abjure its fallacies, seems almost miraculous ! But the simplicity of truth has prevailed. I firmly believe the day not far distant when these principles will receive enlightened encouragement throughout America. Massachusetts generally is Unitarian, its learned men and professors being for the most part decidedly averse to the inculcation of Trinitarian doctrines. Most of the eminent clergymen of Boston have seceded, and refuse to subscribe to the Thirty-nine Articles. Many of the most intellectual and pious strangers, as well as citizens among our acquaintances, agree perfectly in this gospel doctrine, against which I have never yet heard nor read a word to counteract my early prepossession."

It was chiefly through the influence and active aid of Mr. Seaton, and his brother-in-law Mr. Gales, that the church of their faith was founded in Washington, then the outpost of liberal Christianity. Among its warm friends and consistent adherents was Mr. Calhoun, who, on the occasion of contributing generously to the erection of the church, remarked to Mr. Seaton, that "Unitarianism was the true faith, and must ultimately prevail over the world."

"BOSTON, 1823.

" . . . . I close my letter with a few words as to the most interesting visit I have ever yet paid, — to the venerable ex-President John Adams, residing at Quincy, nine miles from Boston. Our good friend John Quincy Adams is here, in the same house with us, and this morning invited himself to a seat in our carriage for the purpose of introducing us to his venerated father. It happened to be an important day, the patriarchal statesman having appointed it to review the Boston Democratic company of Fusileers, who went out for the purpose. We found him sitting to the famous Stuart for his portrait, to be completed on his eighty-ninth birthday. Mr. Adams led me to him and said a few words aside, when I was quite affected by his rising from the sofa, and affectionately kissing my cheek, bidding me welcome to Quincy. He is very infirm, his voice tremulous with age ; but he retains all the dignity which I have heard ascribed to him, with nothing of the *hauteur*. We partook ' with himself, John Quincy Adams, and a younger brother, and a large family circle, of a collation prepared for the Corps of Fusileers, the officers participating with us, the privates occupying another room. We were delighted, and the scene will not easily be eradicated from our memory. On taking leave we were pressingly invited to repeat our visit, and thanked for the compliment of paying our respects."

"December, 1823.

" . . . . You will see that our congressional body take things coolly. After they once fairly enter the arena, however, we shall have no deficiency of warmth, I presume; and we are prepared for an unusual display of eloquence from Mr. Webster, and other conspicuous members, on the subject of the Greeks. My impression is that they push the matter too far in the Northern cities, when they extend their views beyond an expression of sympathy in sufferings incurred in the cause of freedom, and individual contributions for the relief and assistance of a brave people.

" Propositions to alter and amend the Constitution, in time to operate on the Presidential election, will also elicit much declamation ; and, after the ice is once broken, there will be occupation for all the stenographers who attend Congress, — some dozen or two now. You have no conception of the attentions with which the winning, courtly Mr. Clay, and the interesting, agreeable Mr. Calhoun ply the new and old members here. Mr. Macon, with his usual obstinacy, and to be different in detail if not in principle, from his party, is an anti-caucus man, and will countenance no such practice. I suppose he will prove that there were no caucuses in the time of Moses, and therefore there is no necessity for them now. Such is the argument with which he usually winds up his opinions. . . . . I conversed to-day with Dr. Holcombe, from New Jersey, who has been called in to Mr. Crawford, who is extremely low. His general debility has occasioned an affection of the eyes, exceedingly painful, compelling him to remain with them bandaged in a dark room, which will be an incalculable disadvantage when Congress is becoming impatient for the Treasury Report, and when he will require *all his eyes* to make no second blunder. William has seen him this morning, and reports his health and constitution as apparently shattered. He has been bled twenty-three times, *largely*, within three weeks. The physicians apprehend total blindness, the confirmation of which fear would be an irremediable misfortune in a President. My private opinion is, that he will never live to be President. His herculean size and almost entire blindness bring to my mind 'Samson,' as I conceived him to be in my early years. I trust, however, that he will recover, to defeat the insidious as well as open attempts to injure him. Doubly now do we deprecate the event of his being withdrawn from the contest, as we could not conscientiously support his probable rival, a man so unreasonable and exacting in all his concerns, and with whom it would be difficult to transact business without forfeiting independence. Except Mr. Adams, the editors have never thought of any other candidate but Mr. Crawford. The recent conduct of Mr. —— would leave only a choice of evils. He has displayed a vindictive, implacable resentment for an oversight in the publication of his documents, which ought not to have created an emotion of anger, and which was corrected as soon as pointed out to the editors ; but because the whole paper was not made subservient to his particular interests to the exclusion of others, he cannot forgive. . . . . Truth to say, however, I believe that his self-love being wounded was the principal reason for his conduct ; and I begin to think, with Timothy Pickering, that he is unrelenting when either ambition or vanity is concerned.

" The war waxes hot, and it will continue until after the exciting election. Mr. Adams moves neither to the right nor left, but keeps an undeviating course, regardless of the opinion of friend or foe. Mr. Clay spares neither of the editors of the ' Intelligencer ' as such, nor the men personally, whenever opportunity presents ; for they are unaccustomed to bow to any authority save that of conscientious duty, and will teach this Western Hotspur that *they* control public opinion and the 'most sweet voices' he is so anxious to win. General Jackson appears to possess quite as much *suaviter in modo* as *fortiter in re.* He is, indeed, a polished and perfect courtier in female society, and polite to. all. He will, however, if our President, have a most. warlike cabinet, I presume, and will send his Message to Congress by the Secretary of War, flanked by Orderly Sergeants. A more despotic sovereign would not reign in Europe. . . . . . All well with us.

" Your dutiful and affectionate

" SARAH."

" RICHMOND, July 15, 1824.

" MY DEAR SIR, — My friend Mr. William Ruffin, of Raleigh, writes me for Mr. J. Q. Adams's letter to General Smith's constituents. I have no spare number, but you have pamphlet copies. Do send him one and charge it to the good cause. Virginia is firm as the Rock of Gibraltar. My friend writes me (I have it confirmed by another letter by the same mail), that. Mr. Crawford will get the electoral vote of North Carolina. Come out boldly. Trust to God and your country. Crawford and truth will triumph. His friends must be bold, firm, active, and there is no danger of his non-success. The country 's up. Speak out, without mincing or modification. You are the ad-- vocate of the cause of Truth ; speak as her friends ought always to speak when the public weal demands it, — fearlessly and freely. Adams's friends are reeling, and, in all directions, confessing nobly and conscientiously that they cannot support him.

" The time draws nigh. The crisis has come. Three months decide the contest. The country is large, and it takes some time for the voice to reach to our remotest hamlets.

K

"I assure you, in confidence, that all parties here think the *N. Intelligencer* is too mild. Your enemies here are chuckling at your late appearance of giving up to Mr. Adams. Excuse me for my suggestions. I should be the first to call them impertinent and officious if the good of the country was not at stake.

"In haste, yours,

"THOMAS RITCHIE.

"To MR. SEATON."

Mr. George Bancroft relates the following characteristic anecdote of the great Carolina statesman's political aspirations. "When Monroe was about to retire from the office of President there was a great struggle for the successorship. Calhoun desired to be a candidate. Mr. Seaton had a great regard for Mr. Calhoun, but thought his nomination at that time would be premature. One evening as they were walking together by the banks of the Potomac Mr. Seaton reasoned with him, using the argument: 'At the end of your second term you will be still in the prime of manhood. What would you do?' And Calhoun answered, 'I would retire and write my memoirs.'"

The following letter from our great historian and diplomatist is a graceful expression of the feeling entertained by him for Mr. and Mrs. Seaton; a friendship which was mutual and lasting.

"MY DEAR SIR, — If I may judge of your sentiments by the lively recollections I retain of the very pleasant hours it was my happiness three winters ago to pass in your family, I should believe that I am not yet entirely forgotten in the circle to which you and Mrs. Seaton so kindly bade me welcome. It is in that persuasion that I venture to direct my publisher to send you a volume which will reach you shortly after the adjournment of Congress ; and which, I hope, will then find you able to give an hour or two to its contents, and perhaps win a little time from Mrs. Seaton. Of her approbation I should be proud indeed.

" I have been long engaged in gathering material for writing a history of the United States. I dare not own to you how much labor I have given to the preparation. One volume I have completed and printed ; it is that which I have taken the liberty to send you. Accustomed to a large consideration of the affairs of the country, you are eminently qualified to pass an opinion upon the manner in which the work is conceived. I confess my desire that you may find leisure to make the work a subject of careful criticism. Your views would be exceedingly valuable to me ; as the work is, in its design at least, national, I feel a strong hope that it will win your approbation. I beg to be remembered with respectful regard to Mrs. Seaton and your family. How unlike the quiet of the village in which I reside is the turbulent ambition of Washington. Should you and Mrs. Seaton travel to the North, pray promise her from me the richest of our fine moss-roses, and the most delicate of our fruit and flowers.

" With sincere respect, yours,

" GEORGE BANCROFT.

" MR. SEATON.

" NORTHAMPTON, MASS., June 21, 1834."

" September, 1824.

" You will see, dear mother, that Lafayette is expected on the first ; and nothing is heard but drumming, nothing seen but regiments from one end of the District to the other. The Committee of Arrangements, of which William is one, have some very magnificent plans in view, as yet secrets of state. Amongst them one, which, if carried into effect, would be unique, *sub rosa*, of course, viz. to throw a treble arch over the central dome of the Capitol, containing three rows of colored lamps of primary colors, to represent a rainbow. It will require about six thousand lamps, which fortunately can be furnished at a mere *marevedi* in comparison with former cost.

"There is no withstanding public opinion, and William has consented that Augustine, at the head of his company, shall be allowed to meet Lafayette at the District line; so the young Captain and Ensigns are in a way to tread the Avenue with as much precision and dignity as their *fathers*."

An eloquent pen characterizing Mr. Seaton's attributes at this period says: "The course of Mr. Seaton's life from a period little advanced from boyhood was such as to insure, indeed, to necessitate, an intimate familiarity with the men and events of his time, with all changes of public opinion, with all discussions of constitutional law, with all the movements of interest, prejudice, and affection by which the affairs of the world are governed. The thoughts, the passions, the motives of his fellow-men were necessarily with him subjects of scrutinizing observation and intelligent reflection. When he removed to Washington, the sphere of his observation and influence was, of course, greatly widened. The trusted friend and counsellor of the earlier administrations, there can be no doubt that, as he was the depositary of their confidence, he often contributed in no small degree to shape their measures." These advantages, united to the personal charm of Mr. Seaton, had not failed to give him an enviable status in the consideration of his fellow-citizens. His genial cordiality, his captivating courtesy, his large hospitality, and a readiness of beneficence having few equals, had won their individual affection, while their confidence was based on the justice, the candor, the uprightness of purpose and generosity of temper characterizing his daily walk of life.

They already relied on him as their most able coadjutor in every plan having for its object the welfare of the city; and turned to him as their representative on all civic public occasions, whether the duty involved were to offer an address of welcome to an incoming, or to speed the parting President, — to inaugurate benevolent institutions, or to assume the more delicate and gracious task of presiding at social festivals. Possessed of these unusual traits, Mr. Seaton naturally would be chosen to sustain the principal part in offering the city's hospitality to foreigners of distinction; and thus, upon the occasion of Lafayette's sojourn in our midst, upon Mr. Seaton, although in no official capacity, seemed by tacit consent to devolve the special charge of the nation's guest. Those who for half a century were familiar with Mr. Seaton's varied attributes can well understand that his conversational gift, his full intelligence, his noble presence and the seal of distinction with which nature had stamped him, should have fascinated our great French ally, who, versed in every phase of life, — from the brilliant circles about the throne to the camp-fires of our colonial wilderness, — was a keen judge of men; and a sure index of Mr. Seaton's power of attraction may be discerned in the friendship then formed, and cherished for him through life by Lafayette.

Mr. Seaton was Secretary to the Committee charged with the duty of proceeding to Baltimore to welcome and escort Lafayette to Washington. The gastronomic excellence for which the fair Monumental City has ever been famed found an appreciative judge in the illustrious guest, who, on the occasion of the breakfast at Barnum's, Mr. Seaton described as especially enjoying the fine bay perch, six of which he consumed, bread *à discretion*, all washed down with generous Bordeaux; the culmination of his enthusiasm, however, being reserved for the unsurpassed canvas-back duck and hominy; and so constantly was the General in the open air with receptions, processions, and speeches, — the excitement naturally inducing an unusual appetite, — that the consumption of a whole duck would be the tribute paid by him to the excellence of our unequalled Southern winged delicacy, the enjoyment of which a subsequent distinguished traveller, Lord Morpeth, declared to be worth a voyage across the Atlantic.

Among the noteworthy incidents attending Lafayette's reception in Washington was that described in the following letter by Mrs. Seaton, whose modesty, however, did not permit her to express the charm lent by her presence and that of her attendant maidens, to the welcome extended to the General.

"October, 1824.

"DEAR MOTHER, — I don't know how it was, but I certainly figured more than I had any wish or expectation of doing, on the day of Lafayette's arrival. In the first place, I was selected by the committee of arrangements to superintend the dress and decoration of twenty-five young ladies representing the States and District, and procure appropriate wreaths, scarfs, and Lafayette gloves and flags for the occasion, to assemble them at my house, and attend them under my protection to the Capitol.

" I had previously been influenced by various reasons to present a flag to the ' Washington Guards,' of which William is the proud Captain ; and as this was now a duty, I determined to make it a pleasant one, and to avail myself of the dear little children's presence to render my own position less conspicuous by being thus surrounded.

" At eight o'clock a crowd had assembled around the house, and many friends were within to witness the ceremony. The little girls were in uniform, long blue scarfs, hair curling down, and wreaths of eglantine on their pretty young heads. They formed in double line, separating on each side of the front steps, twenty being so disposed, while four were selected — of which J. represented North Carolina and M. Virginia — to bear the flag to the centre of the stone-platform, and forming a star, to await the Priestess of the ceremonies, who, stepping forth arrayed in India muslin trimmed with blue ribbons and lace, and with a nodding but modest plume of the same color, making the most of her height, thus, as nearly as recollected, addressed the Guards : —

" 'FRIENDS AND GENTLEMEN OF THE GUARDS, — This standard is presented to the Washington Guards as a tribute of respect, in the firm belief that the gift will never be dishonored, nor the motto which it bears disgraced by the youngest brother of the company. (*Debellaverunt* over Lafayette and Washington : "They fought together." *Titubimur* in the clouds : "We follow in your steps.") The deep interest which my husband feels in your *corps*, and the high post with which he is honored in it, will always inspire me with the truest solicitude for its reputation and success. Should the day of trial come and events call them to the field, I entertain the most trustful hope that the Washington Guards will be distinguished by a noble devotion to the cause of their country, and that in the protection of wives, children, and friends they will be the *last* to desert their standard.'

"Modesty forbids my description of the reception of this simple little address, and the Lieutenant's glowing reply; suffice it to say, that I was formally petitioned on behalf of the *corps* to allow its publication; being unable to do so, however, from the circumstance of trusting to the excitement of the occasion and having no notes. And so I was saved from the mortification of blazing at the head of the Gazette columns, and can say very cheerfully, 'All 's well that ends well.' I should have liked my friends in Raleigh to see the little States arranged around me; it was a perfect *parterre*, and Judge Cranch, with other elderly gentlemen present, were affected by their interesting appearance and delighted countenances. The picture was complete as they moved off, surrounded by their escort the 'Young Guards,' commanded by *Captain Augustine Seaton*, preceding *my* guard of honor commanded by his father, Captain William Seaton. Augustine's company has eclipsed even the veterans here, and was declared to be the best drilled volunteer corps at the reception of Lafayette in Alexandria. . . . . At General Brown's ball I was presented to Lafayette, once by mine host, once by my husband. On both occasions my hands were most affectionately pressed, though I had my suspicions that my second introduction was like unto the first in the Veteran's eyes, it being next to an impossibility that he should recognize all the ladies with whom he was compelled to shake hands, amounting to thousands during his triumphant tour. . . . . You ask what influence politics have upon social intercourse, — positively none. No individual could have had more enjoyment, or been treated with more attentive politeness by the master of the feast, than I, at Mr. Adams's ball. Mr. Calhoun's family and ourselves are, and always have been, on terms of kindest intimacy. Our cause, however, seems shivering in the wind, and I would not venture a baubee on the Presidential election now, for one candidate or the other, so uncertain does it appear in the perspective. The *Ultras* now court the people with all assiduity. . . . . William has had the onus of the banquet and other civilities offered to the General, and indeed by general consent, the charge of our illustrious Guest's entertainment has mainly devolved on him ; how acceptably he performs the social behest the public voice proclaims. . . . .

" Your affectionate daughter,

" S."

The form of invitation to this historical festival was characteristic of the simplicity of style then prevailing, the one fortunately preserved being as follows : —

" The Committee of Arrangements respectfully request the Secretary of War to dine with General Lafayette this day at the Franklin House, at five o'clock.

" W. W. SEATON, *Secretary.*"
"October 12, 1824."

The Franklin House was kept by O'Neale, being one of the row of houses since known to the old residents as the " Six Buildings " ; and here were gathered those whose deeds had already given them fame, with others whose names were to be imperishably written in their country's history. Mr. Seaton's toast on the occasion was : " The United States and France — their early friendship — may it ever be maintained by mu-

8

tual acts of kindness and justice," — the qualities which so conspicuously characterized the whole life of him who offered the sentiment.

"December 16, 1824.

"Last evening we had the high gratification of entertaining and welcoming Lafayette in our own house, being the only private individuals so honored, as yet. Three hundred and sixty persons took leave of him last evening, being within a score of those invited ; and, although a very crowded party, I hope not an unpleasant one to the old General. He is very lame, and we contrived to keep him seated as much as his extreme politeness would allow. Those persons who had never before been so closely in contact with him were brought forward and introduced ; those who already had been presented availed themselves of their privilege to converse with the hero. My chamber and the large nursery were *deranged* and *arranged* for the occasion, serving as card and supper rooms. We danced in the dining and drawing rooms, the latter opened for the first time, and thus pleasantly inaugurated. I never saw a gayer or, *I* think, a more agreeable party. The guest of the evening was evidently gratified, and we were told from every source that it was enchanting. The leader of the Marine Band came up in the morning and requested to play for us in the evening, which added much to the enjoyment. All the cabinet were with us except Mr. Crawford, who could not come, and the Executive, who was not asked. Mr. J. Q. Adams and family seemed to enjoy themselves as much as our other friends, notwithstanding our wordy war. Every member of the diplomatic corps was here except Baron de Mareuil and family, the French Minister, who are *en grand deuil* for the King of France, and by court etiquette are precluded from society for three months. I regretted their absence, as Madame Mareuil is an excel-

lent and very attractive woman, superior to the generality
of her countrywomen whom I have met. . . . . There has
not been such buoyancy of feeling in my heart for several
years as I experienced last evening, and William and Joseph were rejoiced to see me dance once more. All of our
old friends were here, in great glee, among the members,
except Mr. Macon, who never goes out at night. . . . . Lafayette goes with us next Sunday to the Unitarian church,
being desirous of hearing Mr. Little, of whose fervid eloquence he has heard much. . . . . "

"December, 1824.

" My dear William is from home for a few days in Philadelphia, having paid Lafayette the compliment of accompanying him as far as Baltimore, attending him to the
cattle-show, and receiving, as proxy for Joseph, a pair of
prize goblets, awarded by the committee and presented by
Lafayette, for the two finest *hogs* which were exhibited,
and about which Joseph is quite exultant. . . . . I was
privileged a few days ago to enjoy an unusual opportunity
of quiet converse with the 'nation's guest.' The Marquis
was very intimate with Joel Barlow, and they passed most
of their time together during the stay of the latter in
France ; consequently Mrs. Bomford (sister of Mrs. Barlow,
as you know) is a great favorite of the Marquis ; and I am
of Mrs. Bomford ; and *consequently*, again, I received an
intimation that he would spend a private *en famille* evening
there, in which I needed no pressing to participate. William and the Mayor were to escort him there from the
President's ; and I went solus. I found no company but
the families of Mr. Cutts (brother-in-law of Mrs. Madison)
and General Dearborn, old friends of ours both ; and we
passed a most agreeable and charming evening, from whence
we accompanied the General to the concert. We had much
plain, pleasant conversation, in which the benevolent old

hero participated with all the characteristic ardor of an accomplished Frenchman. . . . . ”

“January, 1825.

“ MY DEAR MOTHER, — The bearer of this note is Colonel G. C., of Georgia, whose name you will perhaps recollect as pertaining to one of W.'s quondam lovers. . . . . He is a decided Jacksonite, and insists that I had a design on his political principles ‘ by ushering him into the presence ’ of Mrs. Jackson, at the great ball given by General Brown on the eighth of January. I introduced him to every one, and he was much pleased with the first *bona fide* squeeze he has attended in the metropolis. The whole city was invited to celebrate the anniversary of Jackson's victory; and I wish it may not be the only victory at which he may have an opportunity of rejoicing, though Mr. Crawford's friends are still sanguine rather than despairing. Much depends on Mr. Clay, and he is scarcely to be depended on. The different candidates are very jocose with each other. At Mr. Calhoun's ball last week I stood among the dancers with Mr. Adams, when Mr. Clay passed in high glee, laughing, and saying he was much in the way of the dancers; or rather, they were very troublesome to *him*. ‘ O,’ says J. Q., ‘ that is very unkind ; you who get out of every body . else's way, you know.’ This dry joke, so evidently alluding to his exclusion from the House of Representatives, was received as merrily as it was given, and they both ‘ laughed long and loud.’ Mrs. Adams came to see me this morning, being the first visit without invitation which has been exchanged since that unlucky stab under the fifth rib. They are all very courteous just now ; but should Mrs. A. be Presidentess, ... she, perhaps, will not forget that her husband was foiled in combat with us even with his own weapon, — the pen. . . . . We received a letter from John S. Skinner yesterday, saying : ‘ *We are dished !*' but I hope not. There is no more reason for despair on the part of Mr. Crawford's friends now than heretofore, and they don't 'give up the ship.'

"We have now completed our homage to Liberty in the person of Lafayette. Congress can do nothing more, asking as a favor, by resolution of the House, that he will add to their obligations to him by accepting a grant of two hundred thousand dollars and a township of land. They are to give him, also, a public dinner at a cost of one thousand dollars. . . . . All well with my little folk, and I am the happiest wife, mother, and daughter in Christendom. With tenderest love to our father and yourself,

"Your dutiful daughter,

"SARAH SEATON."

"February 15, 1825.

"DEAR WESTON, — Lest our paper of to-morrow should by accident not reach you in time for Friday's Register, I use a page of Sarah's letter to say that last evening, pursuant to notice, a number of the Republican members, about sixty-eight or seventy, met in the Capitol to recommend to their fellow-citizens candidates for the Presidency and Vice-Presidency. Of the number present, Mr. Crawford received (including two proxies from sick members), sixty-four votes for President, the rest scattering ; and the old Jeffersonian Republican, Albert Gallatin, received fifty-seven votes for Vice-President. About thirty members of Congress, the friends of Mr. Crawford, did not, from various motives, attend the caucus. Nearly one hundred members of the two Houses are the known and avowed friends of Mr. Crawford, — the remainder are divided among the other candidates, in about the proportion of the following statement, prepared for us by the members themselves ; by which is proven that Mr. Crawford is the *second* preference of nearly all Mr. Adams's Republican friends. You may easily perceive from this why the partisans of the others refused to join in the convention. They thought it best to endeavor to put down by a joint effort the strong man of the nation, and then fight for the prize amongst themselves. They will be foiled. I am sorry that Mr. Macon, and Courier, of your State, threw their weight into the scale of the '*fragments*,' by refusing to join their friends and party in caucus. The galleries were crowded with not less than one thousand persons, and a more orderly or dignified scene I never beheld, the splendid hall being brilliantly lighted. The reporters were all at their places, and everything conducted in the most open manner.

"The factionists are appalled at the firmness of the men who met, and a purer or more sterling body of Republicans than assembled there last night the world cannot produce.

"General Lafayette will leave here for Raleigh about the 23d, but will not take Warrenton in his way, some busybody having put him in such dread of the stage road, and fully persuaded him that he would lose two days. He tells me that he will touch at Halifax and Enfield, having taken up an idea that the latter town is a place of much importance, perhaps derived from conversations with Mr. Branch.

"In haste, with love to all,

"Your affectionate Brother,

"W. W. SEATON.

"WESTON R. GALES, ESQ."

"February, 1825.

" . . . . Having received incessant, though for the most part unaccepted civilities from our friends, and there being an unusual number of respectable and accomplished strangers in town from Baltimore, Lancaster, and Boston, from many of whom we received kind attentions during our Northern tour, we concluded to present our return hos pitality in the condensed and most acceptable mode of a party ; and taking advantage of the morning report from the nursery, " All well," we invited a select and agreeable circle of friends for Tuesday. The evening was boisterous, extremely inclement, but not half a dozen of the invited neglected the summons, from the President's family down to common folk like ourselves. We had most charming music from Dominick Lynch, of New York, whom we met at Saratoga, and who is the delight of every lover of melody. Miss Davis, of Boston, second only to our Mrs. French, accompanied him in his duets, which were sung with entrancing taste and effect. . . . . Among our guests I must not forget to name a Prince, Achille Murat, son to the late King of Naples, who called with Mr. McKim of Baltimore, and was invited to accompany him. We had considerable amusement in making the young ladies designate the Prince among other young gentlemen equally strangers to them, but not one succeeded, and the reason was evident : they associated nobility of appearance and striking elegance of manners with the accident of noble birth, and these were not particularly characteristic of our titled visitor, son though he is, of the dashing " *beau sabreur.*" He has come to this country with the determination to make it his future home, and has applied for the oath of allegiance, — is said to be plainly republican in his principles, and is certainly so in his manners. Old Mr. Macon would not attend the caucus, and did not come to our party, — both very treasonable acts in the eyes of his colleagues, who thought he ought to have departed from all previous obstinacy on so important occasions. . . . . Our visitors remain until after the inauguration, and while occupied with attending dancing-parties every evening with them, and sight-seeing every morning, I have been seriously apprehensive of the death, without the glory, of a martyr in a more noble cause."

" February 24, 1825.

" The city is thronged with strangers, and *Yankees* swarm like the locusts of Egypt in our houses, our beds, and our kneading-troughs !   Mr. and Mrs. Adams are perfectly *comme il faut,* — *he* a little more gay and polite. . . . . . Their last drawing-room for the season was on Monday last, which we all attended, immediately after ascertaining our triumphant election, which spoke in a language not to be misunderstood, the approbation of Congress generally and individually.   We were congratulated on every side, and passed a pleasant evening.   The powers that be, did *not* congratulate us ; probably we had omitted the same ceremony in regard to them on a similar occasion.   We should at least have been as sincere as General Jackson in *his* felicitations on Mr. Adams's accession to the Presidency. It is now ascertained, though not announced, that Mr. Clay has accepted the office of Secretary of State, and Mr. Southard remains in the Navy Department. . . . . The office of Secretary of War will be accepted by Governor Barbour, of Virginia, and Mr. Richard Rush is to have the refusal of the Treasury in place of Mr. Crawford, resigned ; Governor Clinton to go to St. James's.   The great Hal, as the Kentuckians style Mr. Clay, is not our friend and probably never will be, but his friends are peculiarly ours, so that we shall have probably a smooth path for the next four years, as Mr. Adams is evidently in a conciliatory mood, and all the rest of the cabinet friendly.   They have tried, and found it rather inconvenient, to do without the Intelligencer, which will probably hold the same place in relation to the administration as heretofore.   Such are the present indications.

" General Lafayette started yesterday towards Raleigh, but has taken the lower road, which provokes me, his previously announced programme having disappointed W. of a pleasant sojourn with us. We had, the day previous to his departure, an accidental assembling of notable people at our house as morning visitors. General Lafayette, Levasseur, General Bernard, Major Poussin, and the President's family, all calling to take leave. General Bernard is one of the most interesting, animated, agreeable old men I have ever yet seen ; and when his idol Bonaparte is the subject of discussion, his eyes flash with the fire of youth and his countenance is radiant.

" Mr. Crawford and family are well, and have sold their furniture preparatory to their return to their impaired prospects in Georgia, which present no enlivening hope. I most truly feel for their disappointed views, but hold them in increased respect from their noble bearing of misfortune. . . . . I send you a characteristic note from Mr. Custis, who is as vivacious as usual.' "

George Washington Parke Custis was, as is well-known, the adopted son of General Washington, and the grandson of Mrs. Washington by her first marriage. During the many years in which he lived at his beautiful home of Arlington, he delighted in recounting to guests and pilgrims from every part of our own and foreign lands his personal participation in the momentous days of the Revolution, and his memories of the social circle and domestic life of Washington. Countless were the anecdotes of the camp and its patriot heroes ; of the republican court, the beauty and aristocratic elegance of its belles, — while his mansion was a treasure-house of sacred relics of *pater patriæ*. At the foot of a wooded slope of Arlington, on the banks of the river, was the famous spring, a crystal stream gushing from the root of a noble, primeval oak, the grove surrounding which was, during nearly half a century, the resort of gay parties resting from their sail on the lovely Potomac, and of innumerable celebrities seeking respite on the shaded lawn from the turmoil of Washington life. Hospitable, kind, and easy in manner, the presence of the old man venerable was eagerly welcomed at the spring, to which his vivacity, his violin, and exhaustless reminiscences lent an attraction long to be remembered. He was an amateur American *Vernet*, covering acres of canvas with battle-pieces, in which his beloved Chief was depicted on the inevitable white charger; nevertheless, these efforts, startling as specimens of art, were of patriotic interest, as drawn by one who had witnessed the scenes commemorated by his pencil, and had from infancy been familiar with the heroes who had made them immortal.

"ARLINGTON HOUSE, 15th July, 1825.

"MY DEAR SIR, — Old John, the genius of the spring, gave me your card. I should have had the pleasure of seeing you, but that my rheumatic bones gave 'note of preparation' for rain, and I sat down to finish Mademoiselle de Genlis, and left the farm to the comfort of the showers, which I hoped would fall upon it. I could have shown you much improvement in grass, better than Smith's philosopher, who only caused 'two spears to grow where but one grew before,' whereas I have caused them to grow where *none grew before*. You will find the spring a comfortable place for *Aldermen* to retire to from feasting and fagging in the toils of elections and great city affairs, or for you laborers of the type; and if you are not 'worthy of your hire,' 't is not because the sweat of your brains is less than that of your brow, or that you have one moment to rest them for 'lack of argument.' Then come over to the shades of Arlington, where peace and pleasant breezes, good air, good water, and a tolerably good fellow will make you welcome. *Apropos*, have you seen the Bolivar present? You will find it at Gaither's, — a most splendid specimen of miniature painting by Field; a medal well wrought for the state of the arts in Virginia fifty years ago, and the venerated hair of the old chief. Will you propose to the Literati an illustration of the '*Endat Virginia primum.*' Of the last, thereby 'hangs a tale.' I should say *hominem*, but I am only superficial in ancient classics, not having been, like Dr. Johnson, *flogged* enough when at school.

" Adieu, — health and respect,

"GEORGE W. P. CUSTIS.

"W. W. SEATON, ESQ."

"ARLINGTON SPRING, 3d July, 1848.

"MY DEAR MR. SEATON, — I do myself the honor to accept your most kind invitation to dinner to-morrow. ' The sun is making a golden set,' and 'giving promise of a goodly day to-morrow.' May the auguries all be favorable, and the ' Eagle fly on the dexter hand' on the ever-glorious and venerable anniversary of the 4th of July. If my large equestrian painting of Washington will be of any service to you, either in your ceremonials or in your banqueting-hall, or in any way, you can procure it by letter from your very worthy townsman John C. Rives, who has it in charge, to be used on public and patriotic occasions. I shall to-morrow have witnessed fifty-eight celebrations of the 4th July, beginning with the first, under the present government, 1789. May to-morrow's anniversary, with the great and patriotic ceremonies that will attend it, gladden the hearts of all Americans, and may

everything go off harmoniously and happily, is the sincere
wish of

"Dear sir, yours faithfully,

" George W. P. Custis.

"To W. W. Seaton, Esq.

"P. S.   No wafers at the Spring."

"Arlington House, 20th February, 1853.

" My dear Gales & Seaton, — I send you another of
the Recollections, in 'The last Days at Mount Vernon.'
This will probably be the finale, as I am hard pressed by
some of the first men in our country, including the excellent Professor Silliman, to bring out the work entire in
book form ; and as a man at 72, if he has anything to do
should do it as a beefsteak should be broiled, — quickly,
I have no time to lose.   How shall I, my dear sirs, sufficiently express my grateful acknowledgments to the press
of the National Intelligencer, that has published for me so
long and so well, and diffused my humble works through
all parts of the literary world ?

"I am now (since the death of Mrs. Lewis), the *sole
survivor* of the domestic family of the Chief, and the only
human being he ever honored with the title of adopted
son ; as such I feel a bounden duty to transmit my *recollections* and private *memoirs* to the posterity of the Americans
and the world at large, as relations coming from one, who
of much he has told, may say '*et pars fui.*'   I am an old
man, untiring and untirable as a speaker, but dreadfully
annoyed by penmanship ; so that I shall employ a *littérateur*
to arrange the work, and hope to send you a presentation
copy before a great while.   As my very voluminous papers
are in some confusion, I am not sure I have sent you the
Revolutionary letter. . . . . . Accept, Dear Sirs, salutation
and respect.

"From your obliged faithful servant,

" George W. P. Custis."

"ARLINGTON HOUSE, 21st February, 1854.

"MY DEAR COL. SEATON, — .... The story of the *Lost Letters of the Rawlins Book* I have put off to the last. It is a painful subject to me, for it implicates one who while living was dear to me, and whose melancholy end excited much commiseration many years ago. But if I loved my poor friend much, I love the fame and memory of Washington more; and it was my duty as his biographer and member of his family, to place this matter in the only light in which it can ever appear to the world.

"I was charmed by the visit of Mrs. Kirkland. What a fine, handsome woman! I am not, therefore, surprised that you, my dear sir, 'a squire of dames,' should be so eloquent in her favor. . . . . .

"*Apropos* of the railroad and national bridge. Will you not go for the *Jefferson route*, as described in his letter to me more than forty years ago, when he made a reconnoissance from the camp, now Observatory Hill?. . . . Recollect, if you adopt the Jefferson route, the land requisite for the western abutment of the bridge, at the northern extremity of the Arlington estate, will cost you nothing. My love to Gales. Believe me, my dear sir,

"Faithfully yours,

"GEORGE W. P. CUSTIS.

"COL. SEATON.'

"September, 1825.

"MY DEAR MOTHER, — We had yesterday a most kind note from Lafayette, proposing to spend half an hour with us during the last day of his stay here. The half-hour passed quickly in the most interesting conversation, and he protracted the visit until the *hour* had also fled. He spoke to me much of North Carolina, of your kind hospitality to him, of Washington's statue by Canova, which he says is a splendid monument of the sculptor's genius, but is the most inexcusable action of his life, as he sinned both against light and knowledge in making it as much *like me* as the great Washington! But mum to the Raleighites. He dwelt on the magic changes which a few short years had made in our cities, our arts, our wealth, and above all in our population, and in the most touching strain spoke of the spring-time of his youth when visions of hope were strong, and which in age he had the singular felicity of seeing realized.

" Our friend Mr. John Lee, of Maryland, the representative in Congress from Frederick, was one of the committee to accompany Lafayette on his visit to that place, and relates the hero's *sang froid* on the occasion of the carriage being overturned, when he was rolled over and over down a bank, but exhibited the utmost composure, and laughingly resumed his seat and conversation."

" July 12, 1826.

" . . . . You will see noted in the Intelligencer, Mr. Little's intention of answering General Smyth's and Mr. Shultz's proposed substitutes for the Christian Code which happily rules our land. He has during three successive Sunday evenings preached to the most crowded congregations we have ever witnessed in our church, and many of those ' who went to scoff remained to pray.' His arguments were unanswerable, his eloquence most admirable. He has now taken his undisputed pre-eminence among the learned, the pious and wise men of our community, which has hitherto been churlishly withheld by the spirit of bigotry. He preaches a sermon on Sunday next, commemorative of the death of the two illustrious sages who have just preceded him through the dark valley of the shadow of death. On last Sunday he announced from the pulpit the singular coincidence of the decease of John Adams on the same day with the illustrious Virginia patriot, the first received intelligence of which event Joseph handed to him after service ; and in the most delicate and touching manner Mr. Little alluded to the mistaken opinion entertained by many of our countrymen regarding Mr. Jefferson's deistical opinions, which he *disproved absolutely* by reading two original letters from this great man to our famous Dr. Priestley, when the latter first arrived from England, dated Washington, inviting the Christian apostle of liberty to visit this city and confer with him on religious topics ; avowing his entire belief in, and reverence for, the Scriptures, and announcing himself a Christian Unitarian. Mr. Little then dwelt on the warm and uniform faith in Unitarianism professed by the great and venerable John Adams, and very cogently expressed the consolation and encouragement which Unitarians must feel in the knowledge that in all ages the greatest, wisest, and holiest men have been found professing and acting on this faith. There were High Churchmen, *Blue* Calvinists and Presbyterians, Methodists and rigid Catholics composing his auditory ; and what with astonishment at the coincident deaths, Jefferson's letters, and the deductions drawn by Mr. Little, they were ' plussed, — I may say non-plussed.' . . . .

" You see that Commodore Porter is actually in the Mexican service. Mrs. Porter, one of my most intimate friends, came to show me the articles which the Mexican government have entered into with him. *Imprimis*, they guarantee the payment of a claim on the old Mexican government of $ 50,000 or $ 60,000 for destroying privateers ; they put the navy under the absolute control of Commodore P., he selects all his officers ; he locates a certain quantity of land where he pleases ; to be made an admiral at the next session of Congress ; to have a specified liberal salary, his pay to be continued in all cases of illness or necessary absence in the United States, and a pension to his family in

case of accident or death.   These are the leading features
of the agreement. . . . . Remembering father's amused interest in David Crockett's eccentricities, I send him *verba-
tim et literatim* some extracts from a letter William brought
me to read, from the odd but warm-hearted old pioneer.

" 'DEAR FRIENDS, —. . . . I consider the time has come
when every man aught to do his duty I hope the time
will soon come when this man worship will cease.   I am
grattifyed that I can informe you that I beat in nine Countys out of eighteen and I beat 103 votes in the County
that Fitz and myself both live in.   and I beat him upwards of six hundred in the Countys that will compose the
district when divided and of course I will hold myself in
readiness for the next race.   by that time the people will
see the purity of my motive all the people wants is infer-
mation and they will do right   This little *Thing* has been
blowed into Congress by lying and huzzawing for Jackson
in fact I had to run against Jackson as well as this mean
puppy . . . . *he is ready to taike the coller with my dog on
it and the name of Andrew Jackson on the Coller* he will have
the name of beating me on General Jacksons poppularity
but this is not true.   he beat me by writing down wilful
lies and publishing to the world that which ought to sink
every honorable man into insignificants I would rather be
beaten and be a man than to be elected and be a little
puppy dog   I must close with great respects I remain

" 'your obt servt

" 'DAVID CROCKETT —

"JOSEPH GAILES
    and
WILLIAM SEATON.

" ' P S please to correct errs and publish this letter. You
know me   .   D C—' "

The laborious and unintermitting duties of an editorial career allowed Mr. Seaton during his .prolonged life comparatively few opportunities for relaxation away from home, other than the shooting excursions in which he delighted, and which mainly contributed to the health and vigor enjoyed by him to a very advanced age. This is now doubly to be regretted, as the results of his keen observation, candid spirit, and intelligent investigation would be an invaluable picture of men and manners; while the tenderness of his nature, the endearing sweetness of his domestic affections, would be more forcibly portrayed by his own unguarded pen. During a visit to New England he thus writes : —

"PORTSMOUTH, N. H., August, 1826.

" . . . . You will be not a little surprised to find that I have penetrated so far towards the extreme point of the New England coast ; but you will be glad that I had an opportunity of doing so without delaying the longed-for period of my return to my dear wife. I accepted yesterday the proposition of Mr. Harrold (an old English factor resident in Philadelphia, well known to our English friends), to come down with him. Though sixty odd miles from Boston, such is the excellence of the roads and conveyances that the journey is performed in seven hours. I have been' exceedingly interested by the ride, as the road lies through Beverly, Newburyport, and numerous beautiful villages. This morning I spent an hour with Mr. Parrott and his amiable family, who I find had heard that report that is everywhere given of you, and which so often makes my heart swell with pride and happiness. Before dinner I walked about a mile across the Piscataqua bridge into the State of Maine, where at a farm-house I obtained a glass of the New England beverage, hard cider,

and drank it in celebration of my first visit to the eastern-
most State of the Union.   Returning, I found the bridge-
keeper fishing from the bridge for cod, the water being
there sixty feet deep, and taking his line had the luck in a
few minutes to haul up a fine large codfish, much to the
surprise of Mr. Harrold, who accompanied me, and who,
by the by, is even a greater walker than your excellent
father.   This you will credit when I tell you that after
dinner we walked three miles to the fortress at the mouth
of the river, and passed an hour on the rocky shore of the
great deep, whose boundless expanse lay before us, contem-
plating its ceaseless surges as they rolled in and broke on
the cliffs.   I do not think that any one not living on the
ocean can view its vast bosom and heaving billows without experiencing feelings of solemnity and awe, that soften
the heart and awaken all its best impulses.   And if the
heart have anything to love in the world, with how much
force does the tide of feeling turn at such moments to the
objects of its affection.   It is not worth the while, even if
time did not fail me, to endeavor to unravel and describe
those complicated impressions which the sublime view before me, and consciousness of absence from all that my
soul holds dear, at the same time inspired, but while I
gazed my lips involuntarily almost repeated blessings on
you and yours and mine, and rendered absence more sorrowful. . . . . Captain Watson, of the Marine Corps, and
other gentlemen, have called on me, and pressed me to remain; but I must resist their kind and pleasant inducements. . . . . Having finished the day, I give you its history, before I go to bed to pray for your happiness and to
dream of my own."

"NORTHAMPTON, August 16, 1826.

"We reached this beautiful town last evening, and I
must give my dearest wife a brief narrative of the journey

and its transactions. . . . . I shall never be satisfied until I take the ride up the lovely valley of the Connecticut in your sweet company. Charming as it is, I could not enjoy its beauties fully without you; and this place, the most lovely of all, would be enchanting if viewed in your presence. As it is, I feel it selfish to enjoy what my beloved wife is not at my side to partake. But I am writing of myself when you want to hear of your son. . . . . I find Mr. Cogswell and Mr. Bancroft very kind, the former having been in Washington, he tells me, two winters ago, where he knew both you and myself. . . . . I found this morning, from the number of strangers in town, that something was on foot; and behold, the pastor of the new and only Unitarian church here was to be ordained. The church is a very chaste and beautiful specimen of Greek architecture. Several clergymen from Boston were present, among them old Dr. Ware, to all of whom Mr. Bancroft introduced me. My being known as a member of the Unitarian congregation at Washington increased whatever of interest I might have claimed of their politeness, and I was treated with a good deal of attention. Everything, you know, ends in New England with a dinner; and after I returned to the hotel from the church services, which lasted four hours, I was waited on by some gentlemen and taken to the public dinner at the Masonic Hall. All the clergymen and representatives of churches were present, and I was placed near the head of the table. The repast was as cheerful as other dinners; and what would you, or what would any raw Southerner have thought, had he entered after the cloth had been removed, and the wine had circulated a short time, to see a large company standing up at a public dinner, and, with one voice, singing a hymn to the tune of Old Hundred! I declare to you, I never was so impressed in my life. The spirit of devotion which among these descendants of the Pilgrims enters into their festivities and evinces the moral basis of their character, has in it something that commands respect. After the hymn the company separated. I was pressed by Judge Lyman and other gentlemen to accept hospitality at their homes, but I declined for the pleasure of writing to you. . . . . . ”

"Boston, 1826.

“ . . . . I came up yesterday from Salem, the ancient theatre of witchcraft and of faith in sea-serpents, both of which are cardinal points of belief with the good people of the place. Mr. Crowninshield, seeing me on the stage-box as we passed down the street, called on me, took me to his family, who were very earnest in their inquiries for you, and, with Mr. Silsbee, has been exceedingly kind and attentive, showing me everything worth notice in the place, several of which deserve very particular mention, but are reserved until I have the happiness to embrace my beloved wife. I am impatiently waiting the return of Mr. Webster, whom I saw at Ipswich, the oldest settlement in America, where we stopped for an hour. Mr. Webster was attending court, and made me promise to meet him here. . . . . . To-day I heard our great Channing. O, how I wished you could be by my side to listen with me to his inspired accents, as his rapt soul seemed to ascend on high, and his vision to penetrate to the very presence of God. . . . . . Good night, my dearest wife ; may all good angels watch over you and my dear little ones.

“ Your affectionate husband,

“ W. W. Seaton.”

Mrs. Seaton writes to her mother, under date of October, 1826 : —

“ You will see that William is to be orator on the occasion of laying the corner-stone of the new Masonic Hall, the ceremonies attending which are to be especially interesting and imposing, President Adams and other dignitaries to take part in them."

The following extracts from the eloquent address then delivered show how exalted was Mr. Seaton's estimate of the true aims of Masonry, the handmaid of Christianity, of the almost ideal perfection exacted from its sons; the virtues thus glowingly depicted and held up for attainment being nobly illustrated in the life and character of him who paid this tribute to the beneficent brotherhood : —

"You have laid the first stone of a temple to be dedicated to the most noble and the most venerable of all the institutions of human origin. Founded in an early age of the world, by men whose wisdom and sagacity were equalled only by their virtue and benevolence, this institution has survived through successive ages the various revolutions of mankind. Empires have risen, and flourished, and crumbled into dust ; other institutions have one after another sunk into oblivion; while Masonry, miraculously kept alive, even during the long night in which civilization itself was extinct, and the world lay for centuries wrapt in the gloom of profound barbarism, as if rendered indestructible by the eternal principle of good which its immortal founders infused into its constitution, yet survives the lapse of thirty centuries, in all its pristine vigor, in all its sublime principles, in all its mysterious rites, and all the loveliness of its first creation. . . . . .

"I assert, then, that to be a perfect Mason implies little less than to be a perfect man. The perfection of its character comprises within itself the whole circle of virtues, and the whole duty of man, both to his Creator and to his fellow-man. That these virtues impose an obligation on the conscience independent of any social institution is admitted. But we sometimes neglect our duty, not because we are disposed to violate it, but because the obligation it imposes is imperfectly felt, or, for a time, forgotten. . . . . Those institutions, therefore, which enjoin and encourage the performance of our moral duty ; which cultivate the social temper ; which soften the asperities of the human character, and awaken into activity the native philanthropy of man, have a peculiar and happy influence upon society in general.   Of this exalted nature, these excellent principles, and this philanthropic tendency is the masonic institution.   Its solemn rites, its visible emblems, its peculiar symbols, its mystic language, were all designed to illustrate and to inculcate our duty to God, to our brethren, and ourselves ; and while they serve to distinguish Masons from the rest of the world, and make them known to each other throughout the globe, they are, at the same time, ever-present monitors that at once command and instruct us in the discharge of those high and sacred duties to which all Masons stand pledged by the most solemn sanctions. Did I say that these monitors are never disobeyed ? Alas ! we cannot lay that flattering unction to our hearts.   In this respect (I repeat the admission), Masonry shares the lot of all other institutions.   But if it sometimes fails to make a bad man good, it never fails to make a good man better.

" The leading attributes of Masonry are faith, hope, and charity ; but the greatest of these is charity.   Charity is emphatically the great duty which Masons owe to each other, and is one of those virtues which Masons, above all others, are enjoined to cherish and exercise.   Those votaries of Masonry who have not *this virtue* ought never to pollute her sanctuary.   If we approach her altar without it we act impiously against the cause we profess.

" . . . . It is, in short, a compact between certain men throughout the world to perform towards each other, and to each other's families, the offices of charity and friendship, whenever the vicissitudes of fortune place them in a situation to require it. The same principle extends through other relations of society. Citizens are bound to allegiance; but the oath is superadded. Christians are bound to obedience to the Gospel, but they unite in societies and obligations for the observance of their duties. Thus Masons are subject to the common duties of social life; but they have added special obligations to each other, as the citizen to his country, and the Christian to his church.

" Masonry, elevated by the nobleness of its precepts, derives not more interest from its venerable antiquity and surprising preservation, than it does from the land of its birth. In speaking of this ancient institution, the mind involuntarily recurs to the interesting region in which it had its origin. How pre-eminent have been the destinies of that remarkable portion of the globe to which poetry and religion and history and Masonry are continually summoning the thoughts of civilized man. Thence flow alike the primitive streams of our sacred and profane history, in the writings of the lawgiver of the Hebrews, and those of the venerable historian of Assyria. Nay, where but there was the Garden of Eden, in all the virgin glory of fresh creation, planted? Where but there did the sire of the human family first inhale the breath of life? There, too, was the elected spot of earth which bore the footsteps of Eve, in that primeval hour, when

> ' Grace was in all her steps, heaven in her eye,
> In every gesture dignity and love.'

There, also, Chaldean sages uplifted those ' lighthouses of the skies,' from which they scanned the march of the planets, and assigned the stations of the heavenly constellations. There was the land of the patriarchs. And thither the chosen people of God were guided by Moses to establish a theocracy taught them amid the thunders of Mount Sinai, and to build up the holy city of Jerusalem, towards which the devotee, in whatever distant land he lives, bows his head in reverence. There, too, was erected the splendid temple of Solomon, upon which all the skill and taste and wealth of the East were piled in gorgeous prodigality. The same fortunate land witnessed the birth, the life, and death of Jesus Christ, and the miracles which he wrought in attestation of his divine mission. And when the glory of that land was faded away, and the ploughshare had passed over the palaces of Jerusalem, the sanctity of the soil hallowed by every religious recollection made it the arena on which Christian and Saracen hosts contended for the mastery,—the bravest and the best of Christendom flocking thither, in the elevated enthusiasm of Chivalry, to pour out their blood like water for the rescue of the sepulchre from its infidel masters. This land, sanctified by so many recollections, and ennobled by events of such moment to the whole family of man, — this was the native land of Freemasonry."

Mrs. Seaton writes under date of January 8, 1827:—

".... You will see by the Intelligencer that personalities are the order of the day, and that the 'honorable, excellent, worthy, high-minded, and amiable' editors thereof have had their full share of eulogium. 'T is rather an amusing position in which they are placed, attending Congress daily in the line of their duty as stenographers, and laboring in their vocation, to listen to praises from *every side* of the House on a subject in which they are not at all interested except as 'lookers on in Vienna.' The resolution introduced by General Sanders was entirely unadvised and unexpected by your sons, and rather deprecated by them. . . . . Mr. Clay sits rather uneasy, no doubt, to have the propriety of his reasons and causes doubted, when he only exercised his sovereign pleasure. You see that William is accounted a Carolinian, and since poor Virginia and her state rights have been so conspicuously wrong, I suppose he will brook the affront. We want no *fussing* (I believe a legitimate Yorkshire word); if the members choose to quarrel among themselves they must use their own discretion. The Bankrupt Bill, the Tariff, woollens and all, have not excited a tithe of the attention and interest which this merely personal question has given rise to. It is not expected that the bankrupt bill will experience a better fate by being reconsidered after its rejection in the House, which on every score is a subject of regret. Parties will wax hot as the session advances, as there is a great deal of anger and ill-nature in some of the members opposed to the administration ; but we feel sanguine that the fair course pursued by the Intelligencer will carry us safely through the ordeal. Dr. Floyd has become the warm friend of Calhoun, and hates Adams and everybody who thinks differently from himself ; but then he says he loves Mrs. Seaton so well ! ! . . . . . Mrs. Everett and many of the members' wives have been to see me ; but Mrs. Webster is not here, I regret to say, as she is one of the strangers whose society I most enjoy. . . . . . Guns are firing from every point, and great demonstrations of rejoicing are made to celebrate the anniversary of Jackson's victory, and to give *éclat* to the dinner to-day, which has become an entire party matter, and will draw the line of demarcation in social as well as political circles more distinctly than hitherto. . . . . . "

" March, 1827.

" . . . . I have received a long letter from Mrs. Porter,

who sends her kind love to you. She is with her parents, and wields a graphic pen ; but my heart bleeds for her in the state of incertitude to which she may be condemned for weeks or months. The Commodore is blockaded by so superior a force as renders his escape next to impossible ; though,

'What man dare do, he 'll dare ; who dares do more is none.'

" In that state of mind which rejects desultory, miscellaneous reading, as being insufficient to ward off recollections and poignant feelings which every sense of duty warned me to struggle with and overcome, ere they destroyed my peace and health, I applied myself indefatigably to the study of Spanish, by which I have benefited myself and gratified William. I have already found it useful in translating Mexican documents, Spanish papers, etc., for the Intelligencer, and it may be that my interest in everything concerning poor Porter is increased by tracing his preparations and movements.

"You will perceive that the Senate election has gone against us, and that some of our *old friends* have deserted us in our hour of need. Branch, Eaton, and other summer friends, we did not expect to support us. There was great excitement in both House and Senate, and Mr. Webster came up after balloting, to ask what they *could* do in the House to counterbalance the spite of the Senate ; that they were mortified and angry, and would do anything consistent with propriety and principle for our benefit. This is the temper of our friends, and an entire proscription of the course of our enemies, — i. e. the Jackson men. Van Buren of New York is the master spring of all the mischief, though working entirely under ground. Party spirit is now fiery hot, and will increase every day. We have never been so much aware of it, not even in war and embargo times, as it has severed the most intimate links of friendship and good-will.   Mr. S., among our other old acquaintances is decidedly inimical to our interests, his high collective and individual eulogium to the contrary notwithstanding. This morning the line is distinctly drawn for the first time in the Intelligencer, and was unavoidable.   It will make some of the Senators a *leetle* uneasy in their relative journeys home ; but you have no conception to what lengths they went in other things, as well as the sacrifice of old friends.   General Barringer appears to be unsettled, if not entirely changed, in his political opinions, and abused the factions here, and eulogized Daniel Webster in a strain that would have been music to the ear of our friend Lewis Williams, in the last evening he spent with me.   I say *me*, because, in sooth, William turns all this kind of visitors over to me in fee simple, if he should chance to be in the house, which at this exciting and busy season he has rarely been until near midnight.   On parting, the General expressed much fear of not coming again, and hoped that Weston *would* vote this year, and that father would *not* vote against him. He was fiery red-hot for Jackson when he came, and quite the reverse when he went away.   You will see that our friend McLean, Postmaster-General, is always exempted from crime or the imputation of crime, in the sweeping denunciations against the cabinet in one of the city Gazettes. Mr. McLean is a worthy man we think, though led away by partialities. . . . . Colonel John Williams is here, and as usual spends all his leisure time with us.   He returns in a few days to Tennessee, to hard work at the law, being compelled to bend to the fury of the storm, and leave public life until a more tolerant spirit shall prevail, as General Jackson and he divide the State, but, unfortunately for him, not equally.   In our opinion, General Jackson is infinitely superior in magnanimity and other good qualities to his friends.   They are outrageous, and would willingly trample under foot and massacre all who do not bow the knee to Baal. . . . .

"Mrs. Governor Barbour has just called in her carriage on her way to Virginia, to entreat and so strenuously insist on my visiting her for a few weeks, and accompanying the Governor and herself to the White and Warm Sulphur and Bedford Springs, that I could not avoid, without appearing insensible to such urgent kindness, saying that I would consider of it.   She says that if William cannot leave Washington, her husband shall come for me, and we can arrange under their roof our plans, which she certainly painted in pleasant colors, if I could feel interested in paying a visit anywhere unaccompanied by all my children. . . . .

"Our friend Swift, you see, has sunk under the storm, and his family must be the sufferers from his indiscretion, for of nothing more, we are certain, could he be found guilty.   We were surprised and glad yesterday to see him alight at our door from New York.   He is utterly in the dark as to the cause of his dismissal, but supposes it the result of party feelings, as he was always devoted heart and soul to Mr. Calhoun, and needed prudence in the expression of his prepossession.   We felt affected at seeing him a bankrupt in fortune, and *that* he asserts to be the least bitter of his trials. . . . . He fears that his good name may suffer by being superseded at this moment.   He and his excellent wife have suffered much in a short period, their eldest child, a lovely girl, having died during his trial. You will be interested in this, as I know how much you liked him. . . . . With William's and my own united love to yourself and our honored father,

"Your dutiful and affectionate daughter,

"SARAH SEATON."

The domestic affliction to which Mrs. Seaton alludes was the sudden death of a lovely son of six years, interesting in all promise of character, beautiful and engaging in person, who was brought home from his morning canter on his pony, dragging at the stirrup, fatally injured, lingering on earth but a few hours. This blow, so cruel to the parents, was one of the many which Mr. and Mrs. Seaton were called to endure through their long life, and which — in the simple faith and resignation to the Divine Will, the added tenderness of the tie uniting them to each other and to those remaining to their love and care, wrought for them through the chastening — seemed to bring still nearer to perfection the Christian graces that crowned their character.

Joseph Gardner Swift, born in Massachusetts, 1783, was a civil and military engineer of great distinction in the United States service. In 1807 he was appointed to the command of the Academy at West Point, of which school of brilliant soldiers he had been, in 1802, the first graduate. He succeeded Colonel Jonathan Williams as chief of the corps of topographical engineers, distinguishing himself highly in the war of 1812, especially in the defence of New York, for which grateful services that city paid him various flattering marks of approval and thanks. The work for which he will be specially remembered was the skilful and ingenious construction of the railroad from New Orleans to Lake Pontchartrain through an unfathomable swamp, the rails of which he laid on the mass of fossil shell remains found in the depths of the morass ; and of this shell *débris* he also formed the famous " shell road," now the favorite drive near New Orleans.

General Swift was possessed of unusual scientific and literary attainment; was charming in manners, genial in temper, strong in domestic and social affections, an excellent art critic, a devotee to music, singing an admirable song in a rich bass voice, and a keen sportsman. From early years a friendship had subsisted between himself and Mr. Seaton, congenial in so many points of taste and tone of character, which matured in middle age to the intimate affection that lasted to the end of life; and of which the following note is one of the many similar pleasant records preserved in the family.

" GENEVA, March, 1848.

" VERY DEAR FRIEND SEATON, — Thomas March, Esq., of Brooklyn, has proposed an excursion to the south side of Long Island, early in May, to renew, as we sexagenarians may, the joy of days gone by. He, Major Tucker, and myself hope you will smoke a pipe with our party of four. I am mournfully aware of the inevitable relation that subsists between Congress and the Intelligencer, and especially now in these piping times of prospective peace, that may run debate into summer. But we hope that the speed of the political car may allow you to dip a line into this water, and help us to broil a trout à *la* Colonel Hawkins. So think well of this bid to the reel. . . . . Mrs. Swift's respects to Mrs. Seaton, and mine also.

" Ever yours,

" J. G. SWIFT.

"HON. W. W. SEATON."

In 1818 General Swift resigned his commission in the army, as did other officers, from dissatisfaction and wounded pride at the appointment by President Monroe of General Bernard to the charge of the coast defences. This *de facto* supersedure, by a foreigner, of General Swift in the position in which he had earned such distinction created naturally a strong feeling of resentment throughout the army, so sensitively generous in its *esprit de corps*. Subsequently, General Swift's actions were subjected to the crucible of political misrepresentation, from which they emerged unalloyed metal; and it was to that persecution that Mrs. Seaton referred in her letter, and of which General Swift so clearly disposes in the following note :—

" February 18, 1827.

" DEAR SEATON, — My name appears with no good object or aspect in the congressional matter of the 9th inst. Mr. Forsyth calls up the uncandid Report on the Mobile Fort, and enters an extract therefrom on the Journals of the House of Representatives, for the use or abuse of posterity. That report — falsely and in my opinion intentionally to injure — asserts that I, *as United States Agent*, was to divide a profit with Mr. T. and others! The facts: In May, 1818, I, *as United States Agent*, contracted with B. W. Hopkins to build the Mobile Fort. In November, 1818, I resigned my army commission and of course agency. In August, 1819, B. W. Hopkins dies of yellow-fever at his work. In 1820 the executor sells B. W. H.'s contract to Colonel Hawkins, who comes to me and offers me one fourth of the profits for my advice and instructions as engineer how to execute his work. I agree to give them. Am I in this any species of United States Agent, or in any manner or degree censurable? Think a moment on the object and effect of these cuts and thrusts, and think on the humiliating truth that nobody cares for any attempt to justify? So much does love of detraction overbalance inclination to render justice. Compare the eager reading of an accusation with the apathy which a refutation excites! It is quite probable that Mr. Forsyth's extract may be republished or referred to, to prove that I am — anything. I had thought that the asperity of political feeling on the Presidential question had long subsided, so far as it related to persons not filling prominent places. . . . . .

"As ever, your friend,

"J. G. SWIFT.

"W. W. SEATON, ESQ."

General Simon Bernard, born at Dôle, France, in 1779, was one of the many illustrations of the distinction achieved in the French service by unassisted merit. He was educated by charity at the famous Polytechnic school, to which he was making his way on foot, when, overcome by cold and starvation, he would have perished on the road but for the succor afforded by a poor woman, who gave him shelter and saw him safely to his destination. The boy soon showed unusual talent, fostered by such masters in military science as Laplace and Monge; and, winning the position of second lieutenant of engineers, served on the Rhine, under Napoleon, by whom he was promoted to a captaincy. The Emperor, eagle-eyed to discern capacity, and quick to employ it, confided to the young officer an important commission, rewarding his success in its fulfilment by a coveted appointment to his staff. During the "hundred days," General Bernard was placed at the head of the Topographical Bureau, and after Waterloo came to this country with a high reputation and strong letters from Lafayette. His appointment as Engineer in Chief of the United States Army, although certainly an injustice to our native talent, and an undeserved slight to the distinguished Swift, was not without good fruit; and the able Frenchman rendered good service to the country in his military capacity, one of the best known monuments of his skill being Fortress Monroe. After the "three days of July," he returned to France, where he was received with honor and high preferment, being appointed Aide-de-Camp to Louis Philippe, and subsequently Lieutenant-General of Engineers, and Minister of War, remaining in office until the downfall of the Ministry in 1837. In 1839 he closed his varied and honorable career. During his fifteen years' service under the United States government he won, together with his interesting and amiable wife and daughters, the esteem and affection of the society of Washington, the relations of himself and family being especially intimate with Mr. and Mrs. Seaton, in whose home, graced by refined intelligence and open hospitality, strangers, during half a century, found a welcome atmosphere of kindness and congeniality. When, at Louis Philippe's accession, General Bernard returned finally to France, his departure was the signal for many parting compliments and testimonials of regard from the citizens to the worthy Frenchman; and it was on one of these occasions that the honored guest paid a graceful tribute to the virtues of Mrs. Seaton, the scene being thus described by one who was privileged to be present:—

"At a large dinner at the hospitable mansion of Eckington, after the dessert was served and the guest had been toasted, and had replied in warm terms of gratitude and respect to our country, he was called on for a toast, and rising said : 'I will give you, gentlemen, a sentiment which will be echoed in the hearts of all present, as it would be by the society of Washington and all the good and great of foreign courts who have resided in this city, — I give you, gentlemen, Madame Seaton, the accomplished lady, wife, and mother.'

"Edward Livingston, then Secretary of State, immediately rose and said : 'He would relieve his friend, Mr. Seaton, and also their friends, Mr. and Mrs. Gales (the hosts), from the embarrassment of acknowledging this personal compliment, so beautiful, so just, and in such accord with the feelings of all present, by taking the pleasure of that task on himself, on his own behalf and that of his family.' He then proceeded in a strain of delicate and exalted eulogy of Mrs. Seaton, which called forth a burst of applause from the distinguished company present."

"WASHINGTON, December, 1830.

"General Bernard has the honor to present all his respects to Mr. Seaton, and to inform him that, having obtained a furlough to visit Europe, he will do himself the honor to call on Mr. Seaton to receive his commands for France. General Bernard has just received the enclosed article relating to the American claims from the *Constitutionnel*, transmitted to him from General Lafayette, whose desire was that the article should be known to the American public.

"Very respectfully,

"BERNARD."

It was during this absence, thus announced, that the General visited his native town of Dôle, where a triumphant reception awaited the once penniless boy, now the renowned soldier who conferred honor by his presence. This interesting incident is alluded to by M. Poussin, — also a Frenchman, who won high position, professional and diplomatic, in the new Republic, — in the following note to Mr. Seaton : —

"May 14, 1831.

"Dear Sir, — You will no doubt learn with pleasure that this excellent man, General Bernard, who has resided so long among us as to be considered as one of our most distinguished officers, is about to return to his adopted country to resume his highly useful occupations as an engineer. Previous to leaving his country the General visited his aged father residing in his native town, of which occasion the *National* makes the following mention : —

"They write to us from Dôle (department of Jurâ, Franche-Comté), — 'The arrival in our town of the brave General Bernard of the engineers, who has come to us after an absence of fifteen years, has been the occasion of a patriotic celebration. The National Guard, the Sappers, Firemen, the Artillery with a band of musicians at their head, marched spontaneously to meet and greet this worthy citizen.'

"General Bernard begs to be particularly remembered to you and your family.

"Most sincerely yours,

"W. T. Poussin."

William Tell Poussin, a young French engineer, came to this country with letters of introduction from Lafayette, commending his professional abilities to our government, by whom he was employed in various works of engineering, in which he showed undoubted skill. Possessed of talent and many amiable traits of character, he won the esteem of officials and society ; and when the French government appointed him Minister to the United States, the deserved promotion met with signal approbation.

M. Poussin continued to represent France until a change of ministry recalled him home, being, however, reappointed to the same honorable post during the Presidency of the Emperor Napoleon III. He was kind-hearted, and gratefully devoted to those who showed him friendship; to Mr. Seaton, especially, testifying an almost filial affection. "I was blind," he used to say, "and Mr. Seaton made me to see; dumb, and he made me to speak; a stranger, and he gave me home."

Unfortunately, his native impulsiveness had not been calmed down in the reticent school of diplomacy, and betrayed him finally into an indecorous warmth of correspondence with the State Department, which eventuated in his virtual dismissal from our shores; the second occasion in the history of our government, on which a want of the respect due from a foreign minister in his official intercourse had resulted in the presentation of his passports to the offending dignitary.

The circumstances attending the cessation of M. Poussin's diplomatic relations with this country, were in substance as follows:—

While Mr. Clayton was Secretary of State, he received from M. Poussin a note calling the attention of the department to the case of a French resident in Mexico, on whose behalf he desired to appeal from the sentence of a military court held previously at Puebla, by which the Frenchman had suffered in property. After careful investigation into the merits of the case, Mr. Clayton was unable to perceive any legal or equitable grounds for reversing the decision of the tribunal, and so he courteously informed the French Minister. To this communication on the part of the Secretary M. Poussin replied in a very acrimonious note, in which he impugned the integrity of the Court, and more particularly the evidence of Colonel Churchill. To this rude note Mr. Clayton, impelled by courtesy and official consideration for M. Poussin, replied, although his first note to the Minister, sustaining the decision of the Court, was a finality, beyond which he was not really bound to take further action. After defending Colonel Churchill from the aspersions of M. Poussin, and adducing in his favor the approval of General Scott, Mr. Clayton proceeded to controvert, in the most respectful manner, some of the positions assumed by M. Poussin. This drew from M. Poussin a communication so disrespectful and intemperate in language, so insulting in its tenor towards the government of the United States, that Mr. Clayton was compelled to lay it personally before the President, in obedience to whose directions the Secretary of State informed M. Poussin that thenceforth the government of the United States must decline to recognize him as the representative of France. The French government was promptly informed of our action in the premises, the polite suggestion being made, that every facility for M. Poussin's departure would be afforded him, whenever he should be pleased to make known his desire to return to France.

M. Poussin's last insulting note was dated Washington, although he was in New York at the time it was written. Mr. Clayton politely requested his prompt appearance at Washington, to afford him an opportunity of retracting the objectionable language; but no retraction or explanation was ever made, and the French government seemed for a while to sustain the action of its representative, characterizing Mr. Clayton's note as " an imperious summons."

The intercourse of the French government with Mr. Rives, the United States Minister, was interrupted by a refusal to receive him at Court, which action Mr. Clayton met by instructions to Mr. Rives to discontinue his relations with the French government should his exclusion be persisted in, or any explanation be demanded prior to his reception at Court. Our government, added Mr. Clayton in his able despatch to Mr. Rives, was the sole guardian of its honor and dignity, and would, in its estimate of what was disrespectful and insulting, submit to no judgment save its own; and in like manner the government of France was at perfect liberty to act in any manner consistent with its own ideas of dignity. This Mr. Clayton expressed with an aptness and propriety that elevated it above the range of retort.

The following is one among the numerous letters addressed to Mr. Seaton during many years by the impulsive, warm-hearted Frenchman.

"No. 2 Rue de la Ferme des Mathurins.
Paris, 28th March, 1832.

"Dear Sir, — I long wished to inform you in what part of the old continent I were, and that amidst the multiplicity of attractions the two rival metropolis, London and

Paris, offered to a pilgrim from the New World, I were not unmindful of my friends, and of none less so than the gratefully remembered members of your amiable family. I have been constantly in the hope of hearing some gratifying news which I could send you relative to our dear and worthy friend, the good General Bernard. As yet, nothing is done; hope we have, however, that ere long that profoundly scientific and useful man will at last be in position to contribute something towards the improvement of this *Old Society*.

"I had 17 days only to Liverpool, and a most delightful trip over. I travelled through North and South Wales, and some of the most famous and beautiful English counties; but English weather growing too intolerable even for a Franco-American to bear, I decided on leaving John Bull, and arrived in the gay metropolis of the French in March. I was much pleased indeed with Old England, highly gratified, greatly amused and benefited by the journey, during which I met with many courteous and hospitable reception. Having good letters of introduction, I found myself quite at home in the drawing-rooms of the gentry and nobility. My name, (Poussin, should you have forgotten that I am a true lineal descendant of that eminent painter!) my profession, and my character of an American smoothed down all asperities and strong English prejudice. My task was one of the most pleasing of narrating the wonderful achievements of civilization in America; and such eyes! and such wonders! at all which I would say touching the state of our society!! Never in my life have I met with so ignorant people respecting the possibility of the existence of another society as much advanced and refined as theirs, to say the least; and that in America, that savage country to the saying of Basil Hall & Co.!! By the way, I met one day with this truly John Bull at a meeting of the Royal

Society. 'Ah! is that you? I thought you could not long live amongst those Yankies.' 'No!' said I, 'that is the reason I am just going back, for I have found nothing as yet so much to my taste as Yankie habits and laws.' And there we parted, neither foe nor friend; for 'pon my soul! I would not be either. I found scientific men more liberal; indeed, these are of no country. John Bull, Johnny Crapeau, and Brother Jonathan all agree well when they have this freemasonry to cement them. Take this away, and '*Sacre bleu!! God dem, Ros bif, Soupe maigre,* and "molasses and water"' are the best epithets they have for each other. The civil engineers assisted me to witness and explain the mechanical wonders of that immense workshop, as it has been aptly styled. In the paths of science France bears the palm, but in the useful though more humble task of applying the light of modern science to the wants and uses of man, England and our own United States will dispute the prize with the combined world. I think the experience of time will establish the fact, that the inventive genius of America can bear more than a successful comparison with all other countries. Stevens and others prove the fact as to its application to boats, and when locomotives become familiar there it cannot remain a doubt that the Americans will contribute to the improvement of this new mode of land travel in a commensurate manner with that of steamboats.

" France has remained much behind either nation in the application of this new power. No country is more in need of improved communication, and should peace be maintained, public confidence restored, she will take an astonishing start in industry. All elements of prosperity exist within France, only let her get out of this terrible *incertainty,* and she will again be *La belle et grande France.* I speak like an American who knows France, and not from the blood which runs through my veins.

" The venerable General Lafayette is in perfect health, and happy in the settlement of his children. His devoted son is well. Our excellent General Bernard very well, his dear family also, and regretting much America and our Washington friends. You have no doubt seen the noble and generous part he took in common with our distinguished novelist, Cooper, to sustain the excellence of American legislations, in comparison with the elaborated and purposely perplexed administration of the French. The excellent General proved *beyond all doubt* that 'an American pays his personal tax with the labor of less than four days' work ; whereas the Frenchman must work twelve days to pay his !'

"We expect Mr. Van Buren here from London on the 6th April, on his way to the United States, by Havre.

" Mr. Rives speaks of returning home in the autumn.

" Pray to remember me most particularly to Mrs. Seaton, Mrs. Gales, and her worthy husband, to your good neighbor, M. St. Clair Clark and his lady ; and never doubt the sentiments of lasting regards and friendship of your obliged and devoted friend and servant,

" W. T. Poussin, Major U. S. Top. Engs.

"To W. W. Seaton, Esquire."

With the advent of Jacksonism was inaugurated proscription for opinion's sake, and a state of party hostility ensued which not only strictly separated political opponents, but pervaded social relations and severed friendly ties. It was indeed a dark era in the hitherto aristocratic circles of the capital, which had been characterized by elegance of manners and the charm of high-breeding : but now came upon the astonished and exclusive citizens the reign of the " masses." Notwithstanding, however, the extreme bitterness of party spirit ruling political and social events during this "reign of terror," General Jackson himself had the power of appreciating the talent, dignity of character, or individual influence to be found in the ranks of the opposition; and with the sagacity characterizing a great general, appropriated to his own service whatever in the enemy's camp could enhance the reputation of his administration or subserve his ends. Bitter, therefore, as was the war between the Intelligencer and the President, the latter respected the editors of that powerful journal, their virtues and abilities, and deprecated their censure; magnanimously manifesting his sense of Mr. Seaton's position in the community and high personal qualities, by appointing him one of the Visitors to West Point.

A short time preceding the inauguration of General Jackson, Mr. Robert Little, the eloquent Unitarian pastor, preached a remarkable sermon, the text of which was: "When Christ drew near the city he wept over it." Thirty-eight years afterwards, Mr. Seaton spoke of this effort as "a grand sermon, depicting with prophetic force the evil effects of General Jackson's election, — that triumph of demagoguism, ignorance, and radicalism in its worst form, which then deluged the country, defeating Adams, sweeping away Conservative and Tory, gentlemen, and the highest standard of honor, in the tide of unlettered, unmannered vulgarity, from which the country has not recovered; whose fruits are still beheld in this second upheaval of society, when the refined, the wise, must retreat before the untutored empirics who sit in the places of the giants of our Republic."

The amazing contrast between the stately dignity

attending the induction into office of the earlier Presidents, and the scenes occurring at the inauguration of the " Hero of the People," is vividly portrayed by Mrs. Samuel Harrison Smith, whose sketch graphically presents the new order of things, which saddened and terrified the circles accustomed to the elegant decorum of previous ceremonies.

Mrs. Smith was a lady of unusual intellect and cultivated literary tastes, whose active pen painted numerous sprightly and characteristic pictures of Washington society in the days of Jefferson and Madison ; whose charming conversational gift and benevolence of heart won the affection of all who came within their influence, and whose hospitable home was the resort of all who were distinguished for talent or worth.

" When the President's address was concluded," thus proceeds Mrs. Smith's account, " the barricades gave way before the multitude, who forced a passage to shake hands with the choice of the people. General Jackson mounted his horse, having walked to the Capitol, and then such a *cortège* followed ! Countrymen, laborers, — white and black, — carriages, wagons, and carts, all pursuing him to the President's house. . . . . . The closing scene was in disgusting contrast with the simplicity of the impressive drama of the inaugural oath ! The President was literally pursued by a motley concourse of people, riding, running helter-skelter, striving who should first gain admittance into the Executive mansion, where it was understood that refreshments were to be distributed. The halls were filled with a disorderly rabble of negroes, boys, women, and children scrambling for the refreshments designed for the drawing-rooms! the people forcing their way into the saloons, mingling with the foreigners and citizens surrounding the President. . . . . China and glass to the amount of several thousand dollars were broken in the struggle to get at the ices and cakes, though punch and other drinkables had been carried out in tubs and buckets to the people; but had it been in hogsheads it would have been insufficient besides unsatisfactory to the mob, who claimed equality in all things. . . . . The confusion became more and more appalling. At one moment the President, who had retreated until he was pressed against the wall of the apartment, could only be secured against serious danger by a number of gentlemen linking arms and forming themselves into a barrier. It was then that the windows were thrown open and the living torrent found an outlet. . . . . It was the People's day, the People's President, and the People would rule!"

The policy of rotation in office and party proscription, inaugurated by General Jackson, is interestingly discussed in the following letter from Mr. Richard Rush, who speaks as one having authority. This distinguished statesman and diplomatist, whose career is familiar to·every intelligent American, who filled with honor to himself and country the positions of Attorney-General, Secretary of State, Secretary of the Treasury, Minister to France and to England, was noted for his elegance of manner and high-breeding, his charming conversation, replete with instructive and fascinating reminiscences, a tact and vivacity somewhat French, and the finished grace acquired by so long a residence at Courts, in the days when diplomacy was a high art, even science, — when the partition of empires and the overthrow of kingdoms hinged perhaps on the success of an ambassadorial banquet, a *bon mot* over the snuff-box, or a game of whist, the players being Castlereagh and Talleyrand, a Canning or a Metternich, who, with their cards, dealt out crowns for trumps. Mr. Rush was very successful in his negotiation of several treaties with England, especially the important one of 1818, with Lord Castlereagh, relative to the fisheries and our Northwestern Boundary. And it was said, that only by the influence of his personal qualities and the friendship entertained for him by the British Cabinet, was a war averted with England, then imminent in consequence of General Jackson's execution of two British subjects, with his usual defiance of constitutional law and international comity ; being guided by the rashness of conceited ignorance, not enlightened courage.

"SYDENHAM near PHILADELPHIA, September 30, 1853.

" DEAR SIRS, — A short absence over in Jersey has prevented a more prompt answer to your letter, but I take the first chance opening to me since my return to enclose a little notice of Mr. Trescot's letter. . . . . You could have done it yourselves much better. What I say of his secretaryship at London, Mr. Everett himself told me the day I dined there last winter, when you, Mr. Seaton, were there. After you have published this, his diplomatic-reform letter, I may possibly be led to make it the occasion of some remarks on our whole diplomatic system, though I rather fear not ; they would be so revolutionary ; not radical, however.

" I should go against all turnings out of our foreign ministers or consuls, except for downright misbehavior or incapacity, and could give, as I almost dare to persuade myself, sufficient and solid reasons for adopting that course, or rather *coming back* to it, for we had it in effect formerly. The opposite course is intrinsically unwise. It has done mischief, will continue to do it, and finally produce results entangling and disgraceful to us. But our public have got so thoroughly wrong-headed about the necessity of each new President choosing his own foreign ministers, that an elementary discussion would be required to bring back right thoughts, if even that could ever in the least be hoped for. You Whigs are as bad as we Democrats, each side growing worse with time, in this battle for the spoils as the four years come round; so that the subject would be ticklish and staggering, though not unmanageable, if resolutely taken up. Washington even thought that there was no need of choosing the heads of department on party grounds. He put Jefferson at the head of one, and Hamilton of another, when parties were more distinctly marked on principle than now, or have ever been since his day. Jackson advised Mr. Monroe to call to his administration two Republicans or Democrats and two Federalists, the latter name still existing in his time. Washington's practice and Jackson's *theory* were right, under the true theory of our government. The very idea of a cabinet is out of place with us, and the notion that it should be a *unit* still more so. This is for constitutional monarchies, where ministers, not the monarch, are responsible, but it has no legal or constitutional existence here. The very term *cabinet* is of party coinage. The republicans of '98 complained of it as monarchical, as the old columns of the Philadelphia Aurora might show if searched.

"The utmost with us is, that the President may, if he choose, require the opinion in writing of any one of his officers; but all are to do their duty under *his* direction.

"Yet we have arrived at a code of universal partisan proscription, which each party seems equally to approve and practise, under a supposed necessity that every new President is morally and wisely, if not politically, bound to employ as officers from A to Z, abroad and at home, those only who hold his own opinions! This now established practice of universal change every four years, and the terrible contests and corruptions to which it will give birth in our presidential elections, the ratio of each increasing, geometrically, as offices and emoluments grow more numerous and tempting under the prodigious growth of our country, must end in breaking the government to pieces. So it is that the choice of the Chief Magistrate has ever been the great test of popular government. Thus much I have been incited to say in thinking of Mr. Trescot's vain hope of bringing about permanent appointments in our diplomatic service. . . . . I did not intend to let September run out without thanking you, as now let me do, for your acceptable favor, No. 1654 of the Intelligencer, and your more curious number *eight*, as certainly it is. I will bring the latter safely with me to Washington, where I shall probably be, on Smithsonian business, before January comes round. I do not quite like to trust the precious little relic to the mail a second time. In the Intelligencer of September 3d I read Randolph's old unpublished speech against the war, with unusual avidity, for the sake of calling up old matters; and the more, as I heard it in part. The fifth paragraph, a short one of five lines, should end with the word *pity*, I think. That sentence struck upon my ear from the threefold alliteration. 'I ask its (the House's) patience, its pardon, and its *pity*.' What says Mr. Gales's *short-hand* manuscript, which I also remember when it was 'solitary and alone'? It would be odd if that third little word was in the speech, as delivered, and struck out afterwards! I consider the notes appended to the speech as better than the speech itself.   I did not think as much as others of Randolph's genius, and liked his character still less.   There was too much malignity about him, for me, and pretension.   The note about Mr. Monroe is all true, as I could abundantly confirm, in many things.   He was the main propeller of the war in the executive councils, and its main prop there afterwards. . . . . . And now in concluding, I pray you to believe me in old friendship and esteem,

" Yours ever very faithfully,

" RICHARD RUSH."

The Monroe doctrine, which, fifty years ago, as Mr. Rush in the following note says, " surprised " European diplomacy, again agitates and controls the policy of a continent, and by its tyrannous " law of force" precipitated and sheltered the mournful Mexican tragedy, over which the civilized world still shudders and weeps, — the murder of the gallant Maximilian, the madness of a widowed Empress.

" PHILADELPHIA, 22d March, 1857.

" MY DEAR SIR, — I remember the Mr. Stapleton who signs the enclosed slip from the Albion.   He was Canning's private secretary in the days of my negotiations, and a very clever man he was.   He is right in what he says.   Mr. Canning *did*, explicitly and repeatedly, deny the 'Monroe Doctrine.'   He denied it in a solemn protocol, and otherwise, in my negotiation of 1824, he being then Foreign Secretary of England.   Russia denied it, as did France. You may say all Europe was surprised at it.   They could not comprehend it, except as a threat, and holding up the law of force as soon as we were able.   This may be plainly enough seen in the second volume of the work, 'Residence at the Court of London,' which I published in 1845, a copy of which I understand is in the Congress Library.   I refer you to it only as presenting the matter in a nutshell in place of hunting through public documents, should you wish to see the record of it. Stapleton wrote the 'Political Life of Canning,' in three volumes, which I have, but not at hand, as I am staying with a son in town. In one of the volumes you will find the account of the part Mr. Canning took in that whole Spanish-American question, when the European Alliance was for falling foul of the Spanish Colonies.

" Ever yours faithfully,
" RICHARD RUSH.

" MR. SEATON."

In the summer of 1834 Mrs. Seaton writes to a member of her family : —

" . . . . During the past two days we have been in an alarming state of disorder from a dread of insurrection, or rather a dread of the illegal hanging of instigators to mischief. A white man was put in jail a few days since on the charge of circulating incendiary pamphlets. This was the beginning of the disturbance. Mobs have collected to break open the jail, and hang him without trial. Marines are stationed in and around the jail, but there is great apprehension felt, the soldiers from Point Comfort having gone to Baltimore, so that we have no means of suppressing the riot. Snow will certainly be torn to pieces by the mechanics if he be caught, and they are in full pursuit of him. Unfortunately, several hundred mechanics of the navy yard are out of employment, who, aided and abetted by their sympathizers, create the mob, — the first I have ever seen, not recollecting those of Sheffield, and it is truly alarming. I tremble for the consequences of any encounter with mistaken, infuriated men who have set the laws at defiance, and must now be put down by force. The post-office is guarded, but they threaten the Mayor; and you

10

will understand all my fears when I tell you that your dear father has been out during the last two nights, exerting his influence to quell the storm. We have only a handful of troops here, but a company from Annapolis is expected to-night. Last night the rain poured heavily, and probably prevented much mischief, though we hope that the elements of disturbance are somewhat quieted. General Jackson arrives to-morrow and will be prompt to suppress all disorders. . . . . Midnight. Your father has just returned home, and reports that all is tranquil."

This man Snow was a mulatto, at the very head of the respectable colored population, keeping a restaurant much frequented by the good society of Washington. It being reported that he had spoken disrespectfully of the wives of the mechanics as a class, using very coarse and insulting language with regard to their virtue, a mob, a white mob ensued, and the city during several days and nights was at its mercy. All the *gentlemen* of the city protected Snow so far as they could, not believing him guilty, and even had such been the case they were the friends of law and order, and willing that Snow should be dealt with accordingly, but not by the hands of Judge Lynch. Mr. Seaton was not mayor, but of course was called on for aid and counsel; for none ever lived who could offer more prompt service and wiser words, and he possessed pre-eminently the qualities to guide a popular storm, — mildness, reason, and decision. In this instance it was mainly through his personal efforts that order was restored, through the respect with which the people regarded him, and the unflinching courage with which, bareheaded and unarmed, he threw himself into the midst of the mob, controlling by his presence, and the undaunted bearing that finds a responsive chord in the heart of every really brave man, a crowd of excited, maddened men, touched on the most sensitive nerve of honor.

Mr. Seaton had a high esteem for the mechanics of Washington, believing that no community possessed a more order-loving, intelligent, self-respecting body of citizens. He was proud of the confidence of the working classes, sympathized in their needs, protected their interests, and enjoyed the interchange of thought with their practical minds; his constant, respectful kindness to them springing from an appreciation of all intrinsic worth and good citizenship, and being, not the condescension for an especial object, to obtain their suffrages during an election, but the gracious habit of his life. While no man had less of that spurious "pride which apes humility," no one more valued the honors of an ancient lineage than Mr. Seaton. It was indeed a controlling sentiment of his nature; but a citizen of a land where ancestral distinctions and privileges are opposed to the spirit of the government and people, his perfect taste forbade all vain boast of such possession, leading him to cherish it in its true sense, as a hostage to the world so to emulate the virtues of those who had preceded him, that in his hands their escutcheon should suffer no stain.

In 1838 Mrs. Seaton, being in New York, had the privilege of once more hearing in the pulpit Dr. Follen, the learned, evangelical, and beloved Unitarian, whose life, so exquisitely in accordance with the pure and lovely truths he taught, was sadly closed by the burning of the steamer Lexington on the Sound, he being one of those who perished. Mrs. Follen was also widely known for various valuable works, principally on education.

Mrs. Seaton thus writes of this eminent divine:—

" . . . . All of our party went to the sea-side this morning, as the weather, being a little tempestuous, rendered it even more desirable to those who have never witnessed the majesty of the ocean, than a bright, sunny day. I, in despite of the uncomfortable morning, found my way to Dr. Follen's church. He appeared to better advantage personally than when with us. The light came down on his guileless countenance from above, and his simple gestures and earnest eloquence, heightened by the effect thus produced, went right *to* the heart, and I am sure came from it. He is scarcely old enough to be called patriarchal, but he has the wisdom and fervor of one of the Apostles. The music is very unpretending, but soft and sweet, calculated, as all church harmony should be, to prepare the mind for serious impressions. It was Communion Sunday, and Dr. Follen spoke of the mysterious dread experienced by many persons of 'eating and drinking unworthily,' and cautioned them against entertaining superstitious notions of the Eucharist. 'What!' said he, 'is it necessary to entitle you to partake of this comforting sacrament that you should be able to say, "I am pure in the sight of God." "Can any man convict me of sin?" "Am I not exemplary even as Christ was?" No! my brethren; were this so, few would participate, none dare administer it; this sacred rite would cease. It is intended to encourage us to persevere in that self-sacrificing principle which guided our Master on earth, and deserted him not in death: to comfort, to console, to encourage us to follow the example of Christ.' I listened with reverence as 'truths divine came mended from his tongue,' and accepted Mrs. Follen's invitation to go forward with her to the table. The ceremony was shorter than with us, but highly impressive. . . . . I appointed an hour to receive Dr. and Mrs. Follen, and to accompany them to see Mrs. Jameson, the celebrated English authoress, who is now in New York.

" I did not tell you, I think," continues Mrs. Seaton, "that before leaving home I had much gratification in the perusal of the journal kept by Mrs. John Quincy Adams during her journey to Russia, which, despite the deprecatory tone of her accompanying note, I found interesting from the novelty of the scenes described, and the sprightly cleverness of this record of her impressions. I had previously been indebted to her for the manuscript letters of John Adams to his sons, which were so valuable for their condensed instruction and parental wisdom that I obtained permission to copy them for the benefit of my own children."

The note from Mrs. Adams was as follows : —

" MY DEAR MADAM, — I do not know why I should inflict such a penance on you as the reading of my prosy and uninteresting detail of a journey which, in itself, yielded little to amuse the mind or excite the fancy, although it was productive of much unnecessary anxiety, and some serious apprehension during a few short but trying hours. *Such* as it is, I offer it to your perusal : and as it was written in great haste and without any pretence of literary merit, you must be merciful in your judgment, and lenient in your criticism of the silly attempts of your friend,

" LOUISA C. ADAMS.

"7 May.
    To MRS. SEATON."

"You are welcome, dear Mrs. Seaton, to take copies of the papers which I had so much pleasure in lending you, and which I trust will prove a real benefit to your children. Early impressions are the most durable, and children insensibly imbibe principles, which though they may not apparently produce any effect, gradually expand the mind, and operate most favorably on their future conduct. That they may derive all the advantage from these letters which your exertions for their improvement so eminently merit is the sincere wish of your friend,

"L. C. ADAMS.

"I request you will not hurry the copy."

Mrs. Seaton's own letters, and those of her husband to their children, are in many points unsurpassed even by the famous ones of Pitt and the elder Adams; but being precluded the gratification of lifting for the public the veil of family reserve, a few extracts must suffice to show the strength of parental tenderness and wisdom of admonition bestowed by Mr. Seaton on his sons, and which are striking as evidences of his own delicate, honorable nature. This sentiment of honor indeed, fastidious, almost overstrained, being the pervading essence of his life, — a religion in its sanctity.

"MY DEAR SON, — .... I was a little mortified at what I conceived to be indifference to that virtue, punctuality, in not reaching West Point on the day ordered, after the great indulgence extended to you. It is not enough that you escape censure, but you should endeavor to obtain approbation from your superiors. But on this head I will not dwell further. Parents, from their great anxiety, may appear to their children fastidious, and I would not wish

to evince an unreasonable sensitiveness at any slight dere-
liction from rule, and shall, without further admonition,
leave it to your affection for us and just pride in yourself
to attain a high standing. When your steadiness and good
conduct have been sufficiently manifested to Colonel Thayer
to pave the way for such an application, I will write to him
on the subject of your promotion. . . . . Your brother,
you know, is at Georgetown College, and I feel every day,
as his mind and qualities develop, a stronger hope that
he will do well, even distinguish himself.

"It is in truth a happiness to your mother and myself
to witness the promise of his opening character; and more
happy am I to observe it, for it has pleased Providence to
afflict her so severely, that I rejoice doubly in the prospect
she derives of consolation from the good and honorable
career of her remaining children. That you will yourself,
my dear son, prove an added source of this comfort to your
dear and incomparable mother, I ardently hope, and confidently trust. Remember, my dear son, that we are always
thinking of you, and every day talking of you. God bless
you.

"Your affectionate father,

" W. W. SEATON."

"Your letter, my son, has diffused pleasure through the
family, as it assures us of your determination to labor
steadily during the two months previous to June. . . . . .
Do not be lulled into a false security; if persevering effort
can insure your going through, do not fail to try your utmost.
You speak of various novels and romance-writers, as if you
consumed your precious time in reading them. Pray cast
aside henceforth everything that can divert your mind
from the one great object, and resolve to achieve it at
every sacrifice of ease and amusement. You make us very
happy by the standing already acquired in your studies.

Persevere, my dear son, and add this quality to your amiability and integrity of character, and you will have the felicity of knowing that your parents bless the day of your birth, and your excellence will be to them a source of consolation under all the trials which may yet await them. . . . . You have now too many correspondents, and I wish that you would write to them less often and with more care. You should not have mentioned to *any one* that young H—— was dismissed. Never spread even confidentially, much less voluntarily, anything to the disparagement of another, especially a friend. It will spread fast enough. You meant no harm in this instance, and no one has said a word about it; my remark is spontaneous; but remember it as a hint for the future. . . . . You have our daily blessings and prayers. Take not time to write home more than a line, and win the prize of success at all hazards."

"1834.

"MY DEAR SON, — . . . . There is no alternative, without a show of favoritism, but for you to join your regiment. To grant your request, the Secretary thinks would too obviously savor of making the service bend to personal favor. His reasons were fair and rational, and not being able to controvert them I was obliged to acquiesce in their justness. So that we must submit, my son, and, so far from repining at the inevitable, must be thankful that you were permitted to be so long with us. . . . . There was a heavy blow the day after you sailed, and though perhaps not altogether welcome, you had an opportunity of witnessing the most sublime of nature's work, — 'the ocean into mountains tossed.' . . . . And now, my dear son, farewell. You are fully embarked on the career of life, with no guide save your own sense of right, and your own firmness in pursuing it. I fervently trust and, hope, I believe, that these will be sufficient guides so long as you abstain from two rocks on which so many sanguine hopes have been wrecked , namely, cards and conviviality.   They are sunken rocks, not fully discerned till they are struck.   The first leads to pecuniary embarrassment, then obligation and slavery to others, — the second to intemperance and ultimate disgrace. I ask of you, my son, a resolution which will preserve you through life from sleepless nights and anxious days, at least from one of their most prolific causes, — never to incur a debt unless it be under the most pressing exigency.   A man in debt is no longer a freeman ; he loses his erect carriage, his mind sinks under the degrading pressure.   Cards would soon run away with the largest fortune, and are the besetting mischief of the young officers of the army, involving them in drink and ruin.   Under all pressure and persuasion, shun touching them as you would dishonor and death.   Touch them for pastime, and the taste will grow with fearful rapidity.   You may think that I repeat these admonitions unnecessarily often, but, my dear son, if you had seen the number whom I have, in thirty years, swept into the vortex by these enticing pleasures, and ultimately lost to themselves, their families, and society, you would think my anxiety natural.   Idleness so naturally resorts to amusement, and amusements so easily run into excess, that officers in the army are peculiarly exposed to danger.   These are truths of the greatest moment, my son ; keep them in mind, and in time to come you will appreciate their value more highly than you can do now.   But I will not pursue the ungrateful theme. . . . . May a gracious Providence preserve and direct you, and may you be worthy of that direction, prays

"Your affectionate father,

"W. W. SEATON."

Augustine Fitzwhylsson Seaton, the eldest child of Mr. and Mrs. Seaton, to whom were addressed these striking exhortations to virtue, fulfilled the brightest hopes of his parents in all that forms an honored manhood. Rich in talent, inheriting especially his father's gift of graceful oratory as well as beauty of presence, and possessed of the most endearing traits of character, his gallant young spirit was quenched as its light began to brighten the career upon which he had so hopefully embarked. After graduating at West Point, he was ordered to that charnel-house, Fort Gibson, then far beyond the limits of civilization, where with so many other brave hearts his life was sacrificed in barren conflicts with savages. During an expedition in 1835 against the Indians, far into the wilderness on the plains of the Ozark, suffering intense privations, the health of this gallant young Seaton gave way, and in a few weeks the grave closed over a life of brilliant promise. Respected by his command, beloved by his comrades, he died in the discharge of his duty, — a soldier's noblest epitaph.

During the summer of 1838 Mr. Seaton indulged in one of the rare holidays of his busy life, in a flying jaunt to Canada, joining a quartette of friends who dubbed themselves the Pickwick Club, of which Mr. Seaton of course personated the benevolent and immortal President. The respect entertained for Mr. Seaton's reputation and character was most agreeably evinced in the attentions he received from private and official hospitality. The Earl of Durham, then Governor-General of Canada, whose political services and talent as Mr. Lambton had been rewarded by the peerage, and who showed great ability and tact during the alarming complications between England and the United States arising from the " Caroline " and " McLeod " imbroglio, was of somewhat reserved, even haughty demeanor, though of a truly kindly nature, and was noted for the high-bred tone of his social circle, the charm of which was enhanced by the gentle presence and grace of Lady Durham, a daughter of .Earl Grey.

Lord Durham seemed at once to appreciate Mr. Seaton's wide intelligence, knowledge of political history, and distinction of manners ; expressing subsequently to various persons the opinion that he was " the most charming American he had ever met," while the acquaintance then formed by Mr. Seaton with several civil and military members of his Excellency's household ripened into warm regard and frequent correspondence. A few extracts from the details sketched by Mr. Seaton for the domestic circle will indicate the impression made by him on these critical foreigners.

Mr. Seaton writes from "Toronto, July, 1838 ":—

" . . . . A run of four hours this morning across Lake Ontario brought us to the capital of Upper Canada. I begin to be quite anxious to reach the end of our journey, for, truth to say, I am quite tired of the jaunt, and would gladly turn my face homewards if I were not ashamed. . . . . We crossed over yesterday morning to the British side of the Falls, the first time I ever set foot on a foreign soil ; and it was not with indifference that I saw the British flag flying on its own ground, and surrounded by British troops. At the Falls there are about 600 of the 43d Infantry, and at dinner, who should sit opposite to me but Mr. W——, who is here with his regiment. I was at first not able to identify his familiar face, he being in uniform ; he, however, at once recognized me, and during the hour that intervened before my departure he was exceedingly civil, among other marks of it tendering me a letter to his friend Captain Arthur, the son and Aide to the Governor here, as well as letters to some officers of the Guards at Quebec. There is a regiment of foot here, which I shall see parade to-morrow, Sunday being in camp a grand parade day, and shall embrace the opportunity of going to church."

"OGDENSBURG, on the St. Lawrence.

" . . . . I have got so far on my road to Quebec, and through the task which for my sins I undertook of coming from home alone on a jaunt of curiosity. Mr. G——'s letter commanded from Captain B——, of the Guards, at Toronto, very great politeness, as did also Mr. W——'s, from Captain Arthur. This latter called on me on Sunday, though not here a visiting day, and invited me, in his father's name, to see him the next day, which I did. Sir George Arthur, a fine gentlemanly looking man of sixty, received me with much civility, expressing regret that my early departure prevented the attentions he would have been glad to show me. I spent fifteen minutes with him very pleasantly, and went immediately on board the steamer, which reached Kingston at sunrise this morning. While waiting for the Montreal boat, I have run over here to send you this hasty note, with love and blessings for the household, and prayers for your safety in my absence."

"QUEBEC, August, 1838.

" . . . . To-night I set out on my most welcome homeward route, — though the two days I have passed here have been most agreeably occupied in viewing the fine city, and in the enjoyment of kind hospitality. . . . . . On Saturday morning, shortly after my arrival, I received a card of invitation to dinner from the Governor-General and the Countess of Durham, for four o'clock of the same day, — no visiting or company among the English on Sunday, I find. There were present about fifteen persons, military and official, but no American except myself. After a most agreeable dinner, and coffee, his Lordship invited me to drive with him ; so I took a seat in the barouche with Lord and Lady Durham, and Mr. Charles Buller, to whose kind attentions I have been so much indebted. We drove eight or nine miles up the beautiful banks of the St. Charles, — a good deal of chat of course. The next day I went to church alone, my companions declining. . . . . To-day I called to pay my parting respects to the Earl of Durham, and, though engaged with a member of the Council (the famous Mr. Turton by the way), he put him aside to give me an audience ; and so full was he of his official objects here, and of our question and delicate relations with Great Britain, that I could hardly get away in decent time, knowing, as I did, that Turton was waiting to resume his business. This afternoon I have spent in visiting the . striking works, citadel, etc., under the guidance of one of the aides-de-camp, who tendered his services for that purpose at Lord Durham's table on Saturday. I have an hour now in which to take tea with Mr. Buller, — and then on board the boat for Montreal. . . . . But in all this gratification my heart lies in me like lead at my ignorance of home events ; but I must still my anxious thoughts as best I may. . . . . Lord Clarence Paget, I regret to say, is absent on a tour for the benefit of his health."

" WASHINGTON, August, 1838.

" MY DEAR SIR, — Learning from Mr. Gales that you are expecting to wing me on my flight homeward, I send you a word to apprise you of my return last evening to this quiet metropolis, where I wish with all my heart, selfish as it is, that I could have found you still sojourning. I passed New Brighton on Saturday, and while looking with admiration at its delightful position and beautiful edifices, little dreamed that you were one of its inmates. I could have run over to you instead of sweltering in the fourth story of the Astor House.

"I have had a fatiguing but most interesting journey, and was fortunate in meeting old acquaintances (among them Lieutenant West, of the 43d, a son of Earl De la Warre, with his regiment, now stationed at the Falls) and making new ones, which gave me, in addition to your own letters, a key to all desirable society at Toronto and Quebec. At the former place I saw Sir George Arthur, a fine-looking, dignified old officer; and at the latter I saw and conversed a good deal with the Governor-General, whose manner, both at his table and in his bureau, was altogether different from that described by Willis in the last Mirror. I found him anything but reserved, — not only exceedingly conversible, but frank to a degree that rather surprised me, — this, however, was when *tête-à-tête*. The Countess of Durham is a handsome, *not* beautiful, unaffected, and apparently amiable woman, who, with some aid of the imagination, might come up to Byron's portrait of her. . . . . From Quebec I travelled home with great rapidity, my anxiety to obtain news of my family having become painful. Think of doing the distance between Montreal and New York in forty-three hours ! I am stunned by the incessant jostle and loss of sleep of the trip, and feel pretty much, I suppose, as if I had been shot from a mortar !

"I received every civility from Captain Baddeley, and dined with him at his beautiful cottage on the bank of Lake Ontario. I am greatly your debtor for bringing me acquainted with so clever, intelligent, and guileless an old soldier. Adieu. Have the goodness, when you have an hour on your hands which you cannot kill, to write to me.

"Yours faithfully, and sincerely,

"W. W. SEATON."

Mr. Charles Buller, mentioned in Mr. Seaton's letter, a member of Lord Durham's council, was already distinguished in Parliament, being regarded as the foremost among the rising British statesmen; and such weight had he already attained in the estimation of government and in popular confidence, as to bid fair soon to fill the great position of Premier of England. Unfortunately for his country he was cut off in the fulness of his talent and usefulness, to the universal regret of the nation. The following notes from Mr. Buller and the fine old officer of the Guards show their appreciation of Mr. Seaton's attractive powers, their mutual regard being subsequently cemented by pleasant intercourse in Washington.

"QUEBEC, October 22, 1838.

"DEAR SIR,—Your letter of the 1st, coming at the leisurely and dignified pace of an officer of the Guards, reached me only two or three days ago. I am much indebted to you for the very interesting papers you sent me, and Lord Durham desires me to express his thanks to you for the really valuable paper which you were so good as to forward to him.

"I am much obliged to you for your words of comfort to us in our fallen fortunes, and I must say for our friends in the United States, that we receive very much, both public and private. I have been much gratified by your notice of our proceedings in the Intelligencer. The American Whig Press has been of great service to Lord Durham, and acted a most generous part.

" I need not now enter into the propriety of his returning home, as he has explained the necessity of it in his
Proclamation.   I wish he could, as he at first proposed,
have gone through the States and visited New York and
Washington.   But on second thoughts he determined that,
in the present alarming state of the Province, it was necessary that he should go home forthwith, to try if his presence
can do any good.

" I remain a short time behind, and shall go home in the
Great Western from New York.   Whether I shall be able
to get to Washington I know not, but shall make the endeavor.   I am really sorry, in spite of all my ultra-democ-
racy, to see Van Burenism triumphing in these elections.

" Believe me, dear sir, yours very truly,

"CHARLES BULLER, JR."

"GLASGOW, April 5, 1841.

" MY DEAR COLONEL SEATON, — Your kind letter and present have been following me from place to place. . . . . The
fac-simile of General Washington's writing was particularly
welcome ; for, although I cannot be supposed to be so great
a worshipper at the shrine of that truly great man as you
must be, yet the cosmopolitan reverence we bear on this side
of the water to his memory is scarcely less warm than the
patriotic one which electrifies the Union ; among men at
least who have read his life,— *and who has not ?* The plans
on the Boundary question, that knotty point, are very acceptable.   On this subject I am somewhat disposed to think
privately, that you have, in point of *law*, as much in your
favor as ourselves ; but how infinitely you fall short of us
on the score of *equity ! !*   Look at the encroachment, and
think of the object of this, as of all similar portions of
treaties, — to remove as much as possible all inducements
to an unfriendly interference. If you succeed without war,
I will give you credit for diplomatic skill, but not for mag-

nanimity. War, however, I trust is out of the question, — men are too wide awake at this day to deal with its horrors until every other means have been had recourse to to avert it, — and, above all, a war with America ! No ! I, for one, would rather see you usurp the land, and if you can *keep it gracefully*, do so. If the foregoing political tirade should not settle the question in our favor, it will, I trust, induce you to reply to it, and thus I shall get another letter from you, if not the Disputed Territory. . . . . Have you read the Quarterly for March ? There is a' good article on this subject, the impossibility by *the words of the Treaty* of showing which is the northwest angle of Nova Scotia. This is more curious than useful, — proving, however, what a blundering Commission drew it up. Indeed, I think the men who composed it have much to answer for, no less than for all the blood that *may* be spilled in the dispute.

"As to the McLeod affair, we do not dream of it being a source of bloodshed, unless, indeed, you allow Lynch law to prevail, as you have done in too many instances. One thing I have to propose ; namely, that if ever you and I do meet in deadly collision, we will spare each other. . . . .

"Faithfully and devotedly yours,

"T. W. Baddeley, Col. R. E."

The following extracts, referring pleasantly to the impression made by Mr. Seaton in Canada, are from the letters of an English gentleman in the British service. So unusually clever and witty are his sketches of men and current events as to cause regret at the impossibility of presenting them unmutilated for perusal ; but this is forbidden touchingly, though tacitly, by Mr. Seaton himself; for in his remaining correspondence and papers, all that is malicious, — the sting of a story propagating, however unintentionally, some unkind gossip, — the name of the hero of an anecdote implicating, perhaps, not very creditably some of the most prominent men of the day, — all are found carefully erased ; presenting an example of reticence that must be faithfully observed, — a delicacy characteristic of Mr. Seaton's benevolence and kindliness of nature, which never inflicted a wound on the heart or even the vanity of another, which shielded even an adversary from misrepresention or ridicule.

"NEW BRIGHTON, August, 1838.

"MY DEAR SIR,—How you managed to get from Montreal to Washington in forty-three hours must be an affair between you and the Great Western. I shall take the liberty of communicating the fact to Captain Hoskins. Pray offer your services to the Hon. Amos Kendall. But what I am most concerned about is having missed you. You would have passed a pleasant evening at this delightful place. We have lofty and clean bedrooms, a good table, delicious breezes, half an hour's trip to New York offering itself every hour, besides the National Intelligencer, which I, and only I, have the good taste to go to New York for once a day. The funny old fellow at the P. O. who delivers the mail always talks to me.

"'This is not the worst paper in the world,' says he. 'You mean it is the best,' says I. 'You don't take the Globe?' says he. 'Not I,' said I. 'I should be surprised if you did,' says he. 'I once saw Joe Gales,' he began again, 'but I never saw the t' other fellow. What is he like?' 'Just figure to yourself a scalded-to-death corpse walking about,' I replied. 'Ecod, I can just see him,' says he.

"I wrote you a note, and every day did I hope to see you, but, like yourself, you preferred seeing your wife and children. I congratulate them on your safe return. This place has become quite an appendage to New York. The night before last we had an Italian concert, — Fornasari, la Maroncelli (wife of the fellow-sufferer of Silvio Pellico, who lives here), and others. The company leaving New York at seven P. M., and returning at eleven. And last night a party from New York came out, and had a regular ball, bringing their own fiddlers. Think of that! In old times, before the reign of steamers, this would never have been attempted. They might have been driven ashore at Bedlow's Island, or some other country inhabited by cannibals, or all shut up, men and maidens in their dancing gear, in the tin castle of some Connecticut giant. Here am I, writing at my ease in the morning, going quietly to New York at two P. M., to put my letters on board the Great Western, which sails at four, not forgetting a letter to W. W. Seaton, by the great Amos! What revolutions! I had the satisfaction of finding all my old friends here, after an absence of eight years, looking a great deal older than myself. Two or three are here taking Brandreth's Pills. Many are dead, nothing but odd volumes left. . . . . I am off to Montreal for the races. I was sure it was enough for you to present yourself to be well received by the society there. I shall hear of you. Adieu for the present, being unfeignedly

" Your friend and servant,

" G."

QUEBEC, September, 1838.

" MY DEAR SEATON, — I shall confound my enemies with the glorious National Intelligencer which Charles Buller has just shown me. I 'll tell you what I think of you when we meet. But what, under Heaven, has caused you, from whom I expected other things, to disappoint me so perfidiously ? I know nothing that could give me more pleasure than a letter from you, and yet you don't write, you gallant, malicious Colonel, you hero of Bladensburg!

Take that as the heaviest denunciation of my resentment.
. . . . . I have just got into circulation here, and find
it pleasant enough.   Lord Durham speaks in the kindest,
most flattering manner of you, and Charles Buller likes
you better than any American he has yet seen.   I break-
fasted with the latter this morning. . . . . . I find Lord
Durham's dinners very pleasant, nothing awful in them.
A good *cuisine*, attentive servants, and perfect ease.   What
delicious ices! how superior to Kinchy's greasy contrivances!
The day before yesterday we had a charming dinner there.
I had an hour's talk in the morning with his Lordship,
who is in good health and good humor just now, as Lord
Brougham and others have been got the better of.   He is a
man of accurate information and fine judgment, a little like
Mr. Fox in some things,—with whom, by the way, and with
Turton, he was at Eton.   We were about fifty that day at
table.   His Lordship had Mrs. T., a very accomplished
woman, on his right; I was on her right; opposite we
had Lady Durham betwixt two Catholic Bishops in their
rochets and paraphernalia.   I happened to be in a very
talkative mood, and told Mrs. T. and Lord Durham so
many ridiculous stories, and there was so much laughing,
that the lots of Guardsmen present could not choose but
stare.   After dinner we had some good music, and a couple
of rubbers with Sir John D., and I won,—which, you know
is pleasant.   I know of no more agreeable way of winding
up the day than dining with a lord who keeps a good table,
and winning money afterwards from good fellows who have
the grace to pay.   Last night we all went to the theatre,
Miss Tree playing "by command."   Audience rising on the
entrance of the Governor-General and his family, orchestra
playing God save the Queen, curtain rising, and the actors and actresses coming forward to sing the same most
abominably.   You don't do things in that style with Mar-

tin Van Buren! . . . . May my enemies get all they deserve, but may all happiness and prosperity and fame be with you and your generation in *secula seculorum!* We are all mad here about mesmerism, or animal magnetism. The other evening we had a private exhibition at Charles Buller's before Lord Durham. Two Canadian women, one stone blind, were put into the arms of Morpheus in a moment. A young Englishwoman, a servant-maid, was frequently put to sleep, and upon trial it was found that I had the power over her. I witnessed the influence it produced upon some officers of the Guards, — one of whom was taken with spasms, quite sea-sick. It is an odd affair, — I don't know what to think. The Royal Society of London has taken it up, and we are to have a report. . . . . . "

"QUEBEC, December, 1839.

"MY DEAR SEATON, — I have not forgotten you, and never shall, nor anything about so worthy a fellow as you are. I sent you lately an address which it was hoped might serve to conciliate the feverish people on both sides the frontier. I hope, if the National Intelligencer notice the Boundary question, it will strongly point out the wickedness of any individuals, or Provincial or State governments interfering when they are not called to do so, in the management of a question which by treaty and law belongs solely to the governments of the two nations. . . . . . Help us to settle this grave question in a friendly way, I beseech you. I regard the bad and unprincipled in all countries with detestation, but there is no reason why I should dislike the countries they disgrace, or cease to love and honor those whose probity and excellence I know, and whom a cruel fate threatens to render powerless to raise your country to the honest eminence it ought to have. . . . ."

"LONDON, February, 1840.

"MY DEAR SEATON, — I cannot permit the British Queen

to sail without assuring you that I remember you, and with
undiminished affection.   No time will efface the sincere
friendship I feel for you and those most dear to you. . . . .
Some of the rabid Opposition papers ride over every public man in order to damage the Ministers.   This has been
carried to such extremes that it scarce does harm any
longer.   The safe rule is to take no notice òf such attacks.
A man named Westmacott, the editor of the Age, a very
scurrilous paper, aspersed the character of a daughter of
Charles Kemble, upon which, taking a horsewhip to represent judge and jury, the father went to the fellow's office,
and laid the damages on his shoulders in a manner that was
'a caution to Crockett.'   He got sixpence damages, and
the offence was not repeated. . . . . I entertain the kindest
feelings towards 'Yankeedonia,' as the Turks call your country, and neglect no occasion of doing justice to the wise and
good I have left there.   At the same time, when the occasion arises, I express myself in strong terms of what I have
never approved of in the United States.   I do not blame
individuals so much as I condemn the laws, which have
made many men less good and wise than others.   The
frightful effects produced by unrestrained democracy, the
demoralizing effects produced by universal suffrage, never
appeared to me so odious or so striking as they do now, by
contrast with the good breeding, the integrity, the order
and mutual support which all give to each other in this
country, from the highest to the lowest.   Existence is really
a continual luxury to me.   The houses are so commodious,
so clean ; the furniture so apt to every purpose ; the food
and the art of preparing it so perfect ; the servants so honest, so methodical, so obedient, and well dressed, that one
almost regrets the passing over of every day, and would do
so, but for the pleasure which is sure to be reproduced the
next.   Then society is so admirably conducted, there is

such universal good breeding, intelligence, and ease to characterize it, that one cannot conceive of anything more perfect amongst human beings. This city, with its two millions of inhabitants, is a miracle of order and tranquillity. I walked home at two o'clock this morning from a dinner at least a mile, and saw no one but the respectable policemen walking about. The establishment of the present police does great honor to Sir Robert Peel. In the daytime no disorder ever does or can take place. The policeman appears to be looking at nothing, yet has his eye on everything. So that the good walk with confidence, and the bad commit no disorders. . . . . . The idea that there is a strong Administration faction in the United States seeking to embroil the two countries in order to enrich themselves by war expenditures has attracted great attention. All deprecate it, but all know that political considerations are often the cause of weakness in the Federal Government, rendering it the minister of selfish political cabals. . . . . . Mr. Calhoun's influence would, I trust, be directed against it, for a war would be especially injurious to the cotton-planters. . . . . . No doubt is entertained here that if the two national governments are permitted to come to an understanding, everything can be arranged consistent with what is due to justice, and the reverence civilized men owe to treaties. But if the frontier people will not obey the laws of the country, and you cannot enforce your laws, it will be a great public misfortune. . . . . . I pray that Maine may remain quiet. Justice will in the end be done. No English Minister could retain his place one day who would incur the risk of leading England into a war with you for the sake of *enforcing an unjust claim.* . . . . . People here have not the time to make themselves acquainted with the structure of the Federal government, and that it is not directly responsible for so much *brutum fulmen* by a State government like Maine, and when questions are asked of those who know America, it requires a long story which nobody cares to listen to. . . . . Society is an old, quiet, reflecting animal here, and believes that a cause defended by abuse must be inherently weak. . . . . The Royal marriage keeps London in a magnificent bustle yet. It is impossible to get a chance to dine at home. I had the honor of kissing the Royal bride's hand at the first levee, down on my knee, all in toggery, and she has a beautifully small hand. Prince Albert is a fine-looking young fellow, and likely to be popular in England, as he is believed to be uncorrupt, amiable, and honest. Sir Charles Vaughan was at the levee, and looking very well. We often talk of Washington, and he frequently speaks of you. I met Charles Murray, your friend, the other day at Catlin's Exhibition, with the Duchess of Sutherland upon his arm. I also sometimes get a chance of talking about America with the Marchioness of Wellesley, who is attached to her native country. I see Mr. Stevenson now and then and his wife, who is much liked here. And Joseph Bonaparte also likes to talk about America. . . . .

"Ever, dear Seaton, yours most faithfully."

"LONDON, July, 1840.

"MY DEAR SEATON, — . . . . I read your letter with great interest, and your observations on the proneness of governments purely democratic to get into collisions with foreign nations appeared to me so just, and were so admirably expressed, that I took occasion, when talking over such matters with Lord Palmerston the other day, to read the passage over to him, and he expressed his admiration for it. . . . . When I first knew your fine country, a dishonest or a dirty action, whether public or private, was frowned down at once by the stern face of the universal moral public opinion. Universal suffrage was introduced in the name of liberty, and then demagogues began openly to use the many for the exclusive benefit of the few. But from what class were the few drawn ?!!! In countries where there is no distinction but that created by wealth or political power, men will take the shortest road to wealth ; and so it arrives that in a generation or two, the old examples of honesty and moderation in conduct and action become so far a dead letter that they are seldom referred to, and in time the ethics of the Old Bailey come to supplant them. How is a nation in such a deplorable position to be disenthralled from such influences ? It is this insane desire to acquire wealth which has injured Americans so much in Europe that enterprises of the most promising kind are no longer looked at by capitalists. You might as well ask a man to take a share in the small-pox as in an American coal-mine. . . . . As to a war, it almost amounts to wickedness to talk about it. Maine has not risen in the estimation of this country by her blustering. We do not deem that tone an evidence of honest conviction of being in the right. . . . . I congratulate you, or rather your good city, in its worshipful choice of Mayor. My only objection is that the honors so long declined by your Lordship may postpone that constantly promised trip to see how you like old England. No doubt about her liking you. . . . . . "

"LONDON, 1841.

" MY DEAR SEATON, — . . . . . The peaceful relations between our two countries have been further menaced of late, and Boundary matters seem to be subordinate to the imprisonment of McLeod, and to the singular fermentation which the bellicose report of *Squire* Pickens (as the Times calls him) has temporarily produced. The Legislature of Maine, too, with its lofty resolves to " remove the Queen's troops from Madawasca," and its splendid appropriation of a million of dollars (since whittled down to *one man* paid and maintained at the joint expense of Maine and Massachusetts), all these things have fairly dumbfoundered the people on this side. They are beginning to ask, seeing so many big words followed by such small consequences, whether Sam Slick is a romance or not. But their effect on American securities is terrible. . . . . The true way to remove every obstacle *quo ad hoc* is to liberate McLeod. I should hope that the Federal government will begin its administration by frowning upon this irreverence done to justice. . . . . A sentiment of abhorrence for war meets one here at every turn. We do not like Frenchmen, and, having no affinities with the other Continental powers. have little partiality for them ; but the colonies founded by John Bull, and the colonists sprung from his loins are dear to him. It will require great provocation to make him strike the first blow at them. . . . . Mr. Forsyth and Fox have not liked each other for some time past. They are both men of talent, and when they are in the humor, you can get as good tincture of myrrh from them as you can at the worthy Dr. Gunton's. Let us pray that our hearts high and low may be disposed to do each other all the good we can, and to avoid every occasion of raising the arms of Americans and Englishmen against each other. General Harrison's cabinet I know personally, and can bear testimony to their fitness for the important stations they occupy. General Harrison I have met more than once. He was a very handsome man, and a very pleasing, well-informed gentleman. How thankful you must be for having such a true-hearted man at the head of such a cabinet! May Heaven prosper them and your country in peace, and make us all what you and I are, — friends in the best sense of the word.

" Ever yours."

"LONDON, 1841.

" MY DEAR SEATON, — . . . . . Since the very unequivocal declarations made by some of Mr. Van Buren's friends, that the American people ought not to be ground down to enrich the English holders of American securities, it has become impossible to inspire confidence in any securities whatever. Such declaration is considered equivalent to a proposition to confiscate every security held by British subjects, and for the moment the effect is prostrating. That the gentlemen now administering the government of the United States will always be opposed to such flagitious propositions, and that they will produce a restoration of American credit here, I sincerely believe ; but it must of necessity be slow. . . . . For the last fortnight all who take an interest in America have had a gloom upon their minds in consequence of the non-appearance of the steamer President. She left New York on March 11, and has not yet been heard of. The only hope entertained is that she was disabled in a storm, and has either gained Bermuda, or is slowly wending her way under sail and in a crippled state. Who comes here in the place of Mr. Stevenson ? . . . . Such a man, for instance, as Colonel — what the deuce is his name ? — would be worth millions to your country. I met Mr. G—— some weeks ago, looking as St. John the Baptist would do in a wig and new clothes. He has rum manners, although I dare say a very good man. Such men are only fit to keep company with the four-and-twenty elders in Revelations. . . . . We have reached a political crisis here ; a division will probably take place to-night on a motion of ' Want of Confidence ' brought forward by Sir Robert Peel. A dissolution will probably take place and a new general election. . . . . I am happy to say that the wise act of the Maryland Legislature in taxing their people for the interest of a debt created for their own benefit will produce a corresponding wholesome effect here. . . . . It is Jackson-Van-Buren-republican-democratic-universal suffrage philosophy that has done all the mischief, and now that you have an opportunity you must repair it.   Is it possible for that monstrous combination of horrors ever to overpower you again ? . . . ."

"SCARBOROUGH, 1842.

" MY DEAR SEATON, — . . . . . When your Senate shall have ratified the arrangements Lord Ashburton has made with the Washington government, I shall most sincerely return your congratulations.   I see that a very strong opposition will be made, but perceive with pleasure that the American Press advises a ratification.   Lord Ashburton is not yet arrived ; at least, we have not heard of it at this remote watering-place.   Lord Aberdeen is at present with the Queen in Scotland, and my holiday lasts until the decision of the Senate is known, when we shall all make our way to Downing Street. . . . . Providence has favored Sir Robert Peel by giving us a most abundant harvest, and one of the most splendid summers I ever saw.   The disturbances in the manufacturing districts no longer give trouble. The income tax is submitted to with the best grace, and will produce an immense sum, and money is plentiful. The Queen and Prince are universally popular, and nothing is wanting towards rendering the satisfaction more perfect, but the establishment of a regular and mutually prosperous intercourse with your country. . . . . ."

"November, 1842.

" . . . . I have been during this season making a round of autumnal visits at various country-seats in many of our English counties as far west as Devonshire and Cornwall, and a few days ago I left the Grange, a highly embellished place belonging to Lord Ashburton, where, with some prominent persons who take an interest in American affairs, we had a full discussion of the Treaty made by him.   You know what magnificent gardens are kept up at these family places, hot-houses, pineries, &c. There is a very great fancy just now for the introduction and cultivation of foreign grapes, of which singular fine varieties exist, brought from all parts of the world, and some of which, as you may imagine, are very delicious ; but at no place have I met with an American grape. I wish, therefore, to introduce them here, especially the Catawba and Isabella. I have promised cuttings in various quarters, especially to Lady Ashburton, who, you know, is an American by birth, and at whose table I met with boiled Indian corn on the cob, waffles, and other American dishes. Lord Ashburton often talks to me of you in high terms, and Mr. H. M. is very much your friend. . . . . The respectable and prudent men in America are very much pitied here, and it afflicts me that the demagogues and politicians seem to menace you with still further embroilments for an indefinite time. I have always thought that if you could only have one Presidential term under that excellent person, Mr. Clay, with a friendly Congress, that such examples of well-considered measures might arise that the people would become enamored of them, and, feeling the prosperity they would create, would at length give to such men and measures a steady support. . . . . How happily we have got out of our Indian and Chinese wars ! Mr. John Bull has at length his belly full of satisfaction, and expects a regular supply of ammunition for his teapot henceforward. Your commerce will benefit by it, for that Nankin treaty will open China to the whole of Christendom. . . . . . ''

"LONDON, April, 1843.

" MY DEAR SEATON, —. . . . The grape-vines so kindly sent by you have been distributed in the vineries of noblemen and gentlemen in various parts of the kingdom. I hope the Catawba grape will be considered a valuable addition to the best grapes now known in England. I have principally sent them into Devonshire and Cornwall, which I think are our most sunny counties. Some of them are at Lord Mount Edgecumbe's, Sir Charles Leman's, and Sir Thomas Dyke Acland's. I also gave Lady Ashburton a couple at her desire, and a couple of roots to the Marquis of Lansdowne, who has a celebrated gardener at Bowood. If you ever come to England in my time, I hope it may be in the season when you can judge for yourself of the fruits of your kindness. If it is convenient for you to visit us now, you ought not to be deterred by the considerations to which you allude. We here understand that the honorable and good of America are not to be blamed for those evils they have had no share in bringing about, and rest assured, you would have no occasion to feel yourself slighted, but would be *well* received. . . . . . We are all delighted with Mr. Tyler's message on the subject of the Right of Visitation. Your navy has always practised the right of visiting suspected vessels, whether of slavery or piracy, and this country will always practise it. I see by a late speech of Mr. Cushing's that he is as Anti-English as ever, and that his opinions on the Right of Visitation do not harmonize with those laid down in Mr. Tyler's message of February, which I take for granted are Mr. Webster's opinions adopted by Mr. Tyler. . . . . . "

The Sir Thomas Dyke Acland mentioned above was a nephew of a brave officer, Colonel John Dyke Acland, of Pictou, of the British army, who fought during our Revolution, and died, eventually, of the effects of wounds received at Saratoga. His wife was the Lady Caroline Fox, daughter of the Earl of Ilchester, and cousin of the celebrated Charles James Fox. She married Sir John in 1770, followed him to this country, and passed heroically through many dangers in the wilderness for the purpose of nursing her husband, whom she long survived. Her history has been written as one of the celebrated women of those heroic days.

"August, 1846.

"MY DEAR SEATON,—I know how difficult it is to get a letter from you. Mr. M—— says sometimes in his letters, 'Mr. Seaton is going to write to you by the next steamer,' which always enables me to say accurately to my wife, 'Mr. Seaton was *not* going to write to me by the next steamer.' . . . . The death of Harrison was a fatal blow to you all, and led the way, step by step, to the present order of things, from which I hope you will soon be relieved. Many years ago I was thrown familiarly with General Z. Taylor, now in Mexico. You cannot do better than make him your President. I think I never knew one more likely to tread in the footsteps of the great Washington than General Taylor. I think there is reason to apprehend that if he gets engaged too far in that wretched country about Saltillo, he will lose all the advantages he possessed when he crossed the Rio Grande. However, the Mexicans — poor devils!— may be frightened enough to make a treaty of cession to stop your rapacious territorial maws. We are all glad the Oregon is closed. Mr. Polk cuts a curious figure in Europe blustering about 54.40, and then inviting the Senate to ratify on 49. The Senate stands very high in Europe for its judicious management of the affair, and if the defaulting States would only make good their deficiencies, American credit would soon be re-established. . . . . Pray tell me what Mr. Fox does, and what you understand his plans to be. He has discontinued writing to everybody in Europe."

Mr. Seaton thus replies to his friend : —

"WASHINGTON, November 12, 1846.

"MY DEAR SIR,—If it be true, as said, that a certain place, which I trust you nor I will ever see, is paved with good resolutions, I fear much that many of mine may be found there, — among them is the often cherished, but much neglected intention to write to you more frequently ; and this desire was never more ardently entertained than on the receipt of your welcome and very obliging letter. But for my failure, I have a valid apology. During the whole year Mr. Gales has been ill, dangerously so. . . . . Then Congress has been in session nearly all the summer. . . . . You inquired about Mr. Fox, and a month ago I should have written of him in a different vein from the present. You have, of course, heard of his death. He had continued to live in his usual perfect seclusion, and one morning, to my entire amazement, his death was announced. He had had no recent illness, and the suddenness of the event shocked me exceedingly. It now appears that he had been in the habit of using opium very largely, — his servants being under orders never to disturb him until rung for. He had been in his chamber a night, and nearly the following day, before a domestic ventured to enter. He was found in a state of lethargy, from which he could not be roused ; and all medical efforts to revive him failing, he died in a few hours. He was supposed to have taken an over dose of morphine. Thus was a light that might have graced society extinguished, — a fine mind lost, which, from misanthropy and singular eccentricity, was of little comparative value to the world. His remains were attended to the grave by the President of the United States, all the Cabinet, the Diplomatic Corps, and all persons of distinction in the city. His body is placed in the Congressional Cemetery to await the directions of his family for its final disposition. . . . . You were quite right in predicting for General

Taylor a rough road in Mexico, even a long way this side of
Saltillo; but his courage, and that of his troops, has so far
been victorious. His attack and three days' conflict at Monterey remind me of the hard fighting in Spain, where many
similar assaults took place on the fortified towns and positions occupied by the French, by the British army; and
where the same sort of persevering and irresistible bravery
was displayed by the assailants. I am proud of the manner
in which our troops acquitted themselves on the Rio Grande
and at Monterey, and especially the raw volunteers.
They have certainly done credit to their race and lineage,
and that is praise enough. Nor have they found a timid
enemy. The Mexicans have shown more pluck than I
looked for, and have certainly behaved well for so mongrel
a race. But if Taylor is under orders to push his way to
Mexico (City), I fear for the safety of his army. He has a
long march through a difficult country, badly watered, and
poor, with several strong points to carry, and he must
weaken his army by leaving garrisons to secure his rear
communications. What an ill-judged measure was this war,
when everything we are fighting for might have been won
by money and negotiation! Our only solace under it is
the honor achieved by our arms; but this at a terrible sacrifice of life. How nobly the training of West Point has
vindicated itself! This war has settled the wisdom and
value of that institution, and that is one good consequence
of it. I read with great satisfaction and interest your account of your comfortable berth and its agreeable concomi-
tants; but it was almost cruel to tantalize me with the
description, fated, as I am, not to see the picture. A voyage
across, as you say, is very easy now; but how am I, before the period of decrepitude comes on, ever to break away
from the trammels that bind me down here? If I had resolutely refused the mayoralty last June, I might have got

off this summer with my son ; but we are too easily persuaded to keep office, especially one of which I have so
much reason to be proud, — but cannot you visit us ?　I
will return with you, even if I have to resign the mayoralty.
Pray, if possible, come and see us once more, if but for a
month or a fortnight. . . . .

" Yours sincerely, always,

" W. W. Seaton."

In awarding just praise to the graduates of West
Point — the military genius and heroic valor of those
of her sons who, in drawing their sword in the cause
of Southern independence, achieved immortal fame, as
well as the signal ability and undaunted courage of
those who sustained the North, having alike added
fresh lustre to that nursery of arms — Mr. Seaton did
not in any degree seek to depreciate the gallantry of
our volunteers, or the talent and great deeds of Winfield Scott.　If, as some critics assert, Scott's military
prestige culminated at Lundy's Lane, — though Wellington said that his march to Mexico was the greatest
achievement of modern warfare, — it cannot be denied
that the civil talent evinced in his organization of
Mexican society ; the peace he gave that distracted
country, torn as to-day by faction and anarchy ; the
order and content growing out of the presence of his
invading and triumphant army, added laurels to his
name not surpassed in brilliancy by his deeds of arms.
After a series of victories following the great successes
of the gallant Taylor, Scott rode into the grand
Plaza, the folds of the American flag waving from
the palace of the Montezumas.　He had conquered
Mexico, and — a greater victory still — he conquered
the love and blessings of her people.

General Scott, a year younger than Mr. Seaton, the companion of his boyhood, and cherished friend until parted by death, shared with him in Richmond the tuition of the learned and eccentric Ogilvie, Earl of Finlater, and it was doubtless to his teachings, as was notably the case with other pupils of the genial pedagogue, that the future great Captain owed his love of "polite letters." Scott prided himself as greatly on the purity of his French accent, the felicity of his "retort courteous," his critical acumen and apposite quotation, as on his ability to lead serried ranks to victory. And, indeed, his taste for literary discussion and allusion inspired his staff with a salutary terror, as he required his *aides* to be as conversant with the classics as with field-tactics and the science of fortification. A gentleman present described his amusement at the consternation of the General's military family on one occasion, when their chief, in the presence of a distinguished circle, was arguing some literary point, illustrating it by a quotation from Pope, whereupon one of his *aides*, whose usual accuracy was, perhaps, a little obscured by a late dinner, incautiously asked, "Is that from Shakespeare, General?" Scott turned majestically, and, transfixing the unfortunate querist by his severity of look and tone, replied: "Sir, I am deeply humiliated that a member of my personal staff should be so ignorant as to confound Pope with Shakespeare. Be good enough to leave the room, sir!" Scott was an untiring talker; and few persons surpassed him in the charm of those monologues, heaped up as they were with instructive and entertaining reminiscence of his magnificent career, — an interminable parenthesis of anecdote, which in Mr. Seaton's drawing-room often stretched to an hour past midnight,— the General occasionally refreshing his memory by a pinch of snuff, which, in imitation of Napoleon, he carried loose in his vest pocket. His voice was sweet, his countenance and blue eyes gentle in expression, his manner of true Southern courtesy to ladies and exceeding kindness to young people, while, like Saul, "from his shoulders and upwards he was higher than any of the people"; but the severe wound received at Lundy's Lane in his left shoulder partially disabled him, slightly drawing down that side, without, however, impairing the majesty of his height and imposing presence. General Scott held the pen of a ready writer,— rather, indeed, it was thought, to the detriment of his political aspirations, and was not a little vain of his *eloquence de billet*. A note or two are subjoined, as thoroughly characteristic of his tone of expression:—

"MY DEAR SIR, — The Hon. Messrs. Barrow, White, and Green, whom I accidentally met, have engaged themselves to eat oysters and terrapins with me this evening after the arrival of the mail, say at nine o'clock. They were afraid of too much anxiety and depression, but I promised to keep their spirits up by *pouring spirits down*, if there should be an excess of bad news over the good by the mails. I hope for the reverse, — that all that has been bad may be reversed.

"I sent General Clinch to the Capitol this morning to invite you and some half-dozen other friends to join us, but the General has just told me that he could not find you, and I am equally unsuccessful. This is written *ex cathedra* from your editorial chair, and I hope you will obey the wishes of your friends, however short the notice. Come thou then, and rejoice with us.

"Very truly yours,

"WINFIELD SCOTT.

"Wednesday, October 9.

"W. W. SEATON, ESQ."

"MY DEAR MR. AND MRS. SEATON, — I am quite unlucky — I may say, unhappy — in respect to that same fried chicken, — a dish that I do infinitely affect. But I have invited for the day a stranger in the land, Judge Woolley, of Kentucky, formerly of the army, one of Crittenden's friends; and as I am obliged to forego the happiness of meeting the ladies, his Honor the Mayor — also a gallant Colonel, and as such amenable to the call, *Roast Beef*, or *Peas on the Trencher*, as well as to the 2d section — ought to dine with me. The case being plain, I rely upon his *better part* to send him accordingly. My dinner shall be set forward an hour, all the way till three o'clock.

"*Apropos* of late hours, here is a charming epistle of eight pages from Crittenden, complaining that Archer and myself starve him by compelling him to dine regularly with one of us at four.

"And so I make my Sunday morning bow, reserving one more profound for the evening.

"WINFIELD SCOTT."

"WEST POINT, N. Y., September 9, 1863.

"MY DEAR MR. SEATON, — After a long and most pleasing intimacy with your family, it is painful to think it unlikely that I shall ever be again in Washington. Travelling has become in my case difficult, as I am obliged to take with me my go-cart (Brougham), coachman, and valet, with many other 'means and appliances to boot.' My migrations, therefore, must in future be short and rare, perhaps exclusively limited to the fifty miles between this place and

New York. Yet a few days in Washington would enable me to hunt up certain historical matters much needed for the memoirs I have, very recently, undertaken to write. In respect to two of these, I think you may, without much labor, be able to help me, —

" 1. The proposition to abolish the office of Major-General or Commanding-General was often before Congress. In the last instance C. J. (*not* Jos. R.) Ingersoll made an extravagant speech in my favor, declaring that, perhaps but for my services, that body (the one he was then addressing) might not be in existence. This speech was made in his last three terms in the House of Representatives. To the great regret of the public, your Annals of Congress stopped short of that period, and there's not a file of the National Intelligencer within my reach. Probably your memory may be able to fix the date of the speech within a much narrower period, and perhaps my young friend, Miss ———, may be kind enough to copy the short passage alluded to.

" 2. Sir Henry Bulwer, who I think was some two years in the United States, was quite a dinner orator. In some speech, being hard pressed for complimentary topics, he ran parallels between certain Englishmen and Americans, which was read to me, I think from the Intelligencer. Alexander Hamilton and ——— were in one of the parallels, and Sir Walter Scott and your humble servant in another. There was again much extravagance on my subject, in the latter. Sir Walter Scott, it was said, had turned history into romance, and the American, in allusion to Mexico, had done the reverse, &c. Far be it from me to arrogate to myself much of the merit attributed by either of the orators cited, but should be happy to refer accurately to the passages in question. Again I appeal to your friendship for help. Sir Henry's compliment is not found in his dinner speech before the Maryland Historical Society, as reported; it must therefore have been delivered in some other place, or the Commercial omitted it in deference to Mr. Webster, who spoke eloquently on the same occasion. Until within ten days, I felt confident that the speech was made at Baltimore. Did Sir H. make a second speech before that society? Messrs. J. P. Kennedy, Meredith, and Latrobe say not. The Secretary of the New York Historical Society says that he did not speak before that body. . . . . I should say that the passage in question had been wilfully left out. Pardon this tedious note.

"With the kindest regards to Mrs. and Miss Seaton,

"I remain your friend,

"Winfield Scott.

"W. W. Seaton, Esq."

Mr. Seaton, as usual foremost in the recognition of merit, had been especially solicitous regarding the creation, or, rather, revival, of the rank of Lieutenant-General in favor of General Scott, not only for the reason of their long friendship and his State pride in the noble Virginian, but as a matter of justice; this honor, approved of by the majority of his countrymen, having been mainly withheld by the action of a party and political feeling inimical to General Scott.

A prominent Northern politician thus alludes to the circumstance in a bright note: —

"Boston, February, 1858.

"My dear Mr. Seaton, — I hope your Grace is well. As I was not permitted to see Gustavus Adolphus nor Napoleon, I thank the gods that I am a contemporary of yours. Not an annual 'Thanksgiving' ushered into nativity by pumpkin-pies, drums, and fifes, but a daily offering before an altar where the candles of esteem and regard are always burning. . . . .

"I saw Mr. Ashmun the other day for a moment, and we had a word about your Excellency, which would have made your ears tingle and perhaps blush. Do great men ever blush ? . . . . .

"General Scott spoke to me of the Lieutenant-Generalship, and I took the liberty of mentioning how nobly you had acted with the President in this matter. Wrong or no wrong, I could not help it, because it was so just, and like yourself. . . . . I met Colonel Benton here, who was highly pleased. He was well received, and may well be proud of the respect and attention which have been shown him by the 'cold and chilling North.'

"If you will take the trouble to send to the freight depot, you will find a kit of mackerel, which I hope you will enjoy. *If* you do enjoy them, *thank* the gods and *think* of me."

Henry Stephen Fox, whose sad death Mr. Seaton announced to his friend, was born in 1791, the son of General Henry Stephen Fox of the British army, who bore part in the battle of Lexington, 1775. His grandmother was a daughter of the Duke of Richmond, through whom this distinguished family derived from Charles II. and Henry of Navarre. A sister of Mr. Fox married Major-General William Napier, one of the brilliant brothers of that renowned family of warriors. Mr. Fox was a nephew of the great Charles James Fox, whose portraits he strongly resembled, and inherited no small share of the talent common to his race, which, however, in his case was so marred and obscured by eccentricity as to be worth little to its possessor. He had been in the diplomatic career for a number of years in the East, and latterly in South America, whence he was named to Washington as British Envoy, and successor to the handsome, genial, and popular Sir Charles Vaughan. Mr. Fox rarely entered general society, or any house save that of a colleague; his intercourse with the government even seldom passing beyond scant official ceremonies. His habits and dress were singularly at variance with the people and modes around him. He rose at three o'clock in the afternoon, and would appear about six o'clock on Pennsylvania Avenue taking his morning walk.

A gentleman on one occasion meeting him at dusk in the Capitol grounds, urged him to return with him to dinner, to which Mr. Fox replied that "he would willingly do so, but his people were waiting breakfast for him." On the occasion of the funeral of a member of the Diplomatic Corps, turning to the wife of the Spanish Minister, he said, "How very odd we all look by daylight!" it being the first time he had seen his colleagues except by candle-light. He went to bed at daylight, after watering his plants, of which he .was passionately fond, and which he had a mania for collecting, also entomological specimens, and furniture of every description, which constantly arrived in vans from auctions far and near, cumbering attics, cellars, stairways; the immense accumulation found at his death never having even been opened. He died possessed of a large amount of money in bank in this country; and yet with such sums at command could rarely be induced to pay the smallest bill, — resisting, for instance, the claims of the cartmen who brought articles to his residence, which he would allow to be

left on the pavement rather than give the men their
due. This was eccentricity, not parsimony, for he was
known to be even reckless in some expenditures. Like
his celebrated kinsman, Charles James Fox, he played
much and for high stakes at cards, but had not the
reputation of being always prompt in the settlement
of debts of honor. He led the life of a hermit, — his
fear of intrusion amounting to a mania, his grounds
and residence being almost barricaded to keep even
inquisitive eyes at a distance,—and he never entertained, except to give gentlemen dinners, and those
rarely, assigning as a reason, that he " would have to
shake hands with the women "; but he appeared to be
amused *en petit comité*, and knew the gossip of society,
to which he himself contributed not a little in the
innumerable stories circulated of his oddities. He
thought American women pretty, as a rule, but " looking as if they physicked themselves into ill health."
He was scrupulously neat, in nankeen pantaloons
guiltless of straps (for those were the days when such
things were), a coat constructed years before by a Rio
Janeiro tailor, swallow-tailed, blue, with brass buttons ;
a shirt collar nearly concealing the crown of his head,
a large hat suggestive of West India planter or Spanish contrabandisto, and always a huge green silk um-
brella. And yet with this singular costume, and an
exceeding awkwardness of movement, there was· a
musical voice, an air of peculiar refinement, and the
unmistakable impress of a gentleman. He was tall
and excessively thin, with the peculiar expression and
cadaverous complexion of a confirmed opium-eater.
His observation was acute, his conversation at times

fascinating, and he was noted for his wit. One of his famous *mots* was recorded by Lord Byron, who, writing from Naples, says : " I met the other day Henry Fox, who has been dreadfully ill, and, as he says, so changed that his oldest creditors would not know him."

"LONDON, 1847.

"MY DEAR SIR, — .... Your valuable present was handed me by Mr. Curtis within fourteen days of his departure from New York ; a remarkable quick passage, which might tempt you to the chance of a similar wafting across the ocean if you had not taken too firm root in your native land to be moved by any northwester, — which I begin to think is the case. . . . . The conduct of the government of the United States, in the matter of Mexico, has occasioned many reflections to be made by the serious part of English society. That 'repudiating' America should have invaded a younger and neighboring Republic because it had not and could not pay its debts is a measure thought to be pregnant with retributive consequences ; and the sooner you back out of that false step, the sooner you will return to the enjoyment of the high moral reputation you once had. I think Mr. Clay right, that an amalgamation with those corrupt Mexicans will eventually bring about the ruin of all that is moral and admirable in your government. All history points to such results as inevitable, and no Englishman, who feels as he ought to do, wishes to see your country degraded. Pray elect Mr. Clay if you can, or some one not of the Polk school. The people of England have been suffering for their mad speculations. What is to be done with Ireland no one ventures to say. To temporize with that great evil is all that we can do. . . . .

" Ever yours."

In 1840 Mr. Seaton had accepted at the hands of

his fellow-citizens the highest testimony of their respect and confidence in their power to offer, — the dignity of the mayoralty, — which he had declined as early as 1820, and again, in 1834, resisted the following expressed wish of his constituents : —

"WASHINGTON, May 18, 1834.

"DEAR SIR, — For the last two years the propriety of presenting you as a candidate for the mayoralty of our city has been acknowledged by our friends, believing you to be the only individual on whom the respectable part of the community and the party would concentrate their force. In the present state of things, the Whigs must be perfectly blind if they do not see a defeat. before them. . . . . . You are the one whom all good men will support, and I beg to know, in their name, if you will consent to have your name presented for the office. . . . . .   .

"Very truly yours,

"Jo. L. KUHN.

"W. W. SEATON, ESQ."

Mr. Seaton's inaugural address was characteristic of the man, — courteous, regretful for the possible mortification felt by his unsuccessful opponents, modest, yet firm in the intention to uphold his own sense of right, and to do his duty, — the watchword of his life.

Never were the promises of an incoming magistrate more abundantly fulfilled than during the succeeding ten years in which Mr. Seaton was unanimously recalled to the mayoralty, an unprecedented tenure of the office in this country. In his civic administration Mr. Seaton manifested an ability, a fidelity and firmness, an uncompromising honesty and sense of justice in the discharge of his duties, that marked him as a model magistrate. He labored incessantly for the best interests of the community over which he was the watchful guardian, advancing with the most earnest solicitude all movements tending to its moral and intellectual progress; inaugurating projects for its material improvement, adornment, and solid comfort, and with a full knowledge of its people and their needs, devoted himself with unceasing interest and just pride to securing their welfare. By his personal influence in Congress he obtained so many grants and privileges, that the results of his persuasive power became a jest among the honorable members, who predicted that "if Mr. Seaton remained mayor much longer he would bankrupt the national treasury."

Bringing these dispositions to bear upon the execution of his trust, Mr. Seaton's administration was naturally the most successful in the history of the metropolis, the results of his far-sighted views, of his philanthropic suggestions and measures, being visible in the best features of its subsequent prosperity. Early in Mr. Seaton's administration an incident occurred, slight in itself, but striking in its testimony to his loyalty to truth and delicate conscience.

At the expiration of Mr. Van Buren's term of office, the Corporation of Washington obsequiously passed a vote of thanks to the retiring President for the courtesy, liberality, and kindly interest evinced by him towards the city during his administration. Mr. Seaton considered this proceeding on the part of the Councils as derogatory to their self-respect and independence, the fact being notorious that from no previous President had the city received so little benefit or token of good-will, either through the personal

action of the Chief Magistrate or from his recommend-
ations to Congress, the omission of even the heretofore
ordinary civilities and hospitalities offered by the
Executive to the citizens having become a matter of
indignant comment in the community.   Mr. Seaton, in
upholding his magisterial and personal dignity, could
not permit his name to ratify, as it were, not only a
perversion of the true feeling of the society of which
he was the recognized leader, but also an *ex officio*
misrepresentation of fact relative to public measures,
for which, in the corporation archives, he would be
recorded as responsible; he therefore sent in the following veto:—

" . . . . If the fulfilment of this resolution could be
construed as an expression of mere personal good wishes for
a gentleman going into retirement, who had filled the office
of President of the United States, I should not object to
uniting with the two Boards in the ceremony; although, as
a tribute not rendered to Presidents Jefferson, Madison,
Monroe, and Adams, I might deem it uncalled for, and a
precedent not altogether judicious.   But as the terms of
the resolution express a sentiment of high respect for the
official course of the President, and as that sentiment would
naturally be construed by him into one of approbation, my
signature to the resolution would not be in unison with my
avowed opinion, and would be known to the President himself as hollow and insincere.

"Though, therefore, I cannot hesitate as to the course
which consistency and self-respect require me to pursue,
my decision has not been unattended with embarrassment.
By signing the resolution I should virtually retract my
known opinions in regard to the administration of President Van Buren, while, by withholding my signature, I

may appear to aim an incivility at the Chief Magistrate of
the Union, — a misconstruction which I should exceedingly
regret, as it would impute to me a motive repugnant to my
feelings, and to my sense of propriety. But, however unwilling to incur such an imputation, I must meet it in
preference to its more objectionable alternative. . . . . .

       " I remain, gentlemen, very respectfully,

          " Your obedient servant,

               " W. W. SEATON."

The Councils feared that the Democratic party in
Congress would visit upon the city their disapprobation of the recalcitrant mayor; but there is a spirit of
appreciation of right in all men, and so it was in this
case, for the measures for the relief or improvement of
the city never lost a vote by the honesty of its chief
magistrate. This duty had been the more distasteful
to Mr. Seaton to perform, as he had maintained during
former years very friendly and even intimate social
relations with Mr. Van Buren, who always testified
for him personally the highest respect, the following
note being one among similar expressions of kindly
feeling : —

               " ALBANY, April 27, 1823.

    " DEAR SIR, — My friend and partner, Benjamin F.
Butler, Esq., accompanies the Vice-President to Washington, — make him acquainted with Mrs. Seaton and Mr.
Gales. A Southern man would say that he is one of the
finest young men in *the world;* but after the sober manner
of the North, I can only say that he is a young gentleman
of the finest promise and character in this State.

        " Your friend,

            " M. VAN BUREN.

" MR. SEATON."

Mr. Seaton's prolonged career, so inwoven with the social and political annals of Washington, was no less intimately identified with its national and philanthropic societies, which bear on their records the evidences of his unselfish labors and invaluable influence. Among the more noted of those which claimed during many years his earnest interest and constant co-operation was the Colonization Society, of which he was from its inception one of the Vice-Presidents.

"For many years," writes a well-known philanthropist, "Mr. Seaton was an executive member of the American Colonization Society, which ever enjoyed his confidence and regard, and received the powerful patronage of his persuasive pen and influential journal. His personal appearance, the geniality and warmth of his disposition, his unceasing kindness of heart, — all that goes to make up a good and lovely man, — were not only characteristics, but were speaking and visible features of his entire life. His name will always be associated with the early days and eminent men of the Republic."

As the result of the labors of this beneficent society, Mr. Seaton hoped for the gradual solution of the *questio vexata* of slavery; for although by inheritance and association attached to this Southern patriarchal institution, a witness to the general benevolence of its operation and the happiness of the race subjected to its protecting administration, Mr. Seaton yet recognized its coexisting evils attaching to the master and the body politic of the state, the complications and desolating results of which his sagacious mind discerned, but which, with others of the wise and unselfish, he was powerless to avert. With his benevolent nature and keen sense of responsibility, he naturally cared for those who called him master, with the gentle forbearance and kindness to which their condition especially appealed. In the following editorial which the press widely commended as a " Blister for the Tribune," Mr. Seaton, prophetically commenting on the evils of sudden emancipation throughout the South, incidentally alludes to the practical illustration given by Mr. Gales and himself of the earnestness of their philanthropic theories : —

"Our active contemporary assumes imaginary ground for an adversary, attacks a position which was never occupied, and having carried it with great gallantry, rejoices in a victory when there has been no battle. This is a decided improvement upon the tactics of the redoubtable Captain Bobadil, for that hero proposed the *bona fide* killing of his foes, though he never achieved it. The ingenious editor of the Tribune has brought his peculiar strategy to bear upon ourselves by ascribing to us the 'assumption that the South unanimously desires the President to restore slavery.' We disclaim the assumption, for we know it not to be true. . . . . All that we ask of the President in regard to slavery is to let it alone as a policy. . . . . The theoretical abolition of slavery was as much beyond the President's power as it transcended his constitutional right. . . . . There are thousands of masters in the South who would gladly get rid, if possible, of their slaves. The number of negroes offered to the Colonization Society, in every Southern State, for removal to Africa, during the last thirty years, is proof of the fact. . . . . Can the fiercest or most fanatical friend of the negro look with complacency on the overwhelming ruin of the whites of the South, upon the sudden demolition of the whole framework and foundations of society of that vast region? .... Is such a revolution the work of a day, or should it be one of an age? It is not in the interest of slavery we speak, but in that of humanity, of civilization, we protest against the President undertaking to trample on State Constitutions, State Laws, and State Institutions. As for slavery itself, we have long regarded it as a deciduous institution, but it must fall by the action of the States themselves, not by usurped power or convulsion. The editor of the Tribune mistakes if he supposes that we oppose all arbitrary meddling with slavery because we are fanatical advocates of the institution. It is very easy to be generous and philanthropic at other people's expense ;— but we can tell our contemporary, that the publishers of the National Intelligencer have emancipated more slaves at their own cost and out of their own pockets, long before the present agitation, than all the abolitionists put together between the Penobscot and the Potomac, including the zealous emancipationist, the editor of the Tribune."

Thus, in giving his slaves unbought freedom, Mr. Seaton individually carried out the principle to which he so earnestly gave his editorial adhesion, in the humane scheme of African colonization, realizing in his own personal efforts, in the most equitable and unselfish manner, the wishes of Lafayette, as expressed in the following letter to Mrs. Bomford : —

'" January 1, 1827.

" .... I am much obliged to you, dear Clara, for your inquiries after my beloved friends Fanny and Camilla Wright. .... These noble girls have devoted themselves to a noble cause, but I am afraid the smallness of the scale and the shortness of their purse will not effect an end proportionate to their sacrifice of society and friends, for they have turned pioneers in the woods of Wolf River, Tennessee. How much more extensive would be a measure of gradual emancipation in the District of Columbia, however distant might be the assigned term, connected with colonization ! The state of slavery, especially in that emporium of foreign visitors and European ministers, is a most lamentable drawback on the example of independence and freedom presented to the world by the United States. It would be for our friends of the National Intelligencer a glorious task to examine how far those truths can be offered to a generous population, and to take the lead in making them by degrees palatable, thereby softening the susceptibilities partly founded on considerations quite foreign to the main question. I hope Mrs. Seaton and child, whose birth nearly dates with my departure, are in good health."

In relation to the feeling excited among foreigners in Washington on this subject, to which Lafayette alludes, the following note from an esteemed French minister is not without interest. The young prince whose birth he thus wished to commemorate was the posthumous son of the *Duc de Berri,* — who had been assassinated at the opera-house in Paris, — and now known as the *Duc de Bordeaux,* or *Henri V.,* as he is styled by the Legitimists of France, who hope confidently for his restoration to the throne of his ancestors.

" DEAR SIR, — It is my intention, in celebration of the baptism of the young prince who is one day to rule over the Franks, to make free one poor little slave child. I pray, sir, please you, without any mention of my name to obtain information respecting the young slave girl who is spoken of in the enclosed advertisement, to be sold at public sale, by Moses Poor, auctioneer. This communication I desire to be for yourself alone. . . . . .

"I have the honor to offer you the assurance of my distinguished consideration.

"Yours,

"E. Hyde de Neuville.

"Washington, 25 June, 1821.
  "Monsieur Seaton."

No project for the improvement of the city had Mr. Seaton's more cordial advocacy and anxious desire for its success than the Washington Monument Society, of which he was one of the founders, his relations with which dated from the day of its organization, when he was elected Vice-President, the memorandum on the first leaf of its record being in his writing.

"Of that small but select band of patriots," writes one of the officers of the Society, "Mr. Seaton was the only survivor, with the exception of Peter Force, who, in consideration of being as it were *Ultimus Romanorum*, was appointed to fill the vacancy caused by Mr. Seaton's death. Surpassed by none in affectionate veneration for *Pater Patriæ*, the minutes of the Society from the first day of its existence bear tribute to his zeal, his earnest and valuable discharge of all the duties pertaining to his office; his presence at the Board inspired hope, while his judicious counsel, his constant and patriotic devotion to the best interests of the cause during the long period of thirty-three years, contributed mainly to its success."

It was during Mr. Seaton's mayoralty that the corner-stone of the Washington Monument was laid with elaborate ceremonies and much enthusiasm, the occasion being memorable also as the last appearance in public of President Taylor. Mr. Winthrop's beautiful address, felicitous as every effort invariably is of that liberal scholar, trained statesman, and high-bred gentleman, was followed by proceedings so prolonged under the overpowering heat of a July sun, that the President, already indisposed, and who had consented to be present only at Mr. Seaton's earnest solicitation, was overcome, and in fact there received his death-stroke, — as Governor Corwin jocosely declared, "through the malice prepense of Mr. Seaton, who thought that Fillmore would make a better Chief Magistrate." And in truth the Intelligencer, while doing full justice to General Taylor's frank honesty, good judgment, and brilliant soldierly qualities, and by no means indorsing Mr. Webster's opinion that "his nomination was one not fit to be made," yet deemed it fortunate for the country that the accession of Mr. Fillmore should place the helm of state in the hands of a more experienced pilot, this prepossession being abundantly justified by the calm strength and conservative wisdom marking Mr. Fillmore's administration.

However the surviving participant in this generous action may " blush to find it fame," yet, in justice to Mr. Winthrop and Mr. Webster, the following evidence of the modest yet munificent spirit of Northern gentlemen must not be withheld, strikingly illustrative as it is, as well of the cordial kindness uniting the "brother-peoples " during the happy era of good feeling as of the reticent delicacy of a Southern gentlewoman, who, without appeal to the generosity of her countrymen, and declining it even when thus unobtrusively proffered, had maintained the dignity of her position as widow of a President of the United States.

"Boston, October 9, 1846.

"My dear Sir, — I was greatly grieved, before leaving Washington, to learn through some friends of the destitute condition of Mrs. Madison, and resolved to see if something in the shape of permanent and periodical relief could not be provided for her by those richer than myself. I think that means may be procured among us close-fisted, dividend-loving Yankees for buying her a little annuity, say of four or five hundred dollars per annum, for the remainder of her life, if it be thought worth while to do so. In order that we may do this, however, it will be necessary to know her precise age, as that will determine the cost, — and as the *older she is* the larger *the annuity will be* for the same money, it is desirable that she should not use the proverbial privilege of her sex on this subject. Two or three points, then, I should like to be assured of, viz. : —

"1. Whether Mrs. Madison's circumstances are really such as to make such an arrangement desirable for her.

"2. If so, her exact age in years ; if her birthday could be ascertained it might be best.

"3. How such a provision could best be communicated to her *after it is made up*, without occasioning her any feelings of delicacy or mortification, or even obligation.

"Pray do not yet commit anybody to this arrangement, as there may still be a 'slip betwixt the cup and the lip.' But Mr. Webster and I *have a notion* that we can accomplish the matter if we try.

"With kind regards to Mrs. Seaton,

"Yours most truly and respectfully,

"Robert C. Winthrop.

"Hon. W. W. Seaton."

During Mr. Seaton's official incumbency, the reception and entertainment of celebrities naturally devolved on him, the citizens appreciating their good fortune in that the reputation of the metropolis should be sustained by the unfailing hospitality of their civic chief. Among his more noted guests — in addition to Presidents expectant and *in esse*, and unnumbered distinguished citizens and foreigners — may be mentioned General Bertrand, the famous companion-in-arms and friend of Napoleon, who accompanied his imperial master to St. Helena, and whose devotion drew from the illustrious captive the signal praise of being *fidèle parmi les infidèles*. More interesting still, perhaps, was his guest, Charles Dickens, whom a nation welcomed with a spontaneity unsurpassed save in the reception of Lafayette. In the raciness and charm of Mr. Seaton's conversation and manner, in the genial goodness stamped on every lineament of his countenance, the great novelist, the keen reader of every phase of human character, at once recognized the qualities of a man whom to know was to love. The immortal Cheeryble Brothers might seem to have been a prevision of the brother-editors of the Intelligencer, whose unlimited generosity and active sympathy with all suffering and wrong, and whose mutual devotion had already passed into history. Nor was there lacking, to complete the portraiture of the trio, the embodied fidelity, shrewdness, and personal devotion of *Tim Linkinwater*, who lived again in the trusted clerk, the lifelong friend of Gales and Seaton, — Thomas Donoho.

The following notes are characteristic in their expression of friendly feeling on the part of the illustrious " Boz " : --

"WASHINGTON, 16th March, 1842.

"MY DEAR SIR, — I am truly obliged to you for your kind note. I am so constantly engaged, however, that I think I *must* deny myself the pleasure of making an appointment with you, which I could scarcely keep without making a most uncomfortable scramble of it. I will report my knowledge of the lions to you, and you shall judge how I have been shown about.

"In case I should forget it when we meet to-night, may I venture to ask two favors of you, — or rather one favor with two heads.

"It is that you will kindly (if you see no objection) let my friends here know through that channel which is open to you, and over which you so ably preside, that whenever I make an appointment I keep it; and that it gives me great uneasiness and pain to be placarded all over the town as intending to make a visit to the theatre, when I have given no authority whatever to any person to publish such an announcement; and secondly, that travelling as we do, we can never return the calls of our friends, in consequence of their immense number, and our very limited stay in any one place.

"Let me take this opportunity of thanking you, most heartily and earnestly, for the exceedingly kind attention I have received at your hands, and the pleasure I have enjoyed in your society and in that of your family. I need scarcely say that Mrs. Dickens desires me to say as much for her.

"I am, my dear sir, with true regard, faithfully yours,

"CHARLES DICKENS.

"W. W. SEATON, ESQ."

"NIAGARA FALLS, 30th April, 1842.

"MY DEAR SIR, — You will be glad, I know, to receive my hasty report of our safe arrival at this scene of beauty and wonder, — of our being off Western waters and corduroy roads, — and of our looking forward with great pleasure and delight to home. We are perfectly well, and not at all tired by our long journey.

"I have received some documents from the greatest writers in England, relative to the International Copyright, which they call upon me to make public immediately. They have taken fire at my being misrepresented in such a matter, and have acted as such men should.

"They consist of two letters, and a memorial to the American people, signed by Bulwer, Rogers, Hallam, Talfourd, Sydney Smith, and so forth. Not very well knowing. as a stranger, whether it would be best to publish them in newspapers, or in a literary journal, I have sent them to some gentlemen in Boston, and have begged them to decide. In the event of their recommending the first-mentioned course, I have begged them to send a manuscript copy to you immediately.

"We often speak of you and your family, I assure you ; and entertain a lively recollection of your great kindness, and the pleasant hours we passed in your society. Mrs. Dickens unites with me in cordial regards to Mrs. Seaton and your family. And I am always, my dear sir,

"Faithfully yours,

"CHARLES DICKENS.

"P. S. I enclose your son's pleasant and capital letter. Tell him that if he should ever come to London I will 'swing' him about *that city* to some purpose, — being an indifferent good showman of the lions thereof." *

---

* While these words have been in press, that great heart, that teeming brain and loving hand have been stilled, — and to millions whose mortal eyes never beheld him the earth is more sad, the sun less bright, since Charles Dickens went to rest.

The letter referred to from Mr. Seaton's son, then resident in Richmond, is a pleasant picture of Mr. Dickens and of the impression made by him on an enthusiastic, modest young admirer of his genius.

"RICHMOND, March 20, 1842.

". . . . I wrote a hurried note last night, to advise you that Mr. and Mrs. Dickens proposed going to Washington this morning, a delay in the departure of the boat to Nor- . folk preventing their reaching Baltimore so soon as desired ; so they go no farther South. I was amused at the earnestness with which he asked me if I was *sure* St. Louis is farther north than Charleston.

"C.'s letter reached me too late to allow me to comply with your wishes; and though I should of course have attended to your behests, it would have placed me rather more in the attitude of a lion-hunter than I like. Indeed, I have barely escaped as it is. I sent up my card to him, anticipating that I should find a crowd, and determined to pester him with very little of my chat, after offering my services. I thought I might approach him calmly, and like Malvolio, 'quenching my familiar smile with an austere regard of control,' address him in the loftiest style of hospitable welcome. I had only time to frame an appropriate exordium, when his Secretary informed me that Mr. Dickens had been expecting me, and would be glad to see me. Entering the room with somewhat of a tremor, for I knew not whether he would 'roar as gently as a sucking dove,' I was seized by the hand and almost *slung* across the room, and a dozen remarks and questions addressed to me in a breath. For he was entirely alone and writing. In reply, I at first could only gasp, without much power of articulation ; for I suppose few persons feel with more devotion the homage due to the majesty of genius than I. He proposed a walk, and we went to French Gardens. I need not say that I was delighted with his affable, cordial, frank, and conversible manner, a strong proof of which is, that in ten minutes I nearly forgot his distinction as an author, and conversed with him on a variety of topics as they naturally arose. We discussed law, London, negro songs, Richmond, etc. And in truth, if I were to sum up in one sentence the impression he left on my mind, it would be, that he is a thorough good fellow. As you may suppose, from your own feelings, I sedulously avoided the crowded streets, having no idea of being pointed out as having seized Boz immediately and monopolized him. On our return we found several gentlemen, and, with Mrs. Dickens, we walked to Church Hill. She spoke of the pleasure she enjoyed at our house, and their hope soon to see you again. Afterwards we went to the Capitol, but persons crowding in to see them, I made my bow, after a kind invitation from him to call whenever I felt disposed. I saw that he was likely enough to have people around him, and did not see him again that day; though I felt unquiet and restless, I must confess, and could hardly resist going again.

"On Saturday morning I sent up my card, and sat a short time; but he was at breakfast, and expected a crowd of visitors, so did not go out. He had been up late at a supper the night before, and laughed at my reason for not attending it, that I should have been called on for a speech. *He* was, I hear, very happy, and every one else very insipid in their efforts, except Mr. Ritchie, with whom he was greatly pleased.

"At his levee, from twelve to two, I attended to present a lady, and spoke awhile with him. He and his wife offered to bear letters, etc., to you from me, which I declined, and took leave. I knew last night that they were receiving friends, and I could with difficulty keep away from the Exchange. Whether from gratified vanity or a purer feeling, admiration of genius, or simply a liking for the man, I know not, but I do feel very sorry that he has gone. I have never seen a man in whom, in so brief a period, I was so greatly interested. His likenesses certainly flatter him, but they cannot give the charm of his face, his rich expression of humor and merriment when he laughs, — his whole face lights up. And then if he is not a man of fine feeling, no confidence is to be placed in the face as an index of the heart. I do sincerely hope his life may be a happy and prosperous one. . . . . .

" Your affectionate son,

" GALES SEATON."

One feature of Mr. Seaton's municipal administration possesses a value hardly to be over-estimated, — his persistent efforts in the cause of public education. His investigations had developed a deplorable state of ignorance among the children of the city, and a general apathy on this vital subject which awakened his most earnest solicitude. During several years the pages of the National Intelligencer were laden with arguments and appeals in this matter, the facts gathered and recorded by Mr. Seaton having produced the deepest impression on his own mind, and, in truth, startled the whole community. In 1842 Mr. Seaton, in his annual communication to the Councils, in the most express language and strongest terms, urged reform in the existing state of education and the immediate adoption of the Massachusetts school system.

" The recommendation in Mr. Seaton's message, in harmony with the enlightened philanthropy of its author, was in advance of public sentiment and encountered great hostility. Public meetings were held on the subject, and the names of John Quincy Adams, Levi Woodbury, and Caleb Cushing are found among those who stood boldly and conspicuously for reform."

A municipal colleague of Mr. Seaton thus records the value of his services in behalf of education : —

"It was to Mr. Seaton's persevering efforts that the youth of this generation are indebted for the present excellent system of public schools. When he entered on the duties of the mayoralty there were only two public schools in the city; but justly estimating the value to the community of a new and improved system, he continued from year to year to press the subject on the attention of the legislative branches of the government, until it was adopted in the fourth year of his administration, from which time the number of schools has continued to increase until their scholars now amount to nearly twice as many thousands as there were hundreds at the time of his inauguration. Among the many beneficent acts of his official life this will stand pre-eminent; and among the many friends in whose hearts his memory will be the longest cherished there will be thousands who, but for his philanthropic efforts, would have been denied the blessings of education, and the manifold benefits resulting from that mental and moral culture which the children of all classes of our fellow-citizens have since enjoyed, by means of the more liberal and enlightened system which he so opportunely introduced and established."

To Mr. Seaton's unfailing interest in the "increase and diffusion of knowledge," and in every movement tending to moral and intellectual progress, the country may be said to be mainly indebted for the successful realization of the beneficent design of James Smithson in the foundation of the Smithsonian Institution. The following sketch of Mr. Seaton's services in connection with this valuable society is extracted from an eloquent eulogy by its distinguished secretary, Professor Joseph Henry, whose profound learning and benevolent nature Mr. Seaton held in reverential regard, whose name is honored wherever science finds a votary, and whose modesty is only equalled by the value of his discoveries in the operations of Nature's laws:—

"The Smithson fund, paid into the treasury of the United States in 1838, had been, with other moneys, lent by the government to the State of Arkansas, and remained for eight years without appropriation to any object contemplated by the donor. In 1846 Mr. Seaton, being then mayor of Washington, and surpassed by no one in zeal for the public good, and in the influence due to his rare social qualities, his known integrity, and peculiarly winning and unaffected eloquence, united with other gentlemen in urging upon Congress the organization of an establishment which should at length do justice to the benevolent views which had dictated the bequest. Their labors, after much opposition, were finally crowned with success; the good faith of the country was redeemed by an unconditional assumption of the debt incurred by the improper disposition of the fund. . . . . The Institution was placed under the guardianship of fifteen regents, among whom was included the mayor of Washington, a provision chiefly due to the zealous interest which had been manifested by Mr. Seaton in his enlightened advocacy of the enterprise.

"At the first meeting of the Board of Regents he was elected Treasurer, and subsequently one of the building committee. The former office he continued to hold until the time of his death, and during the whole of this period, nearly twenty years, discharged its duties without other compensation than the pleasure he derived from an association with the Institution, and the laudable pride he felt in contributing to its prosperity and usefulness. It is well known that at the time of its organization a wide diversity of opinion existed as to the practical means which would be most suitable for realizing the objects of the legacy. Mr. Seaton, on mature reflection, finally gave his cordial support to the policy which sought to impress on the Institution a truly cosmopolitan character. He strenuously advocated the plan which the Secretary had been invited to submit to the Regents, and which looked to the advancement of knowledge chiefly through the encouragement and publication of original researches, a system which may be claimed, without undue pretension, to have made the Institution favorably known, and to have exerted a well-recognized influence wherever men occupy themselves with intellectual pursuits.

"The relation borne by Mr. Seaton to the city of Washington, the delight with which he watched and aided its progress, a native taste also for artistic embellishment, led him to take special interest in the architectural character of the building and the ornamentation of the grounds surrounding it.

"Mr. Seaton, from his familiarity with the early history of the Institution, as well as from his long experience in public office was enabled to offer suggestions to the Board of Regents, always marked by clearness and soundness of judgment. The social attentions which he was accustomed to extend to the Regents, and to gentlemen invited to lecture before the Institution, were but the expression of his characteristic hospitality; but by thus adding to the pleasure of their sojourn in the capital, he contributed largely to increase the number of its friends and supporters. The columns of the Intelligencer under his direction were always open to the defence of the policy adopted and the course pursued by the Institution, and he rarely failed to soften by the courtesy of his manner and the moderation of his expressions any irritable feeling which might arise in the discussion of conflicting opinions. It would indeed be difficult to say in how many and in what various ways he contributed to the popularity as well as the true interests of the Institution. The Secretary, who was in the habit of conferring with him on all points requiring mature deliberation, may with justice acknowledge that he never failed to derive important assistance from the wisdom of the counsels of this distinguished and lamented citizen, who will be remembered as one of the most constant and enlightened friends and benefactors of the Institution."

One of the most interesting public incidents occurring during Mr. Seaton's official life was the relief extended by the government and people of this country to ill-fated Ireland. The sad tidings reached us that once more that land was stricken by famine and pestilence, that thousands were perishing for bread; and to Mr. Seaton's own overflowing sympathy with suffering, under whatever form or on whatever shore, are due the conception and inauguration of the movement resulting in such imperial munificence of aid.

"Never," writes a gentleman cognizant of the circumstances, "never shall I forget Mr. Seaton's touching expression, and the words with which he met me one morning in the autumn of 1846. 'I declare,' said he, 'that when I left the office last evening and sat down to dinner, and thought of the famishing Irish, the women and children, I could not eat a mouthful. What can be done?

"Taking his seat at the office table, in a minute he handed me a notice calling upon the Irishmen, and all friends of humanity in Washington, to meet at the City Hall, to adopt measures of relief for our suffering brothers."

At the very large assemblage consequent upon this appeal Mr. Seaton was chosen chairman, making an address which aroused enthusiasm not only in his hearers, but was answered and re-echoed from many a distant point throughout the country, Henry Clay, among other patriots, coming from his retirement to preside at a meeting in New Orleans, and to quicken with his matchless voice this gracious throb of our national heart. Mr. Seaton rested not in his active co-operation until, in a month, ten thousand dollars were collected, a ship chartered and laden with provisions and despatched on her errand of mercy. The bark General Harrison, commanded by a Virginian, arrived early in June, 1847, in the port of the Cove of Cork, now Queenstown, — her officers and crew being received with rejoicing wherever they appeared ; and at Galway a magnificent banquet was held in honor of these bearers of glad tidings, a description of which, and of his own maiden essay in post-prandial oratory, is thus narrated by one of the participants in the pleasant occasion, then a very young man : —

"I was waited on by a committee of gentlemen, at Kilray's Hotel, Galway, and invited to a public dinner to be given the succeeding day by the nobility, gentry, His Worship the Mayor, and their Honors the Corporation of the 'Towne of Galway,' at Nolan's Hotel, Eyre Square. It was also intimated to me that I should be expected to reply to a regular toast. How much I felt honored, and how far

' flustered ' by this intelligence, at that tender age, would be difficult to say.

"When the committee, of whom I remember Sir Thomas Blake, of Menlough Castle, and Vicar-General Roche, had shaken hands and retired, I started out for a walk by the banks of the beautiful Lough Carib, and the ruins of Tierland Castle. The delicious air and tranquillizing melody of numerous thrushes, with the exquisite scenery, and its novelty and poetic associations, so drove all thoughts of my speech far from me, that when I found myself the next evening seated at the banquet, I had as little idea of what my speech was to be as I now have of what it was. His Worship the Mayor presided, assisted by the most distinguished representatives of the ' City of the Tribes,' — the Blakes, of Menlo and Renville Castles, the Badkins, the Burkes, the Ffrenches, Lord Wallscourt, of Ardfry, and three hundred other prominent gentlemen.

" The hall was a noble one, draped with the American, British, and Irish flags, a profusion of flowers, while two magnificent bands of British regiments — one of them the famous 43d, or *Faugh-a-ballach* — discoursed inspiring national music.

" The Macedonian had arrived a few days before, and an American bark, the Selma, had that day anchored off Galway, laden with provisions, on the noblest mission to which Heaven ever lent favoring gales.

" The enthusiasm was unbounded, the great Irish heart was lifted up, and swelled almost to bursting, and when, — after a few almost sobbing words of praise and gratitude had ushered in the toast, ' America, the land of the free, and the home of the brave,' and all, rising amid a burst of thundering cheers, had drunk off a bumper, — I heard my name passing from lip to lip and resounding through the hall, any idea of a set speech abandoned me, as it would have done a more accustomed orator. At last, 'when silence, like a poultice came to heal the blows of Sound,' I arose.

" ' Mr. Mayor and Gentlemen — ' Cries of 'Hear, hear,' before I had uttered another word, disconcerted me ; but I remembered that I was but the mouthpiece of my philanthropic countrymen, the speaking-trumpet, as it were, of the bark Harrison, and proceeded without fear. When I sat down, after a speech of half an hour, there was great crowding round me, and hand-shaking, while the health of ' His Worship, William Winston Seaton, Mayor of Washington,' was drunk standing, with three times three, and music by the band.

" When the editors of various papers called to obtain a copy of my address, it would sadly have puzzled me to recall what I uttered during those to me memorable thirty minutes. One point only I adhered to in the speech, — warm laudation of that eminently good man and public benefactor, whose departure our community still mourns, — William Winston Seaton. I gave honor to whom honor was due. I told them to whom pre-eminently the Irish people were indebted. I mentioned the name of that honest, true, heartfelt friend of Ireland and the Irish, by the side of whom, in practical benefits conferred upon their people, a host of their native pretended patriots, craving notoriety, must pale their mirage light.

" I related how Mr. Seaton was the very first to start this Heaven-directed movement in my native land, bent all his energies to the labor of love, and though he had been the means of launching already a victorious armada upon this mission of mercy, even yet he rested nor day nor night, nor proposed to do so, until the last cry of fever and famine in Ireland be turned into tears and prayers of gratitude to God. I told them that he was mainly, if not alone, instrumental, through his personal persuasion with eminent men, in causing the frigate Macedonian to be sent to the relief of our Irish brothers.

"The effect of this just though inadequate eulogy was such that I refrain from the description of the enthusiasm."

Proverbially susceptible to kindness, the ardent Irish heart warmed to Mr. Seaton in gratitude, not only for his unwearied exertions in alleviating their national affliction, but for his constant sympathy and active aid in pen, purse, and kindly words, during his whole life. The story of these services had been borne to their native land by many a son of Erin, so that when for a few brief days Mr. Seaton sojourned in the Emerald Isle, he was welcomed by hospitality from the Lord Lieutenant, the late amiable Earl of Carlisle, and more humble friendly hearths. Among those who had spread the fame of his benevolence was the Rev. Mr. Gill, of Galway, "whom I presented," writes his relative, "to Mr. Seaton, the friend of poor Ireland, whose kind reception and warm-hearted welcome delighted the good priest. He had travelled in many lands, and was an enthusiastic admirer of old families, old traditions, and was especially fascinated by Mr. Seaton's manners and winning presence. 'I seemed,' said he, 'to have known him for many years, and had I heard his voice, with bandaged eyes, I should have believed myself to be in the presence of the head of the house of Seaton, whose guest I was some years ago, while sojourning near his lordship's seat in Scotland; and what is still more remarkable, in personal appearance Mr. Seaton bears a singular resemblance to that nobleman.' "

Among the celebrities whom Mr. Seaton had the

gratification of welcoming to his hospitality was the apostle of temperance, Father Mathew, whose labors were crowned with signal success in this country, and who moved amid the fervent blessings of a million of grateful hearts. The following note expresses a graceful recognition of the honors so worthily bestowed on the modest and holy man : —

"RICHMOND, VA., 22d December, 1849.

" HONORED DEAR SIR, — My sojourn in Washington was so short, and my avocations so numerous, that I was prevented from thanking you previous to my departure for your exceeding courtesy and urbanity. The hospitality of the Catholic pastor, my zealous, learned, pious, and most esteemed friend, the Rev. Mr. Donelan, prevented me from enjoying the privilege of being your guest ; but accept my grateful acknowledgment of your kind and courteous invitation. I feel honored by this proof of your approbation of my labors. I thank you and your amiable and most estimable lady for all those delicate attentions, so pleasing to human feelings, which you and Mrs. Seaton have paid to me so gracefully. The happiest moments of my life were passed in Washington, and are to me forever memorable for the high honor conferred on me by your illustrious Houses of Representatives and Senate. Your great and good President, too, complimented me more than I could even hope for, by allowing me the privilege of dining at his table, and, what I prize much more, by treating me as a friend.

" But amidst all the splendors of Washington, not excepting that perfect model of architecture, the thrice majestic Capitol, the most sublime spectacle I beheld was the President of this glorious and mighty country, unattended and alone, in your public streets, in the true Republican simplicity of the olden time. . . . . .

" I have the honor to be, with the most profound respect,
Honored dear Mr. Mayor,

"Yours gratefully and devotedly,

"THEOBALD MATHEW.

"HON. MR. SEATON."

In 1850 Mr. Seaton retired from the mayoralty,
after an unexampled length of service, peremptorily
declining, on the score of advancing age, the office to
which he had been called with unanimity during times
of high party excitement, "and which it would seem
indeed to have rested only with himself to fill to per-
petuity." An address from the citizens, requesting
Mr. Seaton to reconsider his proposed retirement, thus
urges the wishes of his constituents: —

" . . . . We may be permitted to say that you have conferred large benefits upon our city during your successive
terms of office, and that the extended period of your public
service, so honorably prolonged, furnishes the best assurance, not only of the value of those benefits, but of their
appreciation by your fellow-citizens.   We feel confident that
you have lost no portion of that zeal which, through a long
life, you have manifested towards the city, nor the public
of that confidence which it has always so warmly felt and
bestowed.   Looking, then, upon the past and the present,
we can discover no reason, other than the further sacrifice
of your personal interests and quiet, which should induce
you to decline. . . . . .

"With great respect, your fellow-citizens."

In expressing the gratification derived from this
approval of his official life Mr. Seaton says: —

" . . . . But, gentlemen, I crave relief from the engrossing
labors and anxieties of the office, and however your indul-

gence might be disposed to dissent from the plea, I feel that its increasing duties require to be placed in younger hands. It is not without an effort, I confess, that I resist an appeal from so large a body of my fellow-citizens ; but resist I must, and I pray you to excuse my adhering to the purpose I have indicated. I have not words to thank you for this signal proof of your approbation at the end of so long a term of service. . . . .

"I remain your faithful and grateful friend,

"W. W. SEATON."

Upon the occasion of the inauguration of his successor, Mr. Walter Lenox, in the honors of the mayoralty, Mr. Seaton, after receiving the joint resolution of thanks from the two Boards for the able manner in which during ten consecutive years he had discharged his onerous duties, arose and addressed the assemblage with his usual modest and effective eloquence. " He briefly reviewed the prosperity which had attended the infant metropolis during the past ten years ; highly complimented the Senate and House of Representatives for their liberality towards it ; referred with deep feeling to the Washington Monument and to our public schools, — ten years ago there were two, now twenty ; faithfully and glowingly portrayed the advantages of the Smithsonian Institution ; and, adverting with pride to the fact, that during the ten years of his administration there had not been between himself and the Council a single misunderstanding or unkind word, he reiterated his congratulations upon the choice of a gentleman of such energy and intelligence for his successor. We may say, and without contradiction, that it was one of the most felicitous speeches for a retiring

Chief Magistrate we ever heard, and for its brevity, propriety, and good feeling, worthy of being characterized as a model address."

"Turning to Mr. Seaton's record as mayor," writes still another eulogist, "we find in him a model worthy of imitation. Possessing all the requisites to insure success, — honesty, intelligence, firmness, energy, and perseverance, — he labored diligently, and used all his personal influence and power to make the city what it was designed to be by its illustrious founder. The dignified and impartial manner in which he discharged his duties will ever be the subject of commendation, and those who aspire to places of profit and trust may well take him for their guide and study."

If officially his administration had thus signally gained the suffrages of his constituents, he no less won their heart.

Accessible to all classes, listening with patient sympathy to the story of need or wrong, which was ever promptly relieved or redressed; tenderly consideratè of the humble and poor, these were the qualities which appealed to the sensibilities of all the good and all the suffering.

A friend of fifty years says of Mr. Seaton: "His unbounded benevolence was a household word, and a folio could not contain the record of his disinterested acts of kindness, of the charities that marked his daily path. So well was his liberality known to exceed his official income, that the city fathers several times proposed to increase the mayor's salary; but this, as well as other substantial testimonials of appreciation, Mr. Seaton peremptorily declined and persisted in vetoing.

Generous as a prince, he suffered no appeal to go un-
answered. To the destitute, the stranger, he gave his
last cent. I have seen this, and more. I was present
in his office when a poor man, ill and travel-stained,
came in, and related his case to Mr. Seaton. The eye
of the dear old Colonel softened with feeling, and instinctively his hand went to his pocket, — empty, alas !
for it had only a few moments before been drained for
another poor creature ; but he rose from his seat, sent
out and borrowed a few dollars for this stranger. I
would rather have been that man than the owner of
the mines of California !" And this is only one among
thousands, literally, of similar incidents, unremembered
and unrecorded by himself, and only learned from the .
grateful hearts which invoked blessings on his head.

In Mr. Seaton were united, in a remarkable deg ne,
all the elements of personal popularity, — calm, dignified, engaging manners, a generous temper, exquisite
courtesy and refinement, a genial affability and sprightliness, blended in a person of rare manly beauty, were
among the attractions with which all who had the
privilege of his friendship, nay, all who approached
him, confessed him to be so eminently gifted.

Mr. Seaton's colloquial power was indeed of a high
order. His exceptional personal knowledge of the
secret springs of political and social history and rare
reminiscences of the great actors in public events
during the past sixty years, his varied information,
derived alike from books and men, his originality of
thought illustrated by apposite and pointed quotation,
his quaint humor and fine wit, his freedom from dog-
matic or disputatious temper, were among the traits

which imparted to his conversation an exalted charm, and rendered his society proverbially captivating, — an attractiveness not only recognized among the humble, the great, and wise of our own land, but widely acknowledged by foreigners, "especially the diplomatic representatives of other governments solicitous of obtaining from his lips an explanation of our involved politics, and those sagacious views of public measures which have been known on several noted occasions to materially influence the deliberations of foreign cabinets, and to determine their international policy."

A most touching tribute speaks of Mr. Seaton's conversation, as "wisdom, substantial and gentle. He was an admirable listener. How clearly do we remember his aspect and manner, especially in his office, as editor of the great modern press ! Dear exhibitions were they of his interesting, peculiar self. Who can forget that almost deferential kindness, leading him to interlock his hands, recline back in his chair, and listen to your statement or remarks with that native politeness, the true source of which is benevolence, loving and caring for others ? And so, when he spoke, no one desired to interrupt the calm and precious flow of his ideas. There was a weight of influence in all that he said, more telling than energy ; while manliness, gentleness, and the dignity of a natural grace, were characteristics of his manner, the more artistic from being simple. Dear Colonel Seaton ! Good, noble, brave, generous, kind. I feel now more reconciled to the kingdom of death, for I know you are there to greet me."

In shielding others from the wound which a thoughtless or unkind word might inflict, and in drawing forth to the best advantage the talents and attainments of each, Mr. Seaton's tact was of a delicate grace. Indeed, his manners, without assumption or condescension, suave yet stately and reserved, were those which we are wont to describe as " royal " — although, perhaps, his higher title to distinction resided in the truth of his characterization, by persons from very opposite points of our country, as " the first gentleman in America."   An indorsement of this reputation is related by a gentleman who chanced to be present at the State Department during an interview between Governor Cass and a newly arrived British minister, to whom the venerable secretary said, in his well-known George-the-Third way :   " Have you seen Mr. Seaton ? Eh, eh ? The best we have to show,— best we have to show ! "

There was in Mr. Seaton's manner a certain bearing, something indefinable in his air, which effectually repressed any undue familiarity ; and bold would have been the man who, misled by his geniality and urbanity, presumed to take a liberty with him.

A gentleman whose associations had been those of a provincial town, upon his arrival in Washington, not quite appreciating the dignity underlying Mr. Seaton's playful spirit, presumed to address him in a large circle as "Seaton" ! Mr. Seaton, when next alone with this rather ambitious social neophyte, administered this gentle rebuke : " Mr. ——, you will pardon me, but as I have never in my life taken a liberty with any man, so have I never permitted a liberty with myself, and for the future I must ask you to remember that I am

Mr. Seaton." The characteristic reproof was received in a spirit that proved its recipient to be worthy of the regard with which Mr. Seaton subsequently distinguished him.

This rigid self-respect, enjoining an equal recognition of the rights of other men; the delicate honor, almost a religion in its sanctity, pervading his intercourse with others; the reserve, even reticence, governing his general relation with society, which yet never made him ungenial or uncandid, were the characteristics which mainly conduced to the freedom from all personal enmity or hostile collision with political adversaries, that marked Mr. Seaton's prolonged career. Yet, with this absence of self-assertion existed a quick perception of any infringement on his personal dignity.

Upon the arrival in Washington of General Harrison, previous to his inauguration, Mr. Seaton, partly in his official capacity, made an address of welcome to the incoming President, followed by some remarks of a similar nature in an editorial, which had the effect of exciting the especial ire of Mr. William R. King, of Alabama, afterwards Vice-President of the United States, who, in the Senate, severely commented on them in terms which savored of personal disrespect to Mr. Seaton, and in some degree seemed to impugn the honor of himself and Mr. Gales. Without delay Mr. King was required to offer a full explanation, and in his senatorial seat to retract whatever might be deemed offensive in his remarks, or to give Mr. Seaton the satisfaction usual with gentlemen.

Senator Mangum, having great tact in such matters, was intrusted by Mr. Seaton with this delicate mission, being met, on the part of Mr. King, by Senator William C. Preston. Finally, Mr. King's better feeling asserted itself; he manfully and honorably avowed himself in the wrong; the result of the spirited correspondence was made public, and the friendship between Mr. Seaton and himself, begun in early manhood, was warmly renewed, only to be interrupted by the death of Mr. King.

"While possessed of unswerving firmness and rigid adherence to principle," writes a prominent public man and journalist, "Mr. Seaton was charitable alike in his personal opinions and in his political faith. Bearing no malice, a model of courtesy, he observed in conversation and in his journal the wise proverb, which says, 'Think twice before you speak once,' — and this trait leads me to another quality in which he was also pre-eminent, — a peacemaker; for with his large heart and magnanimous nature, his counsel was always for conciliation and forgiveness, in proof of which I cite the following incident : —

"During the administration of President Tyler, when Daniel Webster was Secretary of State, there was a painful estrangement between the United States Senate, where the Whigs were in the majority, and Mr. Webster. It grew partly out of the fact of Mr. Webster remaining in the Cabinet of Mr. Tyler, selected by General Harrison, after his associates had resigned.; and partly from the policy of Mr. Tyler, which was almost wholly adverse to those who had made him Vice-President. Mr. Webster, however, remained in the Cabinet for the purpose of negotiating a Treaty with Lord Ashburton. The Northeastern Boundary difficulty, long pending, and leading to angry controversy in Congress, in New England, and among the people, and at one time seriously. threatening war, was one of several points settled by this famous treaty.

"Mr. Seaton was deeply pained to see the Whig Senators alienated from Mr. Webster, and was resolved, if possible, to bring them together, and restore their friendly feeling. They met at his own house, surrounded by a large number of personal and political friends, and the hope was, that before the night should pass, 'the good old humor and the old good-nature' of former times would be restored. These honorable and praiseworthy sentiments were more than realized. In the midst of the delightful supper I was requested by Mr. Seaton to remind Mr. Webster that he was about to be toasted, as he was upon the instant, by Mr. Mangum, then President *pro tem.* of the Senate, as '*The Author of the Washington-Ashburton Treaty.*' Mr. Webster, who was never at a loss for the word of inspiration on such occasions, and who often showed greater qualities in private life than in public services, replied instantly, '*The United States Senate, without which the Treaty could never have been ratified.*' Nothing in matter or manner could have been better said or done on either side, and the fruit of Mr. Seaton's tact and kindliness was the restoration of the best relations between the Senate and Mr. Webster. If on earth the peacemakers are blessed, then indeed, for this and many similar services, the memory of good Colonel Seaton will be cherished by all who honor unselfish actions and noble deeds."

Another incident, illustrative of this benevolent wish to restore harmony between dissevered friends and colleagues, is thus related by the late Governor Swain, of North Carolina : —

" Among the thousand anecdotes which Judge Gaston was wont to narrate in connection with his public life, was one in reference to the known kindliness of the editor of the Intelligencer. Perhaps the most brilliant of Judge Gaston's legislative tournaments was a conflict with Mr. Clay on the Previous Question, as a rule of order. Mr. Gaston went into the debate after careful examination of all the points of law and history that had been mooted in the mother country and our own on the subject, and caught Mr. Clay wholly unprepared. Eminent statesman and patriot as he was, Mr. Clay was nevertheless human, and retired from the contest somewhat soured. They did not meet again for many years, the feeling rankling in Mr. Clay's heart, until, during a visit of Mr. Gaston to Washington, they met at Mr. Seaton's dinner-table. They each gave token of recognition, but preserved a stately reserve, until, with an expression well understood by both, the host offered the sentiment : 'Friendships in marble, enmities in dust.' Kind and cordial intercourse ensued, and they were personal and political friends during the remainder of their lives."

Mr. Seaton's intimacy with Mr. Webster, the almost romantic attachment existing between them, has become a record of history, and during the period of nearly forty years but one absolute break occurred in this close and honorable friendship.

This interregnum also hinged upon Mr. Webster's continuance at the helm of state, when his colleagues had resigned their positions in the Cabinet of Mr. Tyler, who, true to his instincts as an old-school Virginia Republican, had a second time vetoed the re-establishment of a National Bank. Mr. Webster's course elicited great severity of comment even among his warmest friends in the Whig party, and his famous speech at Faneuil Hall, defining his position, had drawn from the Intelligencer a criticism rather unusual in strength of expression for the stately columns of that journal. This action on the part of the Whig oracle Mr. Webster felt most keenly.

A few days after Mr. Webster's return to Washington, Mr. Seaton being at the State Department, called to have one of his usual friendly chats with the Secretary, when, to his surprise, his frank greeting was met by an icy and repelling politeness. Instantly seizing the position, and perfect master of himself, he remained for a few moments conversing on indifferent topics, and then withdrew with a quiet dignity not to be ruffled by the haughty temper of a Webster. Conscious that the course of the Intelligencer was justifiable, and never deviating for foe or favor from what he held to be a duty, Mr. Seaton calmly awaited the conciliatory advance, which, from Mr. Webster's sense of justice, and personal feeling for himself, he was sure would be offered.

Meanwhile an embargo was laid upon the usual intimate intercourse maintained between the two families, against which the younger members strongly rebelled, contriving to run the blockade under the very guns of the two stately frigates, which merely exchanged signals of courtesy. Many were the efforts of friends, frequent the private embassies to effect a reconciliation between the belligerents; but Mr. Seaton made no sign, remaining firm in his position that the overture for peace must distinctly proceed from Mr. Webster. At last this estrangement could be borne no longer; and, preceded by his son Fletcher, as a diplomatic *avant courier*, Mr. Webster one evening entered the smoking-sanctum of Mr. Seaton, and fairly taking him in his arms, with one hand-clasp all was forgiven.

There was no friend with whom Mr. Webster's relations were more close and enduring than with Mr.

Seaton, whose affection he had tried in many a conflict of opinion, and had, indeed, grappled him to his soul with hooks of steel. With the exception, perhaps, of Rufus Choate, no one so well as Mr. Seaton had the art of "drawing out" the "Great Expounder"; but Mr. Choate was deficient in an appreciation of the beauties of nature, and still more in that love of field sports, which was so strong a tie between Mr. Seaton and the great fisherman. Mr. Choate would roam about the country with his eyes and thoughts absorbed in the book he ever carried, unheeding the fresh sweetness of morning, or the sunset glory over the ocean; or, which still more excited Mr. Webster's ire, would pass unnoticed the magnificent Durham "short horns," their master's boast. Finally, one morning at breakfast at Marshfield, Mr. Choate coming in tranquilly from a stroll, with his Horace in his hand, Mr. Webster, turning impatiently to Mr. Seaton, said, "I declare to you that I do not believe Choate knows a horse from a cow."

Mr. Charles Lanman, so widely known for his interesting narratives of sporting lore and adventures, as also for other valuable contributions to literature, — among them his delightful private life of Daniel Webster, — thus pleasantly relates his indebtedness to Mr. Seaton's kindness for his introduction to Mr. Webster: —

" Having in the summer of 1850 captured an unusually large rock-fish, at the Little Falls of the Potomac, I had sent Mr. Seaton the spoils with my compliments, which he in turn presented to Mr. Webster. On the following morning Mr. Seaton entered the library of the War Department,

13 *

of which I was librarian, and in a solemn voice, without any explanation, informed me that my presence was demanded by the Secretary of State. I hastened to the Department with a palpitating heart, and entering the 'presence,' was welcomed by the Secretary with these words : 'I am told, sir, that you are a famous fisherman, and I wish to capture a monster rock-fish in your company.' A variety of fishing and sporting adventures with Mr. Webster and Mr. Seaton were the result of this interview. Mr. Seaton's passion for field sports was a marked and widely known feature of his character, and during many years his duck-hunting and piscatorial expeditions down the Potomac were a delight to himself and the various distinguished friends eager to be included in his party; while to hear him recite his adventures on his return home was a pleasure never to be forgotten by those so privileged. Mr. Seaton was an intense lover of Nature in all her multitudinous aspects, and bound me to a promise to report to him everything new and interesting that I might learn on the subjects of hunting and fishing. A little incident will illustrate his long-continued pleasure in the sports of the field, in which his skill was hardly surpassed in this country. A few months previous to his last illness his favorite pointer, the companion of many a delightful expedition, and whose intelligent devotion to his master was a matter of local history, died of old age ; and Mr. Seaton, in paying a tribute to the qualities of his faithful canine friend, said to a gentleman, 'Ah, how much I should like to have a good dog in Ponto's place !' His friend expressed surprise, intimating that at his advanced age he could scarcely be equal to such hardy amusements.

"'I shall be eighty-one years old in two months,' replied Mr. Seaton, 'and not only should enjoy, but it would do me good to go out and bag a dozen woodcock to-morrow ; and if I had a dog, should certainly do so.'"

Mr. Seaton owned a fine farm and shooting-box up among the Alleghanies of his native Virginia, — known by his family name of Winston, — where he would often escape for a few days' relaxation, to breathe the pure air of the wilderness, and hunt the red deer; being always accompanied by fellow-sportsmen, among whom Mr. Webster delighted to be numbered. Those memorable shooting excursions! The ten-miles tramp through the stubble-fields of Prince George, or the havoc among the ortolan along Potomac's reedy banks! By those privileged to share them, they can never be forgotten, when, genial and full of fresh spirit, Mr. Seaton fascinated his very pusher: "willin' to pull all day to hear the Colonel talk." Fortunate pusher! What treasures might have been preserved for history had he noted down the political disquisitions, the discussions of life's grave problem, the wit, the boyish fun which fell from the lips of Daniel Webster and Mr. Seaton over their "double barrels" while rocking in that little skiff! With what heartiness would Webster's contagious laughter awaken the echoes, excited by some quiet stroke of humor or anecdote from Mr. Seaton! This joyous phase of the Great Defender's nature was little known to the outside world, which approached him with awe and bored him intensely. "Why do people always talk law to me?" he used to say; "I know enough law." The world knew Mr. Webster in the Senate, the Forum, grand, sublime in the majesty of his intellectual greatness, but little comprehended the sprightly humor, the playful grace, the tender sweetness which rendered him so captivating in an intimate circle. In his own home, where he was the most noble, regal host; or in Mr. Seaton's drawing-room, singing every known song, — generally impartially to the same tune; or gravely essaying the steps of a *minuet de la cour*, which he had seen danced in the courtly Madisonian era; or joining in the jests of the gay circle, his magnificent teeth gleaming, his great living coals of eyes, — "sleeping furnaces," Carlyle called them, — soft as a woman's; or his rare, tender smile lighting up the dusky grandeur of his face, — then it was that Mr. Webster was infinitely fascinating. He enjoyed the society of agreeable and beautiful women. "I love to hear women prattle," he said. "even if they talk nonsense, — but why will they use such long words? With them every one is 'the most exquisite creature,' 'the most enchanting fellow,' 'the most delicious dancer.' My dear, why can you not say, 'She is comely, — he is agreeable, — he dances well'?"

In connection with this well-known simplicity of Mr. Webster's language, which renders his style a model of Anglo-Saxon strength, Governor Swain related this characteristic anecdote of the genial and learned Judge Gaston: —

"During a period of high party excitement, Judge Gaston made a speech in the House of Representatives which the Federalists regarded with favor, and the Republicans feared might do injury; it was not reported in the Intelligencer. Various gentlemen called on Mr. Gaston, requesting him to write out his remarks for the Federal Republican, which he declined doing, until Mr. Webster came in and would take no denial. Mr. Gaston complained of weak eyes. 'That shall be no obstacle,' said Webster, 'I will act as your amanuensis; walk across the floor, and I will write as you dictate.' Mr. Gaston, who until then had never regarded himself as chargeable with redundancy of style, had uttered but a sentence or two when Mr. Webster stopped him with the inquiry, repeated again and again before he got through, 'Gaston, won't one of those words do? I make it a rule never to use two words when one will answer as well.' "

Mr. Webster liked an audience. An appreciative word, an intelligent glance, especially from bright eyes, and he became inspired. Masterly criticisms of Shakespeare, historical parallels, anecdotes of English statesmen and jurists, learned disquisitions on oak-trees, reminiscences of his own career, varied by clever nonsense, or some story of wrong and scathed affection told with inimitable power and pathos, would keep the circle spellbound far into the night. But it was in touching on more solemn themes, when speaking most reverently and in his grand way of the consoling, sublime promises of the Scripture, that Mr. Webster rose into a wonderful elevation of strength and eloquence. Strongly religious in his nature, — his theological convictions were Unitarian, — he was a daily student of the sacred volume, recognizing the beautiful harmony between Nature and Revelation, dwelling with profound interest on the magnificent prophecies of Isaiah, the unapproachable imagery and inspiration of the Book of Job and the Psalms, but especially on the value of the Gospel of John, or, as he termed it, the " Gospel of Love "; esteeming one chapter of this Apostle to be worth all the disquisitions of Paul, in sorrow or at the approach of death.

The evening before Mr. Webster delivered his great compromise speech of 1850 he spent several hours with Mr. Seaton, who, when his friend rose to go, took his arm, and they strolled pleasantly along. On arriving at Mr. Webster's house he in turn took Mr. Seaton's arm and insisted upon seeing him home. The scene was amusing, Mr. Webster wishing to take the exercise, enjoy his friend's society, and look up at the star-studded sky, now descanting on the wonders of Nature, then repeating passages from the Bible, Milton, and Virgil. Incidents of this character might be multiplied indefinitely, and they prove the power which, in his peculiarly quiet way, Mr. Seaton exercised over every manner of man who approached him; and Mr. Webster constantly sought his society, at his office, at his fireside, while Mr. Seaton enjoyed his cigar, though Mr. Webster seldom smoked.

As is known, Mr. Webster was an unconscionably early riser, — reading, working, making notes for senatorial or forensic onslaught, or the basis of a treaty, before the sun was up, varied by visits to his kitchen, where he delighted to confer with Monica, its presiding Congo priestess, as to the mode of dressing the "bass" for dinner, or salting a round of beef, gravely discoursing to her meanwhile on matters of higher import; or strolling through the market, startling wondering lookers-on by pricing a bunch of parsley in that sonorous voice accustomed "listening senates to command." He had a habit of scribbling notes to Mr. Seaton at this matutinal hour, jotting down some passing thought, making an engagement for the day, and not unfrequently sending *impromptu* doggerel lines, indited while at breakfast on an empty egg-shell. Unfortunately, only a few of these *disjecta membra* have been preserved, but they are valuable relics as exhibiting Daniel Webster in a phase of character not known to the outer world. It may be interesting to record several of these memorable scraps.

" My dear Sir, — I thank you for the summer ducks, which were found delicious. I thank you for the woodcock, and have yet to thank you for other favorable and friendly kindnesses not forgotten.

"Yours truly,

"DANIEL WEBSTER.

"MR. SEATON.

" These are black fish, sometimes called *Tautog*. Monica cooks them thus : —

" Put the fish into a pan with a little butter, and let them fry till pretty nearly cooked, then put in a little wine and pepper and salt, and let them stew. She uses no water. A little more wine, pepper, and salt to make a good gravy.

"So says Monica, who stands at my elbow at half past five o'clock. A good way also to make agreeable table companions of these fellows is to barbecue or broil them without splitting.

"D. W.

"Confidential and Diplomatic."

"My dear Sir, — Mrs. Webster leaves in the cars this p. m. Speaking of a little basket of one half-dozen peaches and two seckle pears, the other evening, — how well-timed it would be, if that little basket, contents as aforesaid, should meet her at the cars !

"I have the honor, with distinguished consideration, etc., etc.,

"Yours,

"D. WEBSTER.

"MR. SEATON."

"Friday Morning.

"DEAR MRS. SEATON,—As I could not accompany Mr. Seaton on his expedition to Piney Point, I hope for the subordinate pleasure of listening to his recital of its incidents, his capture of fishes, his battles with the mosquitoes, etc., etc.

"I wish, therefore, to engage him to dine to-morrow at five o'clock here, at the Burdine Mansion, with one or two friends only ; and I write this to insure your influence on the occasion.

"Mr. Curtis took an abrupt departure last evening, leaving messages of love for your household with me.

"I sent over a letter of Fletcher's, yesterday, and had a kind reply from M——. But she did not 'catch the idea.'

"I shall be obliged to come round this evening, and go into explanations.

"Yours, with the truest regard,

"DAN'L WEBSTER."

"DEAR W. W. S.,—Fish all right for to-morrow. Let them *bask* in Monica's ice-box till the day comes.

"D. W.

"5 o'clock."

"Friday Morning, January 29, 1847.

"MY DEAR SIR,—There happen to be four of General H.'s Cabinet now in town, viz. Messrs. Ewing, Badger, Crittenden, and myself. We dine at my house to-morrow at five o'clock. Mrs. Webster and Mr. and Mrs. Curtis will bring up the number to seven. Our round table holds eight. At breakfast this morning we proceeded to elect by ballot a person to take the vacant place, and great was the satisfaction when it was found that by general concurrence ' Colonel Seaton ' was chosen ! It devolves on me to communicate the result to you.

" DANIEL WEBSTER.

" COLONEL SEATON."

" Wednesday Morning.

" MY DEAR SIR, — Your leader to-day is *Capital.* It is exactly the thing needed, and that tone must be continued. The disturbers of the public peace must be made to feel the force of public opinion.

" Yours,

" D. W.

" TO MR. SEATON."

" I am sitting down, all alone at five o'clock, to a nice leg of lamb, etc., and a glass of cool claret — come.

" D. W."

" BOSTON, June 21, 1847.

" MY DEAR SIR, — We came up from the place of places, three days ago, and have inflicted on ourselves a residence of that length in Boston ; to-day we hasten back to the Old Elms and the Sea. Mrs. Webster has received J——'s letter from New York, and bids me say that she has obeyed all its injunctions, requests, and intimations.

" Our journey was shortened, to our disappointment. Still it was pleasant. We saw many new things and many good people. I can now talk, like an eyewitness, of cotton-fields and rice plantations, turpentine, cypress swamps, and alligators.

" . . . . Think of us at Marshfield, — on our piazza, with now and then a grandchild with us, a pond near, where ' cows may drink and geese may swim,' and Seth Peterson, in his red shirt-sleeves, in the distance. Then there is green grass, more than we saw in all the South ; and then

T

there is such a chance for rest, and for a good long visit from 'tired Nature's sweet restorer.' . . . .

" Yours,

"D. W.

"To W. W. Seaton, Esq."

"Saturday, August 27.

"Mr. Webster wishes much to talk over matters, compare notes, etc. Will be ready for a 'little sociality' on Thursday. Wishes much to make an effort 'to brighten the future,' and will expect the pleasure of a call from Mr. Seaton to-morrow at three o'clock. It is an early hour, but will have the advantage of a long afternoon behind it.

"You shall have a plain New England dinner, and a New England friend or two, besides D. W. and D. F. W.

" Yours truly,

"D. Webster."

"May 2, 1850.

"Snipe-shooting in mittens, with a heavy overcoat and fur cap on, is very amusing. The mercury this morning, five o'clock, at 34."

"Dear Mrs. Seaton, — That you have higher talents than belong to good housekeeping, all know; but that you have any more perfect of their kind, I very much doubt. My convictions on this head, always firm and strong, were rendered still stronger by the admirable piece of salted beef which we had the pleasure to receive last Saturday. I never tasted better. Some friends were with us from New York when it was brought to the table, and they acknowledged that Manhattan Island could not equal it. I was decidedly of the same opinion. It is a wonder if Monica, who does not like to be outdone, does not go some day and have an interesting conference with your cook. She has already intimated as much.

"If the present had been literally a crust or a crumb

from your table, the kindness with which you have offered it would make it acceptable.

"Yours always truly,

"DANIEL WEBSTER."

"February 17, 1852."

"A few slices of Marshfield beef, cured last fall, and put away for family provision for the year.

"I have found it a good lunch for the field or the sea; for although it is rather salt, yet gentlemen engaged in those employments, I have noticed, are not unwilling to be sometimes a little dry.

"D. W.

"April 30, 1851.
"W. W. S."

In September, 1844, a monster Whig meeting was held in Boston to ratify the nomination of Mr. Clay for the Presidency, in which contest, however, Mr. Polk was the victor. Mr. Seaton was one of the delegates from Washington on this occasion, and writes thus pleasantly of the cordial reception extended to him by Northern friends, and especially of his warm greeting from Mr. Webster.

"BOSTON, Thursday, 7 A. M.

". . . . Such was the overflow and jam of every inch of space in the hotels, that I had no chance of a place to write. I found at first difficulty in obtaining even a bed, at the Tremont; but on learning my name the proprietors kindly gave me another person's room. A few moments afterwards I met Mr. Choate, who insisted on taking me off to stay with him; but as they had taken some trouble to accommodate me at the hotel, I remained. The whole town I find alive and running over. Among the many entertainments last night was one at Mr. Winthrop's, to which Choate persuaded me to go, tired as I was, and unwilling to take the trouble of dressing; but thought you would wish it, and acted on the golden rule. I cannot express the cordiality with which I was greeted, and have been by all the friends I have met. At Mr. Winthrop's, had I been Captain Tyler himself, I could not have been made more of. I found there, among others, Mr. and Mrs. Grinnell, and the affectionate inquiries after you, and the fervent wishes that you were here, were very gratifying. Everybody asked for you as if you were first in their affections. I have already had more invitations to dine than I could make good in a week, — Winthrop's, Choate's, a grand banquet at the Mayor's, etc. Mr. Webster came up from Marshfield last evening, and was expected at Winthrop's, but not being yet well, and an arduous day before him, he went to bed early. Having received notice to appear at the Senate Chamber at nine o'clock this morning, among the invited guests, to take part in the ceremonies, and as I shall be in the throng all day, I rose at six, have dressed and taken a stroll before breakfast, and have stepped into a bookstore to write this scarcely legible letter. It is a glorious, bright morning, and the note of preparation is heard on every hand. A great people, these Yankees. One thousand Yankee Whigs, from New York, left in two steamers yesterday for the celebration, and will be here this morning; and others are pouring in from all quarters, fine, respectable-looking men, young and old, — like the Jews of old going up to Jerusalem. I wish you could have seen the procession of the 'Young Whigs of Boston,' last night, with their flambeaux, noble band, and thrilling cheers opposite the Tremont House, as they passed. Next to yourself, I only wish your brother were here to enjoy the sight, and receive the cordial greetings of the good men who love and appreciate him. . . . . .

"God bless you, dear wife. . . . ."

"Boston, Friday Morning.

". . . . Before setting out for Marshfield, I send you a word to advise you of my health and plans merely. Impossible now to give any account of the many people, things, and incidents which have rendered the last twenty-four hours so interesting to me. It is worth coming from home to be made much of, and certainly in that regard I have had everything to gratify me. When I repaired to the State House yesterday morning, whither I was escorted by Abbott Lawrence, who called on me, I found a number of magnates assembled from different parts of the Union, invited guests. Mr. Webster, President of the day, soon after entered, looking magnificent. Several friends who had seen him in the morning told me how glad he was that I had come, and how anxious to see me. He came up to me in the middle of the Senate, and did not hug me, but very like it, saying aloud, that there was not another man in the whole country he would be so happy to meet here, and kindly regretted that you were not with me. Mr. Webster told me what he had decided when he heard of my arrival, — that it was fixed as any decree of fate, and would be vain to say a word against it; that is, to return with him to Marshfield this afternoon, and remain at least until Sunday, if I could give him no longer. We therefore dine with Mr. Paige at two o'clock, and go thence to Marshfield *via* Quincy, where I wish to stop and see Mr. and Mrs. Adams. . . . . .

"The day, yesterday, was a glorious one. Such an assemblage, and such a magnificent spectacle altogether, I never before witnessed. The noblest cavalcade of two thousand well-mounted men formed a part of the procession. I was in an open barouche, next to the first, accompanied by Judge Berrien, Mr. Bates, and Cassius M. Clay. We were cheered at every pause by the crowd, and *Mr. Seaton and the National Intelligencer* had some tremendous cheers at one place. . . . . Mr. Isaac P. Davis has called to say it is time to be off.   I am writing in the chair and at the table of the first Governor Winslow, in the Historical Society's rooms, and I think that my scrawl partakes of the antique around me, being written with an old steel pen made in the time of the Mathers, I should judge.

"There is an autograph letter of John Cotton open before me, about two hundred years old, written to his wife, in which he addresses her as 'my dear wife and comfortable yoke-fellow.'   Take these homely but true words in their fullest sense to yourself, my dearest wife, from

"Your ever affectionate husband,

"W. W. SEATON."

The death of Mr. Webster was the severest social loss ever sustained by Mr. Seaton.   During the prolonged period of their friendship, and of Mr. Webster's almost continuous residence at Washington, seldom a day passed without the interchange of word or note, or social gathering at the house of one or the other. Profoundly as Mr. Seaton estimated the calamity to the country in the withdrawal of the wisdom and weight of Mr. Webster's counsels, which acted as a breakwater in the headlong tide of American affairs, — deeply as he felt the loss to the civilized world of its most comprehensive statesmanship and grandest intellect, — his death was yet more consecrated to his affections, and it was the *friend* whose departure was to cause henceforward a blank in Mr. Seaton's daily life. That he should no more feel the influence of that great mind elevating and strengthening his own, should never more meet the kindly glance of those huge eyes, nor hear again that voice vibrating to him always in tones of affection and sympathy, moved Mr. Seaton to personal and permanent grief. His discriminating affection pays the following tribute to Mr. Webster's many-sided greatness: —

"WASHINGTON, January 13, 1859.

"DEAR SIR, — I have had the pleasure to receive the invitation which you so obligingly convey to me on behalf of the gentlemen of Boston, to unite with them on the 18th instant in celebrating the anniversary of the birthday of our illustrious countryman, the late Daniel Webster. In tendering my best acknowledgments for this mark of courtesy, I beg to assure you, and those for whom you speak, that I feel myself very much honored by such an invitation from such a source, and one which I value the more highly, placed as it is, on 'the intimate personal relations' to which you are pleased to allude as having existed between that great man and myself.

"Happy should I be to obey a summons so flattering. . . . . If, prompted by the occasion, and yielding to the impulse of my own inclinations, I should attempt to speak in eulogy of the great statesman whom we revered while living, and whose loss the country has not ceased to deplore, I might well be deterred from what could not but seem, to those amongst whom he lived and died, a work of supererogation. History has set its seal upon his greatness; and his peerless fame, placed by death beyond the hazards of time and the mutations of opinion, is written on the anuals of his country in characters as bright as they are imperishable. In every branch of the civil service, — whether in the Forum, the Senate, or the Cabinet, he displayed at once the grandeur and the opulence of his massive intellect. The eminence he attained in each of these departments could have singly sufficed to fill the measure of any other man's ambition. It is Mr. Webster's peculiar distinction to

have been equally transcendent in them all. Nor need I
say to those who, like yourself and your favored associates,
were admitted to his private friendship, that he was no less
admirable for the qualities of his heart than imperial in the
endowments of his mind. If in high debate at the Bar, and
on the floor of the Senate, he made it doubtful whether he
more excelled as a jurist or a statesman, his friends might
almost be pardoned if they postponed both to the genial
traits which endeared him to them as a man.

"Renewing to you the expression of my thanks for the
honor you have done me, I beg leave to add how truly I
remain, dear sir, your friend and servant,

" W. W. SEATON.

"P. HARVEY, ESQ., Boston."

Amid all the changes of party, and violence of faction, or the hostilites pervading even social relations,
among the respective adherents and opponents of successive administrations, Mr. Seaton's long life was singularly unembittered by personal asperities. Neither
severe editorial stricture upon official action, nor the
gulf separating him from certain political parties, ever
prevented the recognition by adversaries of his high-
toned character. These tributes to his ability and
candid spirit were sometimes very charmingly paid, as
on one occasion by Mr. Simon Cameron, at the beginning of our Civil War, whose official course was, at the
time, the subject of very stringent animadversion by
the Intelligencer, but who, on rising to return thanks
at a St. Andrews festival, said, with much magnanimity and grace of sentiment: —

" When the toast of 'Secretary of War' was proposed, I
had forgotten that it bore any allusion to myself, especially

when I looked to my left on the face and form of my venerable friend, Colonel Seaton, who, not many years ago, paid me my weekly wages as a journeyman printer in his office; who, for more than fifty years, has been one of the most earnest and powerful defenders of this free government, and who, with great political sagacity combines a purity of character and sincerity of heart, that prove him to be a worthy descendant of a brave and noble Scotch family."

Among the prominent statesmen whose political principles, so widely divergent from those cherished by Mr. Seaton, did not preclude social relations during forty years of a very close cordiality, was Mr. Buchanan. The letters in which he pleasantly speaks of their friendship are the more interesting now that the earthly and distinguished career of the venerable ex-President is also closed. The following is addressed to a member of Mr. Seaton's family.

"WHEATLAND near LANCASTER, June 26, 1862.

". . . . Mr. and Mrs. Seaton are associated with my earliest recollections of Washington, and I shall ever remember them with grateful regard. Mr. Seaton's youthful and buoyant spirit is worth more than a fortune, and must render himself, and those who are near him, happy in his green old age. Although he cannot say that, 'In his youth he never did apply hot and rebellious liquors to his blood,' yet this was always done in the society of choice spirits and with Christian moderation. May he yet live a thousand years surrounded by troops of friends !

" Had it not been for the troubles of the times, I should have passed some months every year of my life in Washington. Its society was more agreeable to me than that of any other city I have ever known. How sadly must this now be changed! For my own part, I am tranquil and contented, and would be happy in my peaceful home were it not for the dreadful condition of the country. Still, I have the consolation of reflecting that I did nothing to promote, but everything in my power to avoid, the civil war now raging.

" . . . . You are, I trust, mistaken in believing me to have been the last of the race of Constitutional Presidents. May you live to see many more of them, and be as prosperous and happy in their day as I wish you to be from my heart!

"I have faith that the kind Providence which sustained our forefathers in the days of the Revolution, and has from small beginnings made us a great nation, will not abandon us in this the hour of our utmost need. . . . . .

"With sincere and tender regard, I remain

"Truly your friend,

"JAMES BUCHANAN."

"WHEATLAND near LANCASTER, September 9, 1866.

" . . . . Though unfortunately never identified in political action with Mr. Seaton, I ever entertained for him a high esteem, as well as a warm personal regard. In the good old days, when the National Intelligencer was the ablest oracle of the Whig party, a difference in political opinion did not interfere with friendly social relations. I therefore knew Mr. Seaton well in the familiar circle, and have never known a more perfect model of a man in private life. Whilst firm in his political convictions and able in defending them, by his manners and qualities he conciliated and secured the esteem and regard of the best of his political opponents. In his social relations he was a charming companion. He possessed an excellent heart combined with a clear and firm intellect. Having a perfect knowledge of the distinguished men of the day of all political parties, his conversation was agreeable, racy, and instructive.

"I shall always remember with the mournful pleasure of an aged man the refined and elegant hospitality of his old mansion in the happier days of former years. . . . . .

"With sentiments of warm regard, I remain

"Sincerely your friend,

"JAMES BUCHANAN."

The following letter may possess an additional interest from the allusion to the famous trial of Judge Peck, of which Mr. Buchanan was one of the Managers; as the manner of conducting that case was referred to as a precedent on the occasion of the recent impeachment of President Johnson.

"ST. PETERSBURG, April 7, 1833.

"MY DEAR SIR, — I now send you my remarks on presenting the resolution from the Judiciary Committee for the Impeachment of Judge Peck. I should regret very much should they arrive too late for the Register, as it would have a very awkward appearance should the debate be published without the introductory observations of the Chairman of the Committee. The greater part of them had been written out at length by Mr. Stansberry. Will you be good enough to supply the omission of a quotation, consisting of one or two sentences in the defence of the Judge, presented to the House in the Session of 1829 – 30. Much as I revere the independence of the Judiciary, and after a review of the case in this land of despotism, I think the Judge's acquittal was a strong one. The tribunal was above all suspicion. . . . .

"Although I have been treated with much kindness since my arrival in St. Petersburg, yet I. feel I shall never be happy except in my native land.   My residence abroad, far from estranging me from my own country, has made me love it much better than ever.   Would that our people were justly sensible of the blessings they enjoy !

" The Emperor of Russia, whatever we may think of his conduct towards Poland, is a sovereign to whom his subjects are devotedly attached.   His private character is without a blemish.   Indeed, his example, and that of the Empress, have done much already to reform the manners of their Court.   He is, by far, the most able and energetic sovereign in Europe.   I am convinced it is his policy to avoid war for the present.   I cannot foresee any change in the nature of the Belgian question which would induce him to assume a hostile attitude.   Besides, the character of the King of Prussia is a guaranty for the general peace; yet it cannot be denied that Europe at present is a magazine of powder, and any accidental hand may apply the spark.   I send you a very important article just published by this government in relation to Turkish affairs. . . . . .

" Will you be kind enough to answer this letter, and give me a little news, local and general?   Remember me with kindness and respect to Mrs. Seaton and your family.   I hope to have the pleasure of again spending happy hours in their interesting society.   Remember me also to Mr. Gales.   I write by the minute. . . . .

" Always truly yours,

" JAMES BUCHANAN.

" WILLIAM W. SEATON, ESQ."

There was, perhaps, no position in which Mr. Seaton appeared to greater advantage than as a presiding officer.   Whether controlling a mass meeting during a Presidential campaign, or addressing a more dignified assemblage of citizens, or as the chairman of unnumbered anniversary festivities, the duties of the occasion were performed with a promptness, unruffled dignity, and acceptability rarely surpassed. His love of the drama, and early histrionic efforts no doubt contributed to the easy declamation, clearness of intonation, and quiet, graceful gesture which distinguished him; and adding to these characteristics a felicitous turn of expression, and remarkably effective wit, it may be conceived that his eloquence would call forth invariable enthusiasm. His fame in this regard was widely spread; and he often was forced to run the gauntlet of post-prandial oratory and political meetings, during his excursions. In a letter from Cumberland, in 1844, while on a shooting expedition, he writes: —

"I have just had a deputation from the Whigs of this good town, saying that, hearing of my presence in their midst, they had appointed a meeting of the citizens to-morrow to hear an address from me. I had rather fight the battle of Bladensburg over again, but of course cannot decline the flattering invitation."

The following little incident, among many others, shows the manner in which Mr. Seaton's appearance among his fellow-citizens was greeted. The occasion was a political meeting during the campaign of 1860.

"At this juncture, Colonel Seaton, the venerable yet active editor of the Intelligencer, entered the room and advanced to the stand. As he passed down the aisle he was greeted by the most tumultuous cheers, which continued unabated for several minutes. When he had reached the stand he bowed gracefully to the assemblage, who gave three tremendous cheers for 'the old war-horse.' The

Colonel was warmly received by the Chair, Mr. Ogle Tayloe, and then turning to the audience, most gracefully acknowledged the flattering reception which had been extended to him, and concluded a spirited address by trusting that, 'whether present or absent, every one knew that
he was heart and soul with the party that hoisted the
Whig and Union flag.'"

"The first evening assembly I ever attended in Washington," writes a prominent *littérateur*, "was one given by
Mr. Seaton to his congressional friends. These suppers were
famous, and worthy of their niche in the social and political annals of the metropolis. The entertainment, though un-
ostentatious, was marked by perfect taste and elegance, and
in view of the men who were thus brought together for an
hour or two of social enjoyment, it was grand and imposing. Webster, Clay, and Calhoun were the leading stars
of the evening, and around them were grouped diploma-
tists, notable citizens, and a score or two of those whom we
delight to honor as the representative men of their time.
With all of them Mr. Seaton was on friendly, generally
intimate terms; for as his abilities and high character
commanded universal respect, so did his affability, generous kindliness, and winning manners retain the affection
of all who knew him socially or in the business walks of
life."

In Professor Joseph Henry's beautiful tribute to Mr.
Seaton the question is asked :—

"Who can forget Mr. Seaton as host? In the gatherings
about his generous board mingled the cordial welcome and
that air of an older and better school which constantly
distinguished him; the kindly and reassuring attention,
unaffectedly bestowed on the least distinguished guest;
the colloquial charm, which extended the fame of his hos-

pitality far beyond the sphere of its exercise. No unimportant part of the charm exercised by Mr. Seaton resided in his engaging presence, — in the winning smile, the bright eye, the gentle voice, the benignity of a countenance upon which a long life of manly effort and kindly purpose had left its impress."

The Hon. A. H. H. Stuart, of Virginia, in writing of Mr. Seaton's power of attractiveness, says: —

"I have always regarded Mr. Seaton as my *beau-ideal* of a true Virginia gentleman, — 'one of the olden time.' To sound masculine intellect and a vast fund of information upon almost every subject, he united an amenity and a grace of manner and expression, which rendered him one of the most fascinating and instructive of companions. On all questions of difficulty I sought the guidance of his counsel; and in hours of social indulgence there was no one who contributed so largely to the enjoyment of his friends. I have heard him often narrate the most striking and piquant incidents connected with our early history, and intended to illustrate the character of such men as Rufus King, Nathaniel Macon, William Wirt, Crawford, and especially John Randolph and a host of those giants.

"But there was nothing sensational about Mr. Seaton. He was not a professed colloquialist. He did not talk for effect, nor attempt to make brilliant hits in the game of conversation. All that he said flowed like a gentle stream, and was intended to minister to the enjoyment of his hearers, not to display his own great powers."

"Mr. Seaton had an especial gift as a *raconteur*," writes Governor Henry A. Wise, of Virginia. "He always made me think of Sir Walter Scott, in his narratives. He had just his genial, manly, open, candid, ingenuous face, and could humor a story with almost equal grace and gusto.

He was always *fresh* and natural, simple and truthful, and wise without being disquisitive. He was a man to be plain and familiar with, and yet to love and honor. . . . . The Biography of 'Gales and Seaton' would be a history of metropolitan life and journalism during six tenths of a century, embracing the lives of all the distinguished men from Mr. Jefferson down to these times, the secrets of Cabinets, the scenes and subjects of Congress and of the Supreme Court, the tenants of the White House, the cycles of parties and of public opinion, and all the tones of the social circles since 1800. What a mass of various interest such a memoir might be made to contain, but it would take a Dr. Johnson to write it and years to prepare the materials.

I knèw Mr. Seaton from the year 1833, when I first entered the House of Representatives. I was elected a member of the Jackson party, in favor of the Union and in opposition to the then raging doctrine of nullification. This brought me in personal affiliation with Mr. Seaton, and soon after, the issue of the removal of the public deposits from the Bank of the United States brought me in still closer affinity with him, and finally the common opposition to the party of Mr. Van Buren, called the Loco-Foco party, united us together in the new organization called the Whigs. That party was truly composed of the old Federalists, the more modern American System party, headed by Clay and Webster, the extreme State Rights party led by Calhoun, and the old Madisonian portion of the Virginia school of Democracy, of which I was always, and am still, an humble advocate.

"This status of mine brought me closer still to Mr. Seaton, and he used to pet me much with his counsel and a place for my speeches in the Intelligencer. We never exactly, or even generally, agreed in our politics, or rather in the ground-work of political opinion, but he was a true old Virginian. He had begun his career with Mr. Ritchie, loved our old commonwealth and her old white-cravat, tobacco-chewing people. Mr. Seaton was fond of his gun, his pointer dogs, and his manly sports. Do you know that I have now a most beautiful descendant of his breed of setters? My boy procured the ancestor pup from Mr. Seaton's gardener, and Mr. Sergeant asked him for the whole pedigree and made my son record it. . . . I used to delight to talk with Mr. Seaton about past events and the old Romans of our country. He told me more of John Randolph than I ever got from any one else, except Benjamin Watkins Leigh. He had a juster view of men and things than any one else of my acquaintance. . . . . The Yankees got all my papers and letters. The last letter I had from Mr. Seaton was when I was Governor of Virginia, — a long appeal from himself and others on the John Brown raid. That I suppose is now in the State archives. . . .

"Believe me most truly yours,

"HENRY A. WISE.

"RICHMOND, July 10, 1867."

The world-wide celebrity attaching to the name of Governor Wise as the dispenser of justice to a great criminal, renders his reply to the appeal above alluded to of especial interest.

"BOSTON, October 26, 1859.

"MY DEAR SIR, — I have written this letter in order that it may reach Governor Wise. Perhaps it is asking too much to have it sent to him by yourself. But it is on a subject which interests us all. There are not too many of us 'national' men left here in Massachusetts, and the action of the court now sitting for the trial of old Brown threatens to blot us out forever. But though we are not of much account here, we feel that we have a great stake in preserving a good understanding with our friends in the other sections.

"Yours very truly,

"AMOS A. LAWRENCE.

"HON. W. W. SEATON, Washington."

"RICHMOND, VA., October 31, 1859.

"MY DEAR SIR, — Mr. A. Lawrence wrote directly to me, and I have replied to him, saying that Brown is in the hands of the Judiciary, — that by our laws no man *can be tried* even, without an Examining Court to inquire whether he ought to be tried, — that the sitting of this Court, I presume, has caused the appearance of suddenness in the prosecution, — that another, the Circuit Court is now sitting upon his trial, and is competent in ability and fairness to try any plea he may put in, — and that the prisoner has all protection, even in his impudent defiance of the justice which surely should visit robbery, rapine, insurrection, invasion, murder, and treason. He shall not be rescued on the one hand, nor lynched on the other; and you know Judge Parker well enough, to say nothing of our Bar, to assure all strangers to our laws and people of the certainty of fair, impartial trial; and if the prisoner be convicted unduly or unjustly, he will be in my hands, as well as in the hands of an Appellate Court. And it is, I regret to say, super-serviceable in Mr. L. to obtrude upon either of us what he would do. I can say to him, in reply to such intimations, that he will find that I will do whatever I may do, about as decisively and obdurately as he could desire, on the one hand or the other. I say this, intimately, to *you* who know me well, the more tartly for *him,* who, I believe was the very gentleman who threw the glove in the settlement of Kansas *per fas aut nefas,* — by Sharpe's rifles or otherwise.

"We are getting impatient under the folly and fanaticism

of the two extremes.   Let Mr. L. keep his sympathy for those who need it more than Brown does, for either excuse for crime or fair justice in its punishment.   Let him restrain the wicked fanaticism at home, not provoke fools among us.   *You* may be assured that justice shall be administered calmly and dignifiedly, and its execution shall be tempered with due mercy ; and the less intrusion there is from the North, the more easily can we act as we ought.

   "Very truly, your friend,

         "HENRY A. WISE.

"W. W. SEATON, ESQ., Washington."

      "RICHMOND, VA., Nov. 1, 1859.

  " MY DEAR SIR, — As I said to you, in mine of the day before yesterday, Mr. Lawrence seems to me super-service-able in his sympathy for Brown.   He, like other conscientious men at the North, who deem themselves conservative too, see that Brown's folly is the result of their own teaching and preaching, and material aid in money and arms, to make war in Kansas.   It has come to this outrage on our borders, and Brown and his comrades are in danger of execution for crimes to which they have been incited by men like Mr. Lawrence.   They now are troubled for the consequences for which they are responsible in conscience, if not in law ; and hence much of their divine sympathy and humanity.   I would not convict Mr. L. on Forbe's testimony, but upon Mr. L.'s own sympathy.   He is too ready in excuse for him, and in distrust of our own judges and people.

  " Brown, I am told, is already convicted, and I shall have soon to pass upon the record of his trial ; and, therefore, can add no more than that I am,

   "Very truly, your friend,

       "HENRY A. WISE.

"W. W. SEATON, ESQ."

For many years it had been Mr. Seaton's ardent desire to visit Europe, especially to tread the soil of Great Britain, for whose history, constitution, true liberty, and glorious people he ever entertained an enthusiastic reverence and regard; England being peculiarly endeared to him as the birthplace of his wife, while Scotland was the cradle of his own race. The unceasing labors of an editorial life had hitherto interposed an insurmountable obstacle to the accomplishment of his wishes; but in August, 1855, he took heart of grace, and crossing the ocean paid· a flying visit to the great centres of European interest and civilization. With his fulness of information derived from sixty years' exceptional study of men and events, he was prepared to form an enlightened judgment concerning the political and social status of European states, and also, as the press throughout our country expressed with gratifying unanimity, fittingly to represent America as her highest embodiment of a gentleman. Unfortunately, owing to the very large and scattered family connection through which his letters were disseminated, but few memoranda were preserved of his " steeple chase," as he called his three months of rapid travel; during which, at the advanced age of seventy-one years, his physical vigor and buoyant spirit enabled him to endure more fatigue, and to extract more pleasure, than is accomplished by many a tourist fifty years younger.

"LONDON, September 7, 1855.

"MY DEAREST WIFE, — That you may hear from me up to the latest hour, I send a brief supplemental letter to mine of yesterday. . . . . . We took the cars yesterday morning for Richmond, where, at the famous Star and Garter, we were received by our Minister in the warmest manner, who accompanied us in our walk over the hill and park, the latter consisting of 1,600 acres, and containing some of the finest trees I ever beheld. To attempt any description of the view from the brow of Richmond Hill — an elevated tract overlooking the valley of the Thames for many miles, and even including the sight of Windsor towers, eighteen miles distant — would be utterly futile for even the highest power of pen, — even my friend, Mr. James himself, could convey no adequate idea of its beauty; as indeed all descriptions of natural scenery are failures, — at least, I have ever found them so. Accompanying Mr. Buchanan and his niece in his carriage, we set out for Hampton Court, calling on the way for Sir William and Lady O., and Miss G., who reside in a beautiful place on the bank of the Thames, adjoining Garrick's Villa, and near Twickenham. . . . . . The palace is a vast extent of Gothic brick building, with turrets, courts, corridors without number, all plain and unadorned, containing no furniture, except a few historical beds, cabinets, etc. The entire suite of the principal story — comprising halls, reception-rooms, staterooms, bedrooms — is filled with pictures, embracing hundreds of portraits, many of which, of eminent men who have illustrated, or rather made, British history, interested me much. It occupied three hours to go the round of this story, dwelling on an occasional object more attractive than others, or lingering at the great windows to admire the most beautiful gardens and grounds. In all this review, Sir William was a very valuable guide explaining these varied objects of interest, — though I had the book in my hand, — as he has long been familiar with them all. Those gardens and grounds! how they would charm you, and how much did I long for you to stroll through them with me! They are laid out in the highest art, kept in exquisite order, filled with *parterres* and rambles, — everything to delight the eye.   But that which would have excited your highest admiration was the famous black Hamburg grape-vine.   If you could but see it !   The trunk is nearly as large as my body, is trained under a space of glass of more than 2,000 square feet, and depending from the vine were 1,600 full-formed and ripening clusters of magnificent grapes.   The palace and grounds were filled with hundreds of people, — among them the boys and girls of a London school, — all roaming about and enjoying the beauties spread before them. . . . . On our return, we passed Pope's Villa, Strawberry Hill, and the church where Pope lies, the tower of which is a striking piece of time-worn antiquity.   But the parks, — the parks ! the beautiful little river, the emerald verdure, and the scores of swans floating about fearless of any harm ! We reached the Star and Garter in time for one of its renowned dinners. . . . . Mr. Buchanan contributed to the gratification of the day in the most assiduous manner, kindly culminating in proposing your health at dinner.   He offers me every facility in his power, and letters to all the great people in the kingdom ; but in using these I shall be very chary. . . . . "

"SHEFFIELD, Saturday Evening, September 15.

" . . . . What a strange thing it appears to me that I should ever write you a letter from this place ; yet here I am veritably in dingy, smoky Sheffield, so deeply interesting to me.   I reached here late this afternoon and set out for the Mount, in search of your Aunt Sarah ; found she had gone for a day to Baslow, thirteen miles off; so, after a stroll, I have returned to the Royal Hotel to jot down some notes of my movements before bed.   The old Tontine, so associated with the history of your parents and your own early recollections, has been pulled down, and a fine market is being erected on its site.   Sheffield, perhaps you may remember, is surrounded by lofty hills, now greatly improved, good well-built streets running up their slopes, and their tops embellished by handsome villas. One of these streets leads up to the *Mount*, which is ornamented with lawns and fine trees, almost a park, descending from a grand-looking edifice as long as our post-office, with columns and porticos, which I supposed to be a palace or public institution, until the cab turned into its gate, and I found it to be a series of private dwellings, in one of which Montgomery lived, and Aunt Sarah continues to reside, and of whose absence I shall avail myself to go to-morrow to Eckington. . . . . I came down to Cambridge from London, and had time only for a few hours to go through some of its numerous ancient colleges, and the fine old chapel of King's College, a beautiful as well as venerable specimen of the impressive Gothic style; but I would rather, if it were possible, describe for you the green velvet grounds and groves and glades, the magnificent. trees that spread away off in front of the colleges, a wilderness of shade, much of it bordering the beautiful little Cam, with its fine, lofty stone bridges, each of them, as seen through the exquisite vistas of old willows, elms and limes, oaks and chestnuts, looking as grand almost as the Rialto. Passing hither from Cambridge, I had near views of the great cathedrals of Ely and Peterborough, and came through Newark, so dear to us all from its association with your father and mother; and how gladly I would have stopped a short time, but it was impossible in this hurried jaunt. Almost the finest mere church in England — that is, any one below a cathedral — is that of Newark, in which, as you know, your honored parents were married. . . . . I do not think I mentioned that, on arriving at Richmond an hour before Mr. Buchanan and party, I filled up the time very interestingly by driving over to Eton College, and going through its aged and crumbling cloisters and its noble old chapel.   These Gothic chapels, with their curiously and richly stained windows, their groined and carved ceilings, inspire an ever-fresh interest.   I must to bed, — my eyes are blinking.   So good-night, my ever dear wife.

"*Sunday Night.* — I returned from Eckington at six this evening, and have just come in from a visit to the venerable *Hartshead,* so important in family history, and familiar to us as household word.   I reached it through one of the little lanes that communicate from street to street, and instantly knew its circular corner and bow-window, — not changed in anything, I presume, except the marks of age.   With what interest I looked at it, and thought over so much with which it is wound up in my heart.   But Eckington! that precious old hamlet, with what feelings did I enter its precincts and walk through its calm little churchyard, — the very embodiment of the immortal one of the Elegy, — decipher its aged and half-obliterated gravestones and pace the aisles of its venerable church! I set out at nine this morning, the train stopping a mile and a half from the village.   There was no conveyance to be had at the station, so, with my overcoat over my arm, I made a merit of necessity and walked.   And soon the spire and time-worn tower of the church hove in view, and the bells were ringing the chimes for morning service.   How sweetly they sounded in the still Sabbath morning, as I advanced by road and field path nearer to the village; and I thought how often your dear father had listened to those same bells, and with what pleasure he described the mode of ringing the changes, the skill and strength required. The good old beadle found me a seat, and the service of the old Church has never, I am sure for many a year, been so interesting to any participant as was this morning's to me.   The lessons were read by Mr. Estcourt, a brother of our friend, General Estcourt; the sermon, preached by a clergyman from a distant parish. After service the sexton accompanied me through the churchyard and pointed out the grave of your uncle Thomas Gales, who, I found, died July 5, 1787, and those of your aunts, — the inscriptions on all of which are entirely legible and unimpaired. I cannot express to you how the well-sung hymns in the church and the standing ·by these old graves affected me. I gathered some small memorials of the place, and, after chatting with the good sexton and old beadle awhile in the nice parlor of the neat, clean little inn close to the church, I set forth on my walk to the station. I passed the little stream in which the catastrophe happened to your aged great-grandfather, and in which your brother Joseph has often cast his pin hook, and fancied that I walked the old and well-worn path by which your father and mother used to take their afternoon stroll to Eckington. I pondered these things as I pursued my way, and they so filled my thoughts that, had the distance been twice as great, it would not have been marked. . . . . . It is bedtime, and I have ordered a cab early in the morning to drive to Baslow to see your aunt. So good-night, dear wife.

·" *Monday Evening.* — A most interesting day I have had, dear wife. When undressing last night, I received a message from the Mount that your aunt, hearing of my arrival, had returned, and expected me to breakfast this morning. So at nine o'clock I found her awaiting me, and I was received with the warmth of a mother; she was much affected, and affected me. . . . . . She remembered most surprisingly every member of the family, even to the third generation. She spoke a good deal of Mr. Montgomery, his excellence, his constant friendship and his deep, enduring affection for your parents and their children. . . . . . I intended leaving Sheffield this afternoon for York, but your aunt appeared so gratified by my visit and so reluctant to part with me, that I deferred my departure until to-morrow and decided to spend the afternoon at far-famed Chatsworth, twelve miles from here. I accordingly took a cab to Barslow, and thence walked half a mile or so through the park to the palace, for such it may with all propriety be called. A part of my drive, for a few miles, lay across the moors, a very extensive range of elevated barren country, consisting of long, sloping undulations without tree or house, but covered with a thick coat of purple heather, with patches of green fern that combine to make it look like vast paintings. They stretch away into Derbyshire, almost to Manchester, and are owned by the nobility, being kept as preserves for grouse and partridge, several coveys of which I saw fly across the road. But Chatsworth! its riches and grandeur and beauties far surpassed any previous imaginings. The grounds, the gardens, conservatories; the fountains, the picturesque, artificial, rocky, rugged cliffs and dells and caves, formed of huge rough rocks brought from the mountain back, which no one would suppose not to be placed there by nature; the great *palmery*, a crystal house sixty feet high, with exotic trees from all parts of the world, the hottest regions, among them a cocoanut-tree reaching the glass dome, — this glass house was built by Sir Joseph Paxton, and furnished the model for the great Crystal Palace of 1851; then the treasures of art in painting and sculpture in the immense galleries of the palace, — all made up a spectacle which exceeded even Windsor in its wilderness of beauty. The graperies far surpass Hampton Court, and their immense extent, the great variety of the fruit, and its astonishing size could but interest me. One species, the Muscat, or Tokay, I am not certain which, had berries more than three inches in circumference. I would have given any price for a few of them for you, had they been purchasable and possible to keep. The clusters would weigh more than three pounds each, maybe five. . . . . And now, dear wife, having finished this crude, disjointed yarn of to-day's proceedings, and it being late, I will 'turn in' and dream of dear home."

"York, September 20.

". . . . I reached this ancient city yesterday, coming round by Lincoln to see its noble old cathedral, hardly equalled by any other in England, and the couple of hours spent in going through it, conducted by a clever guide, richly repay the journey. It is immense in its height and proportions, eight or nine hundred years old, its outer walls much decayed and crumbled, but like all other ancient ecclesiastical houses in England constantly undergoing repair and renovation. In one of the cloisters I saw the, to me, curiosity of a Roman pavement, some fourteen by eight feet, discovered a few years ago in excavating, three feet below the surface ; it is composed of small white and greenish cubes. While in the cathedral, I had the pleasure of hearing *Great Tom of Lincoln*, the largest bell in England, boom out the hour. In the afternoon I came on to Hull ; and the next day, being the last of three days of a great cricket-match between Yorkshire and All England, and I never having seen the game, I resolved to spend an hour or two on the cricket-ground. The match had excited a widespread interest, and an immense number of spectators gathered. How your dear father delighted to describe the game ! It was really an interesting sight. The players numbered about thirty, and what fine specimens of men, so athletic and well formed ! The day was very warm for England, and they were attired in cricket dress. How active and skilful they were with the bat and balls ! . . . . I have spent three hours in visiting the celebrated York

Castle, so connected with family reminiscences, as well as deeply interesting from historical association. Of the famed castle of William the Conqueror nothing remains but the *Keep*, high up on a steep mound, in the middle of the great court made by the surrounding modern prisons and court buildings ; and of this nothing is left but its mossy, crumbling great walls and embrasures, with no roof, and covered all over inside with ivy. But the noble, the magnificent, thrice glorious old Minster ! who would venture to describe it, or the impressions which such a sight for the first time beheld produces ? Westminster Abbey of itself, independently of its monuments, cannot vie with it. There is more curious and elaborate carving in Lincoln Cathedral than in this, but the vastness and grandeur of this great shrine rise indeed to the sublime. The ten-o'clock morning service, which takes place every day in all cathedrals, — honorable custom, — was about to begin, and I stayed through it to hear the chanting, accompanied by the powerful organ. I was standing in the centre of the great transept, looking up at its impressive height, when the rolling volume of harmony struck my ear, and reverberated through the clustered columns and aisles and arches of the vast pile. The only drawback to these relished enjoyments is that I am alone ; that you, dear wife, are not with me to participate in them. I have returned to the ‘ Black Swan ’ to post up my crude diary. . . . .”

An amusing commentary on the ignorance respecting America, pervading even the educated and higher classes in England, was the remark to Mr. Seaton of the Governor of York Castle, who, on discovering his visitor to be an American, exclaimed, with surprise, “ Why, you speak English very well.” “ Yes,” quietly replied Mr. Seaton, “ you speak it pretty well yourself.”

"Edinburgh, Saturday, September 22.

"I am able at last, dearest wife, to write you a line from the ancient, and most interesting capital of Scotland. . . . . . From York we passed through Newcastle and Berwick,— the former a manufacturing place, in a deep dell on the Tyne, dark and smoky as a hundred great chimneys constantly vomiting black smoke from its proverbial *coals* could make it, and has in good preservation an old tower of the time of William the Conqueror. The second, a walled city on the Tweed, a frontier town, which has stood many a siege in the border wars of the olden time, and a place of much historical interest. On our route we stopped two hours, between one train and its successor, to visit Alnwick Castle, the ancient seat, as you know, of the Percys, to which there is a branch railroad of four miles. It is an extensive and impressive specimen of the old feudal stronghold and palace, with its high walls and battlements, and towers and moat. As the home of Hotspur, and a place of so much importance in the civil wars, it could not fail to be interesting.

"We reached this truly noble city at night. It would be impossible to picture to you its great peculiarities and its pre-eminent beauties. A deep ravine — now turned to the most ornate account by grassy slopes and walks and beds of flowers — divides the towering old town from the splendid new one,— the two looking at each other from opposite heights. In a deep walled trench, as it were, in the centre of the ravine, and its sweet though narrow grounds, the railroad runs, bringing the terminus to the centre of the city. When I looked up to the right, towards the old town, with its nine and ten storied houses, it appeared like the dark face of a perpendicular mountain, with long galleries, away up one above the other, of lights, there being nothing visible in the darkness but these lines of glittering windows. After coming up to our quarters in the new town

I sat until bedtime looking across at the novel and striking spectacle. ' This morning betimes we were on the peak of Calton Hill, enjoying the beautiful and most picturesque panorama of the city below, the neighboring eminences of Arthur's Seat and Salisbury Crags, the high-perched old castle on its rocky cliff, all bordered away off, as far as the eye could reach, by lovely fields and the highest cultivation. All these points of interest we have visited, and such others in the old town as Scott's stories have made familiar, and then to Holyrood, — a spot of saddening, most touching interest. Its faded decorations, its gloomy halls, and dilapidated architecture could not be viewed without pain, the mind recurring to the periods of its brilliancy, and the career of its beautiful, unfortunate, and immortal mistress. The once almost peerless chapel is roofless, ruined, and in an almost prostrate condition. It would be idle, however, to attempt to convey to you an idea of these interesting memorials or the emotions they produced. I will now take a walk through the charming new town and resume my memoranda to-morrow.

"*Sunday, P. M.* — . . . . The striking features of this noble city, which I have already seen, have convinced me that in picturesque beauty there can hardly be any comparable to it, and I am quite prepared to agree with G. that in urban elegance the new town has no equal. We have heard of Auld Reekie and its noisome streets and closes so long, that I was unprepared for the breadth of the famous Cannon-gate and High Street of the old town, and the general cleanliness of its thoroughfares. And what a teeming population pouring through its wynds, so decent in appearance, so orderly! The beauty of the new town, its fine long rows of elegant, large, hewn stone houses, the breadth and number of its streets, the beauty and richness of its shops quite equalling Regent Street, all surpass my previous conception. . . . . We shall set out for Glasgow in the morning, *via* Stirling, and Lochs Katrine and Lomond, making it all in one day. . . . . "

"Trosachs Hotel, Monday Night.

" Our progress, dearest wife, is much slower than I expected. We left Edinburgh at eight this morning, and arriving at Stirling at ten, stopped there two hours to view the famous castle and town, the scene of so many romantic events in Scottish history. The castle answers fully in its lofty position, extent, strength, and picturesqueness to all the views we have had of it ; and there was a drill going on within its walls, when we entered, of the 42d Highland Regiment, originally the celebrated Black Watch, in their striking national dress ; that is to say, the lower limbs in no costume at all. The regiment itself is now in the Crimea, but this was a body of four hundred men, enlisted and drilled to send out and fill up the thinning of its ranks by war. From the battlements we see the field of Bannockburn. On our way to Stirling we passed, among other objects of interest, the fine ruin of Linlithgow Castle, where Mary was born. There is no conveyance from Stirling to the lochs except omnibuses and cabs, so in one of the latter we reached this heroic region at five, unable to proceed farther to-day, the steamer not leaving the head of Loch Katrine until the morning. I have taken a long walk up the wild and romantic glenfinlass, and also gone through the ceremony of tea, and now bring my journal up to the close of day. . . . . "

"Head of Loch Lomond, Tuesday.

" We are left here high and dry, for three or four hours, until the steamer from below shall call and take us to Glasgow. . We came over to Loch Katrine this morning, being brought in its little steamer ten miles, up to its head,

in an hour, and thither by coach in another hour.   When
lo ! the Loch Lomond steamer will not arrive for some
hours ; so here we are at the little Scotch inn to kick our
heels and kill the time as best we may, — which I employ
in jotting down a line to you. . . . . The lochs are certainly
very pretty, and the mountains may be termed grand ; but
except for the scenes of imaginary incidents made famous
by Scott's magic pen, they would scarcely be worth the
trouble of coming so far to see, by any one so familiar as
I am with the mountains and lakes, large and small, of our
own country.   The mountains here, of Lomond and Levis,
are a little higher ; but this celebrated Lake of Lomond
does not surpass in beauty or grandeur Lake George, and
there is no story connected with this lake, in all of Scott's
charming fictions, more thrilling than the one related of
Lake George in our romance of the Huron Chief, to say
nothing of the scenes by which that and other of our beautiful inland seas have been commemorated by Cooper.   But
the Helens and Macgregors, and Fitz-Jameses and Roderick
Dhus have imparted a classic character and vivid life to
these mountains which will be perpetuated with all of British origin.   I feel a good deal of it myself, and you may well
imagine that I could not pass by Falkirk, and Bannockburn,
and Sheriff Muir without having my interest in the chival-
ric deeds' enacted on their fields centuries ago keenly excited.   On our way from Stirling, the post-boy diverged
from the public road to drive us through the park of Drum-
mond, — a princely one it is, and such magnificent trees I
have hardly seen in England.   We traversed nearly three
miles in passing through it on the finest road, made for the
accommodation of travellers desiring to see the park, as
well as for the pleasure of the noble owner.   But the
steamer is in sight, so for the present good by, my dearest
wife.   Glasgow will not detain me more than half a day,

as there are few objects in that great but manufacturing city to keep me longer from Oxford, where my dear home letters await me. . . . . ."

"GLASGOW, Wednesday, 2 P. M.

" We reached here last night, after a raw, cold, uncomfortable voyage down Loch Lomond — which I must now admit is very fine and its mountains superb — in a miserable little crowded steamer, thence by rail and another vile steamer on the Clyde, — a dirty stream not twice as wide as the Washington Canal. This is a fine city indeed, and so full of life and business, with above four hundred thousand inhabitants, and large, broad, regular, well-paved, and clean streets lined with splendid shops. I went through a mercantile establishment, Stewart and MacDonald's, — more extensive than Stewart's of New York. I visited of course the old cathedral and its remarkable crypt; but the most astonishing things I have looked at here are the great machine works of Napier, and the immense iron Cunard steamer Persia (four thousand tons), now taking in her vast engines, which I went on board to examine; both were truly wonderful. Wishing, for the sake of Mr. Donoho and my other Irish friends, to tread the soil of old Ireland, and take a look at the Hill of Howth, if nothing more (Donnybrook Fair, the great institution of the island, has been abolished), without going *via* England, I shall take the mail steamer this evening for Belfast and go on board in a few minutes; so farewell, dearest wife. To-morrow I hope to open my eyes on the hills of Antrim, and be able to resume my pen at 'Dublin's fair city.'"

"DUBLIN, September 27.

. "After a calm night and a quiet passage across the Irish Sea, we reached Belfast at five A. M., and taking the cars arrived here at midday, an hour ago. While waiting for the train at Belfast, I drove to look at its beautiful Queen's College, an extensive and very fine Gothic building recently erected. As far as I have seen this place, it is a noble city. Sackville Street, on which my hotel is situated, is a princely one, finer even than Argyle or other of the handsome streets of Glasgow. I write this much before I have seen it, as I must mail these disjointed notes for the American steamer. . . . . And now, my dearest wife, Heaven bless you and all at our dear home.

"Ever your affectionate husband,

"W. W. Seaton."

"Waterford, Sunday, September 30, 1855.

"My dear Thomas, — As I have ventured into the land of the O'Donohues, — the origin of which patronymic I understand to be ' *Hy-dun-na-moi*,' the ' chiefs of the hill of the plains,' meaning the Rock of Cashel, — being, as I have said, in the land of that great, ancient race, I think it due to report the fact to their representative in the distant Hesperia, and therefore while waiting the departure of the train which will take me back to Dublin, I occupy the time in sending you a few words.

"I have been in the island but three days, yet have travelled over not less than six hundred miles of its fine roads, — my limited time denying me anything beyond a cursory glance at town and country in my rapid movements. I came over from Glasgow to Belfast on Thursday morning, thence by rail to Dublin; went through that fine city, including the *Phaynix* Park (seventeen hundred acres) in the afternoon. Friday to Galway (a lively, handsome, busy town, and where I saw good old Father Gill); thence, as there was no ready conveyance across to Limerick, back to Dublin. On Saturday morning took the rail to Cork, one hundred and sixty-four miles, and so by Kilmallock, Tipperary, and Clonmel to this city, whence I shall go by the

way of Glenvallyvally, Kilkenny, Kildare to Dublin and so
to Holyhead. So you see my tour has been pretty extensive, if it has not afforded me opportunity for minute observation. As far as I have been able to judge, the country
fully merits its character for fertility and beauty, and is
capable of supporting in comfort five times its present population. If inferior to the sister islands in agricultural beauty, it is from bad systems of rack-renting, the habits of the
peasantry, the effect of political agitation, agitators, *preju-
dices*, and absenteeism.

"But the late act for selling the encumbered estates will
work a great revolution in the social condition of Ireland, by
abolishing the middle-men, and making the actual cultivator
the only renter and tenant. It has disposed of many large
estates to new hands, and its good fruits begin already to
be perceptible in improved cottages, and neatness of hus-
bandry. Prejudice and suffering have driven so many
hundreds of thousands away during the last ten years, as
to have given a desolate appearance to many parts of the
country, every mile exhibiting roofless, deserted cabins, and
neglected fields. Such must necessarily be the aspect of a
country which has in a few years lost by pestilence, famine,
and emigration one eighth of its population. This emigration, however, has been of vast benefit to our country phys-
ically; for although the emigrants have most deplorably
damaged our *political* interests, they have enabled us to
execute the great works of internal improvement which
could not otherwise have been carried out for many years,
so we must balance the account by placing material advantage against political detriment.

"I was surprised at the general level nature of the
country, at least throughout the midland counties. It was
only hilly or mountainous as we approached the coast, with
two or three exceptions. There is a good deal of stone in

some districts, resembling much parts of Massachusetts, especially in Galway, the derivative of which, by the way, signifies its character, being in the Gaelic, or Celtic, *Guallief,—stony land.*   Speaking of Galway, to show the deserted state of some portions of the island, Father Gill mentioned that in a single village in his parish, where ten years ago there were twenty occupied cottages, there is now but one, — the other nineteen abandoned, roofless, and tumbling down. But, as a young man said to me last night in the coffee-room, ' we have got rid of the agitators and the middle-men, the " Encumbered Estates Act " has emancipated the small holders, the people are attending to their proper business, the country has not for years been so quiet, and it will now, God willing, begin to prosper.'   He spoke very feelingly, and I believe correctly.   I have no doubt, from what I have seen, that under a proper system four fifths of the island might be made a rich garden, equal to England, or even the lowlands of Scotland, which surpass, if possible, England herself in agricultural beauty.   It was melancholy to see so many fields between Belfast and Dublin lying waste, grown up with thistles and weeds.   But a better day is dawning for Erin ; she has peace, and will erelong have prosperity.   I have seen many remains of ancient feudal and ecclesiastical grandeur in the ruins of castles and abbeys.   On the way to Galway I passed Mullingan and Athlone and the Curragh of Kildare.   I have seen the Hill of Howth, and passed old Blarney Castle, where the famous and miraculous stone is ;   but rail trains have little sentiment, for they would not stop to let me imbibe inspiration by a kiss.   The national institution of Donnybrook Fair, where flourished the ' sprigs of shillelagh and shamrocks so green,' and where each b'hoy ' met his friend, and for love knocked him down,' no longer exists ; it has been barbarously abolished.   They tried to revive it at another place, but it proved a dead failure, as they could not get up five fights during the day. Having seen the chief natural curiosities of the island, I have also had opportunities of admiring its great artificial one, for I have been driven in a jaunting-car, — the most extraordinary, most awkward, most uneasy, and most horrible vehicle that the wit of man ever devised.

"I am writing in full view of, and not fifty yards from, an old tower built by the Danes more than a thousand years ago as a fort. It is in good preservation, and now used as the city prison. . . . ."

"LONDON, October 2.

"I came from Waterford to Dublin on Sunday, stopping an hour at Kilkenny. At Oxford I remained two hours examining its noble and unrivalled colleges. At Kilkenny I saw the grand old castle of Ormond, a baronial residence worthy of that great and renowned family. On arriving at Dublin I found an invitation from the Lord Lieutenant, Earl of Carlisle, to dine at the palace, but it would have detained me beyond my time. . . . .

"Yours with constant regard,

"W. W. SEATON.

"MAJOR THOMAS DONOHO."

Mr. Seaton truly appreciated the virtues, the warm heart, the instant sensibility, the wit and delicious humor of the Irish nature, and in return was enthusiastically regarded by his Irish constituents, who found in him personally a beneficent friend, and who never forgot that to his large sympathy their famishing countrymen were indebted for bread. On the occasion of a St. Patrick festival, Mr. Seaton thus alludes to his glimpse of the "Gem of the Sea" : —

"Colonel Seaton, who has so frequently officiated at

similar celebrations, gave great satisfaction by the graceful manner in which he discharged the duties of the Chair. The following toast was then offered and drunk with enthusiasm : —

"'Colonel W. W. Seaton, the friend of Ireland and Irishmen. The alacrity with which he attends on all occasions our national festival, shows that his heart is in the right place.'

" Mr. Seaton acknowledged in felicitous terms the honor conferred on him, and the compliment which his selection as chairman implied.   He paid a glowing tribute to St. Patrick, whose labors in the cause of civilization and Christianity had conferred such lasting benefits on Ireland, and, through its men of letters and missionaries, upon all Europe. A descendant of Scotchmen, he had nothing in common with the people of the sister isle except that he belonged to the same Celtic race. He had, however, always felt much interest in whatever concerned Irishmen, and during a visit to the British Islands a few years ago he passed over from the romantic glens and garden lowlands of Scotland to the green hills and fertile plains of old Ireland, and during a rapid though pretty extensive tour, he was truly glad to find everywhere evidences of improved agriculture and returning prosperity.   He adverted incidentally to some of the causes to which he conceived the amelioration of the condition of the country was due ; and concluded by expressing his pleasure at finding himself once more in festive communion with so many to whose support he had been in times past largely and repeatedly indebted for the highest honors of the city, — honors of which he should ever be proud, and which he believed he could say with truth he would rather wear again, were he young enough, than even the high but harassing ones of Chief Magistrate of the Republic."

"Paris, October 5, 9 a. m.

"My dearest Wife, — My last letter brought my weekly report down to yesterday afternoon in London. . . . . We reached Dover at near midnight, and went on board the Channel steamer, but she could not get out before 3 a. m., when the tide made. It was a rainy, bad, dark night ; the boat a little, confined, miserable affair, not larger than one of our Alexandria ferry-boats, but strong ; the men's cabin not so large as our little front parlor, and into that all the male passengers had to stow, from the bad weather on deck ; no berths but the cushioned bench seats, and no comfort of any kind ; and there we remained packed until we put out into a heavy sea, and then for two hours were rolling and pitching as if the cockle-shell would roll clean over or go under. . . . . I was ensconced on a sort of upper shelf, where I lay witnessing this scene, for sleep was impossible, and wretched enough, but not the slightest sick. We at last got across, and at once took the train, accomplishing in nine hours the two hundred miles between Calais and this most magnificent, most polished city, the undisputed metropolis of the world. We drove to the lodgings of our amiable and able correspondent, Mr. Mann, who instantly and most zealously embarked in my service, and after an hour's industrious search (for the city is excessively full of strangers, and desirable lodgings difficult to find), we succeeded in obtaining rooms in the *Hôtel Choiseul, Rue St. Honoré*, not far from the *Place Vendôme*.

"We have for four hours visited some of the more striking points of this emporium of the grand and beautiful. We walked from the *Place Vendôme*, where stands on the lofty and celebrated column the statue of Napoleon the First, through street after street of colonnades and grand houses to the *Place de la Concorde*, the *Champs Elysées*, till it grew to night, and I have returned to bring up for you a sketch of my movements. . . . .

"Saturday Night.

". . . . Such acquaintances as I have met are as much amazed at seeing me in Europe as I am to find myself here ; and well they may be. The first one who stumbled over me was Mr. H., who, as I was going to a *café* to breakfast, suddenly seized me by the shoulders with such a grip that I doubted not the police with a *lettre de cachet* had got me. 'Of course I must dine with him,' but this I must decline, having no time. An hour after, I met Mme. C. de la B. on the boulevard, who was equally astounded at my apparition and most earnestly cordial. . . . . My attention of course was due to our Minister, whose wife I found at home, — her reception-day.   Were I her father, she could not have given me a warmer welcome, or introduced me to her guests .with more *empressement;* while for you her inquiries were as affectionate as if for a sister. Mr. M. was equally kind. . . . . They pressed me to drive to-morrow to the Bois de Boulogne and dine. The drive I accept, dinner decline. . . . . What a city it is, in its magnificent proportions, finely paved, noble streets, beautiful, lofty, cream-colored, finely cut stone houses, its *Places*, avenues, palaces, *jardins*, grand ancient hotels of the Montmorencis, the Guises, and the old historic names ! And the gardens of the Luxembourg, the exquisite drives, the ever-shifting scene of gay splendor ! The present Emperor has done, and is still doing, more to improve and adorn the capital than any predecessor. He cuts without hesitation through half a mile of an old, confused, crowded district, to open a grand avenue to some other, or to continue some beautiful street or boulevard, upon which is forthwith erected long uniform rows of stone houses. This afternoon I went to the '*Exposition Universelle*'; and great it certainly is, far exceeding the most labored description to convey an idea of its vastness and boundless riches in works of human skill, in every form of fabric, of the loom, of gold, jewels, and porcelain, and thousands of art treasures. Shawls I saw marked ten thousand francs, and lace dresses fifteen thousand francs. I should think such exhibitions so likely to craze the brain of many women who would have to long in vain for such gorgeous attire, that from the mere dictates of humanity they ought to be suppressed. But my candle is burnt out, and I must bid you good night."

"Sunday Night.

"It has rained so steadily all day that I took for granted Mrs. M. would not drive, so I assumed our engagement to be *ex necessitate* released; but I have spent the day as if it had been clear. I began my rounds at nine, and we went afoot and in cabs to many quarters of the immense city, whose greatness and grandeur grow on one at every step; among other places the Jardin des Plantes and the extensive galleries of natural history connected with it. Merely to enumerate the objects viewed during the day would fatigue, not interest you, and my midnight chats, as it were, permit nothing more in detail; but I must mention venerable Nôtre Dame, the Invalides, Tuileries, and above all for a gem of interest, the chapel of St. Louis, — an enclosure, above the base, of one entire mass of richly stained glass, ancient and modern. It was nearly destroyed in '89 by the monsters who broke open the tomb and scattered the ashes of Du Guesclin and murdered their queen, but was restored by Louis Philippe, and is now undergoing further adornment by the present great imperial patron of Paris. Good night."

"Monday Night.

"Soon after breakfast we set out on our daily tour, the morning being occupied with few objects, but of much interest. The first, *Père la Chaise*, the great cemetery for the opulent and eminent, and temporarily, three or four

15 *

years, for the poor, whose remains after the stipulated time
are removed. So indeed are those of all others, high and
low, who have not purchased a ' *concession perpetuelle.*' It
is strictly a great city of the dead, consisting of long streets
of handsome vaults, all above ground, like small stone
lodges of various plans and devices. Every tomb, as you
know, especially of the more humble, being decorated with
chaplets of immortelles, supplied by the shops for their sale
which line the approach to the gates. From the eminence
of the cemetery we had a fine view of Paris in its noble
proportions. . . . . The *Bois de Boulogne* — for thick
wood it is and not open park — was destroyed by the invaders in 1815 for fuel, but was subsequently replanted by
Louis Philippe, and is now of handsome size. The present
Emperor has made a grand avenue out of the city to it,
and has in every way greatly improved and beautified it.
It is of great extent, several hundred acres, furnishing
various delightful winding drives over the finest roads,
which one may pursue for hours without repassing the
same one. . . . . . I cannot accept these pressing invitations, kind as they are. Truth to say, in the evening
I am tired out, and want to dine quietly and enjoy my
cigar. . . . ."

" Tuesday Night.

" It has rained drearily all day, but I faced the weather
to visit the tomb of Napoleon, a most gorgeous and most
impressive object. The body is not yet placed in the splendid porphyry sarcophagus prepared for it, but lies in a small
grated room, in a plain black marble tomb, with his sword
and well-known little cocked hat placed before it. Relics do
not usually have much effect on me, but these personal memorials brought me, in the presence, too, of his actual body,
in such close proximity to that great, most wonderful man,
who had in long years past filled my own soul, as every

other, with deep and daily interest, that I could not contemplate them without emotion, and a good deal of spontaneous moralizing. . . . . This afternoon we set out for the Rhine, and a little tour in Germany. We go at 5 P. M., sleep at Epernay to-night, and Manheim to-morrow. I met Mr. W. B. H. just now, who nearly devoured me. . . . ."

"MANHEIM, on the Rhine, October 11, 1855.

"MY DEAREST WIFE, — When you read the above date you will think I am putting half the globe between us, but in these days of steam a score of hundred miles are accomplished as if by magic, and I am now near my extreme point from you, and hope in a short time to turn my face homewards. We halted last night at Epernay, a principal town in the champagne wine district of France, where I was glad to spend an hour or two in viewing the vine fields, the character of the fruit, the wine-making, it being the height of the vintage, and the great wine-vaults of M. Möet. We rose at six, and before seven had ascended a long hill (the vineyards are generally on the sides and tops of hills both in this country and on the Rhine), and were quickly in a field of two hundred acres, among the gatherers. After satisfying our curiosity we returned to breakfast, when, having still two hours before the train started, we spent them in going through M. Möet's immense vaults. They consist of long arched galleries cut out of the soft chalky stone, two sets, one below the other, and their aggregate length is estimated at six miles, comprehending an area of six acres under ground. There were a million of bottles in the vaults ready for exportation, and almost as much more in various stages of progress, in bottles, casks, and vast vats. M. Möet handed me a silver cup of the juice of the red or tinto champagne, as it ran from the press, which was sweet and pleasant. They cultivate both the white and the black grape for the purpose, but give the preference to the latter,

— both kinds being small and sweet, and good table grapes.
From Epernay we passed through the beautiful and highly
cultivated country of the Marne, and then across some hills
to the still lovelier valley and country of the Moselle, a trib-
utary of the Rhine; and on all the hillsides, for thirty or
forty miles, as far as our road followed, nothing but grape
fields. We reached this place, the head of navigation, at ten
o'clock to-night, but before going to bed make this brief
record of my peregrinations. A little distance from Metz
to-day we passed and had a fine view of the remains of a
Roman aqueduct across the Moselle, of which a hundred or
two yards and many of its lofty arches are standing entire.
I did not mention that on reaching Dover, and leaving it in
the dark, I missed seeing Shakespeare's cliff, but I passed
under it through a railway tunnel!

" At daybreak we go in a steamer to Cologne, or rather
for Bonn, a few miles this side, the famous university town,
where Madame G. is, whom her husband requested me to
see if I came to the Rhine. . . . ."

" DUSSELDORF, Saturday Night.

" *L'homme propose, et Dieu dispose.* I little thought,
when I penned my memoranda at Manheim, that I should
be no farther on my journey than this place to-night,
but such is our adverse fortune. We left Manheim at daylight, — a dismal, rainy morning ; indeed, it has rained almost constantly from the day I left London, — and came on
very well for forty or fifty miles, with every prospect of being
in Cologne by evening ; but it happened to be a Rotterdam
boat, and stopping at the towns to take in freight, lost so
much time that at seven o'clock we were still many miles
from Bonn ; and soon after, the rain made the darkness so
intense that the captain, afraid to proceed, came to anchor
till five next morning, thus rendering my visit to Madame
. G. impossible. We spent two hours in driving about the

curious old town of Cologne, and in viewing its wonderful Cathedral, begun six hundred years ago, but yet unfinished, though four hundred workmen are now employed on it, and there is a hope that it will be completed in fifteen years. While the new portions are going up the old are crumbling away with age. The weather destroyed all the romance of the Rhine, which was nearly the color of pea-soup, and its banks were made dim by the incessant rain. We could dis- cern, however, many ruined castles on their rocky peaks, and many magnificent views as we passed the mountain por- tions. The slopes and mountain-sides were covered with grape-vines for a hundred miles or more, — we can hardly say *vines*, however, as both here and in France the vine- yards resemble fields of green peas, being not higher, and each supported in like manner by sticks. . . . . I doubt if any tourists ever passed a more uncomfortable night on the Rhine, — no bedding, and only the bench seat of stuffed cushion, and of even that luxury few could get a *length*, and most of the passengers sat up or lolled about all night. With Mr. M.'s carpet-bag, and a cushion he found for me, I was among the most comfortable, while he sat up all night. It rained hard, and the cabin, without fire, was very cold and cheerless, — enough so to knock all the poetry about the Rhine on the head. . . . .

" BERLIN, Monday.

" We left Dusseldorf yesterday morning, dearest wife, and reached Magdeburg — so interesting to all juveniles as the place of Baron Trenck's imprisonment — about 7 P. M., a distance of three hundred miles. It was too late to see any- thing of the fortress, as we left it before day to be able to stop two or three hours at Potsdam. We arrived at that cele- brated residence of the great Frederick at nine, and stayed till twelve. We drove out to Sans Souci, and the *new palace*, both built by Frederick ; the former we could only view ex-

ternally, as the royal family were there, but the latter we
went through above and below ; and I found it in many
respects superior to all other palaces I have seen, — I was
forced to leave Versailles unvisited, — even Windsor itself
in its state apartments, which are very spacious, and very
remarkable for their *peculiar* taste. The paintings are fine,
many of the great masters; and everything about the palace
bespeaks the genius of the great designer. The parks are
on a commensurate scale, the trees and drives noble ; but
the lowness and flatness of the land is a serious disadvantage.
In fact, from the Rhine, rather more than three hundred
miles, the whole country, with the exception of a small chain
of hills near the Weser, is as level as a race-course ; much
of it good and well cultivated, but a good deal thin, poor,
and sandy. In some districts we passed miles without seeing a single tree, while scattering farm-houses are unknown,
the cultivators all living in closely built villages or hamlets.
After leaving the palace we went to the church where the
remains of my hero Frederick, and those of his crazy, ruffian
father, are deposited. We entered the little grated cell
beneath the pulpit, and found only the two coffins, side by
side, of thick plain mahogany, but lined, we were told by the
valet de place, with metallic ones, and, placing my hand on
the one in which rests the greatest man of his age, I could
but contrast its plainness with the splendor of that of the
other great warrior (but his inferior), which I had gazed
upon a few days before, beneath the dome of the Invalides.
I was early in life impressed with a great and indelible admiration for Frederick, as a soldier and a genius, and it never
yielded precedence even to the exploits of the wonderful
Corsican. We shall remain here this afternoon to see what
is most worthy of curiosity ; but there is not very much
that specially interests me ; for though a fine city, it is
comparatively new. It is rich in museums, pictures, hos-

pitals, etc., but these are common to all European capitals ; and as I have only time to glance at the infinite multitude of such objects, I begin to weary of such cursory sight-seeing. I should have liked much to stop in Brunswick, Hanover, and Magdeburg, a few hours in each, but could not without losing too much time, or travelling late in the night. From this city we shall to-morrow turn to the south, and after a day or two in that direction shall set my face towards England. Now for a drive, and then home to dinner at the *Hôtel de Russie.* . . . ."

"Tuesday, 11 A. M.

"This morning I find Mr. Fillmore and Mr. Corcoran here, on their way from the south back to France. . . . . I have seen this morning much of the city (it improves on examination and is certainly a fine one) and museums, and regiments of statues and acres of paintings ; but there appears to me a great sameness in these things, similar to those in other capitals. If I had time for careful inspection, I might perceive great diversity, but for me the object would not be worth the delay, even if I could command the time. As I now pass rapidly through these bewildering collections, I am only thinking of when the circuit will be completed and my voyage home begun. I shall set out in an hour for Dresden, that treasure-house of art, and so on to my *ultima thule.* I intended to call on Baron Humboldt, but he is absent from Berlin. By the time you read this, I hope to be on the ocean wending my way back to my dear home and household. . . . . .

"Your ever devoted husband,

" W. W. SEATON."

"MUNICH, October 23, 1855.

"MY DEAREST WIFE, — My brain is so shaken by three successive entire nights without even taking off my coat, and almost without sleep in steamboat and mail-wagons, that both memory and thought are nearly obliterated; but my letter must go in an hour, and I must give you a skeleton sketch of my wanderings since we left Berlin, that rather insipid though large city. We reached Dresden the same night, spent half a day there looking about its pleasant streets and parks, and especially its peerless gallery, and its vaulted suite of rooms in the old palace filled with every variety of *rococo*, in jewels, gold, and precious stones, utensils and ten thousand objects of curious beauty; and at noon set out for Prague, interesting for its historical associations, its peculiarities, its Oriental cast of character. From Dresden the road lay for one hundred miles along the banks of the charming Elbe, combining the grand with the beautiful. We left Prague early next morning, and, passing through Moravia into Austria, arrived at Vienna *the noble* in the evening, and stood on the banks of the Danube. That is truly a grand city, with its stately streets, its palaces, its pleasure-grounds on the ramparts, in every direction, and its magnificent Prater, four miles square, composed of parks, woods, drives, walks, glades, —one vista of it being two miles long, — its music, gay, happy crowds, and brilliant life. Then the palace and beautiful grounds and parks of the glorious Schönbrunn. What would I not have given for you to stroll through them with me! Among other interesting things I visited the burial vaults of the emperors and royal family, all in elaborately ornamented bronze coffins, —comprising those of the heroic Maria Theresa, the Duc de Reichstadt (Napoleon's son), and his miserable mother, Maria Louise.

"On Saturday morning we took the steamer on the Danube for Linz, one hundred and thirty miles, to arrive early the next morning; but the fogs compelled the captain to stop nearly all night, and we did not reach Linz until the afternoon of next day. There was no bedding on board, no accommodation for sleeping, so we lolled about ·on chairs all night, cold and comfortless. At Linz we took an *eil wagen*, and driving all night reached Salzburg next morning. From this interesting and fortified town we set forth in a post-wagon, and after a third night spent on the road, without undressing and with only uneasy, disturbed snatches of sleep, arrived here at daybreak this morning. I have been two hours threading its fine streets, its galleries and other places of curiosity, and find it a magnificent city, highly interesting. I have returned to scratch off this brief summary, to be mailed at Augsburg, for which place we shall depart in a few moments. . . . ."

"AUGSBURG, 7 P. M.

" A pleasant ride of two hours in the cars brought us to this *bijou* of an old Byzantine town, through which and around its ramparts we drove this afternoon. Its most peculiar and quaint old features, surpassing anything I have yet seen, would delight J. . . . . We shall set out early in the morning for Lake Constance, take a glance at the Alps, turn about for France, remain a day in Paris, hasten over to England, run to take a look at Stratford, Kenilworth, and Stonehenge, thence to Liverpool to embark in the Pacific for dear home. I am in great hopes that Captain Comstock has secured me a berth in her; but if he have not, I will agree to sleep on the cabin floor or in the engine-room, rather than wait for the next steamer. Tell J. that I am writing in '*die drei Mooren*,' the oldest inn in Europe, and truly it looks so. Prayers and blessings to all. . . . ."

"PARIS, October 27, 1855.

" . . . . I proceed to post up my brief, disjointed notes of my wanderings since we left Augsburg, whence we went to beautiful Lake Constance, where, as I wished much to get a glimpse of Swiss mountains, instead of turning back through Germany by Baden-Baden, we took a steamer up the lake, and that night by rail and diligence to Zurich, fifty or sixty miles into the country, a curious old towu on the lovely Zurich's waters. This forced travelling by night of course I regret, depriving me of viewing so much interesting scenery; but it is unavoidable. The next evening we were in Strasbourg, and went forthwith, our only chance, to see by bright moonlight the famous spire of its grand cathedral. After a fatiguing run of sixteen hours we reached here late last night, where I found my precious home letters, which so excited me that, notwithstanding my prolonged shaking in the cars, and incessant strain, mental and bodily, for these past weeks, I could not sleep; but after a cup of good coffee I am quite fresh this morning. I am glad to be able to say also that, although it has rained or drizzled every day since I left England, and has been constantly cold as well as wet (they seem to have no conception of warm weather here), I have suffered no indisposition. . . . ."

"Monday.

" I still date from this truly imperial city, but shall leave it to-night. Yesterday was raining and cold, but as it would be ridiculous to return without seeing Versailles, I went thither at 10 A. M., and returned at four. This vast palace and magazine of art, unsurpassed, if equalled, in the world, was worthy of being the culminating point of my continental sight-seeing. The army of statues, the galleries of interesting portraits, each one a history; the ornate grounds on which art has exhausted itself! They beggar language as they outstrip imagination! Inclement as was the day, there must have been ten thousand Parisians, — the *bourgeoisie* and common people, — carried out in successive hourly trains of immense length, filling the galleries and grounds.

In the evening I dined with Mr. and Mrs. M., — their earnest and warm kindness, and indeed overwhelming expressions of affection for you, entirely disconcerted me. . . . ."

"LONDON, Wednesday Night.

". . . . I visited to-day, for the first time, the gorgeous Houses of Parliament, the British Museum, and Sydenham Crystal Palace, and had barely time to make my toilet for our very agreeable dinner, and, the guests gone, I have only a moment to bring up my rough notes. . . . ."

"LIVERPOOL, Saturday Morning.

"Here I am, dearest wife, safe and well, and find a berth reserved for me on the fine ship Pacific, Captain Nye, and I, most ready and willing and anxious to embark for dear home. I reached Salisbury on Thursday evening, was in a cab at daybreak yesterday morning for Stonehenge, — eighteen miles there and back, — so as to be back for the ten-o'clock train for Liverpool. Those gigantic and mysterious remains of an unknown age and race have always impressed me with interest, and there I found them, in silent and solitary grandeur, on the desolate downs of Wiltshire, rendering no account to mortal intelligence of their age, their object, or by whom or what agencies or powers created. I got back to Salisbury to breakfast, not only in time for the train, but for a rapid view of the cathedral, the most beautiful externally, I think, which I have seen in England. So far, however, from being able to stop at Stratford, I did not reach here until midnight, — and now, dearest wife, I must get ready to go on board the ship which, by the favor of an ever-gracious and good Providence, is to bear me across the great waters to her whose prayers, if any can avail, I know will secure me safety. Good night. May good angels guard you and all my dear household!"

"Sunday, November, 4 P.M.

" We left Liverpool yesterday afternoon, dearest wife, and have been all day steaming along in sight of the Irish coast. A fine clear day, but cold. In a few hours we shall take a last look at the shores of Europe and set our faces fairly out upon the dark and turbulent Atlantic. Ten days, I trust, will give to my eyes the shores of my own dear country, where all my treasures are. God grant it, and ever bless you."

In 1859 Mr. and Mrs. Seaton celebrated their "golden wedding," an occasion which drew from many quarters of the land kind salutations, gifts, floral offerings, and congratulatory odes, while the public press expressed very generally the regard entertained for the honored and venerable couple, paying graceful tributes to their virtues, and the courtesy and hospitality which had, during half a century, crowned their home. The two following notes from well-known personages are among many recognitions of the anniversary : —

"HARTFORD, CONN., May 2, 1859.

" MY DEAR SIR, — I was delighted to see in the public papers that you and your estimable lady had celebrated your *golden wedding*, and I felt moved to place your names in a book, where the observance of that beautiful custom is commended. Having missed the opportunity by which I had hoped to transmit the gift, I hesitated whether to send it at all, but decide this morning to commit it to the post ; for though somewhat behind the date, the sentiments of respect and friendship that prompted the tribute are fresh ; and with best wishes for your health and happiness, and for those of Mrs. Seaton and your children, I remain,

"Sincerely yours,

"LYDIA HUNTLEY SIGOURNEY.

"W. W. SEATON, ESQ."

" GENEVA, April 4, 1859.

" DEAR MR. AND MRS. SEATON, — Your 'golden wedding' rejoices me and. many more. Its notice in the public gazettes is greatly to my enjoyment. It brings, too, the reminiscence of our early days in quiet, unpretending patriotic North Carolina, where I also found a jewel ! this adds zest to my greeting. I hope to see both of you again, but this is of the uncertainties ; and yet the hope of it being a reality by and by enhances my pleasure in recalling me to the memory of you both, dear friends. I thank you, W. W. S., for your prompt response to my inquiries about a dear son, and for your invitation to Washington.

" While life endures, I am yours,

" J. G. SWIFT."

In August, 1860, the tie which had for forty-eight years united the editors of the National Intelligencer in so famous, so beneficent, and so close a partnership, was severed by the death of Mr. Gales. " The early tie which had grown between them at Raleigh gradually matured into that more than friendship or brotherhood, that oneness and identity of all purposes, opinions, and interests which ever after existed between them, without a moment's interruption ; and which was long, to those who understood it, a rare spectacle of that concord and affection so seldom witnessed, and which could never have come about except between men of singular virtues. From the point of their editorial union, their stories, like their lives, merge with a rare concord into one. They had no bickerings, no misunderstanding, no difference of view which a consultation did not at once reconcile ; they never knew a division of interests ; from their common coffer each always drew whatever he chose, and down to the death of Mr. Gales there had never been a settlement of accounts between them. What facts could better attest, not merely a singular harmony of character, but an admirable conformity of virtues?"* Possessed of the most lavish generosity of nature, his heart the home of all charitable emotion, Mr. Gales was exceedingly beloved by the community in which he had passed so large a portion of his life, his virtues being appreciated by the whole country, while the columns of the Intelligencer during a period of fifty years bear signal evidence of his intellectual and journalistic eminence. "A very able writer," says Mr. Everett, "there were articles from the pen of Mr. Gales which would do credit to the most accomplished of his contemporaries, and which were often ascribed to different individuals, who from time to time were regarded as the clearest thinkers and most vigorous writers of the day."

As an illustration of the rare unity of feeling and action subsisting between these brother-editors, a prominent journalist related the following incident, almost touchingly characteristic of their habit of doing good by stealth, and the endeavor of each to bear the friendly burden alone. The gentleman in question chanced for the moment to be deprived of resources, and coming to Washington naturally turned to that asylum for the distressed, the sanctum of his friends of the Intelligencer. Mr. Seaton, after discussing the prospects for journalistic venture at that time, said, "We can offer you nothing satisfactory, and unfortu-

* Atlantic Monthly, 1860.

nately just now our pockets are empty; but what we can do for ourselves we can do for a friend, and I will make a loan which is at your service; but it is a private affair between you and myself, not the firm, and I wish that you should not mention the matter to Mr. Gales."

The next morning, a nearly similar conversation ensued with Mr. Gales, who also offered to procure the aid not in his immediate personal power to advance; but when he proceeded, in almost the very words used by Mr. Seaton, to beg that it might be " an affair between themselves, and not necessary to be made known to Mr. Seaton," the gentleman fairly laughed, and noted in his diary this beautiful coincidence of two benevolent natures. The hearty, absolute appreciation entertained by each of these noble men for the attainments and virtues of his *alter ego* was rare in its sincerity, — Mr. Seaton regarding Mr. Gales with unalterable affection, and respect for his talent, who in turn was ever happy in testifying to the ability and singularly winning characteristics of his colaborer, — " My Lord Duke," as he was fond playfully of styling him. A gentleman in alluding to this generosity of affection so closely uniting them, writes: " The press, in commenting on the ability of the Intelligencer, occasionally attributed its leading articles exclusively to Mr. Gales, who was exceedingly annoyed at this injustice, which only excited Mr. Seaton's amusement. I remember more than once finding Mr. Gales quite excited on this subject; and one morning especially he was wrought up to great disturbance. ' See this,' he said, showing me a paragraph; ' this paper, in praising our late masterly series of articles, says they were written by me. Now I say it is false, for every one of them is by Mr. Seaton, and I never *could* write as well as he does.' The controversy was between the government organ, edited by a cabinet officer, and the Intelligencer, and the editorials in question were among the ablest that appeared in that journal during General Jackson's administration, being copied more extensively probably than any other of that period, and admitted even by political opponents to have silenced their adversary."

A month subsequent to the lamented death of Mr. Gales, Mr. Seaton announced that thenceforth Mr. James C. Welling would be associated with him in the editorial conduct of the Intelligencer, with which indeed, during the previous ten years, he had been connected; first, in charge of its literary department, after the retirement from that position of the accomplished gentleman and brilliant writer, the late Edward William Johnston. " Mr. .Welling," adds Mr. Seaton, "was the author of those *Notes on New Books*, which, by their scholarship and ability, would of themselves be a sufficient evidence of the qualifications he brings to the tasks of journalism. Enjoying in the fullest degree the confidence of my late lamented colleague, Mr. Gales, he has equally by his high moral and conscientious character, no less than by his rare attainments, merited my own." Most ably indeed did Mr. Welling meet these flattering expectations. To a fulness of matured thought upon every point of theoretical or practical national polity, and an erudition ranging through every field of science and literature,

Mr. Welling united a force and readiness of discussion with an appreciation of the conservative tone and dignity characterizing the Intelligencer, which gained the marked approval of the constituents of the time-honored journal, and amply justified the confidence reposed in him by Mr. Seaton.

The close of the year 1863 brought to Mr. Seaton the sorrow which was to darken with its heavy shadow the remaining days of his pilgrimage. On Christmas day he laid in the dust the beloved and cherished head of her who had during fifty-four years been the "modest yet shining ornament and charm of his household. Mr. Seaton's union with the honored partner of his life was marked by a mutual tenderness so seldom paralleled, by a devotion so chivalrous on the one part, a reliance so truthful and unhesitating on the other, that it must ever be referred to as the crown and complement of his earthly existence. The loveliness and good report of this conjugal example were treasured, it may be said, as a personal pride and possession by the community in which for so long a period the virtues, the talents, the ineffable grace of true womanhood, as exhibited in the person of Mrs. Seaton, sustained and cheered the toils of her husband in his arduous career." *

"The chronicle of Mrs. Seaton's life may be said to be that of Washington, of which, during wellnigh half a century, she was the recognized head of its highest type of society. Coming to the capital in its infancy, she had witnessed its many changes of rulers, and strange mutations of social circles, outliving nearly

* Professor Joseph Henry.

all her associates of an era we are wont to call the golden one of our republic. Maintaining close friendly relations with all that our own country had offered of good and great, Mrs. Seaton was equally sought by foreigners, who would be drawn to her by their predecessors' report of her charm of manner, her gifts of conversation, and the cordial hospitality that gave her home a special place in the memory of all who visited it. The sprightliness and felicity of expression manifested in her domestic correspondence have been already seen, and the columns of the Intelligencer bore occasional evidence of her graceful pen. Among her correspondents, whose notes are filled with thanks for kindness bestowed and the expression of their friendship, may be found the names of most of the learned and notable who have successively played their part in public life, and passed from the stage, while may be included hospitable and friendly tributes from every chief magistrate of the United States, except one, since Washington. But Mrs. Seaton's highest distinction resided in her moral characteristics, her strong intellect and numerous acquirements being heightened and beautified by the gentleness, benignity, and charity, the unfailing generosity and constant unselfishness, which pervaded the life of this virtuous matron, wise and tender mother, incomparable wife, and gracious lady. While devoted to her own faith, Mrs. Seaton was yet truly catholic in her religious love and charity for all Christian persuasions. Wherever the pure, the virtuous were found, she recognized a kindred soul, and yet Unitarians may be permitted to rejoice that it was the church of Liberal Christianity that developed a faith so true, so enduring, vivified by active benevolence and good works without which the 'Faith is dead also.'"*

The unclasping of the earthly links of this chain of wedded happiness was speedily followed by the severance of another tie, cherished by Mr. Seaton with just pride and fond affection. The National Intelligencer of December 31, 1864, announced to the country, in a dignified and touching valedictory address, Mr. Seaton's retirement from his connection with the press, of which he had so long been an illustrious exemplar. From every portion of the country came a burst of professional and personal tribute to the old man venerable, around whose name were twined the pride, the confidence, the affectionate associations of three generations of men, who of themselves, or through tradition, had come to regard the editors of the Intelligencer as the embodiment of wisdom, truth, benevolence, and justice; who had honored the grand old journal for more than half a century, or from boyhood, and who now witnessed its extinction with deep emotion.

" From every part of the land; from the rugged hills of the North, the fertile plains of the South, the broad valleys of the West, went forth a loving benison for the prosperity and happiness of the then surviving patriarch of the press."

" If the retrospect of a long life," writes Edward Everett, in the last article he ever penned, " usefully and honorably devoted to the service of the country in the highly responsible relation of a leading journalist; if the recollection of confidential intercourse with

* The Christian Inquirer.

the most distinguished statesmen of his day and generation ; if the warm attachment of troops of friends,
and the respect of political opponents, can afford a
solace down the hill of life, few persons could ever be
better entitled to it than Mr. Seaton, who now bids the
public a last farewell."   " The National Intelligencer,"
continues Mr. Everett, " was at its foundation devoted
to the support of Mr. Jefferson's administration, its
politics being consequently what were then called
' Republican,' the epithet ' Democratic ' not having yet
been accepted by the party of which Mr. Jefferson was
the leader. During the ' era of good feeling ' which
followed the war of 1812, and which lasted till the
second term of President Monroe's administration, the
Intelligencer, in conformity with the public sentiment
of the day, gradually dropped its partisan character,
and assumed that independent, national, and conservative position which it ever afterwards occupied.
When the disintegrated fragments of the old parties
were reorganized under General Jackson, the Intelligencer gave its support to Adams and Clay and their
successors in the same line of policy. The Intelligencer fulfilled one of the highest duties of journalism
by the careful and elaborate discussions of great national questions. Its editors, living in constant personal intercourse with the leading minds in all the
departments of the government, and of the foreign
legations, were able to treat the most important topics
of the day, so to say, at first hand, with an unsurpassed
journalistic breadth of view and weight of authority.
The length of time for which the editorship of the
journal was in the same hands gave it a mastery of
the political traditions of the country."

The following eloquent tribute to the value of the Intelligencer was paid while the brother-editors still steadily labored at its helm : —

"Amidst the many popular passions with which nearly all have, in our country, run wild, the editors of the Intelligencer have maintained a perpetual and sage moderation ; amidst incessant variations of doctrine, they have preserved a memory and a conscience ; in the frequent fluctuations of power they have steadily checked the excesses of both parties ; and they have never given to either a factious opposition or a merely partisan support. Tempering the heat of both sides, renationalizing all spirit of section, combatting our propensity to lawlessness at home and aggression abroad, the venerable editors have been, all the while, a power and safety in the land, no matter who were the rulers. Thus it cannot be deemed an American exaggeration to declare the opinion as to the influence of the Intelligencer over our public councils, that its value is not easily to be overrated." *

A prominent Northern editor thus speaks of this setting sun of journalism : —

"We have read the touching words in which Colonel Seaton takes leave of the patrons of the National Intelligencer, and we should be something less than human if we could read this farewell address without emotion. We can hardly recall the time when the names of Gales and Seaton were not associated in our minds with solid ability, sterling patriotism, sound political views, and eminent decorum and propriety of tone. It has been an institution in this land. Amid all the storm of faction, it has shone with the same serene and steady light, a star of hope and comfort to all who loved their country and meant to abide by its Constitu-

* Atlantic Monthly.

tion and laws. It has been consistent, because faithful to principle, never strongly partisan, but always manly and independent. Since the breaking out of the war, the Intelligencer has been conducted with unerring prudence and undeviating ability. During the whole period of our civil troubles the Intelligencer has discussed the grave political problems of the day with an enlightened philosophy, an affluence of historical knowledge, and a wise statesmanship, that have sometimes caused our admiration to be alloyed with regret that such masterly productions were not committed to the charge of something less fleeting than the columns of a newspaper."

During the inflamed political and exasperated personal agitation incident to the late civil war, unceasing evidences of sympathy and approval of the course of the Intelligencer reached the editors from many of the good and wise. A selection or two from these innumerable testimonials of respect will best express the commendation which so greatly cheered a difficult patriotism :—

"BOSTON, June 27, 1861.

"GENTLEMEN, — Please to place my name on the list of subscribers to your very valuable paper. I had almost said invaluable. Though I have not been in the habit of reading it regularly, I know its value from the extracts I have often seen from its columns, from the soundness of the principles it has maintained, and from its regard to truth in every sense of the word. As I am now in my eighty-fourth year, I may not remain long on your list; but I shall as long as I live, because I consider it very important for the national welfare that your paper should be sustained.

"I am respectfully yours,

"JAMES JACKSON.

"3 Hamilton Place, Boston."

"DETROIT, July 15, 1861.

"DEAR SIR, — I have read with care and instruction the able articles in the Intelligencer upon the impending crisis. Their fairness and candor have made a deep impression wherever read in this section. Will you permit me to suggest the propriety of preparing and publishing an article on the subject of *subjugation*. It is entirely misunderstood among the Northern masses ; and there is no source from which a moderate and well-conceived article would be more favorably received, because you are considered by all as truly conservative and patriotic. The Northwest is almost unanimous in the determination to prosecute the war vigorously. The excitement has been so intense that many of our most considerate and intelligent men have been betrayed into rash and unfortunate expressions, which have seriously affected the public mind. It is truly surprising to find that very many of our citizens, blinded by their passions, are misled in regard to the relations which the States bear to the general government. They speak and act as if it were of no importance to encourage and cultivate the Union feeling in the South. They do not reflect that after the Confederates are conquered, the people of the State must govern and control its internal affairs ; in other words, they do not consider the powers appropriately belonging to the general government, and those retained by the States. I think Mr. Lincoln made a great mistake in his inaugural and recent messages by not more definitely and clearly enunciating his views in regard to the future policy to be pursued towards the South. There is no doubt that the enlightened public mind of the Northwest is for preserving the institutions of the South as they are, and when the war closes will willingly agree to a national convention which may consider all the grievances of the different States, real and imaginary, and grant the most liberal redress. What then can be the objection to the proclaiming of this policy now, when its effect might have such influence upon the masses, at least in the border States? It does appear to me that something of the kind is absolutely necessary as an antidote to Lovejoy's poison. His movement is repudiated by all our sensible men, and if this fact could be communicated to the South, it might tend to break its force with them.

"For several years past I have been in a state of political retiracy, but still a close observer of passing events. I have an abiding faith in the stability of the Union, and although I almost despair of success from human power, yet that God who has so long ruled our destiny will not permit this fair fabric to be soon destroyed.

"Dear Sir, truly yours,

"R. McClelland.

"W. W. Seaton, Esq."

"New York, August, 1863.

"My dear Sir, — I have been greatly encouraged and delighted by the perusal of the recent editorials of the Intelligencer. It will be a sad day, should it ever arrive, when the spring which sends forth such refreshing and healing waters shall be sealed. Your review of Whiting's letter and the article under the caption of 'Who are the enemies of the Union?' and that other article, 'The Duty of Public Journalists,' are written with masterly ability. Persevere, my dear Sir, in this course as long as the public will let you. . . . . .

"Very truly yours,

"Hiram Ketchum.

"Colonel. W. W. Seaton."

"Worcester, Mass., November 25, 1863.

"My dear Sir, — I beg to express to you my cordial, most respectful and friendly recollections and regard, and my acknowledgment of the satisfaction with which, through

these anxious and troubled times, I continue to receive
your ably conducted and patriotic paper. The truly loyal,
constitutional, and statesmanlike course to which it has so
nobly adhered commands my admiration; and it is only
in the prevalence of the principles which it maintains, the
certain and speedy suppression of the rebellion, and the
restoration of the Union, that I can see hope for a return
of prosperity, peace, and glory to our now bleeding and distracted country.

"Be pleased to offer to such of your family as may honor
me with their remembrance, the assurance of my grateful
regards.

"Very truly, my dear Sir, your obedient servant,

"LEVI LINCOLN.

"HON. W. W. SEATON."

"NEW YORK, January 4, 1865.

"MY DEAR SIR, — Having learned through the press of
your retirement from the National Intelligencer, I feel it
an agreeable duty to write and congratulate you on the
termination of a long, laborious, and honorable career; and
to express to you my appreciation of your great kindness
to myself for a period of several years.

"When I first began to take an interest in public affairs
the Intelligencer commended itself to my judgment and
taste by the soundness of its political views, the purity of
its style, the elevation of its morals, the accuracy of its
statements, the fulness of its knowledge, and its courtesy
to all. It was therefore with feelings of just pride that I
regarded the admission of my own contributions to its columns, especially as at the time of my earlier efforts I was
personally unknown to both of its editors. When subsequently I made your acquaintance, I found additional reason to be grateful to you for the cordiality of your greeting

and the kindness with which you always welcomed me to your sanctum on the occasion of my visits to Washington. The conversations then held with you are among my most agreeable reminiscences of the Capitol. . . . . In reviewing the many stirring incidents of your eventful past, in recalling the cherished memories of your fellow-laborers in public and private life, who have gone before you to their rest, and in enjoying the repose to which you are fairly entitled, you will probably be content to pass the remainder of your days. I cannot, however, avoid the hope that you may find a pleasant and profitable employment of a portion of your time, in collecting and editing such editorials of the Intelligencer as have from time to time elucidated great questions of public law and policy. Such a work would prove a valuable contribution to our political literature. . . . .

"Believe me to remain, very respectfully and gratefully yours,

"GEORGE MERRILL.

"COLONEL W. W. SEATON."

The following note from the distinguished scholar, the author of perhaps the most charming recent book of travels, "Six Months in Italy," will be the more interesting, as having elicited from Mr. Seaton a reply most touching in its simple pathos and modest dignity. In transmitting this to a friend, Mr. Hillard takes occasion to write : —

" I never was in Washington but once, and Mr. Seaton was the first person I went to see. It is now a pleasure to me to reflect that I have seen him. . . . . From my boyhood the National Intelligencer was the type of a sound, wise, national, conservative journal; and the influence which Mr. Seaton thus exerted was wide and most valuable. We have fallen upon different times, different journals, different men, and influence is now only enjoyed by the papers and the statesmen that represent extreme opinions. I am not one of those who think the change an improvement."

"Boston, January 3, 1865.

"My dear Sir, — .... I cannot let the occasion go by, without a more immediate and personal acknowledgment of gratitude and regard. During these last four dreary years the Intelligencer has been to me a source of comfort, satisfaction, and support beyond expression ; and now that you are to leave it, I feel that something of the daily light around my path is lessened. My heart is heavy unto death at the condition of our beloved land. Clouds and darkness rest upon the future, and I don't see the star behind the cloud. I do not see any statesmanship at all commensurate with the gigantic problems to be solved. We are drifting like the Great Eastern after she had lost her rudder. It is fearful to think of such interests committed to the charge of such small capacities.

"I wish you and Mr. Welling would come to Boston. You should swim in a 'Caspian Sea of soup,' as Sydney Smith said of Prescott. Please convey to him an expression of my warm regard.

"Yours faithfully,

"G. S. Hillard.

"W. W. Seaton, Esq."

"Washington, January 9, 1865.

"Many thanks, my dear Sir, for your very kind letter, the more precious to me, coming as it does from one whose good opinion I value so highly. The parting with my old paper is painful in the extreme. But the untoward circumstances of the times had reduced it to the point of extinction, and no alternative was left me but to see it expire, or to transfer it to some younger men, who thought that, by withdrawing it from the arena of politics and converting it into a news and business sheet, they could make it pay. I would, I confess, have preferred for it the dignity of death; but justice to a few friends around me, who have enabled me to sustain it during three years of vainly hoping for peace and better times, compelled me to part with it. Pride and hope induced me to struggle on against the difficulties that beset me, at the sacrifice of everything I possessed; but I was at last obliged to succumb. The loss of two thirds of my entire circulation by the secession of the South I could have borne; the proscription of the government I could have borne singly; but the weight of the two united was too much for me, and, receiving no compensating support in the North, I was forced to yield. In the high character of the friends like yourself, who have stood by the old journal in its adversity and cheered its editors by their approval and support, I find a consolation which I would not exchange for better fortune, although I end fifty-two years of labor with nothing.

"Believe me, dear Sir, with the highest respect, your grateful friend and servant.

"W. W. SEATON.

"GEORGE S. HILLARD, ESQ., Boston."

Mr. Seaton's heart was deeply stirred by these manifestations of love, sympathy, and reverence which daily reached him from his countrymen. The verdict of posterity came to him, as it were, while he yet could rejoice in this approval of his labors, while his living ear could catch the voices which rose in unison of benediction: "Well done, good and faithful servant."

The prominent features of Mr. Seaton's career of journalism were his candor, fairness, and "an evenness and refinement of temper which never allowed him to question the motives of an adversary." He never tried to enhance his own dignity, or the merits of the cause he upheld, at the expense of his adversary; he never resorted to factious, belittling strife; never mistook malignant bitterness or detraction for vigor and frankness, but carried into the editorial arena his innate decorum and gracious amenity, which not even the acerbities of partisan warfare could disturb.

The distinguished divine, Dr. Dewey, writing of Mr. Seaton, says: —

"There is one thing in his career that ought to be emphasized, that is, his keeping the Intelligencer free from all personalities, not only of abuse, but partisanship. I once heard an instance of this dignified forbearance that struck me very much. When Webster was candidate for nomination before the Baltimore Convention, the Intelligencer was silent upon his claims. Day after day passed and not a word was said. Mr. Webster was impatient under this neglect, where he expected help, considering the well-known friendly and intimate relations between himself and Mr. Seaton, and at length expressed his dissatisfaction. Mr. Seaton's answer was this: 'We established and have always conducted the Intelligencer as an organ of public intelligence and general discussion. We have never lent it to personal predilections or antipathies. Upon the Intelligencer as such I have built up my life, and I desire that it should bear this honorable record of me, and that it should still preserve the same high character after I am gone. And I cannot consent that it depart from this rule which has always governed me, even to express the friendly interest that I feel for *you*.' It was a position of great dignity and firmness to take with such a man and friend as Daniel Webster."

A gentleman for many years intimate with Mr. Seaton thus writes : —

"The care and high sense of honor which he unceasingly exercised in the conduct of the Intelligencer were to me a perpetual source of wonder. Coarse and unkind expressions received no quarter at his hands ; rude personalities he utterly abominated ; and his information was so extensive, so various, as to render it certain that whatever received his editorial sanction would be found new and instructive. His integrity was incorruptible. I was present on one occasion in his office when a man used, in vain, every argument to obtain from him the insertion of an advertisement which Mr. Seaton deemed unfitting for the pure columns of the paper. Finally an amount was offered that would have made many men waver, but Mr. Seaton's answer was this : 'Sir, there is not in the world gold enough to tempt me to insert in the Intelligencer one line which I should be unwilling for my wife and daughters to read.' The instances were numerous also in which he was proof against the temptation of large sums tendered him for permission to publish, as editorials, articles which did not embody his real opinions. With a warm, tender heart, he had the will and courage of a bold and honest man, who knew not what it was to play a double game where principle was at stake.

"Mr. Seaton's modesty reached to a fault, leading him to depreciate the abilities so fully recognized by that public whose political creed and action he had so materially aided to enforce and guide, during sixty years of editorial life. He was sound in discrimination, sagacious in his perception of the bearing of present measures on future issues ; while his tact and facility of expression, with the readiness of long editorial training, made him an exceptionally effective paragraphist ; and in grace and variety as a commentator on passing events he was especially happy."

While these tributes from the public came winged by all heartfelt aspirations, Mr. Seaton's daily path was marked by blessings from those who so long had relied on him as friend, counsellor, and benefactor. Whereever he moved, the earnest greeting, the respectful recognition from all ranks, attested the almost filial love and veneration cherished for the silver-haired old man.

"Mr. Seaton has reached a period of life," concludes an editorial eulogist, "in which a man is permitted to rest from his labors, and to 'adjust his mantle ere he fall.' He is surrounded by 'all that should accompany old age,' as 'honor, love, obedience, troops of friends'; and if love and respect could avert the inevitable stroke, he would enjoy a patent of earthly immortality."

And now the end drew near,—the mantle was adjusted; and this life of two and fourscore years, so replete with all that did honor to our common nature, was to close. The indomitable courage, the hopeful patience, the gentle sweetness, all the harmonized beauty of a noble nature, shone with almost celestial light as he neared the golden shore. "Mark the perfect man and behold the upright; for the end of that man is peace."

Thus, adored. by those nearest him, beloved and revered by his friends, honored through the land, he passed to "a nobler stewardship in the spiritual world," crowned by the tears and blessings of the great, the wise, the humble, the afflicted, the widow, and the orphan, "to whom the withdrawal of his earthly presence seemed a domestic calamity."

"Reserved, even reticent in the expression of his

feelings, the depth of Mr. Seaton's religious nature was hardly known, except as it was manifested in his noble life. To the most exalted reverence and awe for the Almighty Power, he united in a peculiar degree the tender, confiding love of a child. His faith in the future was simply truthful, believing in the recognition of friends; that in one of the 'many mansions' of the Father's house he should be reunited to those loved on earth, and, accepted, pardoned, redeemed by God's mercy, should continue through eternity to minister to His will. Mr. Seaton was one of the founders of the Unitarian Church in Washington, being among the earliest and most zealous to establish and maintain a foothold for liberal Christianity at this advanced out-post, and illustrating by his beautiful and blameless life the truth of its doctrines. His youth and early manhood were passed in the communion of the Epis-copal Church, to whose forms he ever remained at-tached, frequently reading its impressive services with tender reverence; but his theological views changed, founded upon earnest conviction, and he became a Unitarian, and communicant of that church, remaining firm and unchangeable in his belief of the truth of its tenets. A daily student of the Bible, he there found his best rest and encouragement, while deeply enjoying its sublime poems, which he read with the keenest in-tellectual discrimination, as well as devotional fervor."

Seldom has a living presence been hedged about with such an atmosphere of love; while in the wealth of public and private tribute to the memory of this good man — " doubly great, for goodness is great-ness " — the dominant note is that of a rare personal affection.

"There have probably not lived many men," says the Rev. Mr. Angier in his eulogy of Mr. Seaton, "whose characters, public and private, were subject to less deduction on the score of defect or inconsistency. But while all tongues proclaim his merits, I have yet to hear the first word lisped in derogation from his claims upon the love and reverence of his fellow-citizens; and the *tone* in which these are spoken of, the evident personal feeling which accompanies the general award, the warm coloring suffusing the judicial verdict, bear conviction alike to the judgment and heart, that we have in contemplation a man whom it is not only safe, but wholesome, to praise..... And while Mr. Seaton thus inspired the hearts of all who approached him with sentiments of the warmest friendship and esteem, who can doubt that many have been *made* good and noble by his generous appreciation and encouragement? Ah! I doubt it not, how worthy of emulation is such a heart and such an example by all who would most benefit, by most ennobling their fellow-men..... I am persuaded that a greater infusion of these generous and tender characteristics of our venerated friend into the hearts of all who would regenerate and strengthen their fellow-men, would insure a greater amount of success than usually attends the sincerest efforts in their behalf. That the influence of Mr. Seaton for these higher interests of men was extensively experienced, we cannot doubt; and it becomes, therefore, no wonder that there are so many noble minds to pay him reverence, so many loving hearts causing their possessors to rise up and call him blessed. Mr. Seaton's character was of a type of which one longs to see more in the community, — men not wanting in the sterner qualities of the John of the wilderness, preaching repentance, but more conspicuous for the qualities of that John whom Jesus especially loved, — men, who if they *command* reverence, do not less *attract* affection ; whom to love is as natural and easy as to respect is an obligation and duty. With all who knew Mr. Seaton, the heart followed easily the approbation of the moral judgment. Goodness sat on his head as a crown of beauty, as attractive in its loveliness as it was commanding in its majesty."

"Why," asks one of his public eulogists, "why this sorrow and sadness ? Why these tolling bells and emblems of mourning throughout the city ? Why is the name of William Winston Seaton on every tongue ? Because a good man has left us ; one who served the people faithfully and well, whose life was one of usefulness and honor, of whom it has been truly said, that he was without an enemy, — a man illustrious in all those traits of character, those virtues and graces, which go to form the perfect gentleman. Let us remember his patience and equanimity, his dignity and courtesy, his impartiality, love of truth and justice, his charity and loving-kindness, his temperance and forbearance ; let us, in the discharge of our duty, take William Winston Seaton as an example, and so may we hope that in the end our record may be as bright, pure, and angelic as his."

A member of the Burns Club thus pays a tribute to the virtues of his departed colleague : —

"It seems to me eminently fitting that in a meeting

of Scotsmen and descendants of Scotsmen, the death of William Winston Seaton should receive such notice as will attest at least our sensibility at his loss, and our high appreciation of his merits. That beloved and revered name, it is true, does not now need our commemoration, as it has received general and unenvied honors from all classes in this community, and our highest eulogy may, perhaps, sound like the echo of his wide and undisputed reputation. Yet Seaton is a name peculiarly endeared to us; first, as it is thoroughly Scottish ; then as associated with the most various, animating, or affecting recollections — historic, poetic, and romantic — of our fatherland ; but most of all from the personal character of him we mourn, who made the time-honored name of Seaton an acquaintance throughout the length and breadth of the land, among all classes,— 'familiar in their mouths as household words.' . . . . But Mr. Seaton, perhaps, was most remarkable for his smooth, polished, Addisonian periods. He was a very graceful and effective writer at all times, and often rose to a force of argument and earnestness of appeal when great questions of national policy came under his consideration, which could scarcely have been heightened by any speaker or writer of his times. But, great and far-reaching as was his influence through the leading metropolitan journal for more than half a century, the effect of his character, his conversation, and his counsels upon the more active and controlling directors and propagators of opinion was not less important and extensive, and, indeed, cannot be overestimated. Those who have known Washington best, are well aware that its society has always been a region in which nearly as much is done towards moulding and determining great measures of policy, on the part of government or the opposition, as in the halls of Congress. . . . . . Altogether, the standard in such a circle — social, intellectual, moral, and political — is as high as is really ever reached elsewhere. It was in this circle that William Winston Seaton, by the magnetism of his personal character, so pure, so lofty, so amiable and engaging, by his powers of varied and vivacious conversation, by his full intelligence on every question, foreign or domestic, and that combination of gifts of manner, tact, and address, the highest result of which is best expressed in the word *gentleman*, exercised an influence for years which was felt and recognized from the centre to the utmost limits of American society, abroad as well as at home."

A distinguished Northern journalist thus touchingly dwells on Mr. Seaton's winning traits of character:—

" In the death of this venerable editor the country has sustained a loss for which the only consolation is, that he had served all his appointed time, and served well. Eighty years of faithful labor is far more than the ordinary contribution of one man to the good of his fellow-men. . . . . But we cannot part with him or his memory yet. He belongs to us by virtue of a thousand recollections, for which we are indebted to his long life and experience, so that his name will always be associated with the best days and greatest men of the Republic. There was not living in America, two weeks ago, any other man whose mind was such a storehouse of the personal history of the giants of old time in American statesmanship. A man of sound judgment, extensive reading, eminent ability, able to advise and direct, but never intruding his advice, he was in every way fit to be, as he was, the intimate friend and confidential associate of all the eminent statesmen of the past age. There is a parlor in Mr. Seaton's old house at Washington, which, could its walls speak, would be more eloquent than the walls of any other room in America. In that well-known room it was for many years the custom for the greatest men in the country, and the representatives of other nations, to gather in the freedom of social intercourse; and this may be said with undoubted truth, that in those free social conversations and exchanges of thought were born many of the great measures of government which added lustre to the American name; so that that room may be regarded as the birthplace of much of our national glory. We may be pardoned for recalling at this moment the last visit which we made to that historic room. It was in the midst of the war, and the long evening passed into the morning hours, while we sat listening to the venerable patriot, as he recited conversations which had been held there. Mindful, from many such hours passed with him, of the inestimable value of his recollections, we begged him to do a public service by allowing a stenographic reporter to take down from his lips such of his personal memories as he might judge proper and desirable for historical purposes. We had subsequently a correspondence with him on the same topic, and it can never cease to be a subject of regret that the idea was not carried into operation. But the failing health of our aged friend interfered with this last service to the world, and forbade its accomplishment. Would that those silent walls could give us back the impressions which other voices, forever hushed, have made upon them! If there be anything in the theory of the 'conservation of forces,' every atom of those walls would furnish a volume of history, written there by the voices of the great dead. . . . . . But while we lament the loss of the editor, the companion, adviser, and friend of the great men of the past, the originator and assistant in so many of the most important political events in our history, we more than all lament the man. He was rightly loved, for he deserved, and it may be said he commanded, affection. None knew him but to love him. Over his grave will be shed the tears of no ordinary affection. Nor is it improper here to allude to his devotion to the companion of his long life, whose honored head he laid in the dust only two years ago, — a devotion which marked his whole character, the memory of which makes his rest by her side to seem exceedingly welcome. The past is fast vanishing out of sight, and the men of our golden age are becoming, day by day, part of the land they loved. We who survive should better love the dust made up of such precious material. Who shall fitly speak the increase in its value when we give to it such men as this, our best and purest relics of the glorious day?

From the far South comes this discriminating estimate of the value of Mr. Seaton's labors and example :—

"The files of the noble old Intelligencer are a monument which will ever bear testimony to Mr. Seaton's ability, courtesy, honesty, truthfulness, and conservatism, and will show why his society was prized by the great men who adorned our country in its palmy days. For nearly half a century he was at the head of one of the most influential journals of this or any other country, and nearly up to the close of his career gave tone largely to the public opinion of the American people. It is seldom that any political journal has been under the control of two individuals so admirably fitted by genius, education, and practice to impart to it influence and popularity. It is seldom that two editors acting together have been characterized by such high intellectual endowments and such generosity of temper. Mr. Seaton was a gentleman in his intercourse, a scholar in his tastes, and American literature always received encouragement at his hands, and was advanced by his labors. No individual was better acquainted with the history of his country from the origin of the government, nor more familiar with the character, the rise and fall of parties.

His manners were pre-eminently winning, his conversation full of instruction and charm; and no club-room was ever visited with more enthusiasm by statesmen and inquirers of all classes, from every portion of the land, solicitors for information, than the sanctum of his office. His judgment had high influence on all party counsels, policies, and conduct of the day; while with his rare social qualities, his house was the centre of all that was attractive in the metropolis, including political adversaries, who were, however, generally his personal friends. Mr. Seaton was always proud of his connection with the 'art preservative of arts,' and especially must his loss be regretted by the younger members of the profession which he adorned, and for whom he ever evinced a parental regard. Many an old printer 'out of sorts,' many an old *typo* worn out in his service, was welcomed each returning Saturday to the Intelligencer office to receive his pay, and when the days of the old printer would draw to a close, he had the comforting assurance that to those dear to him the same generosity would be continued. Mr. Seaton's long life was a brilliant success, except in the accumulation of wealth, which his integrity, his generosity and hospitality prevented. These qualities, united to his enlarged statesmanship, his philanthropy, his pure and lofty patriotism, commanded for Mr. Seaton the unqualified consideration and respect of a great party, as well as the sincere friendship of so many illustrious men; and his name and fame will be associated with some of the brightest stars that adorn the annals of American history."

In view of these virtues so visibly impressed on Mr. Seaton's entire life, the recital of which might almost be deemed an exaggeration, one may ask, " Was he then perfect ? " A friend who from boyhood to old age has spent his daily life in closest knowledge of Mr.

Seaton, replies : " He possessed more of the great and good qualities of human nature than any man I ever knew ; and never, in my estimation, was there a mortal his peer in all that makes man godlike."

What, then, it may be asked, was the secret of this life of success ? and what may be the value of the lesson learned from its teachings ?

It was not political power or gift of place ; Mr. Seaton possessed not these. It was not wealth ; for his large heart and open hand impoverished his earthly store. The forum knew him not ; the halls of legislation had never echoed to his voice ; he filled no post of Cabinet Councillor or Presidential Chair ; he won no battles on ensanguined field. True, he possessed a stern uprightness that would have guarded the ermine with jealous purity, an eloquence to have swayed listening Senates, signal administrative ability, an intrinsic dignity to have illustrated the highest office, rapid intuition, decision, and a cool courage that would have placed him high in the rank of military heroes. But Mr. Seaton's triumphs were the quiet ones of the closet ; his distinctive influence was the subtile one emanating purely from personal characteristics, from the intangible charm of presence, necessarily impossible to embody and delineate for the appreciation of posterity. The usefulness of his life flowed in a perennial stream, and in the beneficent tenor of its example, rather than in prominent action or salient incident to be segregated for especial record, consists its permanent value. His protecting hand was stretched out wherever his fellow-men were to be helped ; and in the self-abnegation and benevolence of his nature,

in the assimilating sympathies which magnetized all
hearts to go forth to meet him, lay the power which
he exercised over all who approached him; simply by
" the divining-rod of his own goodness," calling forth
the best qualities of others, — the true secret of all
noble influence.

Mr. Seaton was one of the last links between the
illustrious men who framed our Government, and those
who make our history of to-day.   He had seen Washington; had listened to the magic voice of Patrick
Henry.   Can it be wondered that the greatness and
virtues of the Fathers of the Republic should have
been reflected in him who had touched their mortal
garments, who had been glorified by their visible
presence ?

And thus, undimmed by a single unworthy act, in
every word and thought of his spotless life a true
gentleman, duty his watchword, exalted honor his in-
stinct, Christianity his guide, William Winston Seaton
bore his historic name untarnished to the grave; nobly
illustrating the legend of his family arms: —

INVIA VIRTUTI VIA NULLA.

THE END.